BURNING DOWN THE HOUSE

ZOE J. STARK

First published in Great Britain in 2022
Oxford Spires Publishing

ISBN 9798358102200
Ebook AISN B0BJ72Y8LB

Supported using public funding by

ARTS COUNCIL
ENGLAND

For the West Country,
and for all those who look for love
in all the wrong places.

PART I

THE FIRE

'Out of the ashes of this tragedy,
we shall rise to greet the dawning of a new era.'

The Lion King

Nothing says more about a person than what they save from a burning house. When our home was glowing like the desert sun, all of me family were holding onto something.

Me dad had rescued an old monkey cuddly toy, with boxing gloves for hands.

His girlfriend Kirsten had grabbed a bag of knitting.

Gran had her pigmy pig that could predict the future.

And I had a Mary Poppins umbrella that me mum gave me as a kid.

Me family had lined up like suspects in the street, holding on to their prized possessions, the one thing they couldn't leave behind. Or maybe we had all just grabbed the first thing we saw. Who knows.

I had woken up to shouting and smoke. Someone threw a wet towel at me to breathe through. Kirsten grabbed me arm and dragged me through to the landing. Dad, Granny and Destiny (the micro-pig), were all in the bathroom by the open window. I went out of the window first. In me bare feet, I shimmed down the gutter. I found the ladder outside and propped it up for the others.

A neighbour must have called the fire brigade. We heard the sirens as Granny came down the ladder in her flowery nightie. We watched as the fire ate our home, as the bonfire lit up the dark night, taking everything we had with it. The swinging pub sign cracked in two and crumbled like ash from the end of a ciggy. It felt as if all of West Stonecloud came to watch. In the middle of the night. They had come up from the valley; they'd come down from the hills. Every tribe, every class, every race, every species from the Cotswolds had come to witness the Saint's kingdom fall.

The fire brigade leapt out in front of us. They were all in beige, striped with yellow reflectors and wearing yellow helmets. They unreeled a rubber hose and dived into our house, armed with hoses and breathing gear like they were entering a disaster zone. Neighbours brought us their slippers as we got checked over by paramedics. We all wore silver capes, but no one felt heroic. Granny wrestled with Destiny, who was trying to break free.

And then finally, the fire was out.

A woman in brown overalls approached Dad. She was holding a camera by her side.

'What d'you say your name was?' Dad coughed as if he smoked thirty-a-day.

'Kai.' Her face was red. Her breath billowed without fire.

'Kay?'

'Kai! Sounds like pie, but with a K.'

'Right.' Dad nodded. 'Well, K-ai... someone in the village will put us up. Sure we'll find summat.'

Kai turned to look at the fire and crossed her arms. 'Do you remember leaving anything on?'

'No, not at all.' He shook his head. 'So your the one investigating it? K-ai.'

He wouldn't say it. He wouldn't tell her. What about the note we got? What about the letter? Whoever sent them to us must have been involved. I had to say something. 'It wasn't an accident!' I shouted from behind them.

Kai jumped and dropped her camera. 'Shit!' She grabbed the sides of her head.

'Oh, I'm so sorry.' I picked it up for her.

'She doesn't mean us. We didn't do it.' Dad's eyes were wide and his nostrils flared. 'She thinks it's arson.'

Kai turned over the camera, trying buttons, shaking her head. The screen blinked on. 'Oh, thank god. It still works.'

'Of course it was arson, you stupid boy.' Granny wagged her finger at Dad. 'That letter said we should all die and now look. Look!' She pointed at our home, at what was her house. The converted eighteenth-century country pub at the end of a row of houses had disappeared into ash.

'Letter?' said Kai. 'What letter...?'

'Said we should all go to hell. Get out of town.' Granny pointed to the garden wall in front of the house opposite ours. 'Scarlett, take me over there. I want to sit down.'

'I'll be right back,' Kai walked away. 'I need to check-in with the Chief.' She turned around. 'Do you know why someone might want to burn down your house?'

As we glanced at each other, you could feel the finger-pointing.

We all had enemies in the village.

But who wanted us dead?

1

READ LETTER DAY

'What does anyone in this family know about normal?'

The Incredibles

They say there's no smoke without fire. But I thought we were a normal family with normal problems. I didn't think any of us had enemies in the village. But there were little smoke signals the day before, little sparks in the air that I hadn't noticed at the time.

Dad had gone proper-quiet, more than usual. He'd stopped doing deadlifts in his morning routine. Most people wouldn't notice. But me dad's whole life was boxing and body building. I used to call him Mr Incredible when I was a kid. He'd hold me across his shoulders as he squatted: up, down, up, down, floor to ceiling. I can see it now, when I look back: there was no room for his deadlifts. Something heavy was already weighing him down.

One by one, Granny's wails brought us all to the master bedroom that morning. We stood around her bed. Her room was all pink lace, nettings and frills. She moaned and refused to get up, pushing her fleecy electric blanket to the bottom of the bed. She stared up at the wooden beams above her head. 'OOOOO,' she cried, trying to prop herself up. Granny had no teeth in or eyebrows drawn on.

'What's that?' I pointed at a glass of neon-orange slime that dad was holding. 'Looks radio-active.'

'Added Turmeric.' He squatted.

'OOOOOOO!' Granny threw her head to the side.

'What's wrong, Mum?' Dad was permanent-marker tired. Bags sagged under his eyes. No matter how many sit-ups he did, he never could tighten them. But he seemed more than just tired. The bags were carrying more than a lack of sleep.

'It hurts. Summats wrong.'

Dad turned to me with raised eyebrows. I shrugged. 'Tried to get her out, but she says something's wrong with her leg.'

'But it was fine last night, wasn't it?' Kirsten held the morning's post. She was leaning against the wall. Her pig-pink shirt blended into the wallpaper. She was pretending to care. But Gran was work for her - paper pushing.

'Pass me that cushion.' Granny pointed to the chair in front of her mahogany dressing table.

Dad picked up the frilly cushion and put it behind her back. 'Better?'

'I think it's worse.' Granny threw her head back like a terrible actress.

'I've got an early meeting.' Kirsten put a hand on her hip.

'I've got to open the gym,' said Dad. 'I'm already late. Ain't this your area of expertise, Scar?'

'I've got to work too.' I checked the time on me phone. 'But she won't let me help. She wanted you.'

'Want some pain killers, Mum?'

'No - they're useless. This is... ahhhh...'

'Maybe we should call her an ambulance,' said Kirsten.

'Don't you dare!' Granny glared.

'Why not?'

'You'll have me shipped off to that care home of hers!' Granny pointed at me like we were in a courtroom drama.

'It's a nice place, Gran. It's not....'

'Not on your nelly.' She wagged her finger. 'You ain't casting me out of me - own - house.' She pointed to her chest with each word. Kirsten rolled her eyes.

'Mum...'

'Over my dead body.' Gran was the only person I knew who would, legit, snarl.

'We could arrange that.' Kirsten smirked.

I wanted to smack me head against the wall. You can't joke with Granny. That was the worst thing to say.

'YOU.' The point of granny's finger thrust towards Kirsten like a dart. 'You've been trying to get rid of me ever since you got here!'

'I just thought you'd be happier...' Kirsten threw up her arms. 'It was just an option to think about.' She ripped open an envelope as if she was tearing at Granny's hair. 'For god's sake,' she muttered. 'I was just trying to help.'

Granny squinted at Kirsten, giving her evils. 'You're like knotweed takin' over the place. Get your grubby tentacles off me house.'

'I don't want your house! This place is falling a part. The paper is peeling off the walls. You'd have to pay someone to live here.'

'You money-grabbin' little...'

'Granny, you can't say that!'

'Say what? I can say what I like in me own house!'

'Dad?'

He sighed. 'They're as bad as each other.'

Kirsten stood upright and pulled down on her blouse. 'I'm nothing like your mother...'

'No, you're not!' shouted Granny.

'I can't keep living with you both fighting.' I bit me finger-nails. 'Dad?'

'You don't have to live 'ere.' He threw his hand into the air. 'Free country. Nobody's forcing you to be here.'

'How? All me money went on driving lessons and paying you rent.'

'Welcome to the real world.' He folded his arms. 'It's hard graft.'

'You could have moved in with a friend.' Kirsten tightened her ponytail.

'They all went to uni ages ago.'

'What about Rubi?'

'She works at her parent's B&B. Why would she leave the place she works at?'

'Your mum?'

We all knew the answer to that. And I didn't want to live on me own. I didn't want to be like the people in the care home with no-one. For ages, I had tried to get Rory to move in with me. Everyone else had gone to Uni, and he was the reason I'd stayed in the village. I wanted to start a family of me own, maybe move to Cheltenham. Ever since I was fifteen, I had wanted to be a mum. I saved up for a deposit and the first month's rent. Rory said he could double it, and took it to the bookies.

I loved Rory for his dreams, for his Peter Pan like enthusiasm. He said all the right things. He said he'd go small and then only use the profits. But he sank it. Tapped me out. He told me at the pub - eyes glued to his sagging Deliveroo bag he used for takeaway deliveries in Bristol. He said he didn't want to live with me anyway. Said I was too clingy, too baby-mad. He dumped me as he ate a packet of crisps that he'd smashed a pickled egg into. Rubi said she always knew he was a bad egg.

Gran said it was only a matter of time. I never told Dad because I knew what he'd do to him, and I was waiting for Rory to come back. He didn't really mean it. He'd made a mistake and was probably embarrassed, lashing out. When he was drunk, he'd go on and on about wanting kids, having a new start. We both wanted that. But boys don't like to admit it when they're sober.

'Such a drama queen.' Granny snorted. 'Don't know you're born. Lucky to have a family at all.'

I scoffed. 'And you're lucky to have me around, otherwise who'd look after you!'

Granny gritted her teeth. 'I'm not goin' into that care home!'

'You ain't goin' into a care home, for Pete's sake,' shouted Dad. 'Will you stop windin' her up, Scar.'

'I ain't.'

'Was that someone at the door?' Kirsten stared at me.

'Huh?'

'I thought I heard someone at the front door?'

I hadn't heard anything, but Kirsten had better senses than me. 'Postman probably.' I peered out of the window.

'But...' Kirsten held up the post and shook the post already in her hands, so it couldn't have been the postman.

'I'll go,' I said.

'No, you stay 'ere.' Dad walked out of the room and I felt static in the air.

'You wish I was dead, don't you?' Granny glared at me.

'No, Gran.' I tried to stop me voice from sounding like an eye roll.

'Yes, you do. I can see you gritting your teeth. Well... I'd come back and haunt you, mark me word.' She crossed her arms. 'Ungrateful, spoiled children. Give you me house and this is what I get...'

'No one wants your house, Henrietta.' Kirsten paced. 'You don't half make it so bloody difficult.'

9

'You always think you're better than everyone else,' said Granny. 'Nobody cares about me.'

'That's not true.' Kirsten shook her head.

Dad's girlfriend was the only one in the house who spoke proper like the Queen. It always felt like she was looking down on us. Though, she couldn't help it. And we couldn't help sounding like the Wurzels (you're obligated to love the Wurzels if you're from the South West).

I knew Granny was just grumpy from being up all night in pain. We had it lots at the care-home. It's hard to be happy and smiley when things hurt so much. She just needed a little comfort. '*I* care about you, gran. I do.' I sat down on her bed.

'Well you might be the only one, Scarlett.' She took me hand and held it as she stared at her feet. 'Yous got a heart of poet. So big. But drawn to tragedy.'

Granny had always called me a poet. Ever since I was small, she said I had eyes that looked right into people's souls. I could never figure out if it was a compliment or not. 'You're not a tragedy, Gran.'

Dad came back into the room. 'Right Ma, up and at 'em. Time to get out.'

'Wait, what's that note?' I pointed at his hands.

'What note?'

'In your hand.' Kirsten straightened the curtain.

'Probably from the neighbour.' He glared at Granny. 'You've not been workin' him up again, have you?'

'Don't know what you're talkin' about.' Gran stared up at the ceiling. 'S'not like he doesn't deserve it. That bit of land was always ours.'

'If you've been movin' that fence again.' Dad thrust the letter towards her like a sword. 'I don't even know how you can manage it...'

I ripped the note out of his hand and got an electric shock. 'Ow.'

'Scar, give me that back. Right now.'
But I opened it anyway.

I KNOW WHERE YOU LIVE.
DO US ALL A FAVOUR AND DIE.
NOBODY WANTS YOU HERE.
LEAVE! OR WE'LL MAKE YOU.

2

THE MORNING BEFORE THE FIRE

'Think happy thoughts!'

Peter Pan

When we got the note that morning, I guess it shouldn't have been a surprise. We must have upset somebody in the village, and that was common. You won't ever see welcome mats in Stonecloud. They want to keep the Cotswold for themselves, exactly how it was. Even if they ain't native. They think more people equals less space for them. So there's always some sort of drama, some sort of upset about building new houses or Tescos, or dirt bikes, or dog poo, and endangered newt species, just because everybody's looking to keep their Neverland as it never used to be: a museum.

The Cotswolds are filled with people from the city. They come from London with their fairy dust, their money, looking to escape, looking for Neverland. That's why I can't move out of home unless I go miles and miles away from my family. Rent prices went through the roof. They pay shed-loads of cash to hide in the hills, wonder with wood fairies, forage for wild garlic and mushrooms, and live in a golden cottage with climbing roses. But they never think that there might be pirates here. Us natives have never been out of the hills, away from home; a bunch of lost boys looking for their marbles in the nettles.

It was best to ignore the pirates and their death threats. You had to hope they'd go away on their own. People forget so fast, especially if you don't take it too seriously. So I thought of me happiest memory to give me wings. If you can think of the happy things, then you can rise above it all and get to Neverland.

Dad snatched the note back.

'They sound absolutely livid,' I said. 'What did you do?'

'What is it?' Gran got out of bed like nothing was wrong.

'Threat.' Dad put the note into the pocket of his joggers.

'A *death* threat.' I grinned, trying to make a joke of it. 'We're all in for it now!'

'Don't be so dramatic.' Dad frowned at me.

'People round here need to get some perspective.' I got out me phone, but there were no messages. 'Grow up and get over themselves.'

'This, from the nineteen-year-old who watches *Frozen* on repeat.' Gran snorted.

'Only when I'm sick,' I said. 'And I'm 21, Gran.'

'That's even worse!' She flapped her hand at Dad. 'Who sent it?'

'We don't know that do we, Ma. They didn't exactly sign it.'

'Maybe it's your ex?' Kirsten raised her eyebrows at me dad, and nudged Granny's stool under the dresser.

'What! No, it's not. Mum would never do that,' I said.

'I'm just saying...'

'Dad?' I stared at him. 'Dad, say summat. She wouldn't do that, would she?' I waved me hand in front of his face. But he'd taken the note back out and was staring at it. 'Dad?'

'Stop it, Scar.' He batted me hand away.

'More likely to be one of your voters,' I said to Kirsten.

'Oi.' Dad glared at me. 'You watch it.'

'Why can she say that about Mum, but I can't...'

'Put a cork in it. Y'know exactly why...'

Before Kirsten showed up, I thought Dad would never get a girlfriend. He'd been alone for so long. I was super-glad he had found someone relatively normal. She used to take me to swim-practice and bring cakes. A real-life Wendy, looking after us. But when she moved in, it all went Pete Tong. Bit by bit, our entire house changed: rationed, scheduled, controlled. It was like a work camp. But because I was 'old enough to move out', I couldn't say nothing. And Dad actually enjoyed living as if we were in the army.

Light caught in the glass drops of Granny's chandelier. I went back to me favourite memory, back to Neverland. 'Want your slippers, Gran?'

'They're by the door.' She pointed towards the walnut chest of drawers. 'I knew she never should've done it.'

'Done what?'

'Gone into politics. Not a woman's place.' Granny swept her hand towards Kirsten, as if wafting away a foul smell.

Kirsten looked up from her phone. 'Are you kidding me?' Her nostrils blew out like cannons. 'I'm not in politics anymore anyway, remember?'

'Then why are those leaflets by the front door?'

'I need to take 'em to the tip, Mum,' said Dad, still staring at the note. 'I'll do it on the weekend.'

'Been there for months!' She poked her feet into her slippers. 'A right mess.'

'Yeah, I know. I'll do it this weekend.'

Kirsten opened the door to leave and Granny's micro pig ran out from under the bed and down the stairs.

'Pigs shouldn't be in the house!' Kirsten followed Destiny out, with Dad behind. 'She has to be in her pen in the garden! It's not good for them to be inside.'

'I'm not letting her out there with that owl about.' Granny took me arm to steady herself.

Destiny could predict the results of many a-local boxing match in the Shire. She'd been getting a name for herself as an oracle. Granny had been earning a side hustle for a few years. I wondered if Destiny could have predicted the house fire? Granny liked to think of the Saints as entrepreneurs, businessmen and women. When I flunked out of college, I tried to start a business too. I sold leather belts with hand-painted designs on Etsy. Before I knew it, Granny and Dad were both telling me what to do. But the whole thing fell apart. *No Saint gives up that easy,* said Gran. And I wondered if she was right. Maybe I ain't no Saint.

Dad and Kirsten had left me to get Gran into the chair lift. She had on her thick, fluffy pink dressing gown. She strangled me arm with her hand like a boa constrictor. I checked me phone for messages again. No Rory. Nobody. I scrolled through me feed of people I used to know from college, posting skiing pictures or moaning about cramming for exams. They all had more exciting lives than me. More money too.

'Your tea is by the kettle.' I pressed the button for the chairlift to go down.

'You're not going to help me get out of this?' Granny was edging downstairs, bit by bit.

'Nah, I thought I'd let you fall out and roll into the kitchen.' I smiled. 'Tempting...' I walked past Granny on the stairs, past pictures of her through the years, getting younger as I walked down. At the bottom of the stairs, there the random wedding picture of Prince William and Kate.

'What if the person who wrote the letter comes back when you're out?'

'It's just a prank Gran, forget about it.' I chewed on me nails. 'Nothing to worry about.'

'How d'you know? What about that Cox-somebody...? That lady politician,' said Gran. 'She didn't even do nothing. But people got upset about what Kirsten did.' Granny nodded towards Kirsten in the kitchen.

'Your majesty.' I held out me hand, and she took it.

She heaved up out of the chair. 'You're a good girl, really. You always look after me.'

'And we'll be fine. It'll all be fine. Nothing bad is going to happen.'

'Hmmm... but your head is in a fantasy land,' said Gran. 'Too many Disney films.'

'Bad things happen in films too.'

Fantasy films are me guilty and not-so-guilty pleasure. Mum and I built up a DVD collection when I was a kid, watching them every Sunday when I was with her. I wish I could go back and save them from the fire, because you can't replace memories like that.

I watched Gran shuffle into the kitchen, dragging her feet across the black and white lino to sit at the table. Something wasn't quite right with the way she was walking. Something was off centre. Kirsten brought Gran her cup of tea, but she was off too. Something felt wrong in the entire house. I shivered with the cold draft. The edges of the windowpanes steamed with our hot breaths. It felt as if an anchor had lifted and we were drifting. Deep down, the letter felt like bad news, but I didn't want to believe it. You had to believe the best in people, no matter what, and it'll come back to you.

Dad poured his coffee into a red take-away cup branded with his gym's name, *Come out fighting*. 'Take the bins out, won't you?'

'Already on it.'

I put me phone into me dress pocket and stepped on the lever. In the bin was a Horlicks container. 'Plastic goes into the recycling!' I fished it out and waved it in the air before tying up the bag.

'They don't recycle it anyway,' said Granny. 'Big conspiracy. All just gets dumped in the ocean.'

'You gotta stop reading that paper.' I heaved the bag out of the bin and took it to the front door. 'You can't believe what you read!'

I put on me long beige sheepskin coat. It used to be me mum's, so the fake furry collar had matted. I walked outside with the bin bags, towards the side of the house. On the pavement, the council had resprayed a picture of a dog saying: *'Clean it up'*. It was a damp and cold morning in March. Empty, still, lifeless. Smoke floated up from the chimneys like sighs. Golden stone houses had been worn down over time to look like soft, soggy custard-cream biscuits. And the hills lay down easily around them as if they'd given up. On a morning like this, when the mist whispered in the valley, I couldn't believe anyone had the energy to be angry at us.

Me breath blew like smoke. But daffodils were starting to break ground. Soon, the village would wake up with spring. People in big boots would walk through again. The festivals would begin. I was desperate for it all, because if you've lived here since forever like I have, you ain't looking to escape like the townies, you're looking to live.

I unlocked me phone and heard me friend Rubi's voice in me head: *Don't message him. You need to go cold turkey. Make him sweat.* But she didn't know Rory like I did. She didn't love him like I did.

Morning…

I waited for the three dots, but there was nothing. I put me phone in me coat pocket, knocked back the bin lid and threw the rubbish in. Pushing stuff down and out of sight was me specialty. There was someone else who may have sent the death threat to us, and I didn't want to mention it to me family. Perhaps what I had said to me boss had come to nothing. Maybe work would just give her a warning.

I closed me eyes, breathed in the warm wood smoke, and went back to me happy thoughts.

Me phone pinged.

I fished it out of me pocket and smiled, because it was as if he knew I was thinking of him.

Morning gorgeous.

3

THE AFTERNOON BEFORE THE FIRE

'I want to be where the people are.'

Ariel, The Little Mermaid

After we got the note, I set sail for work at Lakeside Care Home. As one of the care assistants, I was the one to make sure they were comfortable. We'd be their legs when they couldn't stand, and their brains when they couldn't think straight. It was the one place in the world where I felt like I was going somewhere, doing something real. Helping. The one place I didn't look at everybody else's lives on me phone and wished I was some place else.

I remember it drizzled on the way in. It felt like I was underwater. I was worrying about bumping into Sophie. What would she say? I had an extra buzz to me, a fire in me belly. I needed to scrub every surface and stretch out me muscles that were screwing up from the stress of it all. In me head, I ran through the names of those who might have sent us that note: Our neighbour Mr Post, my colleague Sophie, Kirsten's old boss, etc. But who was the most likely?

I did most of the hard cleaning before everyone in the home woke up. I was on fire, smoking hot, drenched with the smell of bleach and fake-pine. I felt in control. On top of it. Things were spotless, and I had prepped the morning tea. I couldn't wait for them to wake up and be impressed. I'd be a manager in no time. I'll be able to get onto me own two feet, become somebody important, interesting. I needed to get me life going somewhere, ASAP. Like, yesterday. To get a house, a family.

'Mornin' Gerry, are you ready for a wash?' I held on to her hand.

Gerry had a blue room. Carpets, bedding, curtains: all baby-boy blue. But her room wasn't quite an oasis. It was always oven-hot in the care home, even in our short-sleeved blue shirts. Me hair stuck to the edges of me face and neck.

'I'm not crazy. I know what year it is. I know who the prime minister is.' Gerry's eyes bulged.

'You know more than me.' I propped up her bed.

'I can wash myself, you know.'

'I know, but what a luxury to have someone else do it for you.'

'You're soaking!' She pulled her head back. 'Did you swim here?'

'Feels like it.'

She pulled herself more upright in the hospital-like bed. Gerry would always tell you how you were doing something wrong. But never how to do it right. She had big teeth that she liked to bite you with and red blotchy skin. But she tells it how it is. And I liked not having to guess what she was thinking.

'I knew it was going to rain before it did.' She put on her black-rimmed glasses.

'Did you?'

'Oh yeah, can feel it in me bones. Me arthritis.'

'Do you need painkillers?'

'No, I'm fine.' She flicked her hair.

'Cuppa?'

'No, I'm fine. Stop asking! You're interrupting me. I was going to say something. You know, I can't see out of the window.'

I parted the wavy blue curtains. There was nothing to see but drizzle. I couldn't see the way I had walked in. On the commute, I'd wondered if I could walk into the cow field and not get clumps of mud stuck onto me boots. There was no use trying to drive and park on these pokey roads. There was no room. Winter had soaked into the valley and turned it to soggy bread. I had tucked me black trousers into me socks, but I still got mud on them. The fence in the field out front faded out of sight. The Cotswolds are full of fences to keep you out. You have to know the paths, the secret ways through. Know where to duck and dive over stiles, between houses and cows.

'Supposed to clear up later,' I said. 'But it keeps changing its mind. Wasn't supposed to rain at all today.'

'Makes no difference to me.' Gerry leaned over to turn off her blue bedside lamp. 'Place is dull no matter what the weather.'

'Seems to always rain here. But I guess that's why it's so green.' I put on plastic gloves to get ready to wash her. I focused on the task in front, trying not to think about what I had said to the manager. I didn't want to think about the letter that came, the bags under Dad's eyes, the off-centre walk of Gran, the storm brewing. I had to stop thinking about all of it.

Gerry leaned into me, a hint of a smile. 'I heard you got that Sophie girl fired.'

I dropped the wet cloth on the floor, and it landed with a splat. 'She got fired? Are you sure?'

Most of the time, dementia made Gerry crabby and forgetful. But despite it, she had an excellent memory for Lakeside gossip. She used to be a journalist, and to her, digging up information was a public service. 'That's what I heard. You threw her under the bus.'

'I didn't!'

'Poor girl. I liked her. But she couldn't stand George. Used to beat his wife, you know.'

'I know, but we have to look after everyone here. No matter what.'

'I heard he didn't just beat his wife. His kids want nothing to do...'

There was a cry from another room. 'Be back in a mo, Geraldine.'

'Don't you call me that,' she said. 'It's Gerry.'

On the floor in the next room, like a fish out of water, was Mr Tune. He would never wait for us to help him get out of bed. So he'd always end up on the floor. He was too heavy to be helped up. He was also too big for the inflatable mats we used, so we could never roll him on.

'Oh, Mr Tune! Not again! What you doing down there? Takin' a rest?' I put me hands on me hips.

'Just trying to get going. I'm a shaker and a mover! Used to have me own company.' He tried to get up. 'I got a PhD. And I was an Olympic runner! I did a marathon in three hours.'

'Really?' I raised an eyebrow. 'Three hours? Now, have you hit your head anywhere? Or hurt yourself?'

'All fine, matron! Got good padding.' He patted his Olympic-sized belly like a pregnant woman.

I spotted Gladys going down the bright white corridor. She was striding in that way she does when she's on a mission. 'Hey, Glads!'

She stopped, stood in the door frame and clapped. 'Mr Tune. Not again!' Her semi-permanent eyelash extensions fluttered like butterflies.

'Help me get him up, won't you?' I reached me hand out to her like I was drowning.

'You know we can't, Scarlett!' She leaned on the doorframe and smiled. Her gold tooth caught the light.

'Today's different. Come on.... Look.' I flexed me bicep at her and smiled. 'I'm feeling strong.'

'Oh, good!' Mr Tune tapped his belly.

'Scarlett, we ain't supposed to...' said Gladys. 'You know what Elma would say. Ambulance.'

'For this guy? No way. Light as a feather. Right, Mr Tune?'

'Scarlett, you are me favourite person.' He and I grinned.

'Come on, Glads. We shouldn't bug 'em unless it's an actual emergency.'

'But...'

'Just this once. Promise.'

Gladys checked the corridor. I loved working with her. She never slacked off. Always wanted to help, and all the residents loved her teasing. 'Alright, but only if you promise to swap me Saturday shift with me.'

'For Friday?'

'Exactly.'

'OK, deal.'

I leaned down on one side of Mr Tune, and Gladys leaned down on the other side, looping our arms under his. 'On three. One, two, three.'

I had overestimated me strength and underestimated his size. We got up halfway and hovered as we heaved. I really wanted to help Mr Tune, to get him up, to make him feel right again, to feel like I could manage and lead the way. But instead of going up, I felt him tip to Gladys' side. I heard a shuffle and a slip. Mr Tune fell back down to the ground.

'Shit shit shit! Me hand. I landed on me hand.'

I rushed over to see Gladys. She held her wrist. 'You okay?'

'No no no, I think it's broken. Shit.'

'How do you know?'

'I'm training to be a nurse,' she said. 'I *knew* we should've called the ambulance. Now we definitely need one.'

Gladys's mum picked her up to take her to A&E, and they called me into me boss' office.

'Come on in, Scarlett.' Elma's Filipino accent was stronger than usual, and she was holding onto the lanyard around her neck. 'I wanted to talk to you about a few things.'

She had this clamped-on smile, no matter what she was saying. Like a shellfish that just wouldn't open. She had the potential to be soft and squidgy, but I never could get past her shell. She smiled. I sat down on the low chair opposite her huge, beige desk that swept around her like a bench. I waited to be sentenced, to hear the hammer come down. Me future, down the plughole.

'First, we let Sophie go.' She said it while still grinning, and pushed the computer keyboard away from her.

' 'cause of what I said? Does she know?'

'It's confidential.'

'So she doesn't know it was me?'

'No.'

So it couldn't have been Sophie who sent the threat to us that morning. So if it wasn't her, maybe Kirsten was right...

'But there were a few warning signs that we'd rather stay on the right side of. Which brings me to me second point.' She laced her fingers together and rested her arms on the desk.

'Second point?'

'Don't bite your nails. It's not hygienic.'

'Sorry.' I sat on me hands.

'Now, about this afternoon. With Mr Tune.'

'I was just trying to help. Just trying to get Mr Tune up and I...'

I started me defence, but she cut me off. 'You know as well as I do you are *not* supposed to attempt getting him up without help.' She was still smiling, but shaking her head at me. 'Gladys explained you made her feel like she had to help you.'

'I didn't! She insisted.'

'And when she suggested an ambulance, you refused.' She shook her head and tutted, but was still smiling, so I didn't know what it meant.

'It wasn't like that!' I was on the edge of me seat. 'Honest. Is she OK? Glads?'

'She has a broken wrist, Scarlett. So I'm afraid I'm going to have to suspend you.' For a second, the smile slipped off her face before she picked it back up again. She straightened the computer screen.

'What?'

'It really does pain me to lose three staff members for the next few weeks, believe me. But you put Gladys in harm's way. We take the health and safety of everyone seriously. And that includes those who work here. Not just who we care for.'

'But...' I reached forward to plead me case. I grabbed a seashell she had on her desk. A dusty clam. 'I promise I won't do it again. I promise I'll...'

'I know you were just trying to help Mr Tune. But I need you to *think*. Not cut corners. OK?'

'I just didn't want to trouble the ambulance people.' I couldn't look at her anymore. I tapped the shell on the desk, trying to get it to open up.

'I know. But that was a poor decision. You have to be more realistic and assess the situation properly. When you get back, we will put you through training again. Health and safety and all that. And hopefully, we'd have learned our lesson.' She titled her head to one side as an afterthought, as if somebody had told her she should do it.

'Lesson?'

'Yes, Scarlett. It wasn't you who'd be bothering the paramedics. It was Mr Tune. His fault for not waiting for us to help him. If we don't look after our staff, then there'll be no-one to look after the residents.'

'But...'

She raised her hand in a 'stop right there' signal and her eyes floated wide. I clammed up, retreated into myself. I was so embarrassed. Who was I kidding, thinking I could be a manager? I couldn't even be an assistant without messing up.

'Tammy has agreed to cover your shifts, so grab your stuff and off you go. I'll call you in a few days.'

I put down the hollow shell and got up from the chair. I don't really remember leaving. I sorted of floated out. It was like I'd been cut adrift. Overboard. Two weeks with Granny, and nothing but me own thoughts. I had nothing but the stuff I didn't want to think about.

4

THE AFTERNOON BEFORE THE FIRE

'I want a spell to change my mum.
That'll change my fate.'

Merida from Brave

Me mum lives in the 'rough' part of Stonecloud. A housing estate down near the stream. The village literally looks down their noses at this part of the town. The houses all have wire fences instead of brick walls. There aren't any old houses in golden stone. But nobody in her street cared about what anyone thought, which was good because so much work was needed on Mum's house. There was the shell of a Ford Focus in her front garden: no wheels, no doors, no engine or bonnet. Tall grass grew around it, like it was being swallowed by the ground. It had been there since mum moved in. Everyone in the village had tried to complain to the Council. They called it an eyesore, *Bringing down the tone of the village,* they said. But Mum didn't want to tidy up somebody else's mess. Mum wasn't from around these parts. She was an outsider. She had been looking to escape from London too.

After work told me to go home, I went to see how she was. Mum was me best mate, after Rubi. She wanted us to be close, to be like sisters. She'd tell me everything. We used to have this thing she called *Midnight Madness*. She'd drag me out of bed, giggling, and into the garden to look at the stars. Mum didn't laugh like a normal person - she cackled like a witch. Her laugh was so loud and wicked, you'd end up in stitches too. She still had a baby tooth left, which you could see when she laughed. She said it was the source of her magic, and what made her look young.

But the problem is that there be a good witch and a wicked witch inside me mum. When work said that Sophie didn't know anything about me telling on her, it had made me wonder about Mum. I should check on her more regardless. But there was no knowing which way she'd be. You had to be brave. And I needed to know if the wicked witch was back, to see whether she was the one sending us notes.

Mum answered the door. Her face did lots of weird things I couldn't figure out. 'Scarlett?'

'Hey, Mum.' I dived forward and gave her a tight squeeze. She always said that me hugs were the best, so I gave her a good one that she'd remember. 'You need to get rid of that wreck.'

'It's not hurting anyone,' she said. 'What are you doing here?'

'Wanted to come see you, silly! Me favourite mum.'

'You're not working today?'

'Shift finished early,' I said, not wanting to worry her about me suspension. 'Was a good day. Got a lot done. But...'

'Hold on a sec,' said Mum, closing the door a tad. 'Just got to tidy up a bit.'

'What? Mum! Don't be daft. It's only me. Don't shut me out!' All I could hear was rummaging around. I couldn't believe she'd shut the door on me. It was as if everyone was trying to keep me out. 'I want to get out of the rain.' I pushed the door open and got an electric shock.

She closed the dresser. There was a suitcase near the door. She wasn't wearing her usual fluffy off-white onesie. She had on her white mac coat as if she was going out.

'You going somewhere, Mum?'

'What?'

'What's with the bag?'

'Oh, I got it out to see if it was cabin size,' she said.

'Why?'

'Just dreaming. What you got there?' She pointed to the tote bag in me hand.

'Got you some milk and eggs, just in case.'

'Oh, great!' She came closer and grabbed the bag. 'All out of milk today.'

'Mum, it's freezing in here.'

'I know, I know, the heating's broken.' She rubbed her hands together as if she was hoping she could light a fire from the will of it. She was a bundle of twigs to me, ready to catch. Each time I visited her, she seemed smaller, closer to snapping. 'That's why I've been dreaming about going to hot places.'

I checked around the house. Everything was pale and slumped, like her. It seemed as if it was all sagging, collapsing. Even the Budda on the 70s gas grated fireplace seemed to have let himself go more than usual.

'Where's Jim?'

'Jim?'

'Mum.'

'Oh, don't give me that voice.'

'What voice?'

'That Mary Poppins voice, like I haven't cleaned me room.'

I followed her into the kitchen, looking for signs of Jim and whether he intended to come back. He'd been in and out of her life for years. I was sure he used her for a place to stay. In the kitchen, plates had piled up in the sink. The washing machine had wiggled out, pushing up the brown lino into waves. 'I... I just worry about you is all,' I said. 'Has he left again?'

'I'm sure he'll be back soon. Just another one of those jobs, no doubt. Look, put down the sponge. Stop cleaning.'

'I don't mind, just a quick wipe-over.' I wiped up around the kettle. 'Get the spilt sugar.'

'I just did that.' She took the sponge off me. 'Why don't you sit down and I'll make you a cuppa to warm us up, yeah?'

'Alright.' I watched her go to the kettle and shadowed her. Her breath was visible, and mine. I couldn't help but watch her, to search for the signs. The ones that came before she turned into a wicked witch.

'Mum?'

'Yes, darling.'

'Uh...' I leaned forward on me tippy-toes and put me head on her shoulder. She smelt like incense. 'Can I come live with you?'

She dropped a teaspoon down the crack between the cooker and the cabinet. 'Damn, damn, damn. Stupid woman! Pull yourself together.' Mum always had these talks with herself, this inner fight. She'd fire off insults, work-up to a war with herself. They were like incantations, spells she had rehearsed and practiced over and over again. I always wondered whose spell she was under. Could I break it like Merida in Brave? Maybe it was all part of her curse.

'Ahh, please Mum! Please please please. I promise you I will be the *best* person to live with.'

She turned around and I couldn't read her face again. 'Scarlett darling, why would you want to come live here? Look.'

'I just feel a bit...' I had wanted to say lonely, but I didn't want to look desperate.

'I'm not sure I could afford to.' She turned back to pour hot water into our mugs.

'I've got a job now. Been saving up a deposit to move out. But I could pay rent if you need it.'

'That wouldn't be right.' She frowned and shook her head.

'You look like you could do with it,' I said. 'With Jim gone. I could help out again. Like I used to. Remember?' I started singing: 'Just a spoon full of sugar helps the medicine go down...'

Mum turned around, a mug in each hand, stage-smiling. 'The medicine go doooown,' she sang. 'The medicine go down.' She passed me a mug as she swayed her head. 'You know I love you, don't you?'

Ding ding ding!

The alarm went off in me head. Sign Number One - the witch ain't dead. She used to always tell me she loved me before she lost it, before the spell came over her. The wicked witch was alive and well. So did that mean she was scribbling notes to Dad and Kirsten? It was hard to see her sending us such a thing. But sometimes she'd open an envelope and then throw a glass at the wall. The spell came over her. She'd be the beast, raging. She'd swear and swear and swear that she'd get revenge on me dad.

'You're still taking them, right?'

'Taking what?'

'Your meds!'

'Yes, yes, of course.' She waved me off. 'Oh, you were so cute in your little coat and scarf. Do you remember we made a hat out of a Frosties box and lined it with a bin bag and daisies? You'd run around tidying up and tucking me in like one of the kids. So cute.'

'See, was fun having me here! It'll be fun again.'

'Have you seen here?'

'We've been in worse. Nothing Mary Poppins can't handle.'

She walked to the saggy sofa in the living room and fell into it. 'I'm no good for you, darling,' she said. 'Don't you remember?'

I did.

When me mum and dad first broke up, I lived with her.

Midnight Madness became something way darker. She used to wake me up with a hurricane of boozy breath with something rotten in the eye of her storm. She used to be a train driver. But one day, someone stepped out in front. She'd wake me up in the night to tell me she saw the person's face hit the window. She would dream it night after night. And the face in her dream was always her own. She'd ask me what I thought it meant. But I had no answers.

'It wasn't that bad.'

She was staring at the doors of the dresser she'd closed. Her gaze went so far she could probably see through into next door. 'No, no, I don't need you looking after me, Scarlett.' Her gaze snapped back into the room as if I'd clicked me fingers. 'I'm fine. And you'll be fine.'

'So you'd rather have Jim here than me?' I sat down next to her and lay me head face-down in her lap so it muffled anything I said. 'I miss you.'

She stroked me head and sighed.

'Why's it warmer in here?' I lifted me head up.

'Is it?'

'Yeah, like... I can feel it.' I got up to look around. 'It's coming from the dresser.'

'Scarlett!'

I opened the doors of the old-fashioned wooden dresser, and inside there were lamps and trays and straw and a marbled brown egg. 'What's this?'

'I found it outside,' she said. 'Thought I'd try to give it a good start, you know? I keep hearing this blackbird out the back and I wonder if it's hers, but I can't see a nest out there.'

'Where did you get the lamps from?'

'A friend of mine, in the village.' She leaned forward and pushed the straw up around it as if tucking it in. I never thought I'd be jealous of an egg before.

'Probably dead already,' I said. 'What will you do if it hatches?'

'Look after it.' She adjusted one of the small lamps. 'Then let it go. Best be shutting the doors, though. Got to keep it warm, darling, or it'll never hatch.' I backed away, but as she was closing the doors, I noticed a pile of opened envelopes behind it.

'Mum?'

'Best not mention it to anyone, Scarlett.' She sat back down on the sofa. 'Not sure the council would be happy. Don't want to get kicked out.'

'Sure, I won't say anything.' I needed to ask her. I just had to come right out and say it, and see what happens. Did you send your own daughter a death threat? It was absurd, but me mum could be absurd when the witch was around. I just needed to take a deep breath and...

'Don't bite your nails.' She pulled me hand from me mouth as I sat next to her. 'They'll go back to those bloody stumps you used to have. Awful they were. Looked like I was abusing you.'

I took a deep breath. 'Did you post us a letter this morning?'

'What do you mean?'

'Well, we got a letter. All in red. Told us to die. Wasn't you, was it?'

'What?! Of course not. Why would you think that?' She bolted upright, put her hand to her chest as if I had offended her in a Downton Abbey Victorian Drama.

'Because you hate Dad? Kirsten?'

'Hate?' She blew out her lips and rolled her eyes. 'I can't believe you think that about me. That you'd...'

'I'm sorry, I didn't mean it.' I got up quick, before the second sign that the witch was coming, before she said it was all me fault.

'Hug?' I put out me arms. 'Forgive me?'

She sighed and wouldn't look at me as I leaned down to hug her. 'I'm not a total monster, you know.'

'I didn't say you were. Well, I'll be going...' I stood up straight and checked me phone, but there were no messages back from Rory. He was the only one I had told about being suspended from work. I had that feeling again, of being lost. Like I used to feel when I was a kid. The one when you get lost and you can't find your mum. You cry and reach out to her, but she ain't nowhere to be seen. 'Love you, Mum,' I said. 'I'll call in on you soon, OK?'

'I'm fine!' She crossed her arms. 'You don't need to worry about me. I do just fine on me own. I don't need anybody.'

By the front door on the windowsill, there was a pile of unopened mail and a red pen. I heard Kirsten's voice in me head: 'Maybe it's your ex... Maybe it's your ex.' But then I thought of Mum and the egg, and I shook the thought from me mind like a wand casting a spell: obliterate. Because it didn't matter how bad me mum was, she wasn't a monster. She couldn't help the way she was.

THE FIRE

I LOVE WEST STONECLOUD FACEBOOK GROUP

Ashley Campbell Piece of history going up tonight folks!

Jim Millard is everyone out the house?'

Ellie Lancaster Wow look at him burn.

Dawn Carter Everyone nearby has been evacuated.

Freezing my balls off here @**Geoff Dance.**

Gill Cooper Firemen have arrived.

Kiren Jones 'Firefighter'.

Gill Cooper God - seriously?

Kiren Jones We live in the 21st Century.

Sam Harvey Good job we got a station in the town.

Brian Jones Heard it was arson, did you hear that @bowlyjoe?

Gareth Peel Arson? God almighty. is it that Saint family? Poor sods.

Linn Keating But we can see why, right?

Jill Roberts Why?

Cheryl Williams Nobody deserves that though.

5

AFTER THE FIRE

'We're dead. We survived, but we're dead.'

Dash, The Incredibles.

After the fire, we had to move into a house on the edge of two worlds. I think when you're dead, you should stay dead. You've had your chance. You're already out of this world, and you should stay there, end of. Don't go haunting the living just because you've got nothing better to do. Me friend Rubi lived in a haunted B&B down in the valley. It was an ancient inn, with ribs of wooden beams inside and out. The whole place warped and leaned to one side like it was being pushed into another realm.

When Rubi's parents first moved in, they spent a lot of time trying to cleanse it, trying to get rid of the man rocking a baby, trying to solve his unfinished business. But they soon found out that he wasn't the only housemate they had. So they made a business out of it instead. Me dad had helped them to expand. He converted out-houses and barns and coal sheds into non-haunted hotel rooms. But he stopped short of helping them theme the rooms: The Haunting, Dracula, The Blair Witch Project (that was glamping), and The Cabin in the Woods (which was, yep - in an actual proper cabin). And then there was me favourite: The Shining, a 1970s psychedelic room. You had to snake through a tiny, hedged maze to get to the front door. Inside, it had orange carpets with a black honeycomb print, a bloody typewriter on a desk, a black-and-white picture of Rubi's family in ball gowns and tuxes, and an axe in the door that opened into the bathroom.

Rubi's parents put us up in the cabin. Four people squished into a one-bedroom shack, all stood around in our pyjamas. The wind rumbled the corners as if something bigger was walking through. Trees above us thrashed it out, blowing off leaves and branches that fell on top of the roof, making us jump up to the ceiling so many bloody times we might as well have stayed on it. Granny was sitting in the living room on the sofa, looking like a zombie. Dad was under the sink trying to stop the tap from dripping. I was standing by, ready to help, and Kirsten draped herself between the curtains, looking out of the window towards the main house.

'This place gives me the willies.' Kirsten shivered. 'Not sure I can stay here. I'll never sleep.'

'There's nothing wrong with this one.' Dad's voice sounded far away, in a cave.

'The wind out there just makes it creepier,' said Kirsten. 'Why would anybody want to go on one of those tours they do?'

'Just a load of smoke and mirrors.' Granny flicked her hand. 'Bunch of charlatans.'

'No, they're not.' I waved a spanner at Gran.

'What about that place you're looking after?' Kirsten stared at me. 'The one with the swimming pool.'

'What place?' Granny bolted upright as if she were revived.

'I'm looking after a house for a lady. She's trying to sell, but she's already moved.'

This house was me dream house. It was an old Cotswold manor house. There were roses climbing up the front, and a pool in a conservatory out of the back. I went there to swim and pretend I was rich.

'Would she let us stay there?' Kirsten's eyebrows arched up.

Dad emerged out from under the sink. 'Why didn't I know about this?'

'Uhhhh, I dunno.'

'She told us ages ago.' Kirsten rolled her eyes.

'I don't know how to get hold of her,' I said. 'Her number was on me phone, which is now molten lava.'

I've been kicking myself for not picking up me phone when I left. But all I could see was smoke, and I didn't have time to rescue anything else. I only picked up me old umbrella to help fan the smoke away.

'Maybe her neighbours have her number?' Kirsten peered out of the window again to someone walking by.

'What's *he* doing?' I pointed away from myself and to our neighbour outside.

'Who?'

'Mr Post,' I said. 'There. He just pulled a toolbox out of the bush.'

'A toolbox?'

'Yeah, and... a tripod?'

Mr Post was the neighbour Granny kept arguing with. He was like a raven with his black hair, black clothes, and a hooked nose. In his hand, he had a box. It looked like a toolbox, but was square and fancy. He had a tripod, which made it look like he was going to paint or do a photoshoot.

'That man...' Granny shook her head. 'Y' know, I found him outside feeding that owl. Gave him hell I did. No wonder it stays around town 'cause he's bloody keeping it as a pet! Stupid man.

And it's going 'round town scaring people's dogs and attacking 'em. They're not native, y' know.'

'He was nowhere to be seen last night.' Kirsten perched on the windowsill. 'Which is odd, don't you think?'

'I thought they said he wasn't home? His house was empty.'

'But there he is, in the bushes,' said Kirsten. 'So where was he last night when our house was burning down and his almost went with it?'

'Do you think he did it?' I joined Kirsten by the window, and she raised her pencil-drawn eyebrows at me.

'There's no way he did it! He'd of done it years ago otherwise.' Granny looked away. 'Was one of your voters!'

'What do you mean?' I said. 'You're always at each other's throats. Maybe this was the last straw.'

'Don't you yell at me, Scarlett.'

'What? I'm not yelling at you.'

'You are!'

There was a knock at the door. I went to open it to stop Gran from launching into a rant. Rubi stood in yellow wellies and a tartan wool coat that passed her knees. She was like a crumpled picnic blanket, holding a pile of clothes. Her pink hair-dye was washing out, fading to blonde. Like me, she never got out of the village either.

'Morning Saints! Brought you some clothes if you want them.'

'Ah, that's amazing, thank you. Put them over here.' Kirsten cleared the dining table of mugs and small plates. 'Going to raid the charity shops later. It's so kind of your mum and dad to have us.' She smiled with too many bottom teeth. 'We won't overstay our welcome, don't worry. Scarlett might get us somewhere to stay, isn't that right?'

'I dunno...'

'It's not a problem.' Rubi waded over to the table. I followed close by, ready to lend a hand. 'Honest. It was a quiet week for us.'

I was five-years-old when I first met Rubi at a Halloween party. She dressed up as a ghost and didn't speak to no-one. I went as Mary Poppins because that was the only costume I had. It took me an hour, but she eventually let me hide under the sheet with her and together, we went around the room going 'boo' to people. We laughed so hard we blew snot bubbles. Every Halloween after that, as a tradition, we'd go to parties dressed up as one ghost.

Rubi dropped the clothes as neatly as she could. They were all very flowery, colourful, non-branded, and some knitted. Rubi's family moved to the valley from Stroud and I remember me gran telling me it was good to have friends higher up the ladder from us. But I didn't really see it myself. Rubi's family was just a bunch of hippies with posh accents. Her dad wore a scarf all the time and her mum insisted on everything being biodegradable, and Rubi never liked to wear socks much, or shoes.

'I've got some carrots for Destiny, too. Where is she?'

'Give them 'ere.' Gran waved. 'She's in her pen outback of the house. I'll take 'em to her. I don't like her being there on her own. We should move her 'ere.'

I got close to Rubi, out of earshot of the others. 'You heard from Rory?'

'No, why?'

'I left me phone in the house.'

'Oh no!' She smiled - mocking me.

'Was just worried he might be trying to get in touch.'

'I'm sure he knows. I can lend you mine some time. How you holding up?'

'Never better,' I said. 'It's like a holiday.'

'What have you been smoking?'

'Just one we didn't pack for.' I joined Kirsten in sorting through the clothes.

'Or wanted. It's not like a trip to Spain, is it?' Rubi grabbed a yellow top. 'Whoops. Not that one.'

'Get me a mojito and we'll be halfway there.' I grinned.

'Oh, I could do with a Sherry,' said Granny. 'On ice.'

'It's not even ten AM.' With a jumper in her hand, Kirsten pointed at the clock.

'Considerin' *me* house just burned down. I think this might be *exceptional circumstances*.' Granny held onto her walking stick as if it were a sceptre.

'She makes a point.' I picked up a pair of jeans to check the waist size. Rubi was much smaller than me, so I was hoping they were her mum's.

'Not worried about who did it?' said Rubi. 'The fire, I mean.'

'We got a hunch.' Kirsten picked up a purple skirt that used to be Rubi's and held it to her waist.

'The police will figure it out. They got all those forensics and stuff now. Can't breathe without them knowing, right?'

So far, I had completely underestimated how far someone with a grudge might go. I didn't think for a minute that there would be people who'd want us as dead. But I had the utmost faith in our police. They'd sort it all out. All I could think about was Rory, and whether he was worried about me, and why he hadn't been in touch yet considering everything that had happened.

Rubi sat down next to Gran. 'It would freak me out. I mean, to think someone's lurking in the shadows wanting to...'

'But you live with *actual proper* ghosts.' I said. 'That's got to be worse.'

Rubi frowned and pouted, as she considered it. 'Most of the time, they just want to scare us.'

'Exactly. Maybe the arsonist just wanted to do the same,' I said.

'Or they break things, like that sink there.'

'I thought you said this one wasn't haunted, Jason?' Kirsten turned around to Dad.

Rubi glared at me, eyes wide. 'Just saying we have... You know, ghosts in the pipes. Probably just wear and tear.' Rubi got up and walked over to the kitchenette. 'How's it going under there, Mr Saint?'

'Be a damn sight better if I had me dad's tools,' he said. 'Should have got those from the house instead of that stupid toy.'

We had all regretted not taking something else from the house. I wished I could have taken me phone, and all me DVDs: Disney series, Pixar collection, Lord of the Rings trilogy... Granny wished she'd taken her vinyl records, Kirsten - her box file of bills and admin, and now Dad and his tools. But they were all too big to take down a ladder really. We couldn't have done it.

'I could ask Dad if he has any other tools?' Rubi leaned on the countertop.

'No no. It's just they don't make tools like that no more. Proper sturdy stuff. Last a lifetime.'

'Where are they, Dad?' I leaned on the countertop too.

'Where are what?'

'The tools.'

'Oh no you don't. Don't you even.' Rubi shook her head.

'What?'

'They've not given it the all clear, Scarlett,' said Dad.

'We could ask someone to get them for us?'

Dad pointed a wrench at me. 'Don't you dare go into that house. Y' hear me?'

'Okay, fine!' I threw down the blue top in me hands. There was no way any of these clothes were going to fit me. 'Was just a thought... Got any shoes I could borrow, Rubes?'

'Up in the barn.'

'I'll come with you.'

'Scarlett.' Kirsten came up to me, twisting the skirt in her hands. 'Could you try to get hold of that woman? Go to the neighbours or something. No offence Rubi, but this place gives me the creeps.'

'Not at all. That's our business!' Rubi opened the door.

'I'll try,' I said. 'But I can't promise anything.'

I followed Rubi out towards her parent's house. The wind was blowing at us, clearing out the cobwebs. I ran after her, along the wood-chipped path through the small copse of trees. 'Could I use your phone?'

'Why?'

'Just to check something.'

'Ah, not Rory again. Forget about him. He's no good for you.'

'But maybe he hasn't heard. I just want to message him.'

'Not a chance.' She waved her hand. 'I'm saving you from yourself.'

'We're still friends,' I said. 'It's fine. It's not weird.'

'It is weird! He treated you like shit. I won't be your enabler.' Rubi put on her gloves as she walked.

'He was just upset.' I shivered. 'He didn't mean it. He's had a tough upbringing. You don't know him like I do.'

'You need to get some self respect, lady. A-Sap.'

'I do. I just...'

'He doesn't care, trust me.' We stopped at the dutch door of Rubi's house. There was an Easter wreath on the wooden door filled with colourful eggs. Her family didn't live in the haunted cottage anymore. They had converted the barn next door to live in.

'So who do you think did it? The fire?'

'Oh, I dunno.' I wrapped me hands around me arms.

'There are rumours going around on chats,' said Rubi. 'About some girl called Sophie. People think she did it. Why would they think that?'

'Dunno. Doesn't matter.' I shrugged as I lied, glancing back towards the cabin. 'We won't be with you for long, I don't think.

43

They'll let us back in soon. Damage ain't *that* bad. Mostly cosmetic. Nothing a bit of cleaning can't fix.'

'I know what you're thinking.' Rubi grabbed the door handle and fixed me with her gaze. 'You want to go get them.'

'Get what?'

'The tools. It's a reaaaaallly dumb idea.'

'How bad can it be?'

'The roof could collapse on you. Or the floorboards could give way... Do you want to be dead meat?'

'It'll be fine, trust me. Me dad really needs them. More than you can tell.'

Dad had lost all of his colouring. He was dead-pale - ghostly. His gaze seemed to echo and drag off into the distance like he was in an actual cave. If I could get him his tools, he'd feel better. He'd feel more in control, more able to do stuff, to do something about the situation we'd got in. If I could get him his tools, it would make him happy. It would bring him back to life again. He'd fix our house up in no time at all.

I jumped up and down to keep warm. 'Can we go in?'

'But what about that other house?' Rubi opened the door and a wave of warmth blew over me. 'The one Kirsten wants to stay in.'

'Not a chance. They'll never sell it if us Saints are in it. We ain't exactly the model brochure family.'

6

'One shoe can change your life.'

Cinderella

The next day, Rubi and I walked to me house in the soapy morning sun. I felt it sink down into me. I was a dry sponge soaking it up. I was wearing clothes from the high-street charity shop. Rubi had given me a pair of pumps and a coat that felt like a shammy cloth and smelt like boot polish. It was strange to walk in her shoes. They weren't exactly Rubi's shoes, though. They were ones she'd never worn. Ones her mum wanted her to wear. But she never really fit into them.

'Are you sure you're alright in those?' She stared down at me feet as I shuffled in her pumps.

'Yeah, fine!' They pinched and rubbed at the back, even though they felt alright when I tried them on.

'It was when Mum tried to get me to wear something besides the combat boots.'

'The glitter was a bit of a stretch... But then again, what's with the lipstick?' I pointed to her mouth. 'Who is he?'

'Who?'

'The bloke who's got you wearing lipstick.' I grabbed her arm and made a kissy face.

'Alright gerrof.' She batted me away. 'His name is Ramone. He arrived on Wednesday. But I've not had a chance to, you know...' She elbowed me. 'He's Spanish. Ola!'

'Oh, you've never had a Spanish one!'

'I know. Aren't they supposed to be...?' She put out both her hands as if about to do a robot dance. Then pushed her palms apart while comedy-waggling her eyebrows.

'Rubes!'

'Whaaat?! I heard they're hung like a...'

'Curtain?'

'Ha. Well... He can *drape* himself over me anytime.' She winked.

'Good one.' I rolled me eyes. 'Now I'll never be able to look him in the eye. So what about the other boyfriends?'

Every week, she had a new guy. She had boyfriends in a lot of countries. Not that she got to see any of them.

'Por favor! Maybe I'll drop the others. Long distance never works.'

'Spain is long distance too, y' know.'

'Yeah, I need someone local. But there's nobody in this town, Scar! I'll die alone.'

I wasn't sure Rubi was really wanting to settle. Why else would she keep going for the guests in her parents' B&B? She could just go on Tinder or some other dating app but she never did.

We were walking uphill. The houses looked as if they'd been pushed together. Terraces that seemed squished-squished-squished into one. There were no roads, just tiny paths called things like Shin Bone Alley. The bush on the pavement was budding. A white magnolia tree was dropping flower petals onto wonky paving slabs. As we peaked the hill and passed under the tree, me house loomed ahead.

'Your house...' Rubi sighed and shook her head as she unbuttoned her coat.

'Home sweet home.'

Smoke shadowed the front like a curse had been put on it. The windows on the ground-floor used to have red wooden frames, but they were black. The front door, smashed to pieces, barely hung on. So there was a gaping hole into the house with police tape zig-zagging across it.

'Least the roof's still on.' I shrugged.

'Yeah, lucky you! Ever the optimist.' Rubi pulled me hand away from me mouth. 'There are no nails left.'

'The town's gunna hate us. Letting the side down, aren't we?'

'Who cares! You just lost your house. This isn't a museum.'

'But we're in a heritage area.'

'God, next we'll need permission to paint our faces.' Rubi stood up straight, one hand on hip, and the other wagging. *You may paint your face as long as it's in keeping with the character of the town.*

'Colour reference: Willow BS12 B17.'

'Oh my god, you know the codes!'

'Had to.'

Our house used to be a pub, but then Gramps converted it. It was on the brink of being abandoned and he rescued it. From what I've heard, Gramps got a lot of stick. Old ladies with tiny dogs used to stop me out front, and said things like 'what a pity.' He kept the swinging pub sign, the stained-glass windows and the plaque to keep everyone else happy. On one window, fancy etchings and the words *Smoke Room were* still there.

'That's ironic now, ain't it?' I pointed and smiled. 'But I'm sure it looks worse than it is. Cleaning goes a long way.'

'Better get to it, Cinders.'

'I've cleaned a *lot* worse at work, trust me.'

She raised her eyebrows. 'That reminds me, that Sophie girl everyone's talking about... Did you used to work with her?'

'Uh yeah, I think so.' I walked ahead towards the house. 'Ready to go in?'

'Wait a minute...' Rubi grabbed me arm and pulled me back. 'Was it you? Did you get her fired?'

'No way. Who said that? I didn't get her fired...' I didn't want Rubi to think I was the sort of person who'd throw someone under the bus, who'd rat someone out. Nothing good came from people thinking you were a snitch.

'That might be a good reason to burn down your house. Bit of poetic justice, maybe?'

'She's not like that.' I pulled away from Rubi's grip. 'And I didn't get her fired.'

'Well, she went to school with Tyler from swim practice. *He* said she's a bit...' Rubi crossed her eyes.

'Don't do that.'

'Her nickname used to be Pyro... Bit of a coincidence, don't you reckon?'

'Kirsten thinks it was me mum.'

'What? No way. That's mental. Did she say that?'

'No, but I can tell.'

'She wouldn't hurt you. Why would she think that?'

I shrugged and ducked under the tape. 'She also thinks it could be Professor death over there.' I pointed to the neighbour's house that was joined on to ours and headed off.

'The squirrel-killing guy? Hey, where are you going?'

'Around the back, should be safer.' I followed side of the house towards the garden.

'Wait for me!'

'Hey Destiny!' I waved to Granny's pig, who ran out of her barrel house and up to the edge of her pen. Her paddling pool inside was empty. I made a note to fill it back up. I walked past the row of roses that Granny had clipped back, spiking out of the ground like barbed wire.

The back door was open. There wasn't much smoke damage at the back of the house. But it was as if somebody had swallowed the sun. Like going into a black hole. When I walked into the hallway, the stale and damp smell of soot and smoke almost knocked me over. Ash piled up in the hallway and living room. The walls were stripped to the bare brick. Everything had gone. Even me optimism had a hard time pushing through this. I sighed. Where the hell do you start? The stairs were half there, but mostly collapsed. They were impossible to climb up. In the hallway, there was a trapdoor I didn't remember being there at all, which was odd. I placed me hands on me head and closed me eyes. It was hard to make Dad happy, but there were moments he'd be proper-grinning from ear to ear. They were priceless. They were moments worth trying to get to.

'You can't go up those.' Rubi showed up behind me. 'I won't let you.'

'I know. I'll take the ladder instead.' I turned back around. 'The one we used to get out.'

'But...'

'It'll be fine. The front has the most damage.' I ran out and picked up the ladder that was now lying on the floor next to Destiny's pen. I put it against the bathroom window. Rubi followed me out.

'Scarlett...'

'Hold the bottom, won't you?'

'Your dad would go mental...'

'I won't be long. It's just going back the way we came. Quick, in and out. Bob's your uncle.'

'And Robert's your mother's brother.'

'What?' I glanced down at her as I started climbing up the ladder, the cold metal slipping in me hands.

'My mum says that,' she shouted up. 'No idea why.'

'I love your mum.' I felt the ladder wobble a bit. 'She's so funny. Proper legend.'

'That's because she isn't *your* mum.'

The bathroom window was still open. 'I'm in!'

'Don't be long, OK?!'

'I'll be quick. Promise.'

I jumped up and over the windowsill, and moved the blackened towels that were in front of the bathroom door. I pushed it open and everything on the landing was black and yellow. It reminded me of burnt toast and soggy bread. Fluffy loft insulation had fallen down from a hole in the ceiling. There were no pictures of us left on the walls. I stepped through mounds of burnt plaster and wooden beams to get to the cupboard, using the walls to keep me balance. Rubi would be glad I was ruining her glittery pumps. So far, so good. No creaking. The landing looked robust.

The toolbox was in the boiler cupboard, which was almost untouched. It took a few tries to open the door with all the stuff in front blocking it. As I grabbed the box on the shelf, the lid opened, and it fell over. A hammer and pliers fell out. I crouched down to pick them up. A piece of paper was stuck to the bottom. I slid it out. It was a picture of a baby. But I couldn't remember the clothes or the background. They'd propped me up on some sort of checkered sofa, but not one I remembered Mum or Dad having.

The house groaned and creaked. So I put it in me pocket and closed up the box to get out quick. I closed the cupboard door, but as I turned, the floor gave way. Me stomach dropped. Me legs scraped on the way down, scratching me up. Soot and debris flew up into me face like a black cloud. I caught myself from falling all the way. But I was hanging by me armpits, with me legs dangling downstairs. Darkness surrounded me head.

'What the hell was that?' Rubi shouted from outside. 'You OK? What's going on?'

'Bit of a situation, Rubes!' I started coughing from the soot that was now a dust cloud around me.

'Oh my god! I can see your legs through the window! Your legs! I'm going to go get help.'

One shoe had come off, and I was barely holding onto the other. I tried to pull myself up. But I was too low. Me arms ached. I wouldn't be able to hold on forever. I was dropping lower and lower each second as I waited. Each cough weakened me grip. But the soot was settling. Light was fading in. A glisten in the air. But I couldn't see the toolbox.

'Scarlett! Scarlett! I have someone,' Rubi shouted beneath me. I figured she must be by the kitchen door.

'Who?'

'What's your name?'

'My name's Scott,' said a posh voice. 'I'm Scott! Just moving in down the street. Now I think your best bet is to fall through. The floor is solid here, and I'll catch you. Or at least break your fall.'

'Really? But I'll crush you.'

'On three.'

'Three?'

'Drop on three,' shouted Rubi.

'But what about the toolbox?'

'*Leave* the goddamn box! For God's sake, Scarlett.'

'Right,' said Scott. 'One. Two. Three.'

I closed me eyes, took a deep breath and pulled me arms up into a pencil dive. I felt me stomach jump like on a diving board. Me arms scratched on the way down. I landed on top of Scott. A mangle of legs and arms. His elbow hit me head, but I was pretty sure I'd done more damage. 'Oh my god! I'm so, so so sorry. Are you OK?'

He was wearing an Oasis T-shirt and jacket. He flicked his hair out of his eyes. 'Is this yours?' He held up me blackened, glittery shoe.

'Sorta.' I took it from him. 'Thanks for the soft landing.'

'Not a problem.' He sprang up onto his feet. 'I've got to go, parents are waiting for me.' He rushed out of the door. 'See you around!'

He'd gone before either of us could say another thing. 'Did that just happen?'

'You mean the hot toff saving you? Yeah.' Rubi nodded.

'Oh my god, and to think I crushed him.' I lay back down on the floorboards for a proper swoon.

'He's like your knight in shining armour. Come to save the day!' Rubi put her hands out for me to grab.

'We have to find him. We should have run after him or got his number or...'

'ScarlettScarlettScarlett.' Rubi stepped over me, grabbed me shoulders and shook me.

'But...'

'Please, can we get the feck out of your house before it swallows us.' She heaved me up.

'Yeah, sure, good shout.' We got up, and I followed her out into the sunshine in the back garden. 'Did you see his top? His eyes? Where do you think he went?'

'Who knows?' Rubi stared up at the house. 'I'm just glad we're out in one piece. Your dad would've killed me.'

'I did get one thing from the toolbox that he might want.' I took the picture I found out of me pocket and smiled. Dad wasn't the sentimental type. Not about me, anyway. We never had photos of me in the house. But this. He'd kept this picture of me with his dad's tools.

Rubi took the photo from me. 'Cute.'

'Probably the last picture we own now.'

'What's this on the back?'

LOOK AT HER. ISN'T SHE BEAUTIFUL? I CAN'T BELIEVE WHAT YOU DID, AND I'M NOT SURE I'LL EVER FORGIVE YOU. BUT SHE'S YOUR RESPONSI-BILITY TOO. YOU NEED TO STEP UP. BE THERE FOR HER.

'Ouch.' I pulled an exploding-head emoji face at Rubi. 'What d'you think he'd done? Is Kirsten right? Is me mum holding on to summat?'

'Sounds like your dad wasn't pulling his weight at the beginning.'

Maybe Dad kept this photo as a reminder of what had happened instead, and not for sentimental reasons. Maybe Mum was so mad she'd come after him. 'What about when it says she'll never forgive him?'

'So?' Rubi started walking away, down the side of the house. 'I'd be pretty pissed off. Doesn't mean she'd burn down your house fifteen years later.'

'I guess.' I followed her out into the street, checking side to side. No Scott.

'I know your mum's a bit wobbly, but she's not a monster. Are you sure this is even you?'

'What d'you mean?'

'That date looks like it says 1993 to me.'

I grabbed it off her and read it back. The last number didn't join up and was smudged. 'Nah, definitely says 1998.'

'God, look at you.' Rubi shook her head and pointed at me feet. 'We've got to get you some shoes you can walk in. I can't watch this.'

'These are fine, honest!'

'And you're full of shit.'

7

'A conscience is that still small voice that people won't listen to.'

Pinocchio.

A B&B guest had booked the creaky shack we were staying in. So in the morning, we waited in The Haunted Inn for the Fire Inspector to arrive with the final report. Dad had to duck through doorways like we were in a cave. Tears of condensation dripped down the windows. It smelt like rot and mold, and none of us could take our coats off because it was colder indoors than out. It was like being in a church or graveyard. We were all whispering as if something was in the brickwork, something hiding in the dark wooden beams that we couldn't see. Something we didn't want to wake.

People who are obsessed with the paranormal liked to stay at the Inn, but nobody stayed in the Bishops' Room. Rubi's dad had warned us to *knock first before going in.* The entire house had paper notes taped onto the walls and furniture. They described which ghosts haunted each spot. Random antique furniture stacked up around the room: old lamps, tables, cupboards and dressers. It felt cramped, like there was more in there than just us.

I broke the silence. 'Anyone want a cup of tea?'

'Shhh.' Dad put a finger to his lips, pointed to his head, and then to Kirsten coming out of the bathroom.

'Sorry,' I whispered. 'I forgot.'

Kirsten had on a pair of sunglasses, and her hair was in a storm. She was like a celebrity with a drug habit. We'd heard her heaving in the bathroom, followed by a weird knock, or rapping on wood, which I hoped was not any of the unwanted.

'Don't you have work today?' Dad frowned at me, like he didn't want me around.

'They said I could take time out while the house got sorted,' I lied and scratched me nose. Maybe it was growing? I didn't want to give them more to be worried about. There was enough going on.

'That was good of them.' Kirsten emerged from the bathroom, sat down and put her head in her hands. 'When's she coming?'

'Should be 'ere any moment.' Dad pushed up on a sash window. 'Why's it so much colder in 'ere than out there?'

Dad had forgotten the windows opened only a few inches. Rubi's dad said it was to stop people from jumping out. But Dad kept heaving on the window.

I heard a thump from upstairs. 'Dad, don't.'

'Why not?'

It sounded like a chair was being dragged across the wooden floor above us. We all stared up.

'This ain't no place we should be in,' said Granny. 'The Devil will find us, one way or another.' Granny hadn't said a word until then, and that was unnerving too.

Kirsten stood up. 'Jason. I am *not* staying in this...'

There was a light knock at the front door, and we all jumped.

Dad opened it to the person we met on the night our house was on fire.

'Hi, not sure if you remember me, but I'm Kai, your Fire Investigation Officer. I mean, *the* Fire Investigation Officer.' She held out her hand and giggled without smiling. Before she could shake his hand, she dropped her folder on the floor. 'Oh, sorry, such a klutz.' She bent down and picked it up. 'Just a bit...' She opened her eyes wide and pulled a wobbly-smile emoji face.

'We're all in the front room.' Dad pointed at us. 'That's Kirsten, Scarlett and me mother. But sure you know that.'

'Wow, this place is spooky isn't it?' Kai walked towards us, but stared up at the low ceiling. Her accent was posher than ours. She said all her T's and whatnots. No hint of West Country at all. 'I've always wanted to come and check out the local legend, but now I'm here...' She grimaced.

'Makes you want to do a runner, doesn't it?' I said. 'Kirsten's already half out the door.'

'Don't blame you,' said Kai.

Kirsten had pulled down her jumper sleeve and was twisting it into a knot. She gave a weak smile and pushed up her sunglasses.

'I'd offer to take your coat, but I can see your breath in here,' I said.

'Right. Freezing.' Kai pulled her coat in. 'OK if I sit here?'

'Go ahead.' Dad nodded.

She sat in the armchair by the front window. We all watched her as she read the note taped to the windowsill that said: *A young girl has been seen here waving at passers-by.* Kai raised her eyebrows and cleared her throat. Her smooth, dark bob and warm skin made her seem half-Japanese or Korean or some-thing, and if I were to guess which half of her - it would be her right because her left hazel eye looked like she had something in it, but then I realised it was actually half blue.

Granny was sitting on a footstool in the corner by the enormous stone fireplace. She held onto a walking stick. Her silence was loud to me. Proper-deafening. Nobody said anything.

'Tea or coffee?' I sat upright, poised.

'No, I'm fine, thanks.' Kai waved me off.

'A biscuit?'

'I'll have a tea.' Granny waved her stick.

'Me too, Scar,' said Dad.

When I opened the door to the kitchen, I checked behind it first. When I was sure the coast was clear, I went in and popped the kettle on. It bubbled and roared to life, but I didn't want to wait in the kitchen. Not on me own with god-only knows what. So I went back out to listen.

'Must have been a young 'un.' Dad perched on the sofa, hands placed on both his knees as if he were on a throne or a school kid in the headmaster's office. I couldn't decide which.

'Knew what I wanted to do, so I went straight into it. I've been lucky.' Kai nodded.

Dad raised his eyebrows at me and nodded towards Kai. 'Impressive, don't you think?'

'What is?'

'At her age, in the Fire Service.'

Kai must have been in her late twenties. She looked older, but there was something about the way her eyes shifted, the way she played with her folder, that gave away her age. She was stiff, awkward, a bit unhinged, like she was trying to fit into a mould, to seem more experienced than she was.

'Now I'm not actually doing the firefighting - I'm getting soft, unfit.' She rolled her eyes.

'Bet you're still fitter then this one.' Dad pointed to me as I went back to the kitchen. The kettle had finished boiling.

'There's more to life than the gym, Dad,' I shouted.

'I teach boxin' down at me gym. But she's never been inter-ested.' I heard him through the door. Me fists felt like they were hardening, turning to wood. For years, I had tried so hard to box for him. But he was the one who gave up on me. Said I was too timid, just because I didn't want to hurt no-one. I decided then that the game was demented, and that something was more wrong with him.

'Ah, I love boxing,' said Kai.

'Ever boxed before?'

'I've always wanted to learn,' she said. 'Me dad's really into it.'

'You should come down, join the club.'

'Thanks. Would get me back into shape...'

I put a cuppa down on the table in front of Dad and handed Granny hers. She didn't look at me once. She was staring at the ceiling, along with Kirsten. I dropped myself down on the three-person sofa between Kirsten and Dad, making sure it bounced him the most.

There was another knock, knock, knock. But this time it came from the bathroom door. We all checked to see if we were all in the room.

I cleared me throat. 'So... Do you have any idea who did it?'

For a second, Kai frowned, and then it disappeared. 'Right! The fire. Sorry, got lost a bit there with all the...' She laughed like a bird again. 'Yes, well... The seat of the fire was on the right-hand side of the front door, where there's an electrical socket.' Kai leaned forward, resting her elbows on her knees, waiting for us to say something, but we were all silent.

'Uh, what does that mean?' Kirsten raised up her sunglasses.

'It means it's not a police matter.' Kai fiddled with her pen. 'It's doesn't appear to be arson.'

'What?!' I rose out of me chair, as if someone had pulled up me strings. 'Are you shitting me?'

'Sorry?' Kai's pulled back and raised her eyebrows.

'Of *course* it's arson. You saw the letters!'

'Actually...'

'So you're not even going to look for who did this? They just get to go free? 'cause the fire department sent us some kid to look into it?'

'Scarlett!' Kirsten tugged on me hand.

I froze. Everyone stared at me as if I was the one haunting the house. It was like someone else had said it. I didn't have control over myself. One minute I was happy as Larry, sure that everything would be fine; it would get sorted. And then the next, I had turned into Chucky.

'Sorry,' I said. 'Sorry, I didn't mean it. I'm sure you're doing the best you can. I'm sure you know what you're doing. I'm sorry. That was *well* rude. Out of order.'

'That's OK.' Kai sat more upright, and transformed into a professional instantly. 'I understand that this is a really hard time for you all. But when we investigated, we found an old phone plugged in at that point where the fire began. To compound the issue, your house wasn't wired to current standards either.'

'Nothing wrong with the wirin',' said Granny. 'Me husband put that in himself. Best electrician in town.'

'He wasn't an electrician, Mum.' Dad stared out of the window. 'Knew we should of got rid of that god-ancient phone.'

Footsteps started walking around upstairs, a thud-thud-thud going round in circles and we all held our breath and stared up at the sound until it stopped. When we were kids, Rubi used to tell ghost stories at sleepovers and I'd lose sleep for weeks, because I was probably the only one who knew they were real.

'Now, there appears to have been a lot of paper in your hallway too.' Kai tapped her leg.

'Me campaign leaflets!' Kirsten held the sides of her face.

'Bit unfortunate as that made for perfect kindling, and would've made the fire accelerate fairly quickly.'

Kirsten nodded, holding her stomach. 'Excuse me, I don't feel too good.' She got up and ran to the bathroom.

'Dated appliances are well-known to be a high risk,' said Kai. 'Combine that with perhaps a faulty electrical socket...'

'But what about the note?' I said.

'I don't know what to say about that, except it was bad timing. Have you reported it to the police?'

Dad shook his head. His gaze had fallen inward, to some place else. 'Not sure what they could do when we don't even know who it is.'

'Well, I suggest you do.'

'But how sure *are* you?' I said. 'That it wasn't arson.'

'We are ninety-nine percent sure. We did search for signs of arson. If it was, we'd have found traces of some sort of fuel at your front door. But we found the smoke patterns and the phone. It all indicates to being an electrical fire.'

But the things she was saying didn't ring true. They didn't seem right. How could they not be related? They say you should trust your gut, but I'd had a hard time doing that since Rory. I believed I could trust him, that he still cared about me. But I had heard nothing from him since the fire, even though I'd borrowed Rubi's laptop to message him in every way I could. Maybe I couldn't trust me gut when it mattered. Maybe it wasn't arson?

BRING BRING.

A phone rang in the house, and it echoed around us. We glanced around at each other to see who'd answer.

'Who's that?' Granny put her hands on her hips.

Dad picked up the receiver. 'Hello?' We waited for him to say more. We wanted an explanation as to why the phone was ringing at the exact time we were being told our ancient phone had caused the fire. 'Hello? Hello?' He put the phone down. 'Nobody there.'

Nobody said a thing. Then there was a creak from upstairs. Kai jumped up. 'Right. OK! We'll be putting together the full report in the next few days and we'll be giving you a copy. And if you have any more questions, then just call me, or come to the station.'

'You going? Already?'

'Yes... Sorry... I hope you feel a bit more at ease now, knowing that nobody is out to get you.' She held open the front door, one foot out and looking at the spot she was in where a ghost girl had been seen in the past. 'I can assure you that much.'

'Send that report to me when you can,' said Dad.

'Sure! And I'll take you up on those boxing lessons. I'll be in touch... It's really been great meeting you all.' Kai slowly and carefully closed the front door. It barely made a click, as if she didn't want anyone (or anything) to know she'd left.

'Fuck,' Dad whispered.

'What?'

He gave me a sideways glance and opened his mouth to say something but closed it when the bathroom door opened. 'Well, that's... good news.' Kirsten's face was red. 'I guess no one *actually* trying to kill us is a good thing.'

'I suppose.' Though I wasn't convinced.

'They do these things thoroughly. It's their job to examine it all.' Kirsten sat back down, smoothing down her hair.

'Whose been sendin' notes?' said Granny

'We don't know, Mum.' Dad stared into the carpet.

'Probably to do with her!' Granny pointed at Kirsten. 'Gettin' into politics. What was you thinking? Not a job for a woman.'

'Not this again...' Kirsten turned to Dad. 'I'm going to the shops. I can't stay in here. With them. And her.'

'I'm just sayin' what everyone's thinking.' Gran took a sip of tea.

'I'm thinking I wanna get out of this place too,' I said.

'Two steps ahead of you. I'll pick up some milk.' Kirsten grabbed her leather handbag.

Dad sat down on the sofa, head in his hands. 'I'll call up the insurance company.'

I was still getting my bag together when Kirsten left. Dad raised up his head and stared at me as if I had said Bristol City had lost the league. I felt it too. I felt the dread calling to me, ringing me up and saying: this ain't going to get better, this ain't going to be OK, this is the worst thing to have ever happened.

'What is it, Dad?'

'Nothing, nothing.'

'Dad, I'm not a kid. Tell me.' I sat down next to him. 'You need to share it. You'll feel better. Maybe I can help.'

He got up from the sofa. 'You can't help, Scarlett. There's nothing anyone can do. It's too late.'

'What do you mean?'

BRING BRING. We stared at the phone, and then at each other. *BRING BRING.*

'Ignore it,' said Dad.

'What if it doesn't stop?'

BRING BRING.

'Ignore it,' he said.

'That seems to be your answer to everything.'

BRING BRING

'Why won't you answer?' I said. 'It might be important. Or the insurance company.'

BRING BRING. Dad gave me a squinty-eyed glare and walked away towards the kitchen.

'Why don't you want to talk to the insurance company? Won't they pay out? Why won't they pay out?' I pulled on his arm, and he turned back to face me.

BRING BRING.

'Don't be so ridiculous. It's just a phone.' Granny stomped over and picked up the receiver. 'Who's this?' she shouted. 'Come on, stop messin' about.' She bolted upright.

'No Scar,' said Dad, through gritted teeth. 'Insurance companies don't *want* to give you money. Did you not hear what she said? It was *our* fault. The wiring wasn't legal.'

I didn't hear that part at all. I had just thought insurance companies do their job and made sure you're safe. I had thought they'd want us to live in our house, not on the streets. Don't they know what happened? Aren't they human? Do they not care if we have a roof over our heads? And it made me think of Rory and whether he really cared that he had taken all me money, taken away me promise of a home, and...

'No, I will not! You can't tell me what to do.' Granny slammed the phone down and puffed up her chest. 'Bloody cheek.'

'Who was it?'

She shrugged. 'Told us to go home.'

'But we can't!'

There was a bang above us. Footsteps started thudding down the stairs like they were running. But nobody waited to see who it was because we'd all heard the tales from the Dunn family. We ran out of the house. Unwanted. Chased. With nowhere to go back to.

Second arson attack could be targeting social workers

By Martin Johnson   09:40, 2 April

Two cars belonging to social workers in the town, and a tree at Lakeside Care home, were torched in separate arson attacks in the past 4 weeks. Although, police believe the incidences are connected.

The largest incident saw a car fire spread, setting alight an outbuilding nearby the hospital at around 7.15pm on Monday evening (April 1). Firefighters said the building is a potentially hazardous situation as it is suspected to have contained asbestos, a prohibited heat-resistant building material that can cause chronic lung disease.

This followed a previous incident where an MP's car was set alight in a similar manner two weeks ago. Police have now reported that there appears to be a correlation between the targets, as they have at one point or another worked in or with social care.

Fire crews were called to the first incident where a Nissan Micra had been torched at around 9pm on 1 April, and two crews from the local fire station put out the fire. A tree at Vale Park near the Lakeside Care Home was also set alight on the same night at 8.30 pm.

Jill Revel, owner of the torched Nissan Micra said: 'It's worrying to think that there's somebody with a vendetta against people who work in social care. It's such a tough job to do, but nobody I work with deserves this. We all work so hard and in the best interest of everyone, so it's really upsetting that we're being targeted like this.'

Local MP, Clive Hopkins, whose car was targeted last month said: 'There's been an escalation in incidents and it's devastating to hear that it may be targeting those who are looking to help our community, and to safeguard our children and young people. But I'd like to assure our community that we're doing everything we can to assist the police and ensure the speedy arrest of the person responsible.'

Constable Elizabeth Wright, married to the local MP, said: 'We're confident that we're getting close to catching whoever is behind the attacks. We rely on the community at times like this to keep their eyes open and to report anything suspicious. So far we have been lucky that none of the fires have caused anyone physical harm, but next time, we might not be so lucky. So if you have any concerns, please get in touch with us and we'll investigate further.'

Since police have announced a possible connection, local residents have taken to Twitter to speculate:
@iluvoranges: Saw the huge fireball last night Neighbour tells me it's a vendetta against social workers Can't say I'm surprised. Probably a cover up Vigilante injustice! Power to the people.

@bethechange46: all these people saying theres no smoke with out fire. not true.. Me sister works in social care and she works harder than anyone I know and cares so much but sometimes kids arent happy to be taken away from their neglectful parents no matter how awful the situation STOCKHOLM syndrome.

Police are now launching an investigation.

8

'You think you can do these things, but you just can't!'

Marlin, Finding Nemo

Me dad will fix it, that was me thinking. He was good at fixing things, good at having a plan. He would figure out what to do about the house and the insurance. But the next day, Dad got a call to fix something else. A shower got blocked at his gym. His business was in the middle of town, in a warehouse. It had a red and white sign with *'Come out Fighting'* on it.

I followed him there, hoping to help. He'd tried to make me believe he didn't need it, but he would. It was 6.30am, before opening, so it was empty. It smelt of rubber and stale sweat. I hadn't been down to the gym in a long time, not since the unveiling of the graffiti artwork on the redbrick wall. It was of a huge boxer, mid-punch. We all went down to see it a few years back. Even Rory had come with me then. He was a great boxer. Reckoned he could be the next big thing.

Boxing bags hung like ball sacks, and there were more signs up. They plastered motivational banners around the gym equipment saying:

You get knocked down. You get back up.

Get back into the ring.

Roll with the punches.

We walked past two boxing rings with red and white ropes in the middle of the warehouse. I remembered what Dad had said to Kai about me not being interested in boxing. It made me want to put on some gloves and prove him wrong.

'Wanna spar?' I pointed to the ring.

He scoffed. 'Get the plunger.'

'Where it is?'

He sighed and stormed off. 'Never mind. I'll get it.'

'I would have got it.'

Dad wasn't really talking. He had turned inward like a fist. When we got into the Lady's shower room, he just stood and stared at it. Surrounded by tiles and mirrors, he stood staring at the pool of water, but he wasn't really looking at it. He tapped his foot to an internal clock, to an internal tick-tock. He was always counting. Only ever in groups of ten; his bicep curls, running, brushing his teeth, chewing. Even when you thought he wasn't counting, even when you couldn't hear him count, you could see it. With the way he walked, the tapping of his finger, his blinking, his talking, his everything. The man was a walking time bomb. He was winding up more than ever, and it was getting faster and faster, numbers running like water.

'Is it that bad?' I stared down at the murky pool of water. 'Want me to have a go?'

He snapped his head around and looked at me as if I'd just showed up. 'No,' He squatted down. 'Just pass me that when I ask for it.'

'Hey, boss.' Ceri had joined us in the ladies. 'Hey, Scarlett. Sorry to hear about the house.'

Ceri had been working for me dad on membership for the past few years and was one of the chattiest women I'd ever met. Dad said she was a natural salesman, and she had boosted his clients by ten percent. She was tall but never stooped, as if she knew her height was an advantage.

'Thanks Ceri. It's been a rollercoaster.'

'D'you hear about the other fires?'

'Other fires?'

'Yeah, some over the way.' She pulled her phone out of her pocket. 'Let me find it a minute.'

Dad waded into the stagnating shower. He had on his CAT boots. He pulled up his trousers and bent down with a screwdriver, prying up the grate.

'See that there...' Ceri passed me her pink phone. 'They's all over the place.'

'Is it an April fool?'

'Is it April already?' Ceri shrugged.

'Not a very funny one if it is.' Dad twisted the screwdriver down the hole as we both watched on, poised to assist.

'One of them is the care home I work at.' I picked up the long wire with a bristle on the end. 'The tree out front. A proper shame. It goes so nice in autumn.'

'Do you think it's the same person who did your house?' Ceri squeezed her phone with both hands.

'Wasn't arson,' said Dad. 'They said so.'

Ceri was right, though. What were the chances that all these arson attacks would happen at the same time as we had our fire?

'But what if they're wrong?'

'Don't matter. That's the word.' Dad stood up and put out his hand. 'Scar?'

'I mean, she must be about twelve, Ceri! There's no way that she's got it right.'

'Don't they have to be like... a hundred percent on that sort of stuff?' Ceri moved toward the mirror over the sinks, using it to check her makeup was still in place.

'If someone was really good at hiding it, she could easily of missed it.'

'Scar.' Dad put his hand out to me.

'What?'

'Give me that thing.' He didn't blink and his mouth was turning inward, too.

'Oh, sorry.' I passed him the long wiry twig thing in me hand. He bent back down and threaded it through the drain. When I turned to Ceri, she gave me wide eyes and a clown-smile.

'So... you gunna prove it was arson?' Ceri leaned backwards, holding on to the sink.

'Me?' It had never occurred to me I could do something about it. 'I guess we could...'

Dad scoffed. 'We?!' He left the stick and stood upright.

'Why not?'

' 'cause I dropped out of school, and you barely scrapped through A-levels. You work in a care home, for God's sake. These people they send in, they all have degrees and training...'

Maybe he was right. I washed old people for a living. I wasn't smart enough to figure out an actual crime that had already gone under the radar. We had nothing. No computers or phones to look up stuff. No clues, no leads.

'But if we don't do something, we won't get a penny. We won't have anything. Our house is a goner.'

'Really?' said Ceri. 'Fuck.'

'Scarlett.' Dad was fuming now. 'Can you stop blabbin' our business to every Tom, Dick and Harry.'

'What? Why?'

Ceri stood upright and shuffled towards the door.

Dad bent back down and pulled at the threat of wire he'd pushed down the drain. 'Because I haven't told Kirsten yet.'

'What? Why?'

He tugged on the wire to test it. 'She's got enough on her plate. Ceri, could you grab me a bin bag or bucket.'

'Sure, no problem!' Ceri was already half out of the door anyway.

'Don't matter if there's an elephant on her plate,' I said. 'You know Kirsten'll be super pissed if she finds out some other way.'

'Yes, thank you Scarlett. But she lost her job yesterday, and I think this might just be the thing t...'

'What? How did she lose her job?'

'That bloke she accused last year...'

'Creepy Clive?'

'He got in touch with her work. Threatened 'em. They're worried that they'd get bad press.'

'That's not fair.'

'She was on a casual contract. They can do what they like...' He pulled again at the thread, but it wasn't budging. 'So you need to be nice to her.'

'I'm always nice to her.' I picked up the screwdriver and played with it.

'Extra nice.' He pulled harder on the wire stuck in the blockage.

'We'll be alright... Won't we Dad?! What's the plan?'

'What d'you mean - what's the plan?' He stared at me as if I'd just said boxing was the worst sport in the world. But he often spiralled like this in real life. He never applied what he learned from boxing or the gym to real life shit-shows. He believed the world was set against him, and he stopped fighting it a long time ago.

'To fix it, to get our house back. Kirsten's job. What's the plan?'

'There's no *plan,* Scar. There's nothing we can do. We have nothing. We are well and royally screwed. The Saints are done for.'

He yanked hard and the long wire brush came loose, and he flung backwards into the wall. At the end of the long wire, in the brush, was a snotty-ball of gunky hair. I dry-heaved just as Ceri came in with a bucket.

'Just in time.' Dad lifted the mass of goop into it.

'Scarlett, your friend Rubi's here to see you. Says she's got something urgent...'

'Really?'

'She's by reception.'

But the door of the bathroom banged open and Rubi flew in. 'I couldn't wait.' Her faded pink hair wafted like candy-floss. 'The police have been round. They want you to go in for questioning this afternoon.'

'What, me? Why?'

'The fire at the care home.' Rubi glanced at Ceri, then at Dad, and then at me. 'Someone said they saw you there.'

9

'Tell your boss he can have our house...
when I'm dead.'

Up

There are a number of things you can do to lift someone's spirits. And by god, we Saints needed a lift. At the care home, we'd sing to the residents, draw rainbows with them, let them outside for that extra fag they'd been gagging for. It was important to keep a routine, to stay positive, not to dwell on things too much (like getting suspended from your job, being accused of arson, being interviewed by the police, or made homeless). Best to keep busy, even if you have to spend the morning with the grumpiest woman on earth. Granny was almost exactly like the old man from Up. She had been crabby ever since we lost gramps.

I needed to keep up me driving, so I offered to drive her to the shops before going to the police station. I'd only just passed me test a few months ago - third time's the charm. But the whole family made fun of how I drove. Granny held onto the dashboard the entire drive to the shop.

'Scarlett!' Granny yelled from the tiny yellow car.

'What?' I shouted back from the pavement.

'D'you expect me to get out of this thing by myself, do you?' She stuffed a letter into her handbag.

'What was that?'

'What was what?'

'That.' I pointed. 'That letter. What did you put in your bag?'

'Mind your own business.' She hugged her shiny white handbag to her chest. 'Now, help me up. You've got to get me up the high street or I'll never get to Maggie's today.'

'What you getting again?'

'Balloons! Balloonsballoonballoons. Million times I've said.'

'Alright, keep your knickers on! Just don't get why you won't take flowers. You both used to be florists.'

Granny shook her head. 'You never listen to me. I told you what happened.'

'Yeah, but...'

'Need summat bright and bouncy. Lift her spirits. It would've been her husband's birthday today.'

Granny and Margaret used to work together at the florist in the village. Though it seemed Maggie was always having drama with Granny before she got sick. After she fell, she could only smile and nod. I reckon she didn't know who Granny was, which was probably a good thing. Maybe in sixty years' time I'd be visiting Sophie out of pure guilt for getting her fired. I always wondered what Granny had done to Margaret.

Outside the card shop, there was a Big Issue seller, but I was too embarrassed to make eye-contact, to say sorry, to explain that we were homeless too and so I dug around in me pocket for the only change I had, and I gave it to her, hoping she wouldn't think badly of me. It was only coppers. Inside, the shop was everything-you-can-think-of shop for little presents: homemade soaps, fancy-pants chocolates, picture frames made of recycled plastic buttons.

'You getting a card for Maggie too, Gran?'

'No, that's a bit too far. The man *is* dead, you know!' She snorted and laughed. 'Those. Get me twenty of those.' She pointed at the packet of balloons hanging from the rack.

'Twenty? Ain't that a bit much?'

'Don't be so stupid. I've known her for as long as I can remember.'

'Gran, stop calling me stupid, or I'll....' I walked away from her, swallowing the words like marmite. I was not going to let her get to me. Deep breaths! On the wall, there was a *Home Sweet Home* sign written in flowers. Kirsten told me her Gran had a sign like that and she'd always wanted one. So I picked it up, with Dad's words in me head to be nicer to her, but put it back when I remembered I needed to save to get a new phone and replace all me things, all me films, and clothes etc. Granny shuffled towards me.

'Where d'you think we're gunna live, Gran? Now that we can't go back.'

'I ain't going back to that haunted house. S'not humane.' Gran shook her head. 'Stop bitin' your nails.' She pulled at me hand. 'Filthy habit. Nobody knows where your hands have been. Now, give the balloons to the woman.'

We came out of the Shop of Everything with twenty helium-filled balloons. By some miracle, we got them into Kirsten's Toyota Aygo and drove to Maggie's house. It looked like we were smuggling a circus. We got out of the car and Granny kept checking the grey sky.

'What is it?' I grabbed the balloons out of the back.

'That eagle owl,' she said. 'I heard it hootin' last night, didn't you?'

An eagle owl, like the owl from Winnie the Pooh, had been living in the woods on the edge of town since I could remember.

Whenever we heard stories of it landing on people's heads or taking dogs, Granny always hugged her pet pig, Destiny, closer and would shout about shooting it down. Maybe me mum wasn't incubating a blackbird, but actually trying to hatch another eagle owl to drive me gran mad. Seemed incredibly possible. They've always hated each other.

'Reckon that Edward next door feeds it.' She held onto her handbag. 'They're illegal here, y' know.'

'I know, Gran.' I stopped listening and got lost worrying about going to the police station later. I had kept it out of me mind all morning so far. But it crept into the edges.

'What if it pops the balloons?' Granny had stopped in the road, staring at the sky.

'We better get moving then.'

'You're comin' in too.'

'Why? Does she need help?'

'No, I do. You can spare a few minutes for a poor, old, sick woman.'

'I do all the time. That's me job.'

'We're between visits,' said Gran. 'So you'll need to get the key from under the mat.'

'What? Don't you ring the bell?'

'Best not to get her up. They'd of just got her dressed and downstairs.'

Maggie's house was right on the road. No garden, no fence, just straight in off the street. No introduction needed. It was a small terraced red-brick cottage on a road of old worker cottages and its guttering was sprouting its own field. I bent down, took the key from under the straw mat, and opened the door.

'That's it. Good job,' said Granny, nodding. 'Maggie!' Granny waltzed in, arms outstretched. 'It's your best friend in the whole wide world 'ere to see you.'

I wrestled with the balloons, trying to get them through the narrow, low door.

BANG.

'Jesus, Mary and Joseph!' Granny turned to me. 'Did you lose one of the balloons?'

'Sorry.' I picked a bit of rubber off me foot.

'God's sake. Maggie!' Granny sat down on the faded flowery sofa. Maggie sat in her armchair next to her, smiling with a vacant look, until she saw the balloons. The room wasn't much warmer than outside. Should I get her a blanket?

'Bring them 'ere Scarlett, so she can see 'em. You wouldn't believe how long it took the lady to blow 'em up, Maggie. Lost most of the day. And they cost an absolute fortune! I didn't tell you about what happened to me poor house either, did I? It's a tragedy, an....'

Granny kept her coat on, and I stood by the door, wondering what to do. The balloons drifted back and forth by the fireplace. I zoned out. I didn't have an alibi for the night of the fires around Stonecloud. So Rubi said I should make one up. She'd been listening to podcasts all summer, where prisoners had been set up by the police. So she didn't trust them one bit. Could I really make one up? Should I? What if they found out? Granny's voice droned on in the background until...

'That reminds me...' Granny rooted through her bag and pulled out an envelope. 'See this! Edward's trying to sue me. He's always sendin' me letters, always.'

'What's that?'

Granny ignored me and continued talking to Maggie. 'Do you remember? The ones he used to send me, and now this... He's takin' us t' court, Mags. Son of a bitch.'

'The neighbour?' I walked over to them both. 'When did you get this?'

She ignored me and carried on talking to Maggie. 'Last week, you should of seen him. He's just always been jealous of us Saints. I swear, next time I see him, I'm gunna...'

BANG.

Another balloon got too close to the lamp.

'Damn!' I walked over and pulled the rest of them away. They both laughed.

Granny made a gun shape with her hand and aimed it at Maggie. 'That's what I should do, eh Mags? Bang bang!'

'Is it about that bit of land? Just give it to him.' I went to grab the letter off Granny, but she'd already put it away.

'It's not about the land, you silly girl...' She began playing with the gold locket around her neck.

'What's it about then?'

'Revenge, of course!' She tutted. 'Bloody cheek. We should sue him for those dodgy electrics!'

'I thought Gramps did the electrics?'

She shook her head. 'Edward was an electrician - he did it as a favour but... well, your Gramps had to fix aaaaallllll of it.' She waved her hand like a conductor.

'But...'

'I should tell your dad. He'll send him packin', won't he?'

'No, no, no.' Dad was a bomb, ready to explode. 'Give it time. He might not do it. I mean, what heartless git would sue someone when their house just burned down?'

'That's exactly who he is.' Granny nodded. 'Ain't that right, Mags. See, she remembers.'

'Well, maybe I'll go talk to him,' I said. 'You don't think he had anything to do with the fire, do you?'

'Don't you meddle!' Granny wagged her finger at me. 'You hear that Maggie? She thinks she's Miss Marple or summat. Going round and stickin' her nose into other people's business when it ain't wanted.'

'Somebody's got to do summat and it ain't gunna be the police!'

'And it won't be you!' Granny pushed herself up using her walking stick. 'See you next week, Maggie. Same time. Same place. I'll try to update you on Corrie if I can get a hold of a TV from somewhere. I mean, I am missing all the major events now.' Granny jabbed her stick in the air. 'Won't do, I tell you. Just won't do. Get the door, Scarlett.'

When we got outside, Granny jabbed her stick into me leg. 'Ow!'

'Don't you *dare* speak to him, y' hear me?'

'But we could do summat about it.'

'I'll disown you. No Saint of mine! You hear me!' She jabbed me again. 'Can of worms.'

'Okay. Okay.'

'Silly girl,' she muttered under her breath. 'You ain't got a clue.'

But I did. I had a clue. I had a tonne of them now. What if Mr Post was angry enough to strike a match? Maybe I didn't have to be super-smart to find the arsonist; I just had to be smarter than Mr Post, or whoever. But me whole family was telling me to stay out of it, to leave it alone, like they wanted to see our house stay in ruins. I glanced back at Maggie's front door peeling with paint, thinking about how she couldn't do nothing for herself anymore, how she couldn't clear the drainpipes or fix the damp, thinking about the only company she had was me gran and people popping in for ten minutes. I had to do something. I was done with waiting around for everyone else.

10

'For the greater good.'

Hot Fuzz

G ranny's brother, Great Uncle Nigel, used to write a weekly letter to the Prime Minister. He believed the police were more corrupt than his broken computer hard-drive, and they were all destined for fire and brimstone. He said they were like the Mafia, accosting every bloke who was out for an early morning walk. You needed a brick of money in your back pocket everywhere you went, just in case. But Granny had it on good authority that Uncle Nigel was bat-shit-crazy. She said to ignore everything he said, especially because he was the most likely to be doing something the police wouldn't approve of, anyway. When they found him dead in his flat, he had a wad of out-of-date twenties in his back pocket, and to Granny's upset, they buried him with them.

I walked into the police station. Maybe I should have brought a bribe, just in case. With all the cuts and underfunding, maybe this wasn't a misunderstanding but a funding drive. Uncle Nige believed that was what speed cameras were about. I know Rubi would be inclined to agree. So maybe this whole thing was just a way of getting money in? But I guess I didn't need a bribe on account of Rubi having given me a fake alibi.

'Hi.' I smiled through the glass at a man sat in reception. 'Someone called me dad and asked me to come in?'

'K, love.' He had a high-pitched voice. 'What's your name?'

'Scarlett. Scarlett Saint.'

'Alright Scarlett, take a seat and we'll have someone with you in a minute.'

The station looked like a bank for the Easter Bunny. There were egg garlands and stacks of chocolate eggs behind reception. A4 pictures of eggs stuck to the walls. There was a Happy Easter sign above the door on the way out. If this was a corrupt operation, then they were proper-good at covering it up.

The man who was behind the screen came over to me. 'If you could come this way, Scarlett...'

I followed him into a small, white room with blue padded chairs and a desk that reminded me of school. I sat at the table. A monitor screen was sticking out of the wall next to me. Me heart was thumping in me ears so hard, I wasn't sure if I'd done something wrong or not. I felt guilty or like I was in an exam. I was going to mess it up.

A woman came in. 'So, Scarlett? I'm Liz wright, the Prison Custody Officer here.' I stood up and shook her hand. Freckles dotted her face, so many that they sort of merged. There was a heart-shaped cluster on her nose. 'Take a seat, we just need to ask you a few questions...'

Liz talked about me rights, about codes of practice, but I couldn't really take it all in. I nodded. Liz had a voice that felt like she'd written it in bold, underlined. A teacher's voice. I felt dumb even in how I was breathing.

'Do you know about the fire at the care home?'

I nodded.

'How did you hear about it?'

'Someone showed me. Thought it might have something to do with the fire at me house. But they said it wasn't arson, but we're not sure, we think maybe they missed summat. Maybe the police need to look.' I tried to swallow down me babbling.

'I'm afraid if they have ruled it out as a crime, we can't investigate. We'll keep it in mind, though. You work at the care home, yes?'

I nodded, and there was silence.

'You were suspended, yes?'

I nodded. Getting suspended from work didn't look good on me. I wanted to stick me head under the table.

'Were you angry about being suspended?'

'Angry?'

'Is that why you set the fire?'

'I... I didn't set the fire! Why would I do that? I love those people. We're like family. Like a second home to me. I miss it so much. I just want to go back.'

'Why were you suspended then?'

'Is it really that important?' I clenched me fists. It was as if I was channelling Uncle Nige. All these stupid questions and whatnot. This finger pointing at the wrong person and asking questions when they already knew the answer.

'I think so.' She furrowed her brow.

'But you already know, don't you? So why ask?'

'I would like to hear your side of the situation.' She sat back in her chair. 'We get different views on the same event all the time. This is routine, so there's nothing to worry about.'

'Why? What did they say?'

'You first.'

'Well, I was trying to help a resident off the floor, but he's too big and we're supposed to get an ambulance, but I didn't want to be a pain to 'em, see? I was sure we could do it, but then Gladys hurt her arm and I felt so bad about that. Honest. But I was just trying to help him up. But health and safety...'

Liz was nodding. 'Do you believe they did the right thing?'

'... the right thing?'

'In suspending you?'

'Um, I dunno. I haven't really thought about it. Been busy with me house burning down.' I shook me head in disbelief.

'Do you remember where you were the previous night?'

'Yeah, course.' I wanted to bite me nails, but I didn't want to look shifty. 'You know you're barking up the wrong tree.'

'That's for me to find out.' She smiled. 'So where were you?'

'With me friend Rubi. I'm living with her, since me house burned down.'

'What were the two of you doing?'

'Swimming.'

'Where?'

'There's an empty house I'm looking after nearby.' I gestured in the direction it was in. 'The lady who's selling it asked me to look after it, keep it clean, until someone buys it.'

'Can your friend Rubi confirm this?'

I nodded, because all I could say inside me head was 'of course, it was her idea.' But truth was, I went to the house on me own, pretending to find out if the owner might let us stay there. But I just swam. Alone. Rubi and I have been good at keeping each other secrets. Like that time, when she rear-ended a car of one of her parent's B&B guests, or when she slept with one of the guests and their wife showed up hours later. I told nobody.

'Now, someone made a serious accusation against you, Scarlett. A big one. Someone you worked with said they saw you at the scene. Do you know why?'

'Maybe it was someone who looked like me.'

'Do you know a Sophie Knight?'

'Who?'

'You used to work with her.' The policewoman didn't blink. She didn't take her gaze off me.

'Oh Soph, yeah... oh, right, yeah.' The penny dropped, a silent but definite plop, and I sat back into the chair.

'We're exploring every possibility. We know Sophie was recently let go, wasn't she?'

'Me boss said that she fired Sophie because of something I reported.'

'Sophie knew this?'

'Maybe. One resident even said I got her fired. But I thought nothing of it. Sophie flat out refused to help one resident. She'd just leave him there, in his own you-know-what. He was the nicest man most of the time and we ain't allowed to treat them differently.'

'And you reported this?'

'Wouldn't you?'

The policewoman stared at me. Blank. What she was thinking? She didn't ask any more questions after that. I never discovered if she'd of done the same thing. And now Sophie was trying to frame me. If it wasn't for the alibi from Rubi, I'd have been screwed. I'd probably be behind bars. All because of Sophie. And if she set fire near the care home, if she was already willing to frame me for it, maybe she could have set fire to me house too.

11

'Because when I look at you, I can feel it.
And I look at you and I'm home.'

Dory, Finding Nemo

I used to believe in love at first sight, that moment when your soul mate bumps into you and nothing is ever the same again. Everything spins out from you, and you're swimming in a tide of pure amazingness, afloat on everything that's good. I used to believe in those fairy tales. Truth be told, even though I knew better, I still *wanted* to believe in them. I've had bad luck with picking the wrong ones. Rubi said I was trying too hard. Me ex told me I was like a limpet and the harder he tried to get away, the more I clamped on.

Deep down, I still wondered if it was only a matter of time until I found the one person who'd be me perfect match. Somewhere out there was me perfect person, who'd never want to leave me side; the one person who'd get me. Me soul mate. After a few pints at the pub, Rubi told me to stop watching Disney films all day before talking about her favourite film 'Brave'. But ever since Scott saved me from falling, I'd been floating underwater. I had a weightless sort of feeling that would be the beginning of something big.

I was due back to work that afternoon for the first time since they suspended me. The morning was an ocean. Everything felt so far apart, so far away from me, including the past few days of drama and police interviews. The sky was a hazy pink pond, and the full moon was proper-big like a cartoon shell. I went to the fantasy house I was looking after, the house of me dreams, which felt more like home than any place I'd been in. It was a Cotswold manor, more like a sandcastle with its golden bricks. A rose bush splashed up to the shingled roof. It had a heated pool in a big conservatory off the back. Swimming helps to calm me, to feel free. So I swam lengths underwater on me back, looking up at the sky through the pitched glass roof. I wanted to wash something off me so that when I resurfaced I'd feel different, a new person, reborn, ready to go back to the care home.

'Góðan dag.' A viking was kneeling down by the edge of the pool. I couldn't believe it. It was Scott, leaning on a large, round wooden shield. Chain-metal hung from him, and metal covered his shoulders. His face had two red stripes that slashed down from his forehead to his left jaw.

'Hi.' I gasped for air. 'How d'you get in here? What you doing? Did you follow me?'

'I could ask you the same thing.' He grinned. 'This is me parent's house. We're moving in.'

'Really? Oh wow, that's great news.' I swam to the side of the pool and leant on the cold stone slabs. 'I... You probably don't remember me, but...'

'I remember you.' He didn't blink. I felt heat rising to my face.

'You do?'

'Just to warn you, my parents are here too. Shall I grab your towel?'

'No, it's fine.'

Guys have always said I have great legs, and I didn't want to miss an opportunity to flash me assets. So I pulled myself up and out of the pool, onto the side. I hoped I was a vision of class - more mermaid than whale. But he was busy adjusting his belt so he didn't even notice.

'So...' I twisted the water out of me hair.

'Who's this?' At the doorway stood a couple, and one of them was the officer who interviewed me: Liz Wright.

'Oh my god,' slipped out of me mouth as I ran to get a towel and wrap it around me waist. They were both dressed up as well. He was some sort of king and she was a fortune teller.

'Does she come with the house?' The man smirked.

'Stop it.' Liz slapped his arm. 'She's been looking after the pool. Scarlett, isn't it? I'm Scott's mum and this is his dad.' She reached forward to shake me hand. 'Sorry, not sure why I did that. Force of habit.'

'Ha - force of habit.' Scott's dad span around. 'Good one.' I laughed along, but had no idea what was going on. Maybe Liz was keeping yesterday's interview to herself. 'How strong are you, Scarlett?'

'Sorry? What?'

'You look pretty strong.' Scott's dad tilted his head to one side and rubbed his chin. 'We could do with a hand getting our stuff out of the car. We've been to war, and it didn't make any sense to return our things to a realm that's no longer ours.'

'He means our old house.' Liz rolled her eyes. 'He likes to stay in character for as long as humanly possible.'

'Sure. Just give me a sec to get dressed and I'll be right there.'

'Great! Thanks. Wear what you like. No dress code here as you can see.' Scott's dad pointed to his clothes as he walked away. 'No judgement from us, right Scott?' Scott smiled at me, and followed Liz and his dad out.

When I joined them out front, they were all stood looking in the car through the boot. I was still soaked through. I had me wet cozzy on underneath, but it was weirdly warm out.

'God only knows how we got it in.' Liz put her hands on her hips.

'No, you muppet.' Scott's dad pointed to Scott. 'Go around to the front and push it this way, so it's mostly out. Ah, here she is! Scarlett, come this way.'

When I joined Scott's dad at the boot of the Land Rover, I could see a throne laid down on its back. 'Is that a throne?'

'Good, isn't it?' He waggled his eyebrows. 'Made it from scratch.'

'Except it weights like a million pounds.' Liz pushed it forward. It was almost out of the car, except for the end balancing on the boot. 'It's like he made it with rocks or iron.'

I stared at Scott, but he didn't say a word. He was so different from Rory. So different. Rory would go on and on about his car or what happened down at the pub with darts. But Scott was quiet and solid. Different had to be a good thing.

'OK, so come back around now, you two.' Scott's dad fanned his hand towards him. 'And grab the top of it. Carefully! Scarlett, you grab this end with me. I want us to take it into the garage. Ready?' I nodded. 'Good lass. Right, now on three: one, two, three.' We all lifted and shuffled like crabs across and up the lawn. 'Now Scarlett and I will lower it down and you guys lift.'

We put the golden throne down in the middle of an empty garage. Light flooded in from the garage door and onto the throne like a spotlight.

'Great! One item moved.' Liz pushed back her hair. 'Just another million and one left. We've got to get some wire cutters to cut the lock off the gate. Then we can back-up the car closer to the doors.'

'Might just need some WD40,' said Scott's dad.

'When you moving in?'

'Wednesday.' Scott's dad rubbed a scratch on the throne. 'You know, you haven't once asked us why we're dressed up. Aren't you curious?'

'I uh, I didn't want to be rude or nosey.'

'I like you.' He wagged his finger at me. 'Class act.'

'It's called LARPing? You ever heard of it?' Liz was taking her gold hooped earrings out.

'LARPing?'

'It's a roleplaying game. Great fun. You'd love it!'

'Oh, she would!' Scott's dad clicked his fingers. 'You should come with us. We always need fresh blood.'

'I'm going to get some water. Anyone else want any?' Liz held up an empty water bottle while walking towards the door into the house.

'No thanks.' Scott's dad sat down on his throne, leaning forward on his knees. 'Scarlett, am I right in hearing that your house burned down?'

'Yeah, did Scott tell you?' Scott just stared and watched, arms crossed, smiling. What was he thinking about this whole thing? What was he thinking about me? He wasn't saying anything. He just had these pearly eyes that didn't ebb one bit, and they felt like they were looking right into me, right into me soul, as if he could see what I was thinking.

'Everybody's talking about it. Absolute tragedy. Must be terrible for your family.'

'Worse than people think.' I tried me best not to chew on me fingernails.

'How's that?'

'The insurance company won't pay out, and we can't afford to fix it. We're basically homeless.'

Scott's dad leaned back and rubbed the arms of the throne. 'That is awful. Was it arson?'

'Depends whether you believe the report or not.' I crossed me arms, too.

'So you think it is?' Scott frowned at me.

'Do you?' said his dad.

'I uhhh...'

'Well, we can't let someone get away with that. It's an injustice!'

'But the police won't get involved now because it ain't arson as far as they're concerned. There's nothing I can do...'

'Now, say nothing to Liz...' Scott's dad leaned forward again. 'Scott, close the door. She'd kill me if she heard. But I know some things, stuff that would make you wonder how we're a civilised society at all. But if there's anything that life has taught me, Scarlett, it's that you can't rely on other people to get what you want.' He hunched over like a humpback whale. It was as if anything would roll off his back. Nothing could ever touch him.

'What d'you mean?'

'Take it. You are the king of your own realm. Would a king sit back and let his kingdom burn to the ground?'

'No.' I laughed. 'But, I'm no king.' There was something about Scott's dad that felt familiar, like an uncle or a family friend. He was someone who had a lot to say, who loved to tell people what to do, but in a comforting way. 'Anyway, I'm not sure I'm smart enough to...'

'No, you're a queen! Scott, give her your sword.'

'What? Why?' I said.

'Take it.' Scott held it out to me.

'You need to remember what power feels like.' Scott's dad leant back on his throne. 'You've had it taken away from you, but you need to take it back.'

I tried not to laugh because it was obvious that they did this for fun. I wasn't used to seeing adults playing around. Scott gave me the sword and when I held it, I felt like a kid again with me Mary Poppins' umbrella. I used to point at things with it. I'd talk to the duck's head as if I was Mary. I'd be twice as tall. I was a little kid, running a household, and paying Mum's bills. So if I could do that, then what was holding me back now? Where had that version of me gone?

'Don't hold it like that.' Scott's dad shook his head. 'It's not an umbrella. This is a sword. A sign of might. You hold it up! High! That's it. Queen's don't get bossed about, they take control. They find the rebel and smoke them out. They take matters into their own hands. They rebuild.'

'But, we don't have the...'

'Oh, is she coming to LARP with us?' Liz stood at the garage door, leaning on the frame. I lowered the sword, embarrassed.

'We may have a convert.' Scott's dad grinned. 'It's so much more than a game. I think you'd get a lot out of it.' He slapped his hands together so loud it rang in me ears. 'I got it! You know what we need?'

I shook me head. Scott's dad was a force of nature, a tide pulling you in. I could barely keep up, but he had swept me along with him.

'A fundraiser,' he said. 'We could put on something, or break a world record, or... people will throw money at you if they knew what had happened. We just need to get their attention!'

'That's a great idea.' Scott nodded.

'What for?' Liz took a sip of water.

'For Scarlett here, for her house! We'll get them back in their home in no time.'

'Oh, you don't have to do that.' I bit me nails.

'But I love doing them,' he said. 'I'm always on the telly. It's a great place to get your message out.'

'He's so good at them.' Liz walked over to Scott's Dad and put a hand on his shoulder. 'Got all the press contacts. It'll be huge.'

'We just need a hook. Something unusual to get people interested. Something the entire community would want to be part of.' He draped his legs over an arm of the throne and stared up at the ceiling.

'You're really going to help us?'

'Of course!' He threw up his arms.

'They're great fun.' Liz leaned on the throne, glass of water still in hand.

'But you don't even know us.'

'Ah, I can tell,' he said. 'I know an excellent fish when I see one. Right, Scott?'

'Everyone deserves a home.' Scott tilted his head to one side. 'So much comes down to luck. It's not right what's happened to you.'

I couldn't help myself from staring at Scott and smiling, because he said all the things I had hoped to hear from Rory. He said all the things I had wanted to hear from anyone. I *did* deserve a home. I deserved to be happy, too. He believed I deserved something better.

'Precisely.' Scott's dad stood up. 'That should be our motto or something.'

The tide changed in that moment. I tightened me grip on the sword in me hand as they brainstormed ideas. They felt like people I had met already, a long time ago, but who I'd forgotten. A home I didn't know I had. When people talk about falling in love, they never tell you it can happen all at once with more than one person. But right there and right then, I fell for the entire Wright family.

'Sometimes a person we love, through no fault of his own, can't
see past the end of his nose.'

Mary Poppins

The Saints all stood together in Rubi's driveway, waiting
for our new home to arrive. Me, Dad, Rubes, her
parents, and Granny. Ms Piggy was running circles
around us, digging her nose into the wild garlic on the verge. It
was one of those odd days in April when the wind changes,
making it feel like winter again, and we had our coats back out.

'Dad, have you got that note?'

'What note?'

'The one that told us to die.' I pulled me coat in around me. 'I
want to see it.'

'Miss Bossy's back.' Granny tutted.

I gritted me teeth. This was the problem with living at
home at me age. Everyone still treated you like a kid. I was
called bossy a lot when I was going through me Mary Poppin's

phase. I'd use me umbrella to conduct dance routines and poke the odd kid getting out of line. When I moved in with Dad, he told me to hang up the umbrella. We went to fly a kite on a windless day. We ran and ran, but it never got off the ground. He made a good case about Mary going when Mr Banks had stepped up. He said he was Mr Banks, so Mary could go. But what the film doesn't tell you is that Mr Banks goes back to his old ways eventually, and that included ignoring me.

'Dad!'

'What?'

'Do you have it? The note.'

'No, Kirsten has it.' He was staring at his new second-hand phone, trying to work it. Rubi was chatting with her parents a few feet away from us. They were wrapped up in coats, scarves, hats and gloves, as if they were going to the arctic.

'Where is Kirsten?'

'Should be 'ere any minute.' He growled and put his phone in his pocket. 'Told us to wait. What d'you want the note for?'

'I'm gunna see who wrote it.'

'Don't you dare go making things worse.' He turned his back on me. Everybody was pretending not to overhear. I caught Rubi's parents glancing over. They'd stopped talking.

'Why do you automatically think I'd make it worse? I might be able to find out who is doing it.'

'She thinks a lot of herself, don't she?' Granny bent down to pick up the pig, to stop Destiny from bothering everyone's feet.

'Scar, I won't say it again. Leave it.' Dad took out his phone again and walked toward the edge of the driveway where there was an old broken lamppost I'd never seen lit. He sipped from a bottle of Pepsi that he'd been nursing for days.

I growled then too, me breath like a steam train.

Rubi came over, her scarf gathered up around her mouth. 'Are you OK? You seem different, more aggro...'

'I ain't sitting back and doing nothing no more. Someone's got to get our house back.'

'Ah, fighting talk. I like it! What you going to do?'

'There are three people, I reckon, who could have done it: our neighbour, Clive what's-his-face...'

'Who's that?'

'That guy Kirsten accused of harassment.'

Kirsten never spoke about what ruined her political career. She was a local councillor, a cabinet member for transport and something, and she said a member from another party sexually harassed her. She took back what she said and stepped down. She never spoke about it. She never said why. Maybe she'd made it up; a bit like that time she said she could play the guitar.

' 'ere she is!' Dad pointed up the street at a proper-old double-decker bus coming towards us.

'Is that a...?' Rubi's dad ran over to open the wooden gate wider.

The bus flew down the hill with a tiny, joker-smiling Kirsten behind the wheel. She waved and beeped and pulled into the driveway towards the old barn. The double doors tried to open, but only one sprang back, making the sound of a Pepsi can being opened.

'So, what do you think?' Kirsten opened the driving-booth door, and slid off the seat.

'About what? The bus?' Everyone else looked as equally baffled as I did. Rubi's parents were staring at each other with wide eyes.

'Our new home!' She grinned and threw her arms out like a magician's assistant.

'What?' Dad edged closer, gripping onto his Pepsi bottle as if it were a grenade.

'Well, the person I know... She works for a charity who does up old buses for the homeless. They got halfway through this one and ran out of money. So it has just been sitting there. Come in, come look at it.'

'I ain't livin' in that.' Granny gestured at the bus as if it were beneath her. 'You lost your mind?'

'They said we could have it for a bit, in exchange for helping do it up; get it fitted. We can do that, right Jason? Weekends here and there.'

One by one, we climbed up the steps onto the bus. Granny needed a hand up. The floor was tacky, sticking to our feet. It smelt musty, too. The purple seats, with kaleidoscope patterns, had started to fade. The plastic backs had been melted with lighters and graffitied all over. Dried up chewing gum plugged up corners.

Dad pulled in close to Kirsten. 'I thought we was gonna borrow a caravan from Mike?'

'Don't you think this is better?' Kirsten grinned. 'It has *two* floors.'

'This isn't fit for humans.' Granny held onto a yellow pole. 'Can't expect us to live in 'ere.'

'It's *just* like a caravan, Henrietta, except the beds are *upstairs*.' She pointed as if she was in a Panto. Yellow strip-lights ran down the ceiling on the first floor.

'But it ain't... the kitchen isn't...' Dad was stuttering, at a loss.

'Oh.' Kirsten swiped at the air with her hand and blew her lips out. 'We can do that, easy.'

'But Mike's caravan already has...'

'I can't!' She turned away and mumbled to Dad something about not being able to live in a caravan. 'Not again...'

'Well, I think it's great.' Rubi's dad clapped his hands together. 'It's like a jolly holiday. An adventure.'

Rubi's dad had a panto-like quality to him: large hand gestures, exaggerated smiles and winks, and he always had his hand on one hip. He was one step away from getting out the chimney sweep and tap dancing with penguins. He was the reincarnation of Dick van Dyke.

'But we have enough to do on our house. We can't do a bus too.' Dad was examining the half-constructed kitchen. Kirsten still didn't know about the insurance. She didn't know that we'd be in the bus for a long time and that we were the only ones who'd be fixing our house. But this was more than a bus to her, and at least she was trying to do something.

'I think I quite like it.' I nodded at Kirsten.

'Really?'

'I got you summat too.' I held up the *Home Sweet Home* sign. Even though I couldn't afford it, I went back and got it.

'Oh, I love it! Just like me Gran's.' She clapped and then hugged me - one of those half-committed hugs.

'Shall we go up?' said Rubi's mum. 'Explore the top floor.'

The Dunn's went up first, followed by Granny. Dad watched from behind to see if she could manage. I held Kirsten back.

'Dad said you got that note? The one we got before the fire?'

'The threat? Uh... yeah.' She reached forward to a tote bag on the luggage shelf and then handed me a handful of paper. 'Here you go.'

'What's all this?'

'That's all of them. I took them to work. Wanted to see if it looked like anyone's handwriting I knew.'

'All of them?'

Kirsten's phone beeped, and she pulled it out to look at it. 'No. Just had to go to the doctors...'

'Huh?' She wasn't paying attention to me now, either. I peered at her screen to see what was so important. The text message was all in lowercase and said stuff like - *liar* and *bitch* and *everyone will see you for who you really are.*

'Who the hell's that?'

Kirsten put her phone back in her pocket. 'No one.'

'You get texts too?'

'I don't think it's the same person.' She avoided looking at me.

'Why not?'

'By what they say...'

'What they say? What did you do?'

'You can keep the bus here if you like.' Rubi's dad came down from upstairs. 'We need this part for parking. But we can clear the scrap away from the barn. There would be plenty of room then. Give you a way to hook it up to the mains, maybe.'

'That would be amazing. We can help you out too...' Kirsten followed them off the bus.

On our way out, me first suspect walked past the driveway - Edward Post - our neighbour. When he turned and stopped, he held onto the pair of binoculars hanging around his throat like a noose. 'You can't have *that* there.' He pointed at the bus. 'It's a bleeding eyesore.'

Everyone waited for someone to say something.

'What was that?' Rubi's dad inched forward.

Mr Post's voice was hard to hear. When he spoke, he was a cocktail of cocky and shy. He spent his life telling people what to do, how not to do it, but it was all muttered under his breath like a bitter, grumpy bank man shrivelling up behind a desk. He was like a character straight out of me favourite film.

'I'll be reporting that to the council. Place of outstanding natural beauty and you're ruinin' it.'

'That's rich.' I went up to Mr Post, proper-close, but not so close that his smell could knock me back. 'Where were you when our house burned down?'

'What?'

'You heard me.'

'I was away, visitin' family.' He pulled out a handkerchief and rubbed his nose with it.

'Who?'

'Me son,' he said. 'You know, that fire damaged me house too.

97

I should sue, and then you'll...' He rubbed his nose and started mumbling again.

'I've never seen you with a son.' I stood upright.

'You saying I did it? Don't be ridiculous, I live right next door. I'll have you for this. Deformation. I'll go to the police. You can't go accusin' people...'

Granny marched up to Mr Post. 'You dare. And I'll tell them about your little pet.'

'Me what?'

'That illegal fleabag of a bird you keep feedin',' said Granny. 'You girt plonker. You cretin. You stupid old weasel.'

'Granny!' I put me hand on her shoulder.

'Well, he is,' she said. 'You're right on the money, Scarlett. He's always been after us. And it's not like he can sue us for anything now! We've got nothing for him to take.'

'I ain't gunna stick around listenin' to these bleedin' accusations.' He walked away, mumbling some more. 'You've no right to keep on, and take me land and... the audacity. You stay away from me house. I'll be callin' the council. Mark me words, I'll be sending someone to come...'

Granny turned to me. 'I bet you there's summat else in that house. We'll get him one day, Scarlett.' She patted me arm and walked away. She was right. I had never seen him in a rush to get anywhere. So the fact he'd wanted to clear off so quick made him seem suspicious. Guilty. If I got a-hold of his handwriting and compared it to the notes I had, I bet I could make a match. We'd have our villain, because Mr Post had it in him. He was a textbook villain.

He used to seem harmless, the odd man next door. I always spoke to him because he must be lonely. You see loneliness more when you work in a carehome. You don't wish it on no-one. Mr Post's only visitors were squirrels. But like most here in the Cotswolds, he was at war with nature. He didn't want to be in the wild. He wanted to see nature groomed and trimmed, forced to step in time. He hated squirrels. Said they were pests, invaders, encroaching on his land, eating all the food for the birds in his own back garden. He'd set traps for them and take out a shovel to finish the job. I found him hanging them up once, the bloody bodies from the fence. When I screamed, he said: 'Let's hope the other squirrels feel the same. This ain't their home. Let it be a lesson to you. Don't go where you don't belong.'

13

'They say that you've forgotten that you're a pig.
Isn't that silly? And they even said
that you don't know what pigs are for.'

Babe

G ranny forgot what pigs were for, too. She said her little piggy came to her in a dream, and then she found her the next morning in the back garden, her snout deep in a flowerpot, eating Granny's mint. In her dream, she was told that Destiny could predict the future and so she'd been making dosh off her ever since.

'Stop eatin'.' Granny elbowed me as we stood behind a table at the market. 'Gunna be as porky as the pig soon.'

'But I'm just so hungry.' I picked flaky pastry from me top, and wrapped the sausage roll back up. 'Proper starving all the time.'

Granny and I were at the Farmers' Market in town. We'd set up our table and tent at the random end, where people selling weird art and bric-à-brac end up. We ain't exactly something you get at a market. So we were penned in like cattle into a dark corner on a side street. Our stall is more like what you get at a fair or a travelling carnival. But we got into the Farmers' Market circuit because Granny could fight all day and all night until people got so exhausted they gave her whatever she wanted. It was sheer talent.

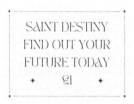

SAINT DESTINY
FIND OUT YOUR
FUTURE TODAY
♀|

You had to write your question for Destiny, because Granny swore she didn't hear good but could read. Destiny would give you an answer by choosing either the *yes* box, or the *no* box (which both had pig-feed in them). Every week, Mr Post came with a pound to wind Granny up, asking questions about who owned the weird bit of land at the back. So far, Destiny had voted in our favour seven out of ten times. But I wasn't here for Destiny this time. I had the threatening letters in me pocket, ready to compare notes. I was here to save our house.

'Scarlett! Look who it is, Liz... It's Scarlett.' Scott's dad shouted from the other side of our table. He wore a stripy shirt and a flat cap, as if dressing for the part of a posh farmer.

'So it is.' Scott's mum came towards us. She was in proper clothes this time too - a long black coat and big scarf wound around her neck like a Mr Whippy ice-cream. 'How are you?'

'I'm...'

'Who are you?' Granny put both hands on the table.

'We've just moved in.' Liz held out her hand to shake. 'Nice to meet you.'

I didn't see Scot anywhere.

'Move to the side, won't-cha love?' Granny didn't take her hand. 'We need space for payin' customers. No room for chitchat. Matter of life and death, y' know, when your house has burned down.'

The herds of visitors that usually came to the market were often curious, poking their nose in for a nibble. But they hadn't been biting all day. They ambled past like sheep, barely interested in what this little pig offered. So for sympathy points, Granny had been telling everyone *everywhere* about the fire. She kept telling me to listen close, hear how she did it. She got her talent for sales from her uncle who could sell you air. She'd shrink in size, act super-frail and quiet, and let a tear roll down her cheek. *Such a performance*, she'd say. *Bring me an Oscar!*

'I heard,' said Liz. 'Absolute tragedy. Been a lot of fires around town lately.'

'Who says?'

'Liz is the Police Officer who interviewed me the other day.' I rubbed me hands together.

'Is that right?' Granny stood upright. 'Got two piggies at the market today, have we?!' Granny laughed and clapped both her hands. Liz raised her eyebrows.

'Gran! I'm sorry, she doesn't mean that.'

'I'm a comedian,' said Granny. 'No crime in that!'

'We have a pound.' Scott's dad held up a coin like it was the holy grail. 'And a question for your fortune telling pig!'

Granny uncrossed her arms and smiled. 'Well, in that case... roll up, roll up, write your question there, and I'll get Destiny out.'

I put food in each box.

'Did you say anything to your family about our idea,' said Liz. 'The fundraiser?'

'Haven't had a chance yet.' Me hand rested on both answers.

'What idea?' said Granny.

Clive began writing his question down. 'Well, we thought we could put on a fundraiser for your family, for the house.'

'We don't want your charity,' snorted Gran.

'We could do something huge like... break a world record, try to make it a big media frenzy.' He handed over the piece of paper. 'That's if you don't mind being on the news or swamped by the media.'

'The news?'

'Yes, nationwide. Maybe worldwide! A story of such tragedy, it'll tug at the public's heartstrings. There's no way they could stand back and not give you their money.'

Clive seemed to know Granny from the get-go, that she loved getting attention. She loved being the centre of such sympathy and horror and fascination. She loved to be noticed. She had no shame.

'Summat big?' Granny nodded. 'Yes, yes, I like it. You're smarter than you look.'

'And you wouldn't have to do a thing,' said Scott's dad. 'Just be your charming self. We've got all the contacts and whatnot.'

'I was born charming.' Granny grinned. 'Me mother used to get stopped in the street when I was a baby. They told her how beautiful I was. Boys were always knockin'...' She glanced down at the paper. 'What on earth is LARPing?'

Scott's dad smiled. I peered over Gran's shoulder to read what Clive had written:

Will Scarlett be coming to her first LARPing event with us tomorrow?

I smiled. 'It's a game, Gran,' I said. 'Better see what Destiny says. Here you are Destiny.' I showed her the question and then I let go of her collar.

'Aren't you all a bit old for games?' Granny pointed at Scott's parents. 'Especially you two.'

'It's more like acting, community theatre,' said Scott's dad. 'Except it's outside.'

Destiny went straight to the *Yes* box.

'WEY!' Scott's dad held up his palm to Liz.

Liz high-fived him. 'She seemed pretty sure of that one!'

'I wasn't sure what I would have done if she'd of gone to the *No* box,' I said. 'What time shall I come over? Do I need to bring anything?' I half heard their answers, but was half distracted by what I was seeing behind them. Me mum was walking out of a building with Mr Post. She was chatting to him and helping him down the step.

'You going to take our money then?' Scott's dad held out a shiny pound coin. Granny took it. 'So see you then? Scott will be glad to see you!'

'I'll lend you something to wear.' Liz waved as they walked off.

'Yeah! Can't wait.' I waved back.

'What you playing at?' Granny elbowed me. 'Keep the feed away from the pig!'

Destiny's snout was close to upturning the whole tub. I pulled her back by the harness. 'Thought I saw Mum coming out of the solicitors.' Destiny tugged at me hand as I stretched me neck to see around the corner.

Granny rolled her eyes. 'That woman! She stole me best vase she did.'

'No, she didn't,' I said. 'It broke. You always say this, but it broke!'

'Well, she ain't no stranger to takin' what ain't hers.' Granny scoffed. 'Like your father.'

'What? What d'you mean? Oh god, here we go. Your favourite person is coming.'

'What?'

'Mr Post... Here he comes.'

Granny crossed her arms and stared at him the whole way down the street. He stared back, as if they were two dogs squaring up to a fight. They both had barks worse than their bites, but there was no knowing who'd bark first.

'They should have you for false marketin',' said Mr Post. 'That pig don't tell nobody's future, except his own, and that's him as sizzling bacon.'

'She ain't going on nobody's plate.' I picked up Destiny and hugged her close.

' 's no life for a farm animal. Bet she ain't even registered.' He used his index finger to clear his ear.

'And, are you?' Granny pointed. 'We shouldn't be lettin' an ass walk around willy-nilly.'

I laughed. Granny was quick and funny when you weren't on the receiving end.

'You've forgotten who you are.' Mr Post bent over, slow as a slug, taking the pad and pen. 'You Saints are anything *but*. All of you. No better than mangy chickens.'

He wrote out his question, and I grabbed it before Granny could, and it said: *Will I get number 23?*

'Our house?!'

He snorted with his laugh. 'I'll get you for everything you got. Even that hole of a house.' He slid a pound coin across the table.

'We don't touch dirty money.' Granny threw it back at him.

I took out the threats we'd got in me pocket and compared notes. The handwriting was the same.

Jackpot.

'You can't afford to be fussy,' said Mr Post. 'I'll tell you summat, if it hadn't of been for that day all those years ago... If he had never of come back, you'd be singing another tune, I tell you.'

'It's you!' I said. 'You've been sending us threats.'

'He's good at writing letters. He's always writing letters. Never shuts up.' Granny took Destiny's lead.

'And you don't, pah!' Visible spit sprayed from Mr Post's mouth. 'Hypocrite!'

'I ain't sent you anything in decades,' said Granny. 'And *I* don't make threats.'

'Don't know nothing about no threats.' Mr Post leaned forwards. 'Except the ones you're always giving me, for just living me life as I choose to live it. And...'

'I've got a question for you.' I grabbed the pen and paper and started writing so hard it was practically an engraving.

'Tell him to sling his hook.' Granny crossed her arms and turned away.

I put feed in the boxes, took Destiny, and then showed Destiny the paper. 'Here we go: *Did Mr Post burn down our house?*' I let go of Destiny's lead.

'What?' Mr Post stood upright. 'Ha. Whole family's the same, ain't it? Everyone else's fault but your own.'

Destiny hesitated for a minute. She went one way, then the next. The air was thick, as if it had been sitting out too long. 'You know what, I've had enough of being pushed around by some grumpy assbucket who ain't got nothing better to do than harass his neighbours,' I said. 'It's illegal, you know, to send death threats. I'm sure the police would like to know about these.'

I shook the notes in the air in front of Mr Post's sheepish face, as our little fortune piggy stuck her head into the box that said: *Yes*.

Mr Post had burned down our house. We were all sure of it.

Destiny had spoken.

14

'You know somethin', Robin. I was just wonderin', are we good
guys or bad guys?'

Little John from Robin Hood.

I was determined to be someone completely different when
I went LARPing with the Wrights. Rubi used to say to me
that if you pretended to be the person you want to be, if
you did what you think they'd do, eventually, you'd become that
person. Eventually, you'd be them.

But I couldn't get Mr Post and Granny's fight out of me head.
There was something they were hiding. And then there was
Mum with Mr Post, those texts to Kirsten, and then Sophie
who'd framed me. There was no way they could be
coincidences.

I needed to leave me life.

Escape.

Become somebody else.

'And, who are you?' Scott's mum, Liz, had both her hands on

her hips. Their dining room was proper-regal, with a grandfather clock in it that didn't work. We were getting ready to leave their house, all of us dressed up as if we were in ye olde England.

I knew who Scott's family wanted me to be. It was who I wanted to be. 'I am Skyla Goode, protector of the realm of Mardon. Loyal to me king, Lord Bannor. All hail Mardon!'

'That's good.' Scott stood, arms crossed, nodding, listening, wearing the same sword, chain metal stuff I saw him in that day by the pool. 'I like it.' He was talking to me, but not looking at me. He gazed up at the chandelier. It's always been this way with blokes. They never really see me, even when I'm the only one there. I figured maybe he was shy. Even though he was taller than the rest of us, he hunched over.

'Thanks.' I readjusted the itchy green dress that Liz had given to me, and loosened the rope around the middle. 'Wasn't too lame?'

'No spot on.' He picked up his round wooden shield off the table. 'What's this?'

'It's a home warming present.' I pushed the tin across their shiny dining-room table, hoping it wouldn't scratch.

'You didn't need to do that.' Liz pried open the lid. 'Oh look, it's shortbread.'

'The M is for Mardon.' I sat down. 'They're empire shortbread!'

'Nice.' Scott took a bite of one. 'These are me favourite.'

I grinned. I knew shortbread was his favourite because it had taken me ages of social media stalking on Rubi's phone to find out.

Scott's dad walked in, adjusting the black and gold Celtic band around his head. 'Hey, that looks excellent.' He was looking at me. 'You're like a mage. I could do with one of those. Hey, maybe we could make you me long, lost daughter or something?'

'Can you do that?' Scott sat next to me at the head of the table.

'I'm game master. I can do what I like.' Scott's dad took a biscuit. 'If that's what Scarlett wants! We're all there to have fun.'

'Yeah, that sounds cool. Would I have powers and stuff?'

'Oh yeah. You can only have a one-handed weapon in battle, but you can do spells.'

'Can I get people to do whatever I want?' I raised me eyebrows for comic effect. 'Because that would be a dream.'

'Sort of.' Scott's dad brushed crumbs from his chin. 'Definitely if you're the daughter of the King! I'm a great person to know.' He winked at me and then pulled Scott's mum to him. 'Ain't that right, me lady?' She laughed as he kissed her on the cheek.

We drove in their Landrover to a field on the outskirts of town with Scott's dad trying to come up with different ideas for the house fundraiser. White clouds followed us there like thought bubbles. I used to daydream all the time, staring out of windows. Dad told me to get me ass out of the clouds. But I was on me way to the biggest daydream of all. I had pretended I couldn't fix me seatbelt, then I pretended it got stuck so that Scott had to lean over and fasten it for me. I imagined him kissing me, shocked and all out of breath. It would be a secret kiss - a moment for just us. I imagined it all the way there.

'Right folks!' Scott's dad pulled on the handbrake. 'It's time to take back what is rightfully ours.' He lifted his hands into the air. 'Are we ready, people of Mardon?'

'At your side, sir.' Scott saluted.

'All hail, Mardon!' Scott's dad banged his fists on his chest.

'All hail Mardon,' replied Scott and his mum.

We got out of the car and unloaded shields and swords and

banners. A silence had come over us. A hush. We were near a forest. The trees whispered like they knew something we didn't. This patch of land had only just been claimed back by the empire, and rebels were rising back up (apparently). I was still finding it hard to take it seriously. It still seemed like a game to me, not a show. They had warned me that there would be no intro. We'd be going straight into a play where they expect us to get ambushed, and that we were to find Lord Bannor's guard before they did.

'Scott? Can I stay with you? This is a bit weird for me.' I followed behind them, into the trees.

'Who?' Scott turned, frowning, hand on his hilt. 'Whom is this Scott you speak of?'

'Huh?'

'I am Ryder Cliftone, son of Oswin Cliftone, defender of the weak.'

Scott pulled out his sword and pointed it at me. At some point in the drive over here when we'd talked about how I needed evidence to prove that Mr Post was the fire starter, Scott had vanished. He was like another person: confident, no-nonsense and making eye contact. This was the guy I'd met by the side of the pool.

But I still felt like me.

'Who is this fair maiden who wanders the woods?' Scott's dad pushed him to one side.

'My Lord, she appeared out of nowhere.' Scott lowered his sword.

'Speak, or have your speech taken from you, maid.' Scott's dad drew his sword and held it to me neck.

From behind us, three men dressed in armour showed up on the path in the woods. 'Lord Bannor, sir!' They ran towards us and aimed their swords at me too. I froze to the spot. The Wright family had disappeared, and I was wondering what the hell I was doing here.

'My name is Skyla Goode.' Me voice sounded pathetic. 'I am no threat to you.' I held up me hands because I didn't know what else to do.

'We are searching for a mage who has a freckle in the crease of her elbow.' Liz's eyes were as round and sparkling as crystal balls.

'My teller here, Ammy Lesbros from Woden tells me I have a daughter, lost here in the forest and I have fought night and day to claim back this land to search for her. Tell me, Skyla Goode, what is in the crease of your elbow?'

I pulled up me right sleeve. There, in the crease, was a freckle I had forgotten about. And in a weird way, I immediately felt seen by them, recognised.

'It is her!' Scott's mum put both hands on her cheeks.

'Daughter, my only daughter.' Scott's dad put his hand on me shoulder. 'I cannot believe my eyes. Today, we will celebrate. Today we will mark the calendar!'

Scott's mum grabbed me hand. Her's was heavy - gold rings with big gems. She closed her eyes. 'She is a mage, your lordship. A powerful mage! Born into Ackermane. You consider yourself a nomad...' She opened her eyes and stared at me. 'But your heart is in the shape of Mardon. Big and strong!'

'I have been in search of Mardon since it came to me in a dream.' I was blurring the lines between truth and fiction, but so were they.

'My lord,' whispered one of the old men behind him. 'Did you hear that?'

'Hear what?' Scott's dad turned and searched around us. 'Who dares ruin this sweet and blessed reunion of royal blood?'

'A messenger in the trees. They speak to us. Someone is coming.'

There was shouting and screaming and the thundering of feet.

'Turn to face them.' Scott took me elbow and swivelled me around.

Scott's mum grabbed me hand, and I squeezed it proper-tight. 'The crown will protect you.'

'What can I do?'

'Take your sword in your hand and be ready.' Liz nodded.

I was ready. I was proper-ready to fight. I was totally ready to *be* Skyla and to defend the crown, the empire, or whatever it was. Skyla was ready to defend the Wrights to the last breath, to take anyone down who came - except... Behind a tree, *she* stepped out as the rebels charged towards the guards, swords meeting padded swords. In her hand, she drew a bow and arrow. Her face wasn't an idea, or a dream. Her face wasn't part of me fantasy-land at all. I was no longer Skyla Goode, but Scarlett Saint, looking at the girl who she got fired, the girl who'd framed her for setting fire to the care home.

Sophie was dressed as a warrior. She had two plaits and a braid crowning her head. She froze for a second as her eyes met mine. When she released the padded arrow, she smiled, and she wasn't firing the arrow at Skyla Goode. Her arrow hit Scarlett Saint in the stomach.

'Fall down.' Scott shouted at me as he waved his sword in the air against someone else.

'What?'

'You're dead,' he said.

'But I don't want to be dead. I need to...'

But Sophie had vanished back into the forest, back into the story. That single arrow had pierced me bubble. I wasn't in no fantasy-land. The Wrights weren't me family. This wasn't no game or play. Scott wasn't about to take me into the forest and kiss me. I wasn't Skyla Goode, defender of the realm, hero and mage to the kingdom. I was Scarlett Saint, homeless, alone, living on a bus, suspended from her job, and part of a family that was probably the most hated in town.

15

'Instead of a Dark Lord, you would have a queen, not dark but
beautiful and terrible as the dawn! Tempestuous as the sea, and
stronger than the foundations of the earth!
All shall love me and despair!'

Galadriel, The Lord of the Rings

I had this niggling feeling ever since I saw me mum with
Mr Post. A dread that weighed me down. Scott's mum said
I should make an official report on Mr Post. Hand in the
notes. It wasn't a coincidence: me mum and Mr Post, Granny
and Mr Post. Something was up. So I went to her house for some
answers first. I owed her that.

Me mum has always been the queen of fads. On a quest to
find that one true thing that could fix her, that one thing that
would sort her out, solve her problems. She has sat in silence for
hours, been laden with crystals, drunk water that was once
touched by a precious, holy emblem. She's taken up painting,

acting, and even flash mobbing. But she never found what she was looking for. This month, she was into yoga. She wanted me to join her in the front room, even though there was barely any space in the middle. She'd do a pose, and I'd copy.

Half-moon. Half-moon.

Hands to feet. Hands to feet.

Awkward pose. Awkward pose.

Eagle pose. Eagle pose.

'Namaste.' Mum put prayer-hands to her forehead and bowed.

'How's that bird? The egg, I mean.'

'Ah, she's gone now.' She folded forward to touch her toes. 'Never hatched.'

'Shame.' I had one eye on Mum and one closed. 'Mum?'

'Yes?' She stretched out her arms, reaching up to the ceiling.

'Why were you with Mr Post the other day?'

She didn't move. 'Who?' Her voice was soft, church-like.

'Our neighbour, Mr Post.'

'When?'

'The other day. I saw you at the solicitors on the high street.'

She lifted one leg up and placed it on her inner thigh. 'Was I?'

'I saw you bring him out.'

'Oh, I don't remember. I was probably just helping him out. He's really old now, isn't he?' Mum put her hands together above her head and looked up at the ceiling. Perfectly balanced.

'Yeah, same as Granny.' I tried to get into the same tree pose but slipped. 'You remember what he did to us, right?'

'What?'

'About that bit of land...' I tried the tree pose again. 'He's trying to get us thrown out of the Dunn's now, too.'

'Well, your Granny isn't an angel.' Mum returned to earth, dropping her leg and arms. 'He has his reasons, I'm sure. They don't even use that basement.' She took a sharp, deep breath, and then opened her mouth wide, stuck out her tongue and breathed out.

'Basement?'

'I mean the back alley...' Hands on hips, she twisted away from me.

'But he's been writing threats to us. I reckon he burned down our house!'

She shook her head. 'Not a chance. He's not a bad man. Far from it. He'd never do that to your house.'

'But...'

'Trust me.' She sat down, crossed legged, hands on her knees, and closed her eyes. 'He's not like that.'

We all think we know our parents. We trust their judgment when we're kids. But now I had experience and distance. I was seven when me mum joined this new religion. There were a lot of rules. For one, I wasn't allowed to call her Mum. I couldn't question anything, and we didn't have Christmas. But she was happier for a bit. I remember that. She'd been going to these sessions to clear her soul. I asked her if I could go into training too. But all I can remember were all these questions, repetitions, confessions, until I couldn't feel anything anymore. At the graduation, in a room full of other kids like me, leaders surrounded us with their eyes closed, hands out, telling us orders, visions, speaking words I'd never heard of before. They pushed a kid back and forth. He lashed out, fighting back, and then they took him down to the ground. I looked to me mum. But she said: 'This is good. That's the bad stuff inside you trying to hold on. But now it's left his body, his soul. We have to fight it out!'

That was when me mum pushed me. But I didn't fight back. I screwed up into a ball and the last thing I remembered was me mum pinning me to the ground, her hair flying up like she was possessed, like she'd got the one thing to rule them all. 'You did it!' She panted. 'You're free.'

That was a long time ago, but when I found a bruise from

Sophie's arrow that morning, it all came back to me. It was in the same place I got a bruise when Mum pushed me down all those years ago. You expect to be hurt by people you don't know, but not your own mum. Trust in her wasn't exactly something I had kept hold of. But I couldn't tell her that. I couldn't tell her that she was putty in over people's hands.

'Who d'you think burned down our house then, if not him?'

'I wouldn't be surprised if your dad did it for insurance money and it backfired.' Her nose was in the air, eyes still closed.

I rolled me eyes. There was no use arguing with her about Dad. She stuck out her tongue and breathed out like a wraith.

'What you doing?'

'Lion's breath.' She opened her eyes and looked at me for once. 'Try it, honey. Supposed to open up your throat chakra and let your face relax. You look tense.'

'Hard not to be.' I stared down at the brown matted carpet.

She did Lion's breath again. 'Come on, you go.' I copied her, and she nodded and smiled. 'That's it. Eyes closed.'

'Mum?'

'Yes, Scarlett?' She sighed.

'Never mind...' I stared up at the light bulb in the ceiling. She really ought to get a lampshade. It's stuff like that which makes people think less of her.

Her shoulders slumped. 'I don't think you're quite getting this.'

'Sorry.' I copied her position, trying to avoid the sofa. 'It's just...'

'What?'

'Why haven't you offered for me to stay here? Until I get back on me feet.'

She laughed. 'Where would you sleep?'

'In here? I'm on a bus, Mum! With Granny. Can you imagine?'

She smiled, shook her head, closed her eyes. 'One day, Scarlett, you'll understand. You're too young to know...'

'I'm nineteen, for god's sake. I can drive, drink, go anywhere. I can get a tattoo...'

'You've never even left the country.' She tilted her head in that patronising way that always makes me want to scream.

'So? What's that got to...'

'Sing to me.' She closed her eyes. 'I used to love it when you sang to me. Such a beautiful voice.'

I reckoned Mum saw me as the same age as when I left her. Time stopped. Maybe she couldn't cope with the fact that she didn't see me grow up. But what if this was actually her way of getting out of stuff she didn't want to do, talks she didn't want to have?

'Stop changing the subject.' I threw a cushion at her lap. 'We lost everything, our house burnt down! Do you get that?'

'Of course I do, honey.' But she didn't. She was too calm to get it. Or maybe she didn't care.

'Kirsten thinks you did it and I am beginning...'

'Kirsten thinks I did it!' Mum went from being this pillar of peace to a bullet of fury. 'That little bitch. How dare she! She's a liar, that woman.' She got up onto her knees, and then to her feet. 'She's lied about me, about that man, about this... who knows what else?'

'Mum!'

She paced the room. 'I just, will she never learn? Where does it get her? She's a pathetic...'

'Mum!'

'What?' She span around.

'Where were you?'

'When?'

'When our house burned down.'

She froze and stared into me soul. '*You* think I did it too?'

'No, it's just I'd like to tell Kirsten...'

'I can't believe you think I'd be capable or would want to... Why Scarlett, baby? Why would you think that?' Her eyes filled up with tears, and the anger loosened in me, but not enough to comfort her.

' 'cause... well...' I got up and went to me jacket, which was draped over the arm of the sofa. I pulled out the photo I found at the house. 'D'you remember this?'

She stood up, took the photo from me, and shook her head sideways.

'Look at the back.' I pointed. 'Remember now?'

'I don't know why you think this means I'd set that fire?'

'What did Dad do that you can't forgive? I need to know.'

She shook her head and stared at the words, examining it again:

LOOK AT HER. ISN'T SHE BEAUTIFUL! I CAN'T BELIEVE WHAT YOU DID, AND I'M NOT SURE I'LL EVER FORGIVE YOU. BUT SHE'S YOUR RESPONSIBILITY TOO. YOU NEED TO STEP UP AND BE THERE FOR HER.

'Do I remind you too much of Dad or summat?'

'What?'

'Is that why you did it? Did he do summat horrible to you? I'm not a kid anymore. I just want to understand why you're so mad. I want to know what happened. I want the truth.'

'Right.' She gave me back the photo. 'Stay there.' She stomped out of the room and came back a few minutes later with letters, thrusting them at me.

'What are they?'

'I didn't want to do this, Scarlett. I wanted to put it behind us. But I spent years fighting with your dad to help. He just wouldn't pay up.'

'This is why you were mad?'

'Then. Yes. But he's your dad, and you're there. I didn't want you to know what he'd done, how terrible it all was. He and *her*. They turned everyone against me. Said I was unfit, but he had no idea what it was like to be a single mum on me own with no support...'

I read the letters, the summons for Dad to go to court, to take custody.

'You didn't want to keep me? You were fighting for Dad to take me?'

'No no no, I couldn't afford you.' She grabbed me forearm and stroked it. 'That's all. When I argued I needed more money from him, he used that against me... He only did it when *she* came along.'

'So why don't you want me now? Now that I need you again and you're better?'

'Scarlett, baby.' Tears filled her eyes again. She pulled back, arms wrapped around herself, and fell onto the sofa. 'Stop it. It's not fair. You know I love you.'

'But...'

'No.' She shook her head. 'I won't hear another word of it. This is so hurtful. Like you're picking at my wounds. I can't bear it.'

'So the fire has got nothing to do with you? Because... you're not mad at them anymore?'

She sat up straight. 'Your dad and Kirsten treated me badly. But I'm not the only one they screwed. There's a line-up, I'm sure. But you have to believe me when I say that I wanted to keep you Scarlett, I just couldn't. They made sure of that. But I would *never* do anything to hurt you. OK?'

I nodded. But I didn't believe she had nothing to do with Mr Post. She was beginning to look like she was on the edge of something bad, and I wasn't going to push her over it.

'Say it.' She sat up straight. 'Say I would never hurt you.'

'You would never hurt me.'

She got up and hugged me. But I couldn't help but tense up, remembering her pushing me all those years ago at that 'gradua-tion'. How scared I was when she hugged me then. I couldn't help but remember her pose - pinning me to the ground and grinning as if she'd taken something precious from me.

16

'Secrets have a cost. They are not for free.'

Spiderman

The secrets I had hung in the corner of me mind like a spider's web. Most of the time, I didn't notice them. I didn't even think they were secrets; they were just things-I-never-told-nobody because I was embarrassed. Some secrets are easier to tell a stranger than those you know.

'So what's the real reason you were out of work?' Rubi and I stood, staring into the black mouth of me house, through the hole where there used to be a door. I'd dragged her there because I had a hunch that there was something more in the house. Something that might explain why me mum was with Mr Post.

'What?'

'What happened?' Rubi crossed her arms. You went back after two weeks off. I figured I'd be hearing all about what

Gerry's been saying, but you've not said a word about any of them.'

'They're putting me through training.' I bit at me fingernail. 'Again.'

Me house seemed taller to me now, a black tower going up into a smoky-grey sky. There was a warm spell. Winds from the south. So Rubi had flip-flops on and I was down to a t-shirt. A web of police tape snapped back and forth, sticking to the wind. The damage was more than I remembered. It was a hole now. An empty, lonely pit. It used to be our home, but it was abandoned, looking more haunted than Rubi's B&B.

'Why training?' Rubi pulled me hand away from me mouth.

I sighed. 'They suspended me before the fire. I did something... Gladys broke her wrist.'

'You broke a girl's wrist?'

'Not on purpose. We were trying to pick up Mr Tune, the big guy, but thought we could do it without help, but that's against the... blah de blah... I just should of listened, followed the rules.' I avoided looking at her and tried to make it sound like it wasn't that bad. No big deal.

She nodded. 'Like the rules that tell you shouldn't go into a derelict, unsafe building when it has burned to the ground?'

'That's different.'

She put her hands on her hips. 'Right. So why didn't you tell your dad? Or anyone? Why not me?'

'I dunno.' But I did. I was embarrassed. Ashamed. I shrugged.

She blew out her cheeks as if she was trying to blow me away. 'It's not that big of a deal, Scarlett. There are worse things. Bigger secrets to have.'

'It wasn't a secret.'

I'd pissed her off. Rubi sucked in her bottom lip as if she'd lost her teeth. It was like that time I went to see Coldplay without her, even though she used to make fun of me for liking them. She was mad and upset, and not telling her had cost me something that I couldn't count up. So I figured I should fess up fast, clean up shop.

'Sorry, I should have said something.' I reached for her elbow. 'There's summat else too... I did get that girl fired.'

'Sophie? How?'

'She wasn't taking care of one of the residents, and I told Elma.'

'Yikes. Do you think maybe she could have done this?' Rubi pointed to the house.

I shook me head. 'I'm pretty sure it's Mr Post.'

'Then why haven't you reported him?'

'I think me mum's mixed up in it somehow. I need to know how bad. I just need to know more. There's a trapdoor in the house. I think I saw it last time we were here. And Mum slipped something about a basement...'

'But what if the floor collapses?'

'We should be able to see it from the door.'

We went through a web of police tape, and up the three concrete steps. Feathers blew around our feet. Tiger striped, light and dark brown feathers. Some small, some big. Inside the house, the fire had chewed away the carpet. There were only bare, blackened wooden floors in the hallway. New chipboard had been put down around the front door to bridge the gaps, and we stood on top of it. I sprang me knees up and down to test its strength. It was solid.

'See, there. A trap door!' I pointed to a small brass handle in the floor, and tip-toed towards it.

'Where are you going?' Rubi pulled me back by me t-shirt.

'I'm gunna go see what's down there.'

'I'm not going in. This is where I draw the line.' Rubi marked an imaginary line in front of her.

Rubi was often 'drawing a line', so much so I wondered if she was a ruler in a past life. But she was a bendy ruler, and she often flexed when pushed.

'OK, I'll just have a peek.' I walked into the hallway as lightly as I could, and pulled open the hatch. Down in the dark, there were red and blue lights in square boxes, but they were far away.

'You gotta be shitting me. No way...'

'What?'

'We have a basement! Can I borrow your phone for a light?'

Rubi stretched a leg over to me and passed me her phone. I turned the flashlight on, and leaned down to look under the hallway where the fire started. In the corner, under our hallway, which was under Rubi's feet, there was an electrical box and smoke marks. I swiped Rubi's phone, zoomed in and took a picture, but it was too dark and grainy. I panned the light around and saw the cellar went beyond our house and under Mr Post's. There were tables skirting the walls with eggs on them. It was as if I had stumbled into some creature's nest. Some eggs were in boxes with fluff. Some were in glass cases with blinking numbers and blue lights shining down. On the walls, he'd pinned up feathers and pictures of different birds.

'Can't believe she missed this!'

'Who?'

'Kai, that fire inspector. She never said it started under the house! And Mr Post is growing birds under here or summat.'

'Growing birds?' I heard a creak and Rubi's footstep coming closer. 'Oh, you mean egg snatching... Oh wait, smuggling. Birds of prey. I think there's a lot of money in it.'

'Is there?'

I remembered seeing it on the news too, when Granny was ranting about the terrorising Eagle Owl and how smugglers must have brought it in. Mum had a suitcase out when she had that egg in her house. Is that why she had lamps in her room and why she was meeting Mr Post? Could this be what she was doing?

'I'm gunna jump down. It's not that far. It's proper low, like.' I lifted myself up, and shimmed me legs over the side.

'Did you hear that?' Rubes eyes were wide egg-whites.

'What?! Is it Mr Post? I thought he was out.'

'No... flapping. I definitely heard flapping.'

'It's fine.' I shimmed closer to the drop. Rubi was a worrier. 'Probably a pigeon.'

I went in with me legs first, into the nest. I held onto the blackened floorboards with me forearms and then dropped. All the tables were away from our side of the house, away from the fire. On the other side of the cellar, there were pictures of birds. But not the sort that you'd ever see around here. There were eagles and hawks and whatnot. In the brick wall in front of a table, there was a gap and some cobwebs. On the table in front, the brick was resting next to a pile of old, browning envelopes. One of them was open. I recognised the writing straight away. Could they be old letters between Granny and Mr Post? The ones Granny mentioned? I picked it up, leaving black finger-prints all over it.

DEAR EDWARD,

I'M SORRY, BUT I CAN'T LEAVE HIM. YOU KNOW AS WELL AS I DO THAT IT'S NOT POSSIBLE IN THIS LITTLE TOWN. THEY'D MAKE OUR LIVES MISERABLE. I KNOW HE'S NOT PERFECT BUT NEITHER AM I. HE SAYS HE'LL STOP DRINKING, THAT HE'LL BE HOME MORE WITH ME AND JASON AND WILLIAM. HE SAID HE'LL BE A BETTER FATHER AND I BELIEVE HIM. I HAVE TO. I CAN'T KEEP WRITING TO YOU ANYMORE. IT'S TOO HARD. I REALLY HOPE YOU FIND SOMEONE BETTER. IT JUST WASN'T MEANT TO BE.

YOURS,

When Granny heard that one of the Royals was having an affair, she was spitting rage for weeks on end. She'd sit upright at the breakfast table, look twice her height, and rant until she was as purple as her dressing gown. It was a disgrace, an abomination, a national disaster. Animals, she'd said. She'd of had them thrown into the street, hung, drawn and quartered. If you'd have snapped her like a stick of rock, you'd see 'Made in Britain' all the way through. She was a royalist, a traditionalist, and a hypocrite. You couldn't get more British than that.

'Oh my god!'

'What? You OK?' Rubi's face appeared at the top of the trapdoor.

I shook me head, and then the letter at her. 'You wouldn't believe it.'

'What? Why?'

'Gran and Mr Post were having an affair!'

'Ewww, recently?'

'It's baffling. They hate each other. But she was gunna leave me grandad. And me dad has another brother?'

'Really? Do you know him?'

'No, first I've...'

Rubi yelped and disappeared. 'Something massive just flew at me!'

She screamed. I grabbed a chair and used it to pull myself up into the hallway. Rubes had her back against the wall. She pointed to the kitchen. The windows were open and an Eagle Owl was perched on the window frame. It stared right at us with glowing amber eyes and feathered eyebrows that curled up on either side.

'It's *the* owl.' I didn't move.

'Bad omen.' Rubi had black marks across her face. 'Me aunt says owls are gatekeepers of the otherworld.'

There was something about the owl, something holy, something that made you want to bend your knee and bow to it. It puffed out its white chin and hooted. It was a low, rounded hoot that sounded as if it was summoning us to a service, calling us to prayer.

'Scarlett, who's in your garden?' Rubes pointed behind me.

I turned and saw Granny standing with her back to us and thought nothing of it. 'Think it's Gran, probably feeding Destiny.'

'But why is she in her dressing gown?'

Gran was staring up at the red brick wall at Edward's house. Destiny was rummaging by her feet. The owl flapped its wings and flew silently out of the window, and landed on the wall in front of Granny. It hooted, but Granny didn't move. I scrambled for the key to the back door and flung it open. Me steps pounded the floor, me jaw clenched.

'Gran!'

She didn't move or speak. She stared at the bird. I ran up to her, and she looked through me, holding onto her locket in her fist. 'What's this!?' I held up the letters to her, me evidence of her betrayal to the family, her betrayal to me Grandad, to me dad, to everyone.

'You's a liar, and a cheat. All of this time, it was your fault. All these secrets. That's why you didn't want me digging, wasn't it?'

She pulled at the chain around her neck. Her hand shook like a feather in the wind as she put her locket in me blackened hand. I opened it up and there was a black-and-white picture of a baby inside.

'Is this him? Is this William? Gran? Come on, you daft cow, say summat.'

She opened her mouth, but no words came out. She was disappearing behind the eyes, fighting through them, but not making it. Her face was dropping on one side as if she'd been poisoned, as if she was being taken down. She collapsed, and I tried to catch her. But the best I could do was cushion her fall. I felt me arm smash into the ground and we both lay at the bottom of the garden as if we'd been ensnared in something we couldn't see.

'Call an ambulance, Rubi, an ambulance!'

'You have me phone!'

The owl flapped its wings as if in slow motion, swooping down. And all we could do was watch as it picked up poor Destiny, squealing. Granny's eyes hooked onto it as it flew away into the grey sky. I screamed at it to bring her back, but we were tangled in a web too thick to move.

17

'The thing that makes Woody special is that he'll never give up on you.'

Toy Story 3

I wasn't about to give up on Destiny. Everybody has one thing that means more to them than anything else. For Granny, that was Destiny. So while Granny was lying in a hospital bed, totally out of it, I was damn-well going to do me best to find Destiny, before she woke up, no matter what.

Destiny was lost but alive. I was dead-cert about it. She wasn't no normal pig. And I was bloody sure she was out there, running around lost, looking for Granny. I couldn't bear to think how alone she must feel, how scared she'd be, how utterly lost and abandoned she was.

But Scott's family came to the rescue. They gathered dozens of locals at the entrance of Millend Wood. It was a small nature reserve surrounded by fields. It was usually a mud pit, but was drying out for spring. The owl was seen the most there.

'Ladies and gentlemen,' said Scott's dad. 'Thank you so much for coming to help us this evening. If you've been lucky enough to have had Destiny tell your future, you'll know what a special little pig she is. But she's even more special to a certain lady who finds herself in hospital this evening.' There was a murmur in the crowd. 'Not only has this poor woman lost her home, and her health, but now she has lost her nearest and dearest. Her time of need is upon us, and this owl-snatching could have happened to anyone of us, to any of our dogs or cats. I'd like to believe that if it happened to you or I, the community would come together to help each other too.'

Scott's dad had an amazing talent for pulling people together. People listened and did what he said. Rubi's parents were listening with their hands on their hips next to Scott and his mum. I saw Rubi in the corner of the crowd, talking. As I shimmied towards her, I could see it was Kai, the Fire Inspector on our house.

'Scarlett.' Rubi grabbed me hand, squeezed it, and didn't let go. Kai waved at me and dropped her umbrella.

'Now, if we could split into three groups and each take a different path.' Scott's dad conducted the group. 'Me son is going to hand out treats Destiny likes, so if you spot her, you can lure her towards you.'

'How you doing?' Rubi pulled me hand towards her.

'What's she doing 'ere?' I nodded to Kai, who was talking to Rubi's mum and dad. I couldn't help but blame Kai for what had happened to us, why we were homeless with nothing.

'She was supposed to be having a boxing lesson with your dad, but then he cancelled because of what happened. Is he at the hospital?'

I nodded. 'With Kirsten. He'll join later... I guess we could do with all the help we can get.' I sighed. 'Have you seen me mum? She said she'd come help.'

Rubi squeezed me hand. 'No, sorry. I cannot believe how many people are here.'

'D'you think you could talk to her?' I nodded and looked over Rubi's shoulder.

'To Kai?'

'About what we saw under the house. See if you can get her to change her mind.'

'Right.' Scott's dad clapped his hands together. 'Follow your group leaders! And let's go find that pig.'

'Who you going with?' Rubi gripped me hand tighter.

'Scarlett!' Scott's dad waved at me. 'You'll come with us through the middle, as she'll recognise your voice.'

I let go of Rubi's hand - like when Granny let go of me hand on the way into the ambulance, strapped in, and being fed oxygen. I felt lost too, like I'd been snatched away and thrown into the heavens.

Scott's mum put her arm around me shoulder and took me up the path, and I noticed other faces I knew in the crowd. I saw the faces of those who'd served us at Tesco, the faces of women who'd swore they'd never speak to Granny again. I saw the Vicar who Granny called a weasel. I saw the faces of people I'd never met, and faces I couldn't place where I knew them. Then there were our neighbours. But the most surprising face of all - Mr Post. He was shuffling up and away with a group, binoculars around his neck. But maybe it wasn't surprising that people in Stonecloud had a sense of loyalty, even to those they couldn't stand.

'How d'you get hold of so many people so fast?'

'Just put a call out on Twitter,' said Scott's dad. 'And in the West Stonecloud Facebook group. Flocked, they did! Don't you worry, Scarlett. We're going to find her. I can feel it.'

Scott walked behind us as I called out to Destiny. I wondered why he wasn't up front with his dad. Or why he hadn't asked me how I was. Maybe he didn't know how to. It was getting dark already, as if someone had drawn a blind but left a night-light on. The path diverged, and we split the group. It diverged again, and then again, until it was me and the Wrights. The next split went down a bit of a hill.

'Scott and I will go this way.' I wanted to get some alone time with him.

'OK - keep your voice up when calling her.' Scott's dad pointed upwards. 'I think that path loops back round to the start.'

'Will do.' I ran to catch up with Scott, who'd already gone ahead. His green jumper was tied round his shoulders, and it blew back like a cape with the wind. His hands were in his pockets. The trees bowed over us, creating a tunnel of branches. I shivered in the evening chill.

'Aren't you cold?' I said.

'No, I get hot when I walk.' Scott didn't look up from the path.

'It's freezing. Wish I bought a coat... Could I borrow your jumper?'

'OK.' He stopped to untie the arms.

'You look a bit like a lumberjack in that shirt, or a cowboy.' He handed me his jumper.

'Is that bad?'

Scott shrugged and turned away. 'Destiny!'

We carried on walking again as I put his jumper on. 'Not much like your dad, are you?'

'In what way?'

'More reserved.'

He shrugged. 'It's easier to let him get on with it. He loves a cause.'

'Is that a bad thing?'

'Do you hear that?' Scott stopped and held his hand up. 'Over there, in the ditch.'

I looked super-close but saw nothing and heard nothing. 'You look different, too.'

'That's probably because I'm adopted.'

'Oh.... Uhhh, sorry? I didn't mean to... Shite - did I put me foot in it? Me head is all over the place with Granny in hospital and Destiny missing.'

It made sense now, why he insisted I needed a home, why the Wrights had been so quick to help me. It explained why he was still at home, why he hadn't moved out yet, because maybe he hadn't had a family very long. He probably didn't feel the same embarrassment and shame most of us feel when we say we still live at home with our parents. But he said nothing, so I didn't know whether I'd said something wrong. Maybe he *was* embarrassed. He carried on walking over the mud that had dried into lumps and footprints. I looked down to see if maybe I could see a pig-print.

'I think I might put up posters of her, y' know? Like in the films. Can't hurt, right?' I jogged to keep up.

On the path ahead, I saw a shadow of something. 'I see her. There!' I pointed.

'Where?'

'There!' I ran, but whatever it was, ran too. 'Can you see it?' I shouted behind me to Scott, as I ran around a bend.

'I see something.' Scott ran up behind me. 'Say her name!'

'Destiny! Destiny! Come 'ere Destiny!'

But the shadow ran and ran down the path, around another corner, and when we caught up to where we last saw it, we'd reached the stile we had climbed over at the beginning, which looked out into a field of yellow. Me dad was standing in it, alone, looking up at the sky. He looked like a lost toy. I leaned down on me knees, breathing heavy.

'That's me dad.'

Scott stopped at me side, panting. 'I'll double-check the path behind us, just in case. Maybe it was just a pheasant.'

'You don't want to meet me dad?'

'Don't you want to get Destiny?' Scott jogged off. Not that I could blame him. Dad looked like he'd seen a lot of years in a very short time. Dog-eared, worn and scratched, and messed about. Abandoned by his owner.

'Dad!' I waved.

'Found anything?!' He held up his palms.

I shook me head.

'How's Granny?' I jogged over to him, the bright yellow rape-seed flicking at me legs.

He shook his head back at me.

'What does that mean?'

He turned away from me as if I had pushed him. He gazed up at the clouds, which were breaking up in the indigo sky. 'They don't think she'll have long.' He slapped his arm. 'Bloody midges!'

'Dad?'

'I've always told her she should look after herself better, but she never listened to me! Always knew better,' he said. 'Blasted woman.' He tried to hide it, but I saw him wipe a tear from his eye and even though I was worried he'd push me off or would try to wiggle out of a hug like he always did, I swallowed down me fear and threw both arms around him. He let me hold him for a minute, patting me arm.

'Pig-headed.' I let go before he did.

'She's a Saint.'

'That's why she loved Destiny so much. Two of a kind.' We both smiled.

'What's that around your neck?' Dad reached for the gold locket I had put on.

'Granny gave it to me before she fell. It's got a picture of Gramps and a boy inside.' I paused for a minute. Should I leave it? Should I let it go? Probably. But then it would all have been for nothing. Granny was trying to tell me something. 'Dad, did you have a brother?'

'What?!' Dad's face turned. It wasn't angry exactly, or lost. It was a look as if he'd been struck.

'Granny had another son, didn't she?'

But his look - it was actually horror, not shock. He was looking into the abyss. It was all the nightmares I'd ever had, all the horror movies I'd ever watched, all the terror I'd ever read, all the monsters under the bed. It was a room that nobody should go into, and I had blundered in like an idiot and turned on the light.

'Never, ever, ask me that ever again. You hear me? He grabbed me shoulders and didn't blink. 'Ever.'

And I wanted to ask him about Mr Post, about Granny, about his brother, but to do it right then would make me a monster. He was going through hell and the last thing I wanted to do was make it worse. I was asking for was more than just history. I'd be asking him to relive something that he probably couldn't take right now. I'd already pushed too much. Maybe Granny wouldn't be dying in hospital if I had just stayed out of it like she wanted.

18

'Life is not a malfunction.'

Short Circuit

Everyone has a button that shouldn't be pressed. A button that will make them explode. Granny had a million of them. She was more like a control panel than a person. I didn't know how they got there. But I wondered if a button could shut a person down.

And had I found it, pushed it?

We had been told that her body was crashing. There was no reboot, and I couldn't get in touch with the manufacturer. No matter how much I tried, or cried, or denied. But I was about to have the instructions posted to me. I was going to be given Granny's very own manual that would explain how she was made.

I sat on me own with her and a million questions. It had been ten days of torture, hoping she'd get better or stop suffering. Dad, Kirsten and I swapped shifts to see her around work. I even went to another LARP event with the Wrights who'd convinced me I needed a break from reality. And she kept holding on. I held her bloated, veined hand and willed for her to wake. Did she squeeze me back? Or was it just because I was squeezing too hard? I wanted the truth so bad, that maybe I was trying to milk it from her? I wasn't ready to let go of her yet. I wasn't ready for them to rub her name off the whiteboard on the wall behind her bed. I took off the gold, penny-sized locket and opened it up, staring at the two faces inside. A babber and his dad. Young and old.

'That's me son.'

I jumped and turned around. Mr Post stood at the threshold of the blue and green patchwork curtains pulled around the bed. He held a bunch of sunflowers. His eyes were red, swollen, as if he'd been trying to rub something from his eyes.

'What you doing 'ere?'

'I'd like to say goodbye.' He sniffed, and without knowing it, he pushed a button I didn't know I had. One of rage and injustice and all the terrible feelings that had been bubbling away just under the surface. And these things I had done so well to push down were forcing their way out. I was on self-destruct.

'What? But you're the reason she's in 'ere!' I whisper-shouted so the rest of the ward wouldn't hear me.

'I ain't.' He stood upright.

'*You* sent her over the edge. *You* sent us letters telling us to die. *You* threatened to sue us, burned down our house and took Destiny with that owl!'

He shook his head. 'I didn't burn down your house!'

Me face felt like it was catching fire. I was crashing, too. I wanted to explode in his face. 'You *hated* her. She didn't want to be with you and so you was gunna make sure she paid for it.'

'You don't know what your talking about... It's not that simple...'

'Really? So making her life hell wasn't in your plan?' I stood up and walked towards him.

'I didn't. Let me explain...' His hands were shaking.

'Scarlett?' Nurse Jill opened up the curtains around the bed. Her eyes were wide and surprised. 'Everything OK? Oh hello, I didn't see you there. You here to see Henrietta?' Mr Post nodded to her. 'What lovely flowers too.'

It was like having a bucket of cold water thrown over me, or a policeman go by when you're speeding. I didn't want her to think I was the monster, that I was the unreasonable one when Mr Post was acting all nice and frail.

'Can I have a few moments with her?' Mr Post gave Nurse Jill his best puppy-eyes. 'We was real close.'

'Of course.' Nurse Jill picked up the empty glass from Granny's table. 'Scarlett? That OK with you?'

'Ummm.' I needed a reason, an excuse that would seem reasonable, and not but-he's-the-reason-she's-dying.

Nurse Jill pulled back the curtains. 'Great, there you go. She's all yours.'

'But...'

'Come on, Scarlett. You can help me for a second.'

I followed Nurse Jill through the oven-hot ward to her front desk. I had betrayed Granny in letting him near her. Mr Post walked over to her bedside, shaking. First, it was a tremble in his hands that spread up to his arms and into his back.

The flowers didn't make it to her bedside. They fell on the blanket at her feet. He grabbed her hand, and that was when Mr Post broke me heart and I hated him for it. I didn't hear a single word he spoke, but I didn't need to.

'Oh, bless.' Nurse Jill held a clipboard to her chest. 'All that love. Did she know?'

I shook me head, numb and dumb. Mr Post wouldn't want her dead. Nurse Jill was right; he loved her. Like a ten-year-old pushing a girl down in the playground. Me granny was good at pushing people's buttons and it looked like they'd been pushing each other's all their lives. Granny knew Mr Post wasn't an actual threat. He wouldn't hurt her or the family or his egg smuggling trade under it. So if it wasn't Mr Post's fault she was in here, it was mine.

'Are you OK?' Nurse Jill put her hand on me shoulder.

I nodded, but I was wiping tears off me cheeks. 'If I hadn't of yelled at her...'

'Oh, darling...' Nurse Jill put her arm around me and spoke to me as if I was a toddler, and I leant into it. 'You're looking at it all wrong. It would have happened whether you were there or not. She was lucky because you *were* there. And I heard you stopped her from really hurting herself. You've always been there for her, haven't you?' I sniffed and nodded, tried to compose myself. 'Now come on, she wouldn't want to see you like this. Where's your pretty smile?'

I gulped back the mess and smiled, because I wasn't exactly sure what Granny would want, but nobody wanted a crying mess around to bring them all down.

'If you ask me...' Nurse Jill nodded towards Mr Post. 'She's one lucky lady to have people who care for her.'

'I'll go see if he's OK.'

'That's a good girl.' She patted me arm. People always think I'm younger than I am. It helps me get the cheap tickets at festivals. But it has its upsides and its downsides. The downsides often outweighed the upsides as nobody would take me seriously. So I did me best to compose myself, stand up-right, wipe me face. I needed Mr Post to answer some questions, to take me seriously.

The ward was crammed, humming with machines. The bedridden watched as I walked past them. Mr Post was silent when I came up behind him. He didn't register that he knew I was there. He hunched over like a robot out of battery.

'Mr Post.' I cleared me throat. 'Why d'you do it? Why d'you send us all those notes?'

He lifted his head. 'I never wanted this.' He wiped his nose with a handkerchief. 'Never never... not for her... never.'

'Then why?'

'I just... I wanted you to leave. You have no idea what it's like. We had something, but then she...'

'She loved you?'

He nodded, and then his body jolted and he bent forward even more.

I walked towards him. 'So when me gramps died, she still didn't want to be with you?'

He shook his head. 'She said she didn't want to remember. That it hurt too much. I had to pay over and over again... No idea how much...'

'Pay for what?'

'That boy in the locket. William.' He lifted his head up.

I held out the locket to him. 'Where is he?'

'William.' He smiled. He reached out for Granny's hand. 'She'll be with him soon.'

'He's dead?'

Mr Post pointed at me. 'Your *grandfather.' His* face turned sour. 'It was him. I know it. He went runabout for a while, and your gran and I fell for each other. But when he came back, it was all over... She pretended William was his. But...' Mr Post was making fists. 'He always knew. That's why he killed him.'

'What?'

'They always said it was an accident. But I knew the truth!'

'So you did hate her?'

'No no, never Henrietta. Not me rosebud. She was afraid of him.'

'What's *he* doing 'ere?!' Me dad was stood behind me, and Mr Post leapt up.

'*He* came to say goodbye.' Mr Post shook his head.

'He's just a neighbour. This is for family only. Family *only*.'

'I ain't just a neighbour.' Mr Post shuffled towards the exit. 'But I'm leavin'. I am going. I have done. I've made me peace.' But then he stopped and looked me dad up and down. 'The apple never falls far from the tree.'

'Get out! Now!' Dad made a move toward him, head and chin forward as Mr Post walked out. I had never seen Dad flare up like that. Mr Post was hitting buttons all over him I hadn't seen before.

'Why d' he say that?' I moved the flowers from the bed to the table.

'He's a meddlin' old man, always saying stuff about Dad, sayin' he...' Dad clenched his fists. 'I've a right mind to...' His face tightened, as if whatever he was about to say got buried deep. 'None of his damn business.'

Problem was, it had been his business. All this time, Mr Post had been part of the family in a weird way and yet, I still had questions. How did me uncle die? What happened to him? I chased after Mr Post, who was shuffling down the lino corridor. The smell of chemicals wafting through. I didn't want to wait, to risk losing another source of answers.

'Mr Post!'

He didn't hear me.

'Mr Post! Edward! For god's sake!' Skyla Goode, mage of the king in Mardon, wouldn't take this shit, so why was I? I ran in front to stop him. I felt bigger and more powerful already. The Wrights had a point with all this LARPing malarky. 'You owe me! I need to know what happened.'

'Don't owe none of you nothing.' He flicked his hand at me and turned away. 'Bunch of thugs.'

I put me hands on me hips and imagined casting a spell over him to talk, and found a real one to use. 'I'll tell the police about your trade if you don't.'

'Wouldn't do that if I were you.' He smirked.

'Why not?'

' 'cause I ain't the only one trading 'em. Your mother, she...'

'Ssshhh, I don't want to hear it.' I closed me eyes. People were all around us. They'd hear us and I didn't want to get me mum into any more trouble. So I whispered. 'I just want to know how he died, your boy?'

'Only when it suits you, eh? Well, your mother was the one who said I should sue you all too.'

'What? Why would she do that?'

'She thought it was wrong, that the land was mine, and... She wasn't wrong... the land was mine... I had ways to prove it... old documents... historic... go way back...'

'Me mum? I don't believe you.'

'She used to live there. Short time, but she did... Things were such a racket. Such a noise, but...'

'Nah, she wouldn't do that to us.'

'She used to live there.' He blew the frustration out of his nose, and I wished Scott's LARPing character was there to take him down. He was so good at swooping in like a Knight in shining armour.

'Yes, I know she did! Are you sure it was me mum?' Why would she do that?'

'Why wouldn't she?' He snarled, as if I had lost *me* mind. 'She knew what happened to William. Disgusted. We helped each other, her and I. Always have. She knew who was right and who was wrong.'

He slid away like a lit fuse. He had sparked off a detonator so there was an explosion of information in me head. Stuff I couldn't un-know. Lightning had struck. Me mum was knee-deep. But Mr Post wasn't exactly a pillar of the community. Maybe he was making it up to get back at us some more, just like Sophie had done? Maybe he hated me mum too and was out to drag her name through the mud? Maybe he wasn't finished pushing buttons in the Saint family.

19

'The fear of loss is a path to The Dark Side.'

Star Wars, Revenge of the Sith

TO ALL THE FREE PEOPLE OF THE REALM,

THE CALL FOR FREEDOM HAS PERSEVERED, BUT OUR ENEMY GROWS STRONGER. THEY THERE, ARE A DIRE THREAT TO EVERY NATION'S SOVEREIGNTY. LORD BANNOR OF MARDON'S LEADERSHIP HAS BEEN THE NOOSE AROUND THE NECKS OF THE PEOPLE FOR TOO LONG! HE WANTS TO CREATE A COUNCIL TO JUDGE THE WAY THAT WE RUN OUR LAND. BUT HOW CAN HE PASS JUDGMENT ON US?

WHEN THEY KNOW US NOT? ONE OF THE FOUNDING CONCEPTS OF THIS COUNTRY IS OUR INDEPENDENCE. HE HAS GIVEN US NO CHOICE BUT TO PURSUE ONE COURSE OF ACTION. THE FIRST IS TO ACCEPT HIS TYRANNICAL HAND OR TO RAISE UP AND FIGHT, FOR OUR WAY OF LIFE, FOR OUR FAMILIES, OUR FUTURES, OUR INDEPENDENCE.

JOIN US.

With Mr Post out of the picture, Sophie was back to being me prime suspect. A few days later, I was with the Wrights for another LARP and I was going to catch her this time, and make her talk. I was sure that Granny was in hospital because of all the stress - the suing, the fire, the homelessness. She was dying, and it was partly Sophie's fault. I was sure of it.

A rebellion had been brewing in the kingdom. Something trickled down into the minds of the people, into their view of the king. They said that Lord Bannon was a tyrant, an unjust king, heartless and cruel. Rumour had bubbled up from fear into rage. I stood side-by-side as daughter to Lord Bannor, ready to defend his name, and his honour, ready to defend the kingdom.

The clouds were like massive explosions frozen in the sky, black and white, with the dark clouds looming heavy like invaders, ready to drop bombs on us. We were in a field. Scott and I were on either side of his dad. All of Bannon's men and women were behind their king, and I felt a pride as I stood there. A presence of something that was altogether. This was our land, our Lord, and there was no way I was going to let Sophie take it from me. Not again.

Sophie kept staring at us, at the Wrights. She kept giving me these looks. I swore she was planning something more, planning to take us all down. I had been watching her all morning as everyone set up, thinking, looking for clues. She was a few years older than me. She had a ring of flames tattooed around her bicep. At work, she'd told me how she'd dropped out of school at sixteen to train to be a tattoo artist. But when the shop shut-down, they didn't pay her wages so she and her boyfriend broke in, and stole the equipment. Arsonist was pretty much written all over her.

'I've got some good news for you.' Scott's dad elbowed me. 'Someone reckons they saw Destiny!'

'Really?'

'On the other side of the woods. It was from a distance. But I reckon it'll be any day now...'

'That's great news...' I smiled a bit and nodded. Because it wasn't going to bring Granny back. She wasn't going to see Destiny again even if we found her. She'd been in hospital for so long and now we were just waiting for it to be over.

'And I have a *great* idea for the fundraiser.' Scott's dad adjusted his belt. 'You're going to love it. I was thinking...' He turned to look at me and frowned. 'Hey, what's up, warrior?'

I stopped chewing on me nails and shook me head. 'Just a lot going on right now.'

'Ah, well, this is the best place to work it all out. He put his arm around me shoulders. 'You angry?'

'Not angry, just...'

'Well, this is the place for it.' He pointed to the rebels lined up on the other side of the field. 'Let it all out! Saved me a billion times when things got rough, I can tell you. It broke my sword! You see them over there?' I nodded. 'You give them all you got, you hear me?'

I nodded again. Scott's dad made me feel protected, more than I ever had done in me life.

'You are Skyla Goode, daughter of the king! You are a mage, a warrior, and you will smite the mighty who dare threaten your home! So I'll ask it again... Do you hear me?!'

'Yes, sir!'

He turned around to face his army. 'We are going to show these traitors exactly what they deserve. There will be justice for us. We will have order and peace at any cost. We will claim back what is rightfully ours. This is our kingdom, *our realm!*'

The two sides roared, beating their shields. He was right. I was going to stand up for myself, to fight.

BOOM.

BOOM.

BOOM.

Scott called out beside me. 'If you get hit on a limb, you lose it. Twice, and you're dead. Any strike to the body and you're dead. OK?'

I nodded, wishing he'd stand closer. But he stared ahead. When I looked across the field, it looked as if he was staring at Sophie. 'D'you know her?'

'Who?' He lifted his shield up.

'Sophie, that girl.' I nodded towards her.

'There ain't no Sophie in this kingdom, your ladyship.' He smirked.

'No one is listening to my orders,' shouted Scott's dad. 'I want second and third battalion in the front. You are infantry.' He pointed at people around me. 'You're our linch pin, Don. Protect the land of Mardon!'

'Load the catapults!'

'Chaaaarrrrgeeee!'

The moment had come. It was a rush of helmets and shields, padded batons and arrows. Feet pounded towards the middle. People yelled. I had eyes for only one person, but she wasn't running at me. She was running to Lord Bannor, her sword above her head.

How dare she go for the king! With each swipe of me sword, I drove towards them both. Swiping left, swiping right, I defended me land. Bean bags catapulted into the onslaught.

I was defender of the realm.

Bringer of justice.

And I was going to save Lord Bannor from Sophie - God as me witness. She ran towards him; her plaits swinging like two pendulums, counting her down to the moment we'd collide. And then she slipped, falling flat onto her face before she even reached him.

I pushed past Lord Bannor with me baton above me head and I slammed it down on her back. She turned around, and I hit her again.

'Stop it.' She held up her arms to shield. 'I'm dead, I'm dead...'

But I couldn't stop. It was as if I had been taken over by Darth Vader, possessed by the dark side. She was going to take out Scott's dad. She was going to attack them. I wanted to save the day. So I kept hitting her, and hitting her, until someone pushed me over and fell on top of me.

'What the hell you doing?' Scott had pinned me down. 'I said one hit and they're out. You're breaking the rules. You'll get kicked out.'

People were shouting all around us. Rain was firing down with the beanbags. I stared at Scott's wet hair dripping down into me face, thinking that this should be one of those romantic movie-moments, but he was frowning at me. 'I...'

He sprang back up. 'Quick, get up! We're losing!' He ran towards a man with his baton held high. But someone jumped onto me back and pushed me down to the floor again. I wrestled with Sophie until her sword was held across me throat, pinning me down.

'Your supposed to be dead.' I pushed up on the sword.

'Tell the judge.' She spat in me face. 'What the hell is wrong with you? You can't beat on people like that.'

'You can't lie to the police and get away with it either.'

'You deserved it. Ratting me out.'

'Was setting me house on fire not enough for you?' I spat back at her and it hit her cheek. She slapped me face, and I grabbed her hand, pushing her back at the same time. 'You burnt me house. And when that didn't work, you set fire to the care home and tried to get me put into prison, didn't you?' I had broken free and pushed her away as I stood up, both of us panting and circling.

'You think I set fire to your house?' She shook her head.

'I should burn your house down, see how you like it.' I pulled wet hair off me face.

Sophie dropped her sword and held up her hands. 'You know what, Scarlett?' I'm sorry... I'm sorry I lied to the police. I'm sorry that your house burned down. But don't blame me for your problems.'

'Blame you?' I laughed. 'You *are* the problem.'

'No, you're the problem. Are you not even a little sorry for what you did?' She moved closer and I flinched.

'I didn't do nothing wrong...'

She laughed. 'Really? Why do you think I didn't look after George?'

' 'cause you're heartless? Lazy? Cold? Inhuman?'

'Oh my god, are you serious?' She shook her head. 'Are you really that clueless? Didn't you think for a moment that...' She turned away, and then put her hands up in the air. 'Well, it's over now, anyway. You lost.'

The rain had stopped. In the field, Scott lay on the floor with many others. His dad was being walked with his hands behind his back, captured by the other side. We were all shivering, dripping, soaked through. The game was over. And I had failed to save the Wrights.

'I wouldn't be on his side.' Sophie began walking away. 'I wouldn't trust him if I were you.'

'It's just a game.'

'If you think this is just a game, then you're more of an idiot than I thought.'

Only one other person has called me stupid, and she was lying on her deathbed, all because someone burned down our house. I felt powerless, embarrassed. A Jedi with no powers, no light sabre.

'Good game, Soph.' Scott ran up to us. 'Now Dad's going to be a nightmare tonight.' He put his arm around her shoulder, and I felt a darker force wanting to bring me down. He was so much more relaxed around her. Why wasn't he the same with me?

'Y' know each other?' I crossed me arms.

'Yeah. What the hell is going on between you two?' He stared at Sophie.

'Scarlett, got me fired.' Sophie raised her eyebrows. 'And she thinks because I told the police I saw her at the scene of the care home fire, that I set fire to her house.' She mock-smiled at me.

'What?' Scott let go of her. 'You thought Sophie did it? No way. She's a lamb. She'd never do that. Sophie is practically a saint.'

'Pah...'

'Hey, Scott, do you remember that LARPing weekend in the Forest of Dean?'

'Yeah, we beat you then! Good times.'

'When was it again?'

'March 16, 17. Why?'

'Scarlett will tell you.' She crossed her arms now.

'That was when me house burned down.' I picked up me sword from the ground.

'Ah, an alibi.' Scott nodded. 'You should say sorry, Scarlett. It's only right.'

I swallowed down the darkness in me. 'Sorry Sophie.' I gritted me teeth. 'It's just...'

'Nope.' Scott waved his arms across each other. 'It's not a sorry if it's followed with 'but'...'

Scott seemed to still be in character, commanding us like we were children, like his dad. He looked me dead in the eye, piercing me, unblinking. He had me in his grip. I was afraid of losing a lot of things. I was afraid to lose me home. I was afraid to lose me gran, myself, Destiny, me mum, and me dad. But I didn't realise I was afraid to lose Scott, that he would think bad of me if I refused to forgive Sophie for lying to the police. But she hadn't forgiven me for getting her fired, either. So I extended me hand for her to shake, and when she took it, I put all me force into shaking it as hard as I could. I wanted her to feel it, to feel how I really felt, that whatever she took from me, *whoever* she took from me, I'd make her pay.

20

'I want to be with you in your dream house.'

Barbie, Toy Story 3

When I got back from the LARP, I found Kirsten sat on her bunkbed at the top of the bus, covered in red paint, holding a box in her hand and rubbing her stomach. I recognised the type of box she was turning over. Kirsten had a dream doll house tucked away in the attic of our burnt-to-a-crisp house. One time, she came home with a grin wider than the doorframe, and a box in her hand just like the one she was holding on the bus. She said she had a new family member and was dead-excited, like proper-excited, more than I'd ever seen her before. Granny complained, saying Kirsten was spending all dad's money, even though Kirsten probably earned more than him. I followed Kirsten up to the loft. It was like being with a kid at Christmas.

She used a duster to clear cobwebs away as she climbed up the ladder. Then she sat on the round rug in front of the doll's house. 'We'll pretend the boxes are the Beverly Hills.' The light-bulb swung above her head like an idea had clicked on. She took out a little dog from the box, and put him in the doll house next to the man, the woman, and the kid. A family from the old days. 'Made for each other, don't you think?'

Kirsten wanted a different sort of family than the one she was in. A new family. There was no old woman in the doll's house, no little piggy, and the kid was a boy. I always felt that if I ever left, there wouldn't be a family to come back to. I'd be replaced by a new one. After the fire, I didn't ask about her doll's house. I didn't want to remind her. I didn't want to make things worse than they already were.

'Ah, the prodigal child returneth.' She put the small box down. 'Feel like we never see you anymore.'

'I'm around.' I swung around the rail at the top of the stairs.

'We could do with your help here.' She laid down on the bed. 'As your dad is with your gran all week.'

'What, now?'

'No, not now. I'm done for the day. Don't feel so good.' She rubbed her stomach again.

'Any change with gran?'

'She keeps hanging on in there.'

'Always been a fighter.' But I secretly wished she'd stop for her own sake. 'What's in the box?'

'New addition...' She shook the box, and it rattled, but it wasn't with her usual glee. 'For the doll's house. I had ordered it before the fire.' Her voice cracked a bit, and she looked out of the window.

'D'you think it's still up there? The house.'

She shrugged, limp and lifeless, like a slinky toy. 'Your guess is as good as mine.'

I bet Kirsten regretted getting involved with us. No job, no house, living on a bus. When Granny was around, it gave Kirsten a bit of spark, someone to prove wrong, a force to drive her, something to prove. But she'd lost all that since gran went into hospital. It didn't matter what I did. I couldn't make things worse for Kirsten. Without Mr Post or Sophie as me suspects, I needed more answers. I needed to know more about Clive. But what came out of me mouth surprised me, too.

'Kirsten?'

'Yeah?'

'Why d' you think it was me mum who set the fire?'

She flinched. 'Sorry about that...' She sat up, swung her legs over the side of the bed. 'That wasn't fair of me to jump to conclusions. Makes me look like a right cow.'

'But, why?' I leaned against the side of her bed post.

'It's not my place to say anything, Scarlett. Not about your mum.'

'Hasn't stopped you before...'

'I'm trying, but it's hard...' She sighed. 'It's hard being on the outside. Not sure what I'm supposed to do sometimes. When you see someone hurting people you care about, it's hard to sit back and just...'

Kirsten loved to wear pink, she loved to take care of how she looked. But these days, she was in joggers and big jumpers like a doll dressed in the clothes of a teddy bear. Something was eating her up, and it made me wonder what it could be. What did she know?

'Me mum has been helping Mr Post to sue us.' I sat down next to her.

'What?! For what?'

'The land at the back.'

'Wow, that is a...' She swallowed and shook her head. 'Really?'

'I think Mum is still upset about stuff that happened with you and Dad.'

Kirsten never treated me like a kid. She treated me as if I was older. She'd be the one to tell me if there was something being kept from me. The air tensed up as I held me breath for her answer. Kirsten stared at the box in her hands. 'What stuff? What she said?'

'She said Dad wouldn't pay maintenance.'

She smiled and shook her head. 'So, it's begun...'

'What d'you mean?'

'Well, you are old enough to make up your own mind...' She looked me up and down. 'Your mum was using the money for you on drinking. Your dad stopped paying to force her to go get help.'

'Really? But she also said that you lied about her in court.'

Kirsten rolled her eyes. 'Oh for god's sake, she's full of it. Some people shouldn't be allowed to...' Kirsten pulled her head back and pulled at her sleeves. 'We didn't take your mum to court. She took *us* to court.'

'For not paying her?'

Kirsten looked up at the ceiling as if picking her words from a library in the sky, as if the heavens might fall down if she picked the wrong one. 'She wanted your dad to look after you full-time.'

'Because she couldn't afford to keep me, she had no money...'

'Sorry Scarlett, but she made it perfectly clear that she didn't want to look after you. She was obsessed with her boyfriend at the time. And he... Well, you know the rest. Your dad took you.'

'But why would she say...?'

'Because she doesn't deserve to be a mum!' Tears pooled in Kirsten's eyes. 'Some people just don't. I'm sorry, Scarlett, but they don't. Life is unfair. Your body may be able to produce babies, but it doesn't make you a mum. That's earned. You were more of a mum to her than she was to you. There are poor women everywhere who should be mums but aren't. It's just the way the world is.'

'It's not her fault, she ain't well.' I pulled at granny's locket around me neck. 'She regrets it. She keeps saying how she wishes she could have me there.'

'Does she?' Kirsten held me hand, but I pulled it away.

The thing was, I wasn't sure. I didn't want to believe it because that would make me mum a liar. And if she was lying about that, then what else could she be lying about? 'So that's why you thought she sent the notes? Set the fire? Well, you're wrong. Mr Post sent the notes.'

'He did?' Kirsten fiddled with her jumper. 'Actually, in the end, I thought it was Clive who'd sent them. Along with the texts. But...'

'D' you think he set fire to our house too?'

'No, because it wasn't arson.' Kirsten threw up her arms. 'Just Saintly stupidity.'

'It...'

'OK, for the sake of argument, say it *was* arson... Clive wanted to destroy my career, and he's done that and he'll keep doing that. He said he would. Somebody who'd set fire to our house would want to hurt all of us, and there's only one person with that much motive. There is only one person who has a vendetta against each and every one of us. One person who can't be trusted.'

She didn't have to say her name. 'You're wrong. You've just wanted to get rid of her ever since you moved in. But you can't. She'll always be me mum.'

'I know.' Kirsten's shoulders slumped. 'Trust me, I know.' She got up and pulled down her top, smoothing it out, staring at the paint on it. 'And I'm sorry about that, Scarlett. Me mum was like yours and I'm still having to deal with what she didn't do every day.' She sighed and put her arm on me shoulder. 'She doesn't deserve you, Scarlett.'

'I'm all she's got.'

She nodded and opened up the plastic rubbish bag that we'd

hung up on the side. 'I guess it's pointless saving this.' She put the box inside the bag.

I waited until she was outside before I went into the bag to look into the box. In shredded paper there was a little baby on all fours, mid-crawl. She had wanted a new family, a new beginning, but now she'd given it up. It reminded me of life with Rory. How we used to talk about where we'd buy a flat. I'd scroll through Rightmove and dream of little fingers, and Rory and I swinging them up and down. He'd call me 'her indoors' and 'the Mrs' and I loved it. I wanted a 1950s picture-perfect life. I thought we were made. But maybe it was a good thing to let things go, for Kirsten to stop dreaming. Because in those moments in the attic, maybe she wasn't really living in our house with us. She was tucked away into a fantasy, into a perfect family that didn't exist.

21

'The problem is not the problem.
The problem is your attitude about the problem.'

Pirates of the Caribbean

Maybe the reason I hadn't figured out who'd set fire to our house was because me attitude had been all wrong. Maybe I wasn't trying hard enough, or maybe I was ignoring something that I shouldn't. Maybe there was another suspect who I wasn't willing to name yet because it would turn everything I ever believed upside down, because it would go against the laws of nature. It would be worse than piracy. It would be cruel, barbaric, monstrous.

Rubi was taking me to Kai's house. Except, Kai didn't live in a house, she lived on a canal boat. When Rubi and Kai spent the day searching for Destiny, they'd hit it off. Really hit it off, like best-buds apparently. She'd invited her to take up boxing lessons with me dad. Rubi said it was to help me. She said it was to get Kai to change the report. But it was more than that. She kept talking about how nice Kai was, how funny, and how I would love Kai too, and how Kai was better than anyone she'd ever met, including me. Well, she didn't say that but she didn't have to.

'Seriously, Scarlett, she's got this mad obsession with pirates. It's so cute.' Rubi's arm hooked through mine. She was lit up, glowing. Her pale pink hair was almost luminous. I held tighter onto her arm. We were sticking to each other but I didn't want to let go. A heat wave had hit a few days ago. I couldn't sleep on the bus for the stickiness of it.

The canal water was deep and black. Fog was rising from the water as if it was smoking. The sky was glowing embers behind the blackened trees, and I was burning up.

'So we're here to get Kai to reopen our case?' I tried to remind Rubi of the real reason we were there.

'I think she'll do it for us.' She searched the path ahead. 'Kai's always saying how much she hates seeing people suffer because of the insurance companies. She feels so bad, I think. She really wants to help as much as she can.'

'How old is Kai?'

'Bit older than us, 26, 27.'

'Funny. She seems older.' I kicked a pinecone. 'Dad said he sees her every day at the gym, and he's always talking about her, and now you...'

'You're just jealous. There it is!' She pointed to a canal boat up ahead, windows glowing orange in the twilight.

'How do y' know?'

'It's the one with the pirate flag.' She broke away from me. 'She told me this super sweet story of the time her mum spoke the entire day in pirate because Kai's birthday is on pirate day. Oh, and she also has a parrot!'

'Me uncle had a budgie!' I caught up from behind her. 'Called it Elvis as it had a funny quiff at the front.'

'I remember.' Rubi nodded. 'Kai's parrot is called Captain Morgan... like the rum.' She elbowed me.

'I get it, I get it.' I rolled me eyes.

The barge had a hanging black flag with a skull and cross-bones on it. There were barrels as plant pots on the roof, a wooden wheel, and portholes for windows. And then there was its name, painted onto the hull - The Black Pearl. Rubi stretched one leg onto the boat and knocked on the front door. Kai answered as if she'd been behind it, waiting.

'Ahoy, maties!' Kai stepped back from the door. 'Come on in.'

We climbed down the stairs and into the boat. Kai was in her normal clothes. She had a Motörhead t-shirt on and black jeans, and a bandana on her head. Rubi and Kai pretended to spar by the door. I watched them box the air to show me what they'd learned from me dad. But the words floated around me. The boat was cramped, with the ceiling practically on top of me. The panelled wood made me feel like I was in a coffin. I wanted to leave when I thought we might go down with the fishes.

'Oh my god, I'm so sorry.' Rubi had her hands on her cheeks. Kai held onto her chin and laughed to the point where she snorted like a pig, and then Rubi started laughing too.

'I knew you were competitive, but to take me out before-hand, that's smart!'

'You OK?' Rubi held Kai's face to look at the damage.

'I'm fine. Now, what do people want?' She opened kitchen cupboards, searching. 'I have tea... or tea... or shiver me timbers, would you look at that... tea!'

'Hot hot hot!' There was a green, long-tailed parrot in a cage near the door.

'Oh ignore her.' Kai waved. 'She's been complaining about the heat all week.'

'Got anything stronger?' I peered into the cupboards full to the brim with flour.

'Sorry, I don't drink. There's a weird bottle of black stuff my mum used to have...'

'What is it?' Rubi sat down at the table as if she'd done it before, and I followed her.

Kai shrugged. 'Could be poison for all I know. Rum maybe?'

'Oh, we have one of these.' I pointed to a box that looked like a mini treasure chest.

'Family heirloom.' Kai pulled out a bottle. 'From Italy, I think. My mum went there once...'

'Hot hot hot!' The parrot flapped its wings.

'Think ours would've gone up in the fire...'

'Hey, I'm really sorry to hear about your gran and everything...'

'Thanks, yeah. It's been a tough time.' I fanned me face. 'So do you live here with your mum?'

'I used to. But she died a while ago now.'

'Oh, I'm...'

She waved her hand again. 'I like to talk about her. She was this big hippie, obsessed with water gods and crystals and auras and pirates.'

'She sounds cool.' Rubi leant forward, propping her head up on her hands.

'She was.' Kai smiled.

Rubi and Kai were in their own little water world. It felt like I was watching two goldfish, and I was the big giant human head peering in. 'I brought you something.'

'What for?'

I remembered someone saying to me that if you thank someone first and then ask them for their help, then they're more likely to do it. I took a fire extinguisher that had been made into a vase out of me bag and handed it over. 'Here it is. Something for the table.'

'Ah, thanks!' Kai picked it up and turned it over in her hands.

'It's amazing. Thanks so much. Really, I'm super touched Scarlett.'

'You're welcome.' I grinned. Hole in one. 'Just a thank you.'

'What for?'

'For helping us look for Destiny and the house stuff. Means a lot to the whole family. Especially after everything that's...'

'Hot hot hot.'

'Captain! Shhh.' Kai almost dropped the vase. 'Rubi says you guys are investigating the fire at your house. You think someone might have known how to make it look like an electrical fire? From the basement?'

'Is that possible?' I sat up straight. Kai always gave me this feeling that I was still being interviewed, assessed, as if she was eyeing me up as the arsonist.

'Aye, anything is possible.' She put on a pirate voice. 'But who would do that? And why?'

'Scarlett has this neighbour who's...'

'Nah, it ain't him.' I shook me head.

'Really? You sure?' Rubi sat back, frowning. 'Well, what about that politician and Kirsten?'

'Kirsten seems to think that he's had all the revenge he needs.' I crossed me arms.

'But what about the text messages you said she's getting?'

Kai put a glass of water down in front of me and I didn't realise until I saw how thirsty I was. 'Honestly?' I took a gulp of water. 'I think they might be from me mum.'

There are some things you don't want to admit you're thinking; some things that just sort of float at the back of your mind like a pirate ship in fog. They shouldn't be there. They're thoughts you shouldn't be having, that when you get close enough, they suddenly show themselves, looming and unavoidable. And before you know it, they're aboard and taking over the ship.

'What? No way.' Rubi blew out her bottom lip like a flag in the wind.

'There's just something familiar about 'em.' I finished the glass of water.

'But what about Sophie?'

'Who is Sophie?' Kai passed Rubi a glass of water.

'She lied to the police, saying she saw Scarlett set the fire at the care home.'

'What?' Kai tripped on the way from the sink, but caught herself in time.

'That was close.' Rubi smirked. 'Almost had a wet t-shirt contest.'

Kai laughed, embarrassed, and put her glass down on the table. 'I'm so clumsy...' She sat down opposite us. 'So this Sophie girl. Why would she do that?'

'Scarlett got her fired,' said Rubi.

'But she's already had her revenge, right?' I pulled me top out that was sticking to me. 'Like Clive. Except hers backfired.'

'Not quite that simple for arsonists.' Kai was back to her teacher-voice. 'Depending on why they're doing it, they'll have a history of setting fires. They'll have done it before.'

'Oh interesting.' Rubi gazed at Kai again. 'You know, Big Matt knew her, said they used to call Sophie 'little pyro' when she was a kid, always melting stuff with a lighter.'

'Hot hot hot!' Captain Morgan flew back and forth.

Kai's boat was a hot spot, pumping out heat. I wanted to ask if we could go outside, or if I could take all me clothes off, or me skin or something to stop me from feeling like I was melting on a furnace. I couldn't think straight. All I could think about was me mum and if I could see her doing it.

'She might just have a thing for setting fires.' Kai stared at her own hands, turning the fire extinguisher vase around and around. 'It might not all be about revenge or fraud. Some people just love setting fires, or they love to see them being put out or...'

'Why on earth would anyone want to do that?'

Kai shrugged. 'I don't think they even understand it. It just makes them feel better. To feel closer to people or to save the day. Usually their upbringings...'

'Oh, Sophie grew up in care, didn't she?' Rubi nudged me.

'It's not Sophie. She's got an alibi.'

'Oh.'

'That's why it's got to be me mum.' I shook me head.

'Well, *if* it was arson.' Kai stared at the vase. 'And I say *if* for argument's sake. This person would have to be pretty skilled and have access to the basement...' Kai looked up at me. 'I mean, realistically Scarlett, could your mum have done it?'

'She'd lived there before. And she was helping Mr Post with stuff in his basement.' Sweat was trickling down me forehead, along the side of me ear. Kai was irritating me. I never usually sweat, but I was the only one.

'Stop, it's mental.' Rubi's hand was on me arm, and I shook it off.

'Scarlett.' Kai leaned towards me. 'Think about what you're doing. If you accuse your mum, she would go to prison. Is that what you want?'

'I want me home back! I want to get back to normal. We're all falling apart without it. If she took that from us then...' I pulled up the bottom of me top, and bent down, wiping me forehead with it to soak up the waves of sweat coming over me.

'Hot!' The Captain squawked.

'But maybe it's like you said. Maybe me mum didn't want to hurt us. She just wanted to be part of the family or summat...'

'Scarlett, I don't think it was your mum.' Kai put both hands down flat on the table. 'I know it's not my place. But take it from someone who's lost their mum. You will lose her if you go down this road.'

I swallowed down anything I really wanted to say, and it tasted salty, a big gulp of the sea. I picked up a leaflet from the table. It had me dad's gym on it, and I used it to fan myself. 'I'm just saying maybe it was... But, let's say I found out who it was. Would you be able to change the report? To say it was arson.'

'The likelihood of it being arson is tiny,' said Kai. 'I'd have to look into it and investigate, based on what you found.'

'So y' could?'

She turned to stare at Rubi, and I couldn't understand why no-one else was burning up except me and the parrot. Why was no-one else was dripping with sweat or could feel the heat? I peeled me top away from me stomach, billowing it back and forth to get some air. But it didn't seem to do anything, it didn't seem to be enough.

'Sorry.' Kai sighed. 'But I can't guarantee that I would re-examine...'

'What?' I stood up, still inflating me top, filling it with air as if I was about to blow up. 'Why not?'

'There are many reasons...'

'You're just worried it'll make you look bad.'

'No.' She stood up, too. 'I'm worried that if I reopen it for you, it won't be in a professional context. That I will get questioned by my boss. It's not black and white. Do you know how many people get stuck in your situation? I would love to help them all, tell everyone it was arson so that their insurance companies wouldn't screw them over, but I can't. I'll lose my job, my home, everything I have. I don't have a family I can rely on like you. It's just not...'

'HOT HOT HOT.' The parrot flew around the cage.

Rubi put her hand on Kai's arm. 'It's OK, we get it. Don't we, Scarlett? We don't want you to lose what you have.'

'Why is it so hot in here?' I paced up and down the boat. 'How can you guys bear it?'

When I first got Rubi as a friend, when I uncovered the ghost under the sheet, I'd struck gold. I had found treasure - me own shiny, red ruby. Nobody else knew she was under there. This kind, funny, shy girl. She was me best friend and nobody else's. I was the luckiest person in the world. And since everyone had left Stonecloud, gone to Uni or off travelling, never to return, she was me only friend left. Seeing her side with Kai was like watching someone else stumble across the X-marks-the-spot. Someone else could see the treasure, and if I wasn't careful, I was going to find myself on the wrong end of a looting, and I'd lose Rubi for good.

'I have a fan I could put on?' Kai pointed to the corner. 'Might help a bit.'

'Yeah, thanks.' I sat down and Kai turned on the fan. The breeze blew over us and I drank it in. The buzz of the fan filled the silence for a few minutes.

'I wish there was something...' Kai was gazing at her feet, shaking her head. Rubi reached over and touched her arm.

'It's OK. I'm sorry. Must have got overheated. Like Captain Morgan here...' I smiled. 'I'm just a bit... you know. With granny in hospital and everything.'

'I really wish I could do...'

'It's OK.' Rubi nodded.

But it wasn't OK. Not even a bit. Without reopening the case, without someone ruling it as arson, we could never go back home. The whole of granny's life would be wiped out in a matter of weeks, and we'd have nothing left. And I stared at Rubi to tell her this. But she wasn't looking at me.

22

'What would you do if you were stuck in one place and nothing you did mattered?'

Groundhog day

The heatwave had passed, and we were back to spring-like temperatures - up and down. But there was nothing in the forecast about pigs flying. I had given up hope when a sighting of Destiny had been called in. At first it felt like we'd already done this day, we'd already been there and done that and come out with zero. Now we were on repeat. It was all pointless. We were searching for something that didn't exist, chasing our tails.

But what if Granny was only holding on for Destiny? If we found her, then maybe she'd be at peace and let go? She'd stop fighting and suffering, stop dragging out the agony. But when I got to the farmer's rapeseed field that was glowing as bright as the sun, it wasn't like last time at all. A big white van was parked up on the verge. People in coats and wellies grouped together. Scott, his dad, and Liz were chatting with a TV crew.

'There she is. Scarlett, come here!' Scott's dad waved to me. I walked over and he put his hand on me shoulder. 'Isn't this great?' He grinned. 'It's BBC South West. They're going to cover our search for Destiny and get the word out about our fundraiser for your house.'

'Really? That's great.' A camera was pointed at me. A microphone boom loomed above us. Everyone around me was chatting except Scott, who was staring at his phone.

'Told you he could do it.' Liz nodded.

'Thanks so much.' I faced the busy crew. 'I mean, that's just...'

'So you're Scarlett?' A lady in a suit and a lot of makeup pointed at me. 'Do you mind if we interview you all on camera?'

'Sure.'

'Great! We'll count you down....'

I saw Dad and Kirsten pull up with the Dunn's in their VW car. I waved. The TV lady turned towards the camera. 'Here in West Stonecloud, it's Groundhog day, as we join local MP, Clive Hopkins, on the search for a not-so-lucky fortune pig called Destiny.' She turned to face us. 'Scarlett, can you tell us what happened when you lost Destiny?'

'She was taken from us.' I took a deep breath. 'I went outside to see me granny who was having a stroke and then the eagle owl that lives 'ere swooped down and grabbed her, and took her off.'

'That must have been awful to watch.' She nodded.

'T' was a nightmare!' Me accent sounded more like a farmer than ever.

'I hear Destiny is somewhat of a local celebrity?'

'She's a treasured part of our community.' Scott's dad put his hand on me shoulder again. 'But most of all, she's a part of the Saint family. Ever since she was taken, the Saints have had the most terrible bad luck. If they don't find Destiny soon, who knows what might happen!'

He was bending the story, trying to link the lost pig to the fire to help spread the word about the fundraiser. I watched Dad and Kirsten talking to people as they went past, as if they were local celebs. I didn't see me mum anywhere...

'You lost your house in a terrible fire too. Is that right, Scarlett?'

I nodded. 'We're livin' on a bus at the moment 'cause...'

Scott's dad squeezed me shoulder. 'Like many people. The Saints had house insurance, but were hoodwinked by an unlicensed electrician and so didn't see a penny. It could happen to any of us. As a community, we're determined to put things right, to find Destiny, and to get the Saints back their home, which is why we'll be launching a fundraiser. In the summer, we're inviting the community to take part in a competition. Huge prizes have been donated by celebrities in the area.'

'And how confident are you in finding Destiny today?'

'I've no doubt.' Liz clapped. 'With a community effort like this, we can bring her back home where she belongs. Pets are like children, and nobody should have to go through losing one of their own.'

'It is heart-breaking. And Clive, how do you feel about the upcoming local elections?'

The name Clive echoed in me head as if it was on repeat. Over and over again: Clive, Clive, Clive. But I didn't put the two together. Me brain did not see how Scott's dad could be the same man. Not until I saw Kirsten's face as she saw us, all facing the camera as the presenter asked questions. Her gaze saw tsunamis and earthquakes and volcanic eruptions and horrors of war, as she shook her head and backed up and pushed past people to get away. Nobody saw her but me. And it was as if it had happened before. As if I had seen it all before somewhere, some place else, and it wasn't real.

'OK, that's great,' said the presenter. 'We'll get some shots of people searching for the pig. Fingers crossed!'

'Clive Hopkins?' I stared at Scott's dad, waiting for some sort of hint or glint, or reaction that would prove it either way, but there was nothing. He just turned and smiled.

'That's my name. Don't wear it out!'

'But I thought you were the Wrights.' I shook me head.

'*My* surname is Wright.' Liz put her hand to her chest.

'What's your surname, Scott?'

'Wright.' He nodded.

'Why ain't it the same as your dad's?'

'It's Scott Hopkins Wright. Just use it more like a middle name. Why?'

'But...' I shook me head as if trying to remember or see someone else, but it was only ever the same goofy man.

'Well, we'd better get a move on if we're going to catch Destiny.' Liz got Destiny's treats out of her bag.

'We'll each take a group. Alright Scarlett? We'll get her! Don't you worry. Got a good feeling about this.' Clive and Scott walked towards the group where the camera crew were standing.

'Scarlett, have you seen Kirsten?' Dad came up behind and me heart sank.

'No, sorry.' I held me breath, bit me nail.

'She can't of just vanished! She's not answerin' her phone either.' He stood on his toes to look over people's heads.

'Did you tell Mum to come?'

'Yeah, but not heard back.' He walked off again towards crowd.

'How's Granny?' I shouted after him, but he didn't hear me.

'Everything alright?' Liz put her hand on me arm. The warmth brought me out of the cloud in me head. I put me hand on top of hers. She was so great. Scott was lucky to have her as a mum. Always there, no matter what.

'He's Clive Hopkins.' I stared at Liz. '*The* Clive Hopkins.'

'Yep! Your local MP, here to serve.' She grinned.

'Me dad's girlfriend is Kirsten Keenan, she...'

'What?' Liz took her hand off me arm. 'You're related to Kirsten Keenan?'

'She's me dad's girlfriend.'

'Your dad's girlfriend?' Her face reddened. 'She ruined his life!'

'It ruined hers too.'

Liz shook her head and glanced up at Clive on the hill. 'Oh god. Clive's going to be crushed when he finds out.'

'What? Why?'

'You were like the daughter he always wanted. But if Kirsten is...'

'Kirsten is me dad's girlfriend, not me mum or anything. I'm not even sure I...'

'But she's your dad's *girlfriend*.' It was as if she was broken, stuck on repeat.

'I know. Just don't tell him. Not yet...'

We were both watching Clive as he pointed and waved as if he was conducting an orchestra. He was fired-up, ready to go. The air was crisp, clear, the sort where you can see for miles. And I didn't know what to do, what to think, what to believe.

'Do you believe her?' Liz whispered.

'Ummm, I had always pictured him to be some sort of sleaze bag, but he's, I... But I can't believe Kirsten would make something up that's so...'

'It's not her fault, I don't think. So don't blame her.'

'What do you mean?'

'Clive knew her from school, and...'

'He did? She never mentioned that.'

Liz started to walk up towards the crowds, and I followed her. 'Small towns. Whatever she told you... She may *actually* believe it. But it doesn't mean it's true. We used to come across this a lot with our foster children. The things that happened to them. The things that they'd seen. It just did stuff to them we can't understand. They're trying to process it, you know?'

'You think summat happened to Kirsten?'

'Clive said she had a rough time at school. This awful reputation with the boys for being... well, a bit... she got called Kinky Kirsten. She was only twelve. I mean, no twelve-year-old gets a name like that unless something happened to them.'

'She never talks about her past or her family.' I nodded. 'Not really.'

Liz straightened up, a step away from being in her police uniform. 'Well, we've loved having you around, but you may need to have a rethink about the LARP because it's just going to make things worse for your family.'

She started to walk off, and I grabbed her arm. 'But it's not me fault.'

'I know, but we don't want to make things worse... Your whole family is going through such a rough time. Let's just focus on today and find Destiny, OK? Which we will.'

'Please. I'm not a kid. I can do me own thing. Don't punish me for summat that I didn't do.'

'Of course not! I wouldn't dream of it. But Kirsten is clearly a very troubled woman, and...'

'I don't know what I'd do without you guys.' I could feel tears coming up. Liz had been more of a mum to me these past few weeks than mine or Kirsten combined.

She hugged me sideways. 'Aw... Well now, we just *have* to find you your pig.'

I lost track of the minutes, and who was saying what, and who was going where and taking what route. Maybe Kirsten got it wrong? Perhaps it was Mum harassing her and not Clive? Or Kirsten *was* traumatised from some other thing that happened to her? Liz was more experienced in this stuff than I was. Rubi was always going on about false confessions on these crime podcasts and how troubled people often believed things that didn't happen or weren't true. False memories. Maybe that was Kirsten. Mum was like it too - her memories were all over the place. You could never trust her to get things quite right. Her past drinking made sure of that.

Everyone had scattered around the fields of sunshine, but there was something odd in the air, something brewing. Someone grabbed both of me arms from behind, tight, and came close to me ear.

'Was *that* who I think it was?' Dad's voice was quiet, but angry.

'What d'you mean?'

'Don't you play stupid with me.' He turned me around. 'That's him, isn't it? That's why Kirsten's done a runner.'

'I didn't know. Honest.'

He let go of me arms and stormed off into the field, calling for Destiny. His head bobbed above the flowers. A chill came into the air out of nowhere as I ran after him. In a matter of minutes, I felt like a six-year-old again, chasing after me dad, who didn't want nothing to do with me.

'Dad? Dad? It wasn't me fault.'

'You can't see 'em again.' He marched at speed.

'You can't tell me what to do. I'm 21 for god's sake.'

'Scarlett, I'm serious.'

'But they're helping us, Dad. Didn't you see what they're doing? They did all this. And they're helping us get back our house. They wouldn't do that if they were bad people.'

'I don't want nothin' that piece of filth touches.'

'But if you gave 'em a chance. You'd see what they're like and...?'

He stopped and turned to face me. 'Then what? We'll all just say Kirsten made it up? Are you mad? Why would she do that?'

'Maybe she didn't mean to. I mean... look at what Mum does. She doesn't remember right. Maybe Kirsten is the same. It's not on purpose. Maybe it's Mum that is doing stuff to Kirsten? Got her fired.'

He shook his head and laughed. His face was grey in a sea of yellow flowers heads. The bags under his eyes looked as if they were ready to collapse into his cheeks. 'I can't keep doing this, Scarlett. Leave your mum out of it.'

'Why won't you talk about it? It all points to Mum. All of it! She must have been the one who got Kirsten fired.'

'I don't want to talk about stuff that went on with your mum.' He turned and marched off again. 'It doesn't matter now. It's all over with.'

'No, it isn't. Did y' know she was helping Mr Post to sue us? Did y' know that she is sending shitty text messages to Kirsten?'

'Destiny!' Dad shouted, refusing to listen to me.

'I bet I could prove it.'

'Scarlett, your mum isn't right in the head.'

'I know, and what if she set the fire? You said it yourself, she's not well... Wait, is it... snowin'?' I stopped to look up. 'In April?'

The sky had clouded over. It hung heavy over us, brewing. Big flakes of snow flew towards us, making it harder to see. Dad was pretending to look for Destiny, but really, he was putting all his effort into trying to ignore me. He acted like nothing was going on. He was trying to outrun me, trying to run away from me like he always did, as if he wanted nothing to do with me.

'There's a basement under the house.' I kept up with him, trotting behind, skipping over lumpy ground. 'The neighbour had access to it - and Mum was friends with him. Did you know that? What if she sparked the fire from down there when he was away?'

'Why?' He stopped again and turned. 'On this godforsaken planet, would your mum set fire to a house with *you* in it? Her own flesh and blood.'

'Because she never wanted me anyways.'

'Who told you that?'

Dad's phone rang, and he answered it before I could answer him. 'Kirsten? That you?'

Someone was staring at me from across the other side of the field. It was Rubi and Kai, and they were waving and jumping up and down. A little pink piggy ran down the path between the green stems towards us. 'Destiny! Oh my god! There she is! Destiny!'

And I swear that Destiny's feet didn't touch the ground. It was as if she'd flown towards me, her head almost at the height of the flowers. I held Destiny up to the sky like a trophy for Dad to see as she wriggled and snorted, happy to see us.

A flurry of snow blew up around us like a tornado. Dad was staring at me, blank. He wasn't moving, but something in him had finally collapsed. I hadn't heard what he said on the phone or who it was, but I didn't have to. I knew at the very moment we'd found Destiny, we had lost Granny.

23

'You want me to be the bad guy?
Fine, now I'm the bad guy.'

Mother Gothel, Tangled

Granny didn't want a normal funeral. Even in death, she made life difficult. She used to be a florist in the village. But there was some sort of drama and she swore off flowers for life, and apparently in death too. She wanted Destiny to lead the parade down the church aisle. I couldn't help but wonder if Granny was having her last laugh. That was what I liked the most about Granny. She didn't care what people thought of her. She never backed down. She fought for herself. Funny, ain't it? How when people are alive, all you can see are their faults. But when they're dead, all you see are their strengths. The traits you wished you had.

I agreed to take Destiny down the aisle, even though she'd refused to budge all morning. Dad and I waited at the church entrance together, waiting for people to arrive. He had taken to drinking like a fish these past two weeks as we prepared for the funeral. He never drank before, not that I saw. Not in me lifetime. But if you lit a match, he'd have gone up like a witch burning at the stake. I don't think he even noticed that I was barely around. I spent most of the past few weeks with the Wrights. Did he feel guilty like I did, that Granny had died alone, that none of us were there when she went?

The Dunns showed up with Rubi, who was wearing a long flowing dress me gran had liked.

'Any sign of Kirsten?' Rubi took me hand.

I shook me head. 'I don't think she'll show.' Two weeks had gone by since we'd seen Kirsten on the edge of the field, running away from Clive. Nobody had seen or heard from her. Just a message from her sister to tell us to leave her alone. Kirsten had vanished. She'd abandoned us. Just like me mum. They were all the same. Except Liz. Scott's Mum had sent me a text every day to see how I was, especially when she found out Kirsten had gone.

Rubi twisted her hands. 'Did you tell your dad about the doll you found?'

Rubi and I had gone to Gran's favourite pub to raise a glass of whisky to her memory, and I told her about the last time I'd spoken to Kirsten, about the red paint and the baby in the bin. Rubi rattled the ice in her glass and stared at me, unblinking. She asked me whether it was definitely red paint - maybe something worse had happened, maybe somebody else had died too. Rubi was good at putting things together. It never occurred to me that Kirsten might have been pregnant or even trying.

'Have you seen him?' I nodded towards Dad. 'I think one more thing would send him over the edge.'

'I think he's already over it.' Rubi took a service leaflet that had Granny's young face on it.

Dad's eyes were bloodshot. His face was as grey as the stone of the church that towered up to the sky. We stood in its shadow, looking out at the graves sinking, as if they were falling in slow motion. We used to come here when we were seventeen, drink cider and laugh. It felt like another life. The clock above us had stopped at 6.08, but it was actually 2 pm. The service was about to start.

'D' you believe in heaven, Rubes?'

'Yeah, I think so.' She was flicking through the order of service.

'D' you think me granny's there?'

'Reckon she'd be complaining that the pearly gates were too showy.' Rubi elbowed me. She always made me smile. When Granny's wicker-basket coffin drove up to the front, Rubi grabbed me hand and squeezed it. 'Ever the trendsetter your Gran.' She squeezed me hand tighter. In silence, we all watched men in tails lift me gran's coffin and position themselves at the carved wooden doors.

'Are you ready?' The vicar put his hand on me shoulder. He was too young to be one.

I held onto Destiny's lead and watched everyone else go inside. Dozens of people were inside the church. Scott waved slowly at me from the front. I waved back. It was sweet of him to be there for me. I could rely on him. Liz had texted to say she wished she could come for support, but considering me dad's state, I had asked her not to come. Destiny was looking up at the coffin like she knew who was in it. Two men held open the doors, and we walked in silence up the aisle, in a church I believed would be empty, but was filled with the village.

Me feet tapped along the red and black tiles. I watched Destiny as we passed the pews and didn't look at anyone. Lights filtered in through the stained glass windows in front. I wondered whether Granny got married there, whether she got baptised, and I felt guilty that I didn't know, that I might never know. I heard the doors behind us swing open, and Destiny changed her mind about walking forwards. She turned around and ran so hard and so fast that she pulled me with her. I held onto the lead. And smacked into the men at the front of the coffin before letting go. It all happened in slow motion like a broken piece of time: the buckling of legs, the running pig, the coffin toppling down to the ground, the thud of her inside, the looking up to see that Destiny was running towards me mum who stood at the back of the church.

'Bravo!' Someone clapped. 'Bravo!'

It sounded like Granny, but I was pretty sure Granny was dead. I had heard her fall in the coffin. It came from someone at the back of the church, in the last pew, but I could only see their hair, which was way darker than Granny's.

'I'm so, so sorry.' Mum held the sides of her face like The Scream painting. 'Scarlett, are you OK?'

Like Kirsten, Mum had been AWOL for weeks. And I didn't realise until she walked in that I was capable of making a scene, that it didn't matter who was watching. The nerve she had to show up, in that moment, at a funeral of the woman she so obviously hated. I snapped out of staring at the woman in the back and turned to her. 'Why d'you care?'

'What?'

'Ladies and gentlemen!' The vicar gestured to the organ player. 'Please give us a few minutes and talk amongst yourselves while we sort things out.'

It's dead-easy to spot a villain in a kid's film. They'd be wearing black, have squinty eyes and a deep, raspy voice. But sometimes a villain can be a woman, who appears incredibly tanned, pretending to be a mother, trying to keep you locked up in a tower, in order to take your youth. Or they can be wolves with big teeth, and big eyes, and claws, dressed up as grandma, waiting for Red Riding Hood to come on home. The wolf had arrived, and I wasn't going to let her take down me house. I was done being her little pig. Like Granny, I wasn't going to be kicked about no more. I marched towards me mum. 'Come to make sure she's dead, have you?'

'What? No.' Mum stared at the pallbearers kneeling to pick up the coffin. 'I came for you. I've not heard from you in so long, Scarlett baby. I was worried. I wanted to be here for you.'

'For me? That's rich. You're the reason she's dead.'

'What?'

'I know everything, Mum. Everything.'

'What d'you mean?'

'You were helping Mr Post to sue us.' I pointed at the man himself in one of the pews. Destiny ran to the woman towards the back, wiggling her tail as I watched the top of this woman's head as she pet her.

'Sue you?' Mum stopped walking towards me and froze.

'Do y' know how much that stressed Granny out? Why else d'you think she had a stroke? You're the one who got Kirsten fired too, aren't you?'

'I wouldn't do that, Scarlett baby.' She shook her head.

'But you'll harass her with text messages?'

'What text messages?'

'Stop it! Don't pretend. I know they're you. They *sound* like you. I've heard you speak like that before. Give me your phone, I'll prove it. You're a wolf; a wolf in sheep's clothing.'

'Hold on a minute. You can't judge me, you don't know the half of it...' Mum's back rose as if she was filling her lungs, getting ready to huff and puff and blow me accusations down.

'Ladies.' The vicar took me by the elbow. 'Please, could you both take a seat so we can start the service?'

'One minute.' I held me index finger in the air.

'Kirsten lied about *me*.' Mum held a hand to her chest. 'She got *me* fired - said I was drinking when I wasn't. Your Gran stole that land just like they stole me stuff. I never got back me Mum's jewellery, they never gave me anything...'

'Boo hoo!' I tipped me head from side to side. The lady at the back laughed. Just like Granny would've laughed. A slight snigger at first, and then a full-on cackle. 'So that's why you burned down our house so we would lose everything you thought was your right? And you did it so that we couldn't claim insurance.'

'What?'

'You knew about the dodgy electrics and the basement...'

'You can't claim your insurance?'

'Ladies.' The vicar tried to usher us with his hands. 'Please, everyone's looking.'

'I'm almost done; we're almost done.' I threw up me hands. 'Where have you been, Mum? We're homeless. You took everything. Even Granny. You win! You huffed, and you puffed and you blew our house in, and now we live on a bus. I hope you're happy.'

'Why would you think I'd do that?' She asked without the baby voice or anger, just a neutral voice that I wasn't used to hearing.

' 'cause I found out the truth. Dad didn't steal me away, Mum. You lied to me.'

'Who told you that?'

'Kirsten.'

'That little...' She glared at Dad and puffed up her chest again, ready to blow. 'Well, if the truth is what you want...'

Dad stood up, shaking his head.

'They're no Saints either. Your dad wouldn't have you.'

'What?' Me question echoed in the church as the organ stopped playing.

'That's right. I tried me best, I did. But it wasn't good enough. So I went to court to get your dad to take you on because he wouldn't. He wanted nothing to do with either of us. But then Little Miss Kirsten came along and...'

'Dad, is that true?'

'I... only at first.' He'd frozen again, wordless, looking at the crowd. Me mum had just blown down the last thing I had, the one person I thought had fought for me, who would get in the ring for me. And when I felt myself split open, it wasn't for sadness or pity, it was fury. I was done being the piggy in the middle. Done being a Saint. I had descended from wolves, so it was about time I acted like one too.

'Well, I guess it's a good thing that Kirsten lost the baby, considering you can't stand being a dad.'

'What?'

'Scarlett!' Rubi stood up with her eyes wide. 'That's not right, we don't know for sure.'

Even me Mum had shrunk back with horror, her hand over her mouth. It was terrible but they were all terrible too, and unlike them, I had done nothing but tell the truth.

Mum walked towards me. 'I'm so so so....'

'Save it. I'm done feeling sorry for you!' I was shouting but me eyes were pooling, and I took a deep breath, me own huff, to blow everyone down around me. 'I never want to see you again. I never want to hear from you again. I don't want to know your name, ever. I want you out of me life for good. Both of you.'

Mum had no more puff in her. She backed away a little, but then walked forward again. 'OK.' She nodded. 'I'll admit it. I set the fire. I burned down your house.'

The entire village started talking, conferring; a hum, like a distance chainsaw. A melody of shock and horror and disbelief as if we were on Jerry Springer.

'Wowie,' said the woman with Destiny. 'Didn't see that comin'...'

'I will go to the police station right now, and hand myself in.' Mum turned around, announcing to the crowd. 'Yes, yes. It was obviously me. I'll go. I can fix it. I can do it.'

Bit by bit, she walked away from the coffin. The entire village watched, clocking her every move, the gears in their mouths getting louder and louder. She opened the door, took a glance back with a look that felt a million miles away, and she left.

'Ladies and gentlemen,' shouted the vicar, bringing them all back to the procession. The coffin lay at the front. Without meeting anyone's gaze, I marched towards the woman at the back. I wanted Destiny back, and I wanted to find out who the hell this woman was who was interrupting me granny's funeral as if it were some sort of show, some sort of circus. Me breathing heaved in me chest; me jaw was a vice. I was ready to throw everyone out. When I reached the end of her pew, the woman lifted her head up as she picked up Destiny from the ground, and she grinned at me with that wicked look in her eye.

It was Granny.

And all me anger just went 'poof'. But it wasn't Granny as she was when she died. It was a middle-aged version, without wrinkles or white hair. Whatever this was, it had been sitting in the back row, clapping and laughing. I stood, staring, dumb struck. It couldn't be her. I had heard her body fall in the coffin. I was losing it, surely.

'Y' know what?' Granny picked up Destiny. 'Reckon your Mum's lying.'

Me eyes almost fell out of me head when she spoke.

'Sit down and shut your mouth. You'll catch flies.' She laughed and slapped her leg.

I sat down and realised she wasn't there. Not quite solid. She was more like tissue paper: thin and see-through. I grabbed Destiny's lead and noticed she was gazing at Granny, too. They had finally been reunited.

'Granny?' I whispered, but people still turned around to stare at me.

'Shhh.' She put her finger to her lip. 'It's starting.' The organ picked up again, and she stood up to get a better look. She'd always said she wanted to see her own funeral. But I didn't think that I'd be able to see her watching her own funeral. And what a fuck up it was, but she was clearly loving every moment.

I clutched onto Destiny's lead so tight that me nails dug into me hand. Why Granny was there? Why had she come back at this very moment, in the worst moment? Or was this the final straw? Maybe me sanity had been hanging on by a thread and this was the last thing to bring me house down? I was numb, me brain like figgy pudding. The nursery rhyme me mum sang to me as a kid went round in me head as people spoke about a woman who should have been dead but was standing right next to me:

This little piggy went to market.

This little piggy stayed at home.

This little piggy had roast beef.

This little piggy had none.

And this little piggy went weeweewee all the way home.

PART II

INCOMING MESSAGE…

Scarlett,

I want you to know that it wasn't

her, it wasn't your mum.

I know, because it was me.

It was me who set the fire.

She's innocent.

1

_____

'Souls... don't... die.'

The Iron Giant

Most people wouldn't of believed me. Hell, I didn't believe me. Scott didn't believe me. Not even Rubi, who was raised in a haunted house. She believed in her ghosts, but couldn't believe me gran would be just the sort to haunt the crap out of people. They all gave me that look like I used to give me mum. And there was no way I was going to get put away because of me gran. So I zipped it.

After her funeral, I looked for her everywhere. When I moved out of the bus, I looked back to see if she'd appear at the window. But it was just Dad staring at me, saying nothing as I packed up and left. It was Liz who took pity on me. She said she couldn't stand by and watch me go through what I was going through. Everyone needed someone to step in. What a gem. When I moved me stuff into Scott's house, into the spare room with their costumes and scenery, I looked out of the window to see if granny was in the garden, pruning. When I saw the Wright's piano in the sitting room, I half expected to hear her singing *Roll Out The Barrel*. She loved to play the piano, but she loved to play people more - to press at their minor keys, pushing them until people screamed at her. I felt like an instrument too, highly strung.

Everyone treated me different after. And I guess that made sense, because everything was different. I had two parents who didn't give two shits about me, and a family who felt sorry for me. Mum and Dad had never wanted me around. On some level, I reckon I'd always known. But when it gets said, a part of you gets destroyed. And it ain't a quiet passing. It's violent. Explosive. It was like that part in the Iron Giant when he thinks his little friend is dead, and the robot goes nuclear out of grief and starts destroying everything. When Mum confessed to burning down the house, it was the final straw.

The woman I thought loved me was worse than dead. She was a figment of me imagination. They were right. I had been living in a fantasy land. My entire life. My family. It was all a lie. Why would I believe a single thing they said? I couldn't trust them. My family were pathological liars. That was why they were nowhere to be seen. Not one of them could face up to the truth and so they'd all run off. Not one of them could face up to what they'd done, who they'd hurt. I was ashamed to be honest. I was ashamed to know them, to be related to them. People like Kirsten, me dad, me mum, they had ruined lives with their lies. They had destroyed good people. It wasn't fair. They shouldn't be allowed to get away with it.

The Wrights were the only ones who didn't treat me different. Instead of backing off or telling me to rethink, they gave me hugs and sympathy and a way out. Liz spent hours with me, watching movies and doing pedicures, listening to me rant about them. They were angry too. They saw what I saw: me entire life had burned down to the ground. But the Wrights made me believe it was a good thing, that maybe in the ashes, I could have a new life, a new beginning. They said they would help me get back onto me feet. Salt of the earth.

When I got to their house, I felt as if I'd landed on another planet. They were a proper family. No eating in front of the telly, and they had napkins at dinner. They were proper-posh, and I ain't going to lie, it was alien to me. It was hard enough, pretending to be posh, acting as if this was something I did every day. It got even harder when Granny turned up at dinner with the Wrights and sat at the end of the long, shiny wooden table as if she were the queen. She was sporting a salmon-pink skirt suit with a matching hat.

'Scarlett!' She threw open her arms. I glared at her and looked away.

'I give it a 8.2 in technical, and a 9.5 in creativity.' Scott's dad waved his fork.

'So what's that... a 8.8? or 8.9?' Liz added up on her fingers.

'Is that aniseed?' Scott chewed and looked up. 'It's... different.'

'Utter shite, he means.' Granny leaned forward. 'Ain't that the truth?'

I glared at Granny again. Maybe the stress of dinner was getting to me. She wasn't there, not really. And it would be best if she wasn't.

'Don't ignore me, Scarlett!' Granny hit the table.

'So wait, are you saying it's creative, but doesn't work?' Liz carried on, unaware of the extra guest. Nobody moved. The Wrights were obsessed with the Olympics. They had a scoring system for almost everything - including tea (which they called dinner). Like the Olympics, you got scored on two things: technical ability and creativity. You added the two scores and divided them up to get your overall score.

'Scarlett?' Liz looked to me.

'Oh go on, tell her.' Granny picked up a fork and examined it. 'Tell her it smells like a clogged drain.'

'I think it's lush! Proper delish!' I stuffed a large forkful of pasta into me mouth to fill it up and nodded.

'Oi.' Granny got up from the table. 'Stop ignoring me!'

Liz was searching our faces around the dining table. I pretended to study the time on the grandfather clock until Granny stepped in front of it. Clive was re-tucking his napkin into his shirt. Scott was adding salt. 'I'm calling it.' Liz raised her hand. 'Give me a real score. I can take it.'

'Oh, I'll give you a score.' Granny stood right next to Liz. I tried me best to blank her because it would look weird if I was staring into space and nobody else was seeing her. But Granny turned around, lifted her dress and mooned us.

I put me head in me hands, pretending to rub me face, trying to hide me reaction from her because that was exactly what she wanted. That, and probably to show off her now-young ass.

'It's a valiant effort.' Scott held up a glass of water. 'But it's a 5.5 for me.'

'Oooo, I get it now.' Granny stood next to Scott. 'I'd give him an eight out of ten. Tasty bit of stuff. No wonder you were keen to move in so soon.'

'Still...' Scott's dad smirked. 'Better than your score for the time you tried to tap dance. You hear about that, Scarlett?'

Scott kicked him under the table.

Scott's dad dodged sideways. 'Ah, missed! I see your football skills still need a lot of work. Anyway... What does it matter? Scarlett's practically family now.'

I'd only been with them for a few weeks, but I couldn't help but grin. Scott and Clive cleared and stacked the plates. Liz showed no hint as to whether Clive knew Kirsten was me dad's girlfriend, that she was the one had caused them so much hell. Ruined their lives. I'd have known, surely? No-one had seen or heard from Kirsten, so maybe we could forget it?

'Family?! Pah!' Granny picked up a fancy plate from the dresser behind Liz.

Shit.

'Of course, always wanted another girl around the house.' Liz smiled as Granny lifted the plate above her head with both hands.

'No!' I jumped up. 'Don't.'

'I need to talk to you.' Granny waved the plate around. 'Matter of death, you know.' She laughed at herself.

Both Scott and Clive had stopped to stare at me.

'I'm sorry,' said Liz. 'Did I say something wrong?'

'Oh no, sorry, I think I miss-heard you. I thought you said something about water. Hahaha. Let me get the plates.' I took the plates from Scott and grabbed the one Granny was holding up in the air. 'I'll clear up. Take them to the *kitchen*.' I nodded to Granny to follow, and she vanished.

'I'll help.' Scott grabbed a glass.

'No, no.' I shook me head. 'Let me. It's the least I can do.' I tried to sound less like a farmer and more classy. 'You've been lifesavers. And thanks again for giving me a new phone. Not sure how I've survived so long without one.'

'Hopefully it's not giving you jip.' Clive sat back down. 'It always used to do weird things with me back when I used it. God, it really is an old phone. I'm amazed it even works.'

'That's because you're technically challenged.' Scott rolled his eyes.

'I reckon it's because you dropped it on one of your midnight excursions.' Liz rolled up her napkin.

'That's not my fault.' Clive leaned back. 'I sleepwalk, Scarlett. Sometimes, I even try to sleep drive! Can you believe it?'

'Really? Isn't that dangerous?' Plates in hand, I hovered by the kitchen door.

'Super dangerous.' Liz turned to face me. 'If you ever see him roaming about. Come and wake me up.'

'And if you ever see him in the car, take the keys off him,' said Scott.

I heard something clang in the kitchen. 'Will do!' With me back, I pushed the door into the kitchen open.

Granny sat up on the white marble countertop. 'Dahling!' She was putting on a posh accent. 'Look at me! I mean, just look at me!'

'Shhhh.' I put the plates down next to Granny. 'What *are* you doing 'ere? You're supposed to be dead.'

'Dead fabulous y' mean? You wouldn't believe the people I've met. So many famous people and they all think I am hilarious!'

'Are you sure they're not laughing *at* you?' I turned on the tap to drown out our voices.

'No, they adore me! I'm an R/D, a recently deceased. We're hot stuff, y' know?' She hopped down and paced around the room. 'I've been telling 'em all about how we grow roses now. They can't get enough.' She looked at the open rack of herbs in the corner and screwed up her nose. 'And I said to 'em if ya.... Oh, forgot to mention.' She pushed me new old-phone towards me. 'You got a message.'

'You ain't here!' I shook me head to see if that would make her disappear and sighed. 'You ain't 'ere.' I picked up a napkin, thew it and it didn't touch her. 'See! You're just me loopy brain going mental. Oh God, I'm going to end up like Mum.' I put me hands on me head. 'Should of seen it coming.'

'It was there from the get-go! From birth.' Granny smirked. '*But,* you daft cow, if I was your loopy brain, how is it I know you got a message, and you don't?'

'Got a point.' I glanced at me god-ancient-phone-that-couldn't-even-get-on-the-internet to see a message blinking.

'So, you haunting me?'

'You betcha! Being dead is quite good, y' know... I mean, look at me bosoms - look!' She pushed them side to side and then squeezed them. 'They don't sag, and neither does me neck.' She pulled at the skin around her throat. 'And nothing hurts anymore. I feel a million pounds.'

'You're dead.' I unlocked the phone. 'Aren't you?'

'Well, of course I'm dead, stupid.' Granny swung her legs back and forth. 'Whose got Destiny? She OK?'

'Rubi's got her. She's fine.' She was right about the message, and so I opened it. 'So d' you have unfinished business or summat?'

'This ain't a movie birdbrain... Anyway, I don't *do* business... But now that I'm pushin' up daisies, I *am* incredibly wise.' She held up her nose to the ceiling. 'Summat happens when you go six feet under...'

I ignored Granny to read the message:

> Scarlett, I want you to know that it
> wasn't her, it wasn't your mum.
> I know, because it was me.
> It was me who set the fire.
> She's innocent.

'Who's this? Who sent me this?'

'See, told you your Mum's full of it. I knew all along that woman was bad news. From the get-go. She was always givin' me these looks, these odd little sideways glances, and I thought to myself, she's gunna do you in one of these days. Mark me...'

'Wait a minute. Are you saying Mum didn't burn down our house? Why would she say she did?'

'Ain't it obvious?'

'No!' I threw out me hands. 'Course not.'

'That woman wouldn't burn anything she could steal first. And your mother couldn't stage summat so...' She waved her hand in the air like the queen waving to her people. 'Clever.'

'Do y' know who sent this?' I waved the phone.

'I *am* a fount of wisdom but I ain't all knowin'. If I was

Columbo...' She crossed a leg over the other. 'I'd say y' know this person.'

'And why would you say that? Whose Columbo?'

'No one would send that message unless they cared about you, and...'

The door swung open. 'Everything alright in here?' Scott frowned at me.

I put me phone down and smiled. 'Uh yeah, sure.'

Granny had gone, and I felt me back ease up. But Scott set off me nerves too, in a different way. He was the strong-silent-type who also was hard to figure out if they even like you. Rubi said that was me type, the hard-to-get ones, the not-even-sure-they-like-me ones. But she ain't always right. Scott showed he cared - he came to Granny's funeral for one. And he was always inviting me to watch stuff with him. We'd sit in Scott's room, which was full of computer screens and equipment. He had a black wall that looked like a blank screen. He was into movies like me, but old ones. His entire room was like being in a black and white film. He had a wall of posters: The Godfather, Jaws and Pulp Fiction, and he had been introducing me to the 'classics' and none of the 'kid's stuff' I liked. I always tried to get close to him, like a magnet, as if we were being pulled together by an unknown force. It was as if we were meant to be. But we still hadn't made it over the line, and I was holding back because I didn't want to ruin it and scare him off. But we'd been getting closer, bit by bit. Maybe I could trust him?

'You've got to rinse those first.' He pointed to the plates.

'Oh sorry, we used to... umm... Never mind...'

'Are you sure everything is alright?' He walked towards me.

I stared up at him, thinking about what Granny had said. 'Actually...' I lifted up me phone and showed Scott the message.

'Wow.' He put his hands in his pockets. 'Do you think it's true?'

'I dunno. Maybe.'

'She'd be a saint after all, then.' He nodded. 'If that's the case.'

'What d'you mean?'

'Well, if that's true.' He leaned against the counter. 'Your mum just sacrificed her life so you could get back your house.'

'What? No. That can't be true.' I shook me head. 'She would never do that. She's always been about number one.'

Because if it was, then it was all me fault. Me mum would be in prison, waiting for a trial, all because of me. All to save a house I didn't want no part in anymore, a family I'd disowned. She wouldn't do that, would she? If Mum wasn't the arsonist, if she wasn't the wolf, I'd be back at square one. Worse than square one. I would need to save her.

2

'Because of the wonderful things he does,
we're off to see the Wizard...'

The Wizard of Oz

To get Mum out of prison, I was going to need me own Rubi slippers. Rubi was wearing her red coat and yellow wellies, looking like a five-year-old in front of the tunnel on the track. I hadn't seen so much of her lately, since I moved in with the Wrights. The path was waterlogged because June had been a washout so far. Her reflection shone in the puddles. She stood in front of graffiti that said *Make a Wish* in big bubble-writing. People had written their wishes around it, and some had come back to say thank you for making their dreams come true.

I was awake all night, wondering if I should-or-shouldn't do something to save Mum. And if so, what? That phone message had changed everything. What she did changed everything. She was on her way to prison because of me. And with Granny showing up, dead, maybe there was more to life? Maybe I could get some otherworldly help? Get me own wizard.

Rubi waved and ran over to me. 'I'm pretty sure I just saw the biggest rat I've seen in me entire life. Can we go? I've got to work at the B&B soon. Mum'll kill me.'

'Oh, but I need courage. Please come with me.' I took her hand. 'I really, really need you.'

'Where?'

I pointed behind her. 'In there.'

'What? Hell no. I'm not going in there. It's pitch black! Giant mutant rats will eat us.'

'But I really need some extra help right now.' I raised me eyebrows. 'A little magic...'

'But you hate the dark, too.'

'I know, I know, but... I'm desperate. I feel so bad about me mum. About everything. And it can't hurt, right?'

'It can too. It's a fricking long tunnel, Scarlett. And then there's the dark... Do we have to go all the way?'

'Nobody's wish came true by going part way through it.'

'Oh god.'

'We'll walk real fast, OK?' I threaded me arm through hers as if we was off on the yellow brick road. 'And don't leave me side. It'll be just like that time we went skinny dipping. A bit of a shock at first, but then... All's gravy.'

'I don't call three tick bites, all gravy.' Rubi snorted. 'That doesn't help at all.' We stalked towards the black hole. 'What do you want to wish for?'

'To get me mum out of prison.'

'You might need more than Lewis for that!' Rubes sighed. 'OK Dorothy... lead the way.'

'No, you're Dorothy.' I nudged her. 'I'm the lion. On account of me hair.'

We marched like Dorothy and the Lion going into the forest. We were swallowed by the tunnel, into its drippy mouth.

'It's too quiet in here.'

'Then talk!'

'About what?'

The sound of something dropping echoed in the tunnel. 'Oh god, anything.' I grabbed her tighter.

'How's living with the Wrights?'

'Oh, I love it.' I bit me fingernail. 'They're like proper, y' know? A proper-proper family. If you get what I mean.'

'Hmmmm.'

'What?'

'Nothing.' I couldn't see Rubi to read her face. 'And work?'

'Some more training, but alright... Liz says I should train to be a police officer. That I've got the deductive skills. But I'm thinking I might try me business again. Scott said he could help. But not sure...'

'What does Scott do?'

'He's looking for work. Can't seem to catch a break. He went to Uni, so he's overqualified for a lot of jobs.'

'Soft hands, eh?'

'He's just really smart, too smart for a lot of stuff we do.'

'Hmmm.' Rubi's voice trailed off again.

'He only got adopted when he was fifteen, so I reckon he just doesn't wanna leave yet, maybe not until he has his own family.'

'Did he say that?'

'Not exactly like that...'

'Are you sure you're not just seeing something that isn't there? Like with Rory.'

'I didn't make up stuff! Rory told me he really wanted to be a dad.'

We picked up our feet along the path in front of us, trying to avoid tripping by feeling our way through. We listened for any signs of Lewis. I always felt sorry for Lewis for being so alone. Legend has it he ran away from home, took shelter in the tunnel and died. When they found him, they said his eyes were wide open and his face in awe, as if he'd seen the face of God himself. And if you walked through the tunnel to the end, and made a wish to Lewis, he would grant it.

'Scarlett?' Rubi's call echoed around us as if we'd entered an extra dimension.

'Yeah?'

'I think you have to ask Lewis out loud.'

'Really? OK. Uh, hi Lewis, I'd like to ask for a favour, a wish...'

'Did you hear that?' Rubes grabbed me arm tighter.

'Hear what?'

'I thought I heard something up ahead.'

'Stop it. Stop freaking me out.'

We stopped and listened, but heard nothing. 'Probably just another rat or something.' She shivered. 'Let's keep going.'

'I uh, Lewis? I don't want me mum to go to prison, so could you help us find out who really set fire to me house so we can get her out? Thank you.'

'Yes, thank you, Lewis. Amen.'

'Amen?!'

I heard a noise in front of me too. Rubi got out her phone and put the torch on. But it was just rubble and shiny walls and darkness. The walls dripped and echoed. We walked in silence, listening to our breaths and the dripping, wondering when we'd see the light at the end. Something more was in the tunnel, something was watching, thinking. And the darkness there was so familiar to me. Was Granny paying another visit?

'Scarlett?'

'Yeah?'

'Can I make a wish too?'

'About what?'

'There's someone I really like.'

'Oh, really!'

'They even live here. Bonus.'

'What will your other boyfriends say?' I nudged her. 'They'll be gutted.'

'Well...'

'You got over Ramone quick, or is it a rebound?'

'I'm not even sure they like me back.' Rubi inhaled deeply. 'It's just... They aren't me usual type, and you might be a bit...'

'It's not Scott, is it?'

'No! Course not. But it's...'

'Oh good! No man could get between us, but I think Scott would be an exception. He held me hand last night. And it took everything I had not to pounce on him. To take it slow, like you said.'

'You should take it slow,' said Rubi. 'Don't give them everything from the get-go.'

'Ah, I hate taking it slow. I think I love him already. I fell asleep and woke up with him stroking me head.'

'Cute.'

'Me mum used to do that too, put me right to sleep...' I sighed. 'She tried, y' know? She tried to be a good mum to me. She just had problems. And now she won't even see me. They say I'm not on the approved list.'

'List of what?'

'Visitors. How am I supposed to stop her?'

'When's her court date?'

'Dunno. Because she pleaded guilty, it's going to this final court for her sentence. But you'd never guess who *is* seeing her...'

'Who?'

'Mr Post!'

'Really?' A clang echoed in the tunnel. We stopped and clamped onto each other. 'You know what - why don't you ask Mr Post to get you on the list.'

'You reckon he would?'

'Worth a shot.'

'I still can't believe she's done this.' I tutted, and the tunnel tutted back at me. 'Granny thinks I must know who really did it.'

'Granny?'

'Uh yeah... I mean, I just talk out loud to her when I go to bed.'

'Aww.' Rubi squeezed me arm. 'I wonder if she hears you.'

'She never heard me when she was alive!'

'Ha, oh god.' Rubes smothered her laugh. 'Sorry I shouldn't laugh.'

'It's fine, I'm fine, I think...'

Seeing Granny hanging about was making me wonder, though. If it was Granny, she'd be looking to scare the hell out of me in this tunnel. What if I was imagining her? Or maybe I fell off me rocker like Mum? It made me think of when Mum kept seeing the person who jumped in front of her train. When she thought it was her that jumped in front of it. In me head I heard me dad's voice: *she's not well, she's not well, she's not well.*

Did it run in the family?

'I think I can see it,' said Rubi. 'The end.'

There was a small glow in the distance. Bit by bit, it got bigger and clearer and brighter. Gravel crunched under our feet, and a warmer, drier air blew in.

'I have a question...' said Rubi. 'Did, uh... did your dad ever have any other kids?'

'What? No.' I pulled away from her a bit. 'Why d'you say that?'

'Me parents said something the other night.'

The light at the end of the tunnel was growing, bleaching the darkness. 'What? What they say?'

'Overheard them, remembering some woman who went searching the village for him a while back. Made a fuss around the town. She had a kid with her.'

'A kid? Maybe he just owed her money?'

'Maybe. Then there was that photo you found, and I

thought… Anyway, I'm not sure me parents will have your dad much longer.' She cleared her throat. 'He just drinks all day on that bus and tries to fight with the ghosts. Guests keep complaining. Think he might ruin business.'

'Sorry.'

'Not your fault.' She sniffed. 'Just thought you should know.'

Rubi's question had clicked together in me head like shoes tapping: there's-no-place-like-home. What sounded insane at first took up space in me head. If I was an unwanted kid, maybe there was another.

'Y' know Rubi, you're such a smart cookie.' I crossed me arms as we made it towards the light. 'You said the date on the photo looked more like 93, and not 98. Maybe you're right, maybe it's not me.'

'Didn't want to say in case it offended you, but it did look boyish too.' Rubi smirked. 'But didn't your mum say she wrote the stuff on the back?'

'Umm… sort of. She looked confused, as if she didn't remember.'

'Well, maybe if this kid exists, they're the one who burned down your house.'

'To get revenge on me dad!' I stared at Rubi, who was staring at her feet. 'And if I can prove someone else did it, then me mum would go free, right?'

'Oh, thank god we're out!'

I hadn't noticed the end of the tunnel. We were through. Me mind was still tunnelling away at the thought that maybe, just maybe, there was another Saint out there.

Rubes gazed at the tunnel entrance as if she was taking in a cathedral. 'Do you think it worked?'

I was staring at her as if she was me wizard. 'What?'

'Your wish!'

'Ah shit, we forgot your wish, Rubes…'

'That's OK.' She turned away. 'Doesn't matter.'

'Let's go through it again.' I edged towards the entrance, feeling bad for getting distracted. 'Run it and shout it out real loud, like.'

'Nah, it's not right now... missed the moment.' She walked off with big steps. It was too late. I'd already done the damage. She chanted. 'Lions, and tigers and bears, oh my! Lion, and tigers, and bears...'

'Oh my!' I ran after her and away from Lewis, who had just granted all me wishes, and I sent one back in me mind for Rubi, hoping he might hear.

3

'Sing sweet Nightingale. Sing sweet Nightingale.'

Cinderella

I woke up to Granny singing Shirley Bassey in me ear along with the birds. She had always fancied herself as someone who was never discovered. A gem in the rough. A princess in the basement, who just never got her Prince Charming and her castle.

'Come on, cinders, rise and shine! Time to get back to work.' She pulled at the sheet on me. It was too hot for duvets. The heat had me body sticking to itself. It chaffed and rubbed, like two people fighting to get their own way.

'I'm on the afternoon shifts this week.' I squinted and tried to squat her. 'How do I turn *you* off?'

'Y' know, today's the day.'

'For what?'

'To see Edward.'

'What? How? Have you seen him?'

'You'll see.'

'How?' I sat up on the side of the bed.

Granny started singing again and twirled around in a flowing silk gown in front of the painted castle set the Wrights used in their LARPs. She denied knowing anything about another kid. She'd disappear if I brought it up, so she must be lying. There was only one person who I figured might know and actually tell me, and that was me mum. And I needed to see her and convince her not to throw her life away, too. But I wasn't allowed to visit. Not yet. I hadn't tracked down Mr Post to put me on the visitor's list. It was like he'd vanished, too.

'Y' know, I'd forgotten about that song. Used to sing it when I was young, when I was part of a group.'

'What group?'

'What group?! We was the Stonecloud Players. I was on vocals. I could have been famous, y' know, but then *life* got in the way...'

I rolled me eyes. 'Why you here?'

'Why are *you* 'ere?' She put her hands on her hips. 'Just tryin' to punish your da even more?'

I blew out air as if trying to blow out a candle. Maybe that was partly true. Maybe part of me wanted me dad to show up, make a scene, prove he wanted me. If he really believed Clive had done anything to Kirsten, then he wouldn't let me stay here. But he hadn't come to my rescue. So what did that say? I didn't want Granny to know that I was glad she was there. She'd be unbearable and would leave if she knew. It was nice to have her around, to have someone who wanted to be with me. Well, I think she wanted to be with me, but maybe she just wanted to haunt me. Better than nothing.

On the way to work, I stopped by Mr Post's house. It reminded me of all the times me friends at school would knock on his door and run away. But now, years later, I needed him to answer, and he didn't. I wonder if that was me fault, too. The weather couldn't decide what it should do, rain or sunshine. First-thing in Stonecloud, people were out watering their desperate plants, and I caught a dandelion's wish and made one when Granny wasn't looking. I'd been trying me best at work, trying to keep in line and not get above myself like last time. I tried to keep me personal life separate. But it was hard not to let it get personal, it was hard to keep it separate in such a small town.

I cornered Tamara, the new temp. 'Where's Gerry?'

'Gerry? Oh, she's gone.' She didn't look at me as she emptied the bins, pulling out bags and stuffing them in a larger one.

'To another home? Or gone-gone.'

'Gone-gone I'm afraid. Sorry.' She let the bin lid slam shut. The hollowed inside echoed like a drum through the hall. She hadn't bothered to wipe the bin over; it was streaked with water marks running down. That was the problem with working in a care home. You're always looking after people at the end of their lives and you just don't know when that might be. One minute they're telling you they love you and you were like the daughter they never had, and the next... they were being dragged out in a bag, too.

I stared at Granny, who'd followed me into work, thinking about her body in the ground and the one in front of me. She wasn't really here. Maybe she was just a memory I couldn't let go of, because if I did, I'd have no-one. She was looking over the shoulder of Jim who was doing a crossword puzzle, and she was shaking her head at his writing. Jim kept looking up at her, and then he put his head in his hands.

'Everything alright, Jim?' I knelt down next to him.

'D' you think people linger around after they die?'

'What makes you say that?'

'Well, I'm starting to think that maybe poor Gerry didn't make it out of here in the end like she wanted.'

'Really?'

'Or perhaps she's looking to swipe me crossword one last time before she goes, just to prove summat to me.' He wagged his pen like a teacher. 'She was an odd woman.'

'Some men don't know when to quit.' Granny rolled her eyes. 'As thick as two short planks.' She had no patience for old men. She had no patience for old people full stop, not even herself. 'I could give him a nudge, y' know, push him over to this side. Just say the word!'

'No!'

'No, what?' Jim was frowning at me.

I stared at him and then at Granny. 'We can't speak ill of the dead, Jim, no matter how hard they were to live with, yeah? She was in a lot of pain, that's why she was grumpy. Not her fault.'

There were a lot more empty chairs in the main sitting room. It felt more like a hall. They'd taken away the pictures of flowers on the walls, and the books in the bookcase and the clock. They'd been talking about decluttering, but they had taken the home out of care home.

Jim shrugged. 'Did I tell you who came to visit yesterday?'

'You did! Your sister came, didn't she?'

'She did! She brought my favourite. Shortbread! Want some? I'm Scottish y' know.'

'I'd love some.' I took the box. 'Uhhh... box is empty Jim.'

'See, dim as they come.' Granny raised her eyebrows. I shot her a look, hoping it would shut her up.

'Oh, sorry.' Jim took back the tin to look inside. 'D' you know who else is comin' today?'

'No, who else is coming?'

'Stonecloud Players!' He smiled, and Granny turned her back to me so I couldn't see her face. 'You ever seen 'em? They was proper popular around these parts, but they only do private gigs now 'cause they're all ancient like me.' He started laughing.

'Me gran used to play with them, I think.' But Granny was avoiding eye contact with me to confirm.

'Oh, what was her name?'

'Henrietta Saint.'

'Ooooh.' He smiled as if he was a cat who got the cream. 'Henrietta Saint. What a magnificent chest she had!'

'Jim!'

Granny span around with her face beaming and standing up as if she'd won a Grammy.

'Oh, and her voice! She sang Shirley Bassey better than Shirley Bassey herself! The lungs on her. I remember this time she sang *Baby, come and light my fire*.'

Granny's smile slipped and her eyes went wider than the widest sea.

'Did she ever tell you what happened?'

I shook me head.

'Almost took the whole place down with her pyrotechnics.' He slapped his leg twice. 'Curtains went up - woosh! And we all had to throw our beers at the stage, but then people were throwin' hard liquor and... Well, you can guess...'

'Was everyone alright?'

'Oh look, 'ere they are! That guy was there. He'll tell you I ain't makin' it up.'

'I didn't think you were.' When I turned behind me, there was Mr Post at the front door carrying an instrument case. I couldn't believe it. This was what Granny was telling me. I had been trying his door for days, ringing the bell. But like that morning, he never answered. But here he was, showing up at me front door.

'Mr Post!' I waved at him. He glanced up, but then back down again. I walked right up to him. 'Mr Post!' But he still wouldn't look at me. 'Thank you for coming to me granny's funeral. I know she'd have been glad you were there.'

'Pah!' Granny stood next to me. 'Couldn't care less! The man's a moron...' She put her hands on her hips.

'How did you know he was going to be 'ere?'

'Who you talkin' to?' Mr Post glanced around us.

'Oh, so I do exist!' I clapped. 'Well, good morning to you, too.'

'What d' you want?'

'I wanted to ask you for a favour.'

'Why should I do anything for you?' He put down his instrument case.

'Do it for me gran, then. Please!'

Around me, three other people younger than Mr Post were setting up with guitars and brass. Then a woman in her forties and in a bright red dress and feather boa came through the door.

'Is that who ended up replacing me?' Granny pointed. 'She's soooo... Good god! No wonder.'

'Look, Mr Post. I don't expect us to get along, but I know you're seeing me mum, and I know you care about her. So if you really cared about her, you'd help me see her.'

'Why? Why would I do that? So you can go abuse her some more?' He bent and opened up his case.

'No, I want to say sorry. I want to stop it. Please, Mr Post. Believe me. It wasn't me mum's fault. I know that now.'

He looked me up and down as if assessing me weight, as if assessing whether I'd fit into the slipper. 'I'll see what I can do.'

'Really? Ah, thank you! Thank you! I miss her a lot. And if I can just see her and convince her to take back her statement...'

'She ain't got long, y' know. So don't go messin' around.' He shuffled his music sheets together.

'What d'you mean?'

'End of the month.'

'What is?'

'Until she goes to court.' He shook his head as he stared up at me as if I was short of a brain cell or two. 'Thirty first.'

'Is that it? But that's so soon.'

He pulled out his trumpet and held it like a weapon. 'Go sit down.' He pointed to the chairs. 'We're 'bout to start.'

All the residents gathered in the sitting room and they started playing. Mr Post had lungs for the trumpet. It blasted through me like fanfare, as if I was being called in to see royalty. I only had twenty-six days. That was it. Twenty-six days to save me mum from being locked up for something she never did.

I had to walk out of the room because Granny was singing at the top of her lungs over the Shirley Bassey sing-a-like at the front, convinced that she could do a better job. So I left the sitting room, and I slumped down in the empty corridor, thinking about how Gerry used to pace it when she was waiting for a cigarette. She'd shout at me to hurry: 'Quick, it's almost midnight. I'm gunna turn into a pumpkin if I don't get out soon.'

4

24 DAYS UNTIL COUR

'I would go most anywhere to feel like I belong.'

Hercules

I would go anywhere for the Wright family. Even if that meant doing something I hated - camping. We'd spent all day at a LARP and all evening drinking ale around a fire. I felt more like Skyla Goode every day. When it came to finding out who burned down me house, the odds were against me but the gods were for me. Why else would Mr Post show up just when I needed to ask him something? Me wish in the tunnel must have come true. Granny's ghost wasn't lurking about for no reason. Destiny had been found because her part wasn't over. The gods were working to help me free me mum. And it was the gods who sent me the Wright family too, just when I needed them.

Liz and Clive had both raised their eyebrows when they overheard Ryder Cliftone (AKA Scott) asking Skyla if she wanted to share a 'shelter' with him. They turned in early to give us 'lovebirds' some time alone. I'd wrapped myself up to keep the mozzies from finding a way in. Scott was looking for gaps in the clouds to show me stars and tell me about how they were born. And I said maybe stars were the mozzie bites of space, which wasn't exactly romantic, but Scott laughed.

On our way to the tent, we spotted glow worms along the way. Little green lights, a sign, a message from beyond. I had planned to get real-close to him, but he got straight into his sleeping bag. I was cut off, chewing me nails and sweating. I took out a bottle of whisky. With each swig, we got closer. It was as if I'd unscrewed the cap off Scott, because his words started flowing out like he'd been letting them age in barrels.

'What d'you reckon? Does it look like me?' I held out the baby photograph I found in Dad's toolbox.

'Hard to tell in this light.' Scott squinted. 'Bring the torch closer.'

I put the torch light onto the baby photograph. 'Looks more like a boy, don't y' reckon? All that blue. People were still very traditional about things then.'

Scott shuffled over in his sleeping bag. 'Hmmm...' He shut one eye to focus. 'And you don't recognise anything in this photo? What about the handwriting?'

'It ain't me mum's. I forgot she does these funny e's that look a bit like eyes and they ain't here.'

A snore thundered through the air a few meters away, and I laughed. Then it happened again. Scott put his hands on his head and gazed up at the ceiling of the tent. 'Heaven help us.'

'Is that for real?'

'There's something about camping...' Scott sat up. 'Especially after a long day pretending to be king.'

'He seemed to be extra...' I was searching for the right word.

'Dickish today?'

'No, no, just tense?' I stared down at the baby photo in me

hands, running me fingers along the edges. 'As if something was bothering him.'

'The power goes to his head. Like he thinks he is some sort of Greek god! Did you see what he ordered Sophie to do? He made her put up all the staging on one side of the field and then halfway through, made her move it.'

'Gees, bet she was pissed.' Scott showed no signs or hints about him and Sophie. Did they used to be something? Did he have feelings for her? Before Rory, I went out with a guy who couldn't keep his eyes off other girls. Then I found out he started seeing me friend Flora behind me back, and I lost two people that day.

'I don't think he's ever forgiven her for trying to overthrow him ages ago...' Scott picked up the glass bottle of whisky. The snoring picked up speed, followed by some rustling and a zip, up and down.

'What was that?'

'Probably nothing.' Scott put down the bottle and lay down on his mat. 'We should go to sleep.'

I didn't want him to go to sleep yet. I needed more time, more chances to get close to him. 'I'm gunna have a look. I can hear voices. Maybe it's another coo. Didn't you say sometimes game stuff happens at night?'

'Yeah, but not this time of night...'

I wiggled out of me sleeping bag. The damp was already rising from the ground. 'Oh, come on. Let's go have a look!'

'Nah I'm good.' He turned away from me. A wind flapped the tents like flexing muscles.

I sighed and put on me boots. 'Well, at least your dad would be happy if I intercepted a coup against him.'

I unzipped our tent slowly, so nobody would hear. The inside was getting wet. The opening flap gave me a good lick as I got out. I followed the voices. A small, red glow bobbed a few metres away, and I headed towards it. Two people were getting hot and heavy up against a tree. Maybe if I threw myself on Scott like this, we'd be like these two. But I was still trying to play it cool. How did they figured it out? Who took the first leap?

Me eyes adjusted to the dark. It was Liz, Scott's mum, being pushed up against the tree. But it wasn't Clive who was on her. I backed away, using Scott's dad snoring as a guide back to the tent. I don't remember getting in, but Scott had his back to me as I sat on me sleeping bag, legs crossed, waiting. Should I say something? Did I see what I thought I saw? It didn't make no sense.

'Did she see you?' Scott mumbled without turning to face me.

'No.' I turned on me torch. 'What are you wearing?' Scott had a headband pushed down around his eyes and ears, as if he wanted to see or hear no evil.

'Wanted to sleep in.' He turned and pushed it up onto his brow. 'It keeps the light out.'

'How long has it been goin' on?'

'The sweatband?'

'No, your mum and the Knight.'

'A while.' He took the torch off me and turned it off.

'Y' know about it? Is it part of the game?'

'What do you think...' The silhouette of him turned away.

'Your poor dad. Does he know?'

Scott shook his head and sighed. I didn't need the torch to see him now. Scott seemed to glow, as if out of this world, like he'd had a strength hidden inside of him that just needed a little help to come out.

'But she knows that y' know?'

He nodded. 'Do you think I should tell him? She says it won't last long. That it's just a passion thing. Not a love thing.'

'She talks to you about it?'

'She tells me a lot of stuff. Says I'm the only one she can speak to. She gets me to cover up for her too.'

'Why d'you do it?'

'She just needs to get it out of her system. No point breaking up an entire family over it, if it means nothing.'

Maybe he was right. Why risk it? Why break up the family over something that could go away on its own? There'd be no more LARPs, no more ranking family dinners, no more house with late night swimming. No more Friday night pedicures and movies. What would happen to Scott? What would happen to me?

'I guess all families have their thing.' I took a swig of the whisky. The darkness gave me courage too.

'Yeah.' He propped himself up on one elbow. 'I'm so glad you're here, Scarlett.'

'You are?'

'Of course.' He shuffled closer and I gulped. 'Now I don't feel like the only dumb one.'

'Oi!' I threw the bottle cap at him and he caught it.

'Aye, watch it.'

'Would you ever do that? Cheat?' I held me breath.

'Hell no!' He took the bottle from me. Me shoulders relaxed. 'Can't imagine why she would risk hurting people like that.' He shook his head and took a swig. 'They are still way better than some carers I used to have. Some parents too.'

'Do you remember your biological family?'

'Only me mum. She was a bit like your mum. Just everything worked against her.'

'Where is she now?' I spoke quietly, scared that I might spook him and he'd stop speaking.

Scott lay back on to the ground and gazed up as if he could see the night sky through the tent. He sighed again. 'I like to imagine that she's on some remote tropical island somewhere, with a cocktail and a smile. She always told me stories before bed, and the way she told them, they remind me of you.'

'Me?'

'Yeah, you get really Italian with your hands.'

'Italian?'

'You're always throwing them around like this...' Scott threw his arms around like he was throwing lightning bolts.

'I do not!' I laughed. Me moment had come. I leaned over to hit him as if we were kids in the playground, and he kept mocking me. He grabbed me arms and pulled me down towards him. Me heart was growing, going from zero to hero, and the gods were here with me, rooting me on, and I was thanking them that Granny wasn't ruining it for me. I wanted to grab him and kiss him, quick and hard, but he leaned up, and both our heads smacked together.

'Ow!' He grabbed his head.

'Ah, smooth.' I squinted and rubbed me forehead. 'I'm such an idiot, I'm so sorry. I've always been clumsy. I blame the whisky.'

His face crunched together in pain. 'It can be our thing, like Hercules and Pegasus. They headbutt when they see each other.'

'So you *do* like kids' films!'

'Only the best ones.' And me heart melted all the way. Maybe he was me perfect match. He put both hands on the side of me face, and brought me towards him so our foreheads touched. 'Headbutt.' He smiled, lips together. Scott and I were the same. Divorced from our own bloodline, holding on to the one family unit we could. It was like looking into a reflection pool.

'Hold on.' I pulled back. 'Do y' know your real dad?'

'No, why?'

I glanced at the photo on the floor of the tent, and then at Scott. 'Were you born around here? You don't think we could be related...'

'No way, that's crazy.' He pulled me towards him again, as if for a kiss.

'Is it?' I pushed him away. 'Sorry, I can't...'

'What?'

'I should clean me teeth again.' I crawled away. 'I'm not sure I did a good enough job.'

'Scarlett... We're not! We can't be... This is ridiculous.'

I got out of the tent with me wash-bag to escape. I cleaned me teeth until the gums started bleeding, until I was sure that Scott would give up and go to sleep. Because the feeling had struck me, bolted me upright, like a eureka moment.

Maybe we were related?

Maybe that was why I felt this draw to him? There was this pull that felt out of this world. Maybe he was hiding it from me because he was looking for revenge on me family, on me dad, on me? Maybe he was the one who set fire to the house? If there was one thing I knew about gods and myths and Greeks, it was that there was always tragedy and a bit of incest.

5

21 DAYS UNTIL COURT

'I didn't come all this way to see you quit.'

Cars

I went to find Dad. I needed to know for sure if I had a sibling. And I needed to know if it was Scott. Dad was an abandoned car, rusting next to the train tracks - all shell and no engine. Dad sat on the concrete floor with a wall holding up his back, his gaze on the train-line. Clouds above him plumed like exhaust smoke. Fat pigeons with manky legs circled him. Granny said he'd be here, but she didn't say he'd be a sad sack of broken parts. But I needed answers, for Mum, for Scott, for me, and the buck stopped with him.

'What you doin' 'ere, Scar?' He didn't lift his head to look at me.

'What *you* doing here, Dad?'

'Rememberin'.' His eyes flickered on a little, as if I'd tried the ignition.

'Remembering what?'

'Your Mum and I met 'ere at this train station. Y' know that?' He didn't see me shaking me head. 'She had these huge hoop earrin's. Like a ring toss they were. She was about to start her shift when she got one...' He spluttered. A smell like petrol wafted from him, fuelling up on the wrong stuff. 'She got stuck, on the door... and I had to...' He laughed until it went silent.

Granny stood to the side. I raised me eyebrows at her, but she only shrugged. 'Dad? Dad?'

'Your Mum was a right old...' He shook his head and wiped his eye and took a deep breath.

'Dad, I wanted to ask you summat.' I knelt down.

'Y' see that there.' He pointed to a bit of scrap metal on the side of the tracks. 'That there is a part of a Chevvy. Guess how I know that?'

'How?'

'Me pops. Used to quiz me for hours. Gave me parts and I had to tell him what car it came from. And y' know what he did to me if I got it wrong?'

'What?'

'No, no, no I won't tell you.' He shook his finger and poked the ground with it. 'I won't. It's a disease.'

Granny was staring down at the train track as if bored with the whole thing. I don't remember much about gramps. All I can remember from him is in pictures. A bloke with tattoos and a pipe.

'Dad? Did you have another kid?'

'Don't bother.' Granny paced up and down.

Dad muttered. 'It's better to know nothing. It's better to hide in the dark. I wasn't found in the dark.'

Granny shook her head, walked up to Dad, and stared down at him. 'It's no good. I've seen it before. There ain't no way you gunna get sense out of him.'

'But I have to try. I have to know who it is. Dad? Do I have a brother or sister I don't know about?'

'Why? What's it to do with you?! None of your business!' He shook a pigeon away from his leg.

'Business?'

'Y' know, I don't know why I expected more from you.' Granny tutted even though Dad couldn't hear her. 'Me sister always said you were bad seed. Maybe she was right...'

'Better off without me.' Dad closed his eyes. 'You too for that matter. He should have finished me off. Like this pigeon here. A pest. Can't live with a leg like that. Can't provide for its little birdies. Practically beggin'. Better if we helped it out of its misery.' Dad pushed the pigeon into the tracks, but it flew off.

'So I *do* have a brother or sister?'

'Don't know which. Your Granny might know. But she's dead.'

'Granny?' I turned to look at her, but she was walking away.

'Stupid Jason, idiot Jason, useless Jason...' Dad muttered imitating a lady's voice, and then he laughed. 'Her hair! D'you remember when she accidentally dyed it orange? Like a traffic cone!' He slapped his leg.

'I thought she looked more like Beaker from The Muppets.' I smiled.

Granny twirled around. 'I thought I pulled it off, actually.'

' 'ere yeah.' Dad smiled, closed his eyes, and nodded off for a second. 'Saints. All a bunch of muppets, aren't we?'

'Speak for yourself!' Granny put her hands on her hips. 'I could have been famous.'

'We have our moments.' I rolled me eyes and stood up.

Dad nodded and dropped his head. 'I always knew I'd be a terrible dad.'

And it was as if the car door had just swung open and hit me. I didn't want to do this. I didn't want to be the one that had to get this car moving. It was always me who had to push, try. But I was done chasing after something that didn't exist. I was done.

'You know, Dad, it ain't hard. If I had a kid, I'd never let them go. I'd fight for them with everything in me because I would never, for a single second, let them think they weren't wanted.'

'Not that simple. I...'

'Scarlett.' Granny shook her head.

'I didn't know what I'd been made in to.' Dad stared down at his hands. 'Whose blood did I have? Who is on me hands?'

'I think we should go now.' Granny fanned her hand in the air.

'Blood?' I knelt down again, leaned closer to dad. 'Did you set the fire? To the house? For insurance? Is that what this is about?'

'Don't be so stupid.' He tutted and rolled his eyes like Granny.

'No, you're the stupid one! You're always telling me, telling people to fight, to get up and get back in the ring, no matter what. You're always going on about facing fears, yourself, but... You're a hypocrite. You've done nothing but run away your whole life.'

'I changed, I did...' He nodded and stared at the tracks.

'So what d' you call this?' I pointed at him.

'You don't understand.' He shook his head as if looking for the loose screws. 'Some things can't be fixed or fought.'

'You can try. Don't you want to be the hero who keeps going no matter what?'

'Yous in a fantasy land, Scar! Get real. Stop watchin' all those stupid elf films. Me life is the stuff villains are made of.' His face brewed darkness. 'Heroes have money and shit, and good up-bringings. But we... I mean, look at us.' He grabbed me wrists and brought me close to his face. 'We have nothing. No house. No family. No life. No-one who cares. They all go, all of 'em, sooner or later. Nobody sticks around.'

I pulled away from his grip. 'No Dad, you have no-one. I have people who care, people who are trying to save our house.'

He laughed. 'What a joke. They usin' you. You're a Saint,

Scar. Your grave's been carved. Some day you'll figure that out. Nobody sticks around. They all leave. You ain't no different.'

'I ain't no Saint! I don't just leave when things get tough. I stick it out.'

'Yeah, even if it means getting walked all over.' He grunted and turned away.

Granny had disappeared too, leaving us all alone. No-one around at all. A train plummeted through the station, not stopping. When it left, it echoed through, leaving a void behind. Dad had stopped talking, stopped trying. He'd never said much about anything before, but drink had made it pool out of him, black like an oil spill. And I turned away from him and abandoned him on the platform. I left him to rust away, left him open to the elements for his self-punishment, just like the Saints before me, and the Saints to come.

6

20 DAYS UNTIL COURT

'After all, you can't lose what you never lost.'

Mary Poppins

You feel like a prisoner when you visit one, a proper-criminal. But maybe I was? Mum wouldn't have been in prison if it wasn't for me. I pushed her over the edge. When I got there, they asked me to hold up me arms as they patted me down, to open me mouth so they could check inside. Maybe I should tell them. Confess. *I* should be locked up, not me mum. I was the guilty one.

At Granny's funeral, I had both lost and found me mum. But can you lose what you never had? She wasn't there for me most of me life. She couldn't be. But when she had confessed to burning down our house so we could get it back, she showed me she could be me mum, but it was at the cost of losing her, too.

The visiting hall was like an airport waiting area. It was like be surrounded by people afraid of flying or excited to welcome people back. A woman with long fingernails tapped the table in front of her. A man stepped in time. A family talked low, like far off engines. They were all focused on the doors. But me eyes had spotted someone else arriving, using a different door than the rest of us.

'What you doing here?' I spoke out of the corner of me mouth.

'I want to see how she's doing.' Gran sat at one of the round tables, her back as straight up as a pole. 'Mighty curious.'

I rolled me eyes and sat down on a stool, crossing me arms. 'Still not gunna tell me if I have a brother or a sister?'

'I told you, I don't know...' She dismissed me with her hand. 'Could be a boyish girl or a girlish boy.'

I wasn't in the mood for her today. She wasn't helpful. I had no idea if Scott was related or if I was paranoid. I got up and walked to the shop.

'What can I get you?' The server was dressed in blue, like a flight attendant.

'Oh, I dunno...' I scanned the shelves.

'You can get as much as you like.' She rearranged chewing gum on the counter. 'It's a great icebreaker if you're feeling nervous.'

'How can you tell?' I smiled. 'Will it help her forgive me?'

'Who can stay mad when they have a mouthful of chocolate? Whose it for?'

'It's me mum.'

'And what does she like?'

'I don't think you have it.' I hopped up and down to see.

'Might have some tucked away, out back.' She pointed to the side door. 'What is it?'

When the prisoners started coming out, I had me head down, cleaning the table with me sleeve. Everyone stood up, and there were hugs and kisses and smiles. Mum came out wearing an orange bib over her blue jumper. I gulped and glanced down at the five packets of chocolate I bought, and the sandwich, and the Diet Coke, and the crisps. It wasn't enough. There would never be enough.

'Mum!' I smiled, but it split me dry lips.

'Scarlett!' She opened up her arms. 'Give me a hug. I can't believe you came. I never thought you'd forgive me. Never in a million years...' Bony shoulders stuck out of her. She had less weight on, and I wondered if she'd lost something more.

'She shouldn't of.' Granny crossed her arms.

'Forgive you?' I was confused.

'Oh.' Mum grabbed the sides of her face. 'You bought my favourite. Ferrero Rocher!'

'And a sandwich with crisps. So you can make a crisp sandwich.'

'Oh, my favourite!'

'Do you have everything you need? Toothbrush, books? Music? Does it get cold?'

'I'm fine. It's all fine. Don't worry. You're always thinking of me, aren't you?'

Granny snorted. 'Girl had no choice, you wacko!'

I turned to give Gran a glare.

'What is it?' Mum leaned over the table to hold me hand.

'Nothing, nothing.' I stared at her hand holding mine, and I grabbed hers even tighter.

'Weather bad?'

'Raining. Got stuck behind a tractor on the way here. Got me umbrella though! Mary Poppins back to save the day.' Mum took her hand away from me, but I reached back over the table for her. 'Mum, I'm so sorry. This is all me fault.' I swallowed down the lump in me throat. 'I didn't mean what I said at the church. It was a hard day and confusing and I didn't want to...'

'Shhhhh sssshhh.' She glanced from side to side.

'I know you didn't do it.'

'What do you mean?'

'Quit it Mum. I got a note from the *actual* person who did it.'

Granny leaned in. 'Oh, I want to hear what she has to say to this.'

Mum looked at the spot where Granny was sitting and squinted.

'Mum?'

'I can't talk about this, Scarlett.' She glanced around her again as if she was smuggling something through security. 'We're talking about... shrinking your jumper, aren't we?' She raised her eyebrows and nodded her head towards the prison officers.

'Uhhh, sure. Me jumper.'

'Well, I'm your Mum.' She nodded as if reminding herself of this, and opened the packet of crisps. 'And I've not been a very good one. I know that. I've not been able to give you a good jumper. And I just wanted to help you get a new jumper. I may not have been the one to ruin it, but I didn't do much to make sure it was looked after.'

'But, it's too... expensive.' I raised me eyebrows.

She had opened up the sandwich and started layering the crisps inside. 'Granted, I'll have to put in some extra hours to pay for it, but that's what mums do.'

'Why not Dad? He should pay for it, not you.'

' 'cause you need him around.' She pushed the sandwich together and took a bite.

'He's not around right now. He's drinking himself into a coma.'

Mum just stared at me, chewing. Her nostrils flared. She wasn't going to answer.

I crossed me arms. 'I don't get why you're in here when you haven't been proved guilty yet.'

She shrugged and bit through a Ferrero Rocher before she'd

finished her sandwich. 'You only get bail if you run a red light or steal or smuggle birds or something.' She flashed her gaze at me, a spark of rebellion inside.

'Mum, were you and Mr Post...'

'What?' She held out the box and offered me a chocolate. 'Business partners? I helped him out from time to time. Just when things got tough, you know? I was good at looking after them. Was a bit like therapy for me.'

'See, I knew it!' Granny hit the table. 'She deserves to be locked up!'

'You know what, Scarlett?' Mum gazed at the spot granny was sitting. 'You have this weird energy around you.'

'What do you mean?'

'Like every now and again, it sort of flares up like an explosion. And I can almost hear it, but it's so far away from me...'

'She's always been off her rocker, this one.' Granny got up and moved to the other side.

'There it goes again. To your right.' Mum pointed directly at Granny, who gave stuck out her tongue at her. Mum sighed, crossed her legs and arms and sat back. 'I *sound* crazy, don't I?'

'You can't be in 'ere.' I shook me head. 'It's not good for you.'

'It's not for long, hun...' She took another bite of her sandwich.

'But you'll go to prison for a *long* time Mum, don't you get that? I feel you don't understand how serious this is.'

'I do, I do...' She had her mouth full. 'It's just...'

'You don't want to come out, d' you? You'd rather stay stuck in here than see me. I guess prison is an easier excuse for you.'

'That's not fair, Scarlett. It's not about you. I'm doing it for me too.'

'For you?'

'Nothing new there.' Granny snorted. 'She's always been selfish. All about number one.'

'That's rich, coming from you.' I stared at Granny.

'Huh?' Mum glared at me. 'My lawyers are going to get me out of prison and into a hospital. I could finally get the help I need and be in a safe place.'

'How?'

'They think I have good evidence to show that I need some help, and that I wasn't in my right mind, which... Well, you know how I've not been right ever since that woman jumped in front of my train.'

'Understatement of the century.' Gran picked her fingers.

I nodded, and Mum glanced at where Granny was sitting as she ate the last piece of her sandwich. I sighed because it felt somewhere at some point I had lost something again. 'So you're not doing it so we can get our... me jumper back?'

'Can't it be both? I never dealt with it, right? I see her face all the time. In here, I've figured out why.'

Mum had a look in her eye. One that she used to get when I was a kid, when I would put on me Mary Poppins' hat and pick up me umbrella. Mum believed her problems started because of this suicide. So if she could do something about it, she'd be better. But she didn't remember that it all went downhill before that. Mum was already falling off. This just knocked her to the ground.

'Why?'

'It's because I had seen her before. I *had* seen that face before, and it wasn't mine.'

'Are you sure it's the same person, Mum?'

'Why?'

' 'cause you've also said it was one of the neighbours, or the woman from that morning show, and the bus driver you used to know. You've also said that it was a long-lost cousin and a lady from Lidl.'

She sighed. 'What's it like to have a psycho for a mum?'

I smiled and dropped me shoulders. It must be so hard for her. 'I wouldn't trade it.'

Our time was up. Guards were calling. The gates opened. Time for her to board the plane. People were getting up from the table, kissing, hugging. I completely forgot what I wanted to ask her, what else I had wanted to say. Mum got up, too. I walked over to her and hugged her. I didn't let go because it might be the last time. If I kept holding her, maybe it would stop her from falling apart completely, maybe she'd change her mind and decide she could get better, that I could make her better.

'Oh, don't cry, Scarlett.' Mum squeezed me tighter. 'It'll be OK.'

'It's never been OK.' I sniffed. 'No house is worth losing a Mum, y' know.'

'But I'm already so lost, darling. You know that. I want to be different, better, for you.' She let me go. 'It's never too late, is it? Come back to see me, won't you?'

I nodded as she walked away to join the queue of prisoners waving at their families. The room became quiet, like we were seeing people off who might never come back.

Was it too late? I wasn't a kid anymore. I'd never been a kid with her. But that wasn't her fault. 'Mum, who was it?!' I shouted. 'Whose face was it?'

She turned around, her eyes wide. 'She was the same woman who'd come to the door asking for your dad.'

'What?'

'She had a kid with her, too.'

'A boy or girl?'

She shrugged. 'Dunno. To hard to tell. But I lied. Said he didn't live there!' She was walking forward, bit by bit as people were being led away. 'It's my fault what happened to her. We could have been there for her. She must have...'

'It's not!' I shook me head. 'It's Dad's.'

She blew me a kiss before being put back into cuffs. It wasn't a coincidence that me mum thought she killed the mother of me dad's kid. A kid no-one had met. Did I believe her, or was she just seeing her own guilt hit the train? The guilt of having turned her away, having lied to her. Maybe this was why me mum wanted to plead guilty. She thought she deserved to go to prison. All because of the woman she hit. Me mum never knew what was best for her. I did. Mary Poppins did. We always knew. And I knew I had to find the actual person who set fire to me house before me mum turned herself into a martyr.

7

16 DAYS UNTIL COURT

'Sometimes anger can help you survive.'

Storm, X-men

Rubi's mum

Hi Scarlett,

urgently need your help!

Please come ASAP!

I legged-it over to Rubi's in the morning. The sky was a tired-grey, the colour of a once-white t-shirt that had gone through too much. A storm was on the way. The trees were already waving it in. The storm was named Jason, and that couldn't be no coincidence. It was a bad omen to have a storm named after your dad. There's something about storms that makes people lose their shit, turns them into mutants, and me dad was no exception. We could only watch to see what the storm would bring.

I was so knackered from me evening shift I tripped over me

foot on the way. There was that earthy, lingering smell like yesterday's tea. I heard Dad's slurred-shouting before I got to the B&B. A group of people stood around the bus: Rubi, her parents, Kai, and even Granny. They were all wearing rainbow hats and holding flags - apart from Granny. Me dad stood facing them, wearing shorts, a bare chest and a face that was brewing.

'I helped you build this whole damn stupid place!' Me dad threw his arms up.

'Yes, and we're so grateful, honestly.' Rubi's mum had her arms out as if calming a horse. 'The man who did that isn't the one shouting at us right now.'

'You're scaring our guests away.' Rubi's dad marched forward.

'That ain't me. You're haunted!' Dad laughed. 'It's her!' He was pointing at Granny, who was dressed in a pink silk ballgown.

'We've been getting bad reviews for weeks. We just can't afford to keep you here, Jason. You'll drag us all down with you!'

'You always thought you was better than me, didn't you?' Dad's lipped curled. 'And you...' He pointed at Rubi as if striking a bolt in the air. 'This was your doing, wasn't it? Me daughter put you up to this?'

'Huh?' Rubi turned to Kai next to her.

'What the hell's going on?' I stepped in.

Dad span around on his heel like a tornado. 'You!' His hand pointed to me. 'This is all your fault. Your the one who chased Kirsten away. She never would've lost that babber if you hadn't of brought that piece of dirt into our lives. She tried so hard with you....'

'He makes a good point.' Granny swished her dress.

'Shut up muver!' Dad held onto his head.

'Muver?' I glared at Granny. A distant rumble travelled through the air.

Rubi adjusted her hat. 'He thinks your Gran is haunting the house. He keeps yelling at her.'

'Oh.'

I stared at Granny and then back at Dad. I wanted them both to clear off. I didn't have time for their pity parade. I needed to go to the library to look at birth records or something. But I had nothing to work with because they wouldn't give up one iota of information to narrow it down. The Saints were always making things worse.

'Look.' Rubi sighed. 'We can help you find somewhere else to park up, maybe? I'm sure there are places...'

'I know some. I can take you.' Kai held on to Rubi's hand and nodded, and I stared, because Rubi and I didn't hold hands.

'I don't need your help! I don't want help from a bunch of fairies.' Dad jabbed his finger in the air towards them like a sword.

'What the hell does that mean?!' Rubi's dad turned red. 'You better not be referring to my daughter.'

'Right, that's it! You're done.' Rubi's mum drew her finger across her neck. 'I'm calling the police.'

'What you talking about?' I turned to Dad, then Rubi, and then Kai.

'Oh, you didn't know, Scar?' Dad leaned forward to slap both his legs. He stood up straight and pointed at Rubi. 'She's a lesbian! Her and Kai are an *item*. Found them kissing after one of me lessons.'

'Well, I didn't know that!' Granny gazed at the sky.

Kai closed the gap between her and Rubi, stepping forward. 'I'm sorry we shocked you, we didn't...'

'Don't say sorry!' Rubi's mum put her arm around Rubi's shoulder. 'You don't have to be sorry for anything.'

I'd known Rubi since I was five. We used to talk about marrying a prince. We'd kiss her doll called Herman the German, we played Beauty and the Beast, we'd stare at posters of

233

Jim Morrison together and make collages of his face. 'She can't be.' I shook me head. 'She likes boys...'

'Not no more.' Dad threw his t-shirt over his shoulder. 'She...'

'You are not allowed to speak about my daughter!' Rubi's dad squared up to mine. 'We are proud of her.'

'Well, lucky you! More than I can say about mine,' said Dad. 'Oh wait, I guess I don't have a daughter as she's disowned me. Adopted another family.'

'Scarlett's still here.' Kai cleared her throat and let go of Rubi's hand. 'She wouldn't be here if she had left. Isn't that right, Scarlett?' She cleared her throat again and stared at me, but I couldn't answer. 'I'm here too. We all are, but...'

'I don't need your pity.' Dad paced the gravelled parking lot.

'It's not pity.' Kai cleared her throat again and looked at her feet. 'It's...'

'I know pity parades when I see one. Bunch of morons.' Dad stormed off and zig-zagged away towards the bus.

Guilt. Kai was trying not to say it. She felt guilty, and she should. She'd turned our whole lives upside down and she wouldn't do nothing about it. She had ruined everything. She had done us all in by ruling it as not arson. Our house, me dad, Rubi, me... It was like she'd taken away parts of me life. Rubi stared at me. Her eyes glistened as I stared back, waiting for what was being said to register in me brain or for her to deny it. It was as if I'd been struck by lightning, with me hair on end from the shock of it.

'Scarlett?' Rubi walked towards me. 'I'm sorry. I tried to tell you, but...'

'When? When did you try to tell me?'

'In the tunnel. But...'

The bus jolted backwards and stumbled in and out of gear. 'He's not sober enough to drive!'

'I'll drive him.' Kai's voice shook as she ran towards the bus.

And I hated her. I hated how she ran, how she just rolled in out of nowhere, how the rainbow-coloured hat fell to one side of her head, a hat that I should of been wearing. I turned to Rubi, lost in the mess of stuff that had just stormed into me head.

'Why? Why would you not tell me? Who do you think I am? Do you think I would take it bad?'

'I wasn't sure. You were just so...'

'And you and Kai? How long?'

'A week... I only just told my parents.'

'Well, I guess we weren't as good as friends as I thought we were.'

'What does that mean?'

'I barely see you anymore. It's always Kai. Now I know why!'

'You're jealous?'

'You weren't trying to help me at all, then? You were just trying to get closer to her!' I pointed to Kai on the bus. The engine revved up.

'You know what Scarlett, you're right. We clearly aren't that good a friends, because when I told my parents, they were *happy* for me. So happy for me they actually threw me a party. They didn't make it all about themselves.'

'What?'

'All you can do is talk about you, and Scott, and your mum, and the fire. You're obsessed. If you'd have taken any interest in me life, you'd probably of found out sooner. But whatever...'

'Ouch!' Granny twirled. It started to rain. A few drops to start, but heavy, the sort that soaks you in no time.

'I'm going inside to have some cake.' Rubi turned away. 'Because I deserve it. It's not every day that you come out, and I will not let you rain on my parade.'

'You can't blame the rain on me!' I shouted after her, but she wasn't listening. 'This ain't me fault!'

I'd lost so many friends when they all went to university. They all moved away. Got left out and left behind. I never believed I'd lose Rubi because she was still in Stonecloud. But when she walked away, I remembered the time her family took me to Disneyland when we were kids. It was so long ago. We were both obsessed with meeting Mickey Mouse, wearing our headbands with black mouse ears on them. Rubi was feeling sick because she got overexcited, and I squealed when I spotted Micky from the queue of *It's a Small World*. Micky went around the back of a gate and then took off his head. I screamed. There was a bald man inside. I felt betrayed. Lied to. Afraid. It was a loss I couldn't even figure out. Me favourite thing in the entire world didn't exist, it was just an actor. A person I didn't know.

I watched the bus back out of the driveway. Kai stared at me out of the corner of her eye. Her head bowed. She put her hand up in a slow wave as she took Dad some place where he wouldn't bother anyone.

Granny walked towards me as I stared up into the rain that was soaking me t-shirt until it was see-through. Her ballgown was bone-dry. 'Don't I look fabulous? D' you think Rubi will have me at her party?' Lightning broke across the sky, followed by a rumble so close that it set a car alarm off. Someone or something got hit. 'Great thing about being dead is I can't get rained on. But for you...' She handed over me Mary-Poppins' umbrella. I took it from her. Why she was being nice to me? Did I know anyone at all?

'Are you really me gran?'

'What you talkin' about? Course I am, you daft cow.'

'So you're haunting Dad too?' I didn't see the point of putting up me umbrella.

'Hauntin's a bit of a strong word... I'm tryin' to help.' The rain got harder.

'Why? He's the reason me mum's in prison, the reason she's lost it. He pushed her over the edge. He's the reason this kid of his might be out to get us. Everything that's happened is his fault.' I wiped the water off me face.

'He's me boy. He's not all bad, y' know. What happened to him... it was my fault, really.'

'What?!' I had to shout over more thunder.

'It's complicated.'

'So? So what!' I yelled through the sound of the rain pelting it down on the cars in the driveway. I used me umbrella to point at her. 'You're dead! What does it matter to you?'

'It does matter to me. I don't want you thinkin'... It's just... It's the sort of thing that breaks a family. And it broke ours. Broke your dad. You're always helpin' your mum. You're always feeling sorry for her, acting like she's helpless. But your dad's got problems too.'

'What problems? Don't see nothing or hear nothing about no problems.'

'Then I'll tell you. No more hiding stuff. Just the truth. Think you can handle it?'

And on cue, lightning bolted across the sky as if Granny and I had summoned something, opened up hell or cracked opened the heavens. I was fed-up of having to second guess the past, having to figure out what the hell happened to the Saints and why we'd ended up like this. Maybe now I'd get some answers.

8

15 DAYS UNTIL COURT

'Sir said we're diggin' to build some character.'

Holes

Granny told me to meet her on the Severn Bridge because she was going to do some explaining. She was going to fill in some holes for me, because she wanted to save dad. Nobody thinks they got holes in their story. Not until someone comes along to fill them. But I had been falling into holes for weeks now. From the brother I didn't know about, to the uncle who died as a kid, to whatever Granny was covering up about the past, about Mr Post, Dad...

The bridge was a skeleton of white and grey, stretching itself along the horizon. Granny was walking ahead of me, stooped. When she started haunting me, she looked younger, like I had seen her in photos. But on the bridge, she was as I remembered her, as if her body couldn't handle the weight of everything.

'Why did you take me all the way out here?'

'I got me reasons.' She tossed her head. 'Y' see down there?'

She pointed to a bit of land under a red cliff that was topped with a grey layer. It wasn't a beach. It was grass and mud and rocks, merging into the brown lapping of the river. A blanket grey sky laid out above.

'Your Gramps had this metal detector. Used to come 'ere with your dad every Sunday. He was obsessed with finding treasure. Absolutely obsessed. He thought that one day, he'd get filthy rich.'

'Bit of a dreamer Gramps was, then?'

I could almost see it. Dad and Gramps scanning the ground, picking things up and then tossing them away. I could almost see a boy and a man, swinging their rods in rhythm together, like divining rods, counting down to their next discovery.

'Oh, your Gramps had *it*, whatever it was. I've seen him pull off miracles. He had this way of making you feel as if...' She looked up at the sky. 'It was as if he fed off the moon and the stars and slept on the wind. He had a voice that turned into a melody that people would almost dance to and they'd follow him into whatever mad scheme he had next. He once lifted a car right off his friend, y' know that?'

'Seriously?' I followed her as she wandered.

'The jack failed, and the car fell on top of Barry's chest. He lifted it off him to get him out.'

'What's that got to do with Dad?'

'I want to make sure you get the whole picture. The good and the bad. It don't matter whether you change your name to Miss Piggy, you've still got Saint carved into you. And you've got your dad in you whether you like it or not. We all do. We all have bits of the past, getting down in our business.'

'Like you now.' I picked up a rock and threw it into the river.

'Yeah and you got me in you, too.' She snorted.

'Oh god! Say it ain't so.'

'You've got me chest... great knockers.' She honked her boobs and gave a joker-smile.

'Gran! Be serious.'

'I am!' She stood upright. 'Be grateful you didn't get your mother's ironin' board!'

I rolled me eyes.

'But you've also got your Gramps in you.' She shook her head. 'And that's...'

'I do?' There was a chill in the breeze, and so I hugged me arms around me.

'Yeah, head in the clouds, and you just can't stop digging either... You never met him, not really. He was brave and courageous. He was strong and commandin'. But there'd be days when he woke up and I could see it right away - this sort of gapin' hole that would open up inside of him. Like a valley in his stare. I could never fill it. Nor could your dad. That's when we'd lose him. Your Gramps would go out for hours with your dad, forcin' him to dig and dig and dig. Rain and snow.' Granny was animated, acting out the weather. 'On bad days, I'd go out the back garden and find him digging up the lawn, swearin' there was a faint signal. Holes with ladders down 'em. As if he were trying to dig to the centre of the earth. And some days they'd find things. Some days your dad would come back, a bouncin' little boy, 'til he almost hit the sky. They'd find a watch or a coin. Your Gramps would hoist him up on his shoulders and carry him like a champion.'

'Sounds...'

'Then sometimes he'd come back with a bruise, with mud all over him. Your dad would say he fell. But I knew it was 'cause he'd fallen into that hole. The one in your grampa.'

'He hit him?'

She wasn't listening to me. She'd launched into storytelling mode, and I was to be her audience. 'And then poof!'

'Gramps disappeared?'

She nodded. Granny was right. I didn't know me gramps. Dad never talked about him. Granny only ever talked about his adventures on boats and rigs and the time Gramps bred horses for betting on. I only had stories and pictures of an old man who looked a like a Santa you wouldn't wanna mess with.

'For how long?'

'A year.'

'Where did he go?'

Granny shrugged, and leaned on the railings. 'Off chasin' rainbows probably, or holes.'

'That's when you and Mr Post had...'

'Oh, it was delicious. If you're ever miserable with a man, have an affair. Nothing like it!' She grinned.

'Gran!'

'So shoot me! I thought your Gramps was gone for good. Part of me thought he'd died...' She walked away again, and I followed.

'What happened when he came back?'

'Your Gramps didn't care whose baby it was. He promised he'd stop diggin'. He promised he would stay at home and stop chasing wild dreams. The holes in the garden filled with water, like ponds 'cause even though he stopped digging, he never filled 'em in.'

Granny's gaze faded, seeing nothing around me, and her hands came together in knots. But I didn't want to say nothing to bring her back because I could see she was having to go some-where, having to relive something that no one should have to live through once.

'Your dad left the back door open one day.' She sighed and gazed up and away from me. 'I asked him to keep an eye on his brother.'

'What d'you mean?'

'Like I said, Scarlett. There are things that break or make a family. And there are things that make or break a person. This broke all of us. Forever.' Granny grabbed at her chest. She stood upright as if she was about to sing an anthem. 'I found me little boy, face down in the water. Face down in one of the holes in the garden.'

It made so much sense now. I had seen people stare at us in the village, whisper, avoid us, and I didn't know why. Where we live, rumours grow with the blackberries, leaving you with stained fingers if you pluck them. Ever since I was a kid, this one had stained me family. 'But Mr Post said it was Gramp's fault.'

Granny shook her head. 'We told people he died fallin' down the stairs. We didn't want people... It wasn't his fault. It was mine. I should of been the one watchin'. Your dad, he was just a little boy too, see? And he was fallin', and I couldn't dig him out. I'm not sure your dad ever got out of his hole. Y' know that toy he saved from the fire?'

'The monkey with the gloves? Was it from Gramps.'

She shook her head. 'It was William's. Your dad never could let it go. He never let that monkey out of his sight after what happened. As if that could undo it all.'

That explained why I wasn't allowed to play with it, why he lost his shit whenever I took it. The night of the fire, Dad went back for it. That was why Dad never let me play in the garden. That was why he made me learn to swim, proper-swim, and lost it when I struggled to learn. He didn't want me to drown. But why did I feel like I was, anyway? Why did he leave his one of his own kids to fend for themselves, but not me?

'We took his ashes 'ere. I didn't want to bury him, not in a hole. I wanted him to blaze like a star. Be free.' Granny was gripping the sides of the bridge, standing tall. A breeze blew back her silver hair, and it waved back to a darker colour. 'That was when your Gramps started drinkin'. Proper. He loved that boy. Takes a special type of man to love a child that ain't even his. And your dad... He seemed to be startin' something... I think he wanted to be punished.'

'Are you tryin' to make excuses for him?'

'Not excuses. Reasons.'

I shook me head. 'People have tragic stuff happen to them all the time. That don't make them abandon their children.'

'You don't get it, Scarlett. It's not that he didn't want you. He didn't think he was good enough to be a dad. He was trying to save you from himself.'

'Save me?' I tutted. 'Did a great job of that. He could have been better. I see it all the time. All these people have horrible things happening to them and they choose to make good of it. They become better people. Their kids become better people, too.'

'If you'd have done that to your brother... If you'd witnessed the aftermath... his father... then you...'

'Well, I guess I'll never know, 'cause you won't tell me who me brother or sister is. I guess they were properly saved from the family, eh? Where I'm now all messed up. Maybe Dad was right the first time, better off without him.'

'You're right. I was wrong to do that. To keep it a secret.'

That was the first time she had ever proper-apologised. There was one time I thought I had heard her admit she was wrong, but then she corrected it to 'sorry you're so stupid.' She held onto me hand and then kneeled down in front of me. 'Forgive me, Scarlett, for I have sinned.'

'For god's sake, Gran. Get up. You look like you're proposing.'

'But I don't know how to confess... Hail Mary and all that.'

'I ain't the pope! I can't cross you and make it all right.'

'But I need forgiveness.'

'So you *do* have unfinished business!'

'I was the one who kept 'em away - her and the kid. Your dad didn't know she came by, came lookin' for him, and so I pretended he didn't live at the house. Like your mum did. And I burnt the letters.'

'What? Why?!'

'She was bad news. She had this funny look about her...'

'Look?'

'That gap in the eyes. The hole. Like your Gramps. And your dad... Well, he had a tendency, y' know. A sickness. And he was doing so well at the time, teetotal. More than your grandpa could, and thought maybe this would... I didn't want him to suffer, to fall... Not again. I couldn't lose another.'

'What was her name?'

'Who?'

"The woman who came to the door?'

'Mari Tammii.' She squeezed me hand. 'But it ain't Mary with a y, it's got an i on the end. It's not British.'

I sighed. 'Come on, get up Gran.'

'I am a wicked, wicked woman, and I should burn.' She stood up and looked out to sea.

'Yeah, you probably should.' I smiled.

She laughed, not loud, but just like a gentle lapping.

'Did you do it? Did you set the fire?'

'What?' She frowned.

'You said it was someone who cares about me. And there aren't a lot of those. Maybe it's your unfinished business? Some weird sort of purge of family history?'

'No no. I'd never do that. Anyway...' She gave me this wicked sideways look and a joker-smile. 'I wouldn't care if your mum took the fall for it.' She laughed hard, a raspy strangled-laugh as if it had snuck up on her.

'You're right Gran, you are a wicked, wicked woman. I hope I haven't inherited your heartlessness.'

She gave me a look I couldn't read. Magically, sunglasses appeared on Granny's head, big sparkly ones, that she pulled down over her eyes. And she walked away from me on the bridge, fading away, but getting taller and less saggy, more filled in, solid.

'Granny?'

'Scarlett?!' She didn't turn around.

'You're not gunna leave me too, are you?'

'Gotta go sometime, love. Will get sick of you soon.'

I ran up behind her, like I should have done when I saw Rubi walk away. 'Stay until I find them, yeah? Until I find Mari.'

She lifted the glasses up onto her head. 'You've spent most of your life looking after me, Scarlett; most of your life getting me up and down, and bringin' me tea and cuttin' me nails. Didn't you?'

I nodded.

She smiled. 'I was always there. And every day, *you* left to go to work, to see friends, to live life.' She stopped and stared out again, to the river edged in mud that looked like a giant hole full of water. 'It was always you who left me.' She nodded. 'It's just the way it is, see? It's always the children who leave. And we's the ones who are left behind, waiting for you to turn back, to see us. We's always 'ere, waiting.'

Granny had holes too. Her eyes swam in them. I threw me hand out to her like it was a lifebuoy, to grab her hand, even though I knew it wasn't really there. And she took it.

9

8 DAYS UNTIL COURT

'Love is never wrong and so it never dies.'

The Lion King 2

When I first started living with the Wrights in their kingdom, it was an oasis. So much space and room. It was picture-perfect. But it started getting crowded with me in it. I kept finding clothes left everywhere, shoes stranded in every room in the middle of the floor, ready to trip me up. All their stuff was in the way, under me feet. And it didn't matter how hard I tried to clear up, to get the oasis, the calm, it was a losing battle.

But it kept me busy when I wasn't at work. It gave me excuses to avoid Scott. Whenever he came up to me, I had a load of washing to do, or a hoover in me hand. It may not be a crime in the animal kingdom to fall in love with someone you're related to, but it's definitely a crime here. I needed to find out if Scott was me long-lost brother with a vendetta. Granny had given me a name. But I'd gone back to day shifts at work, which made it too difficult to get to the library computers, and I couldn't ask to borrow Scott's laptop.

'How was work today?' Scott blocked me on the stairs, as I picked up Clive's slipper.

'Fine, fine, thanks.' I tried to get around him.

'Right.' He didn't move aside.

'How's job huntin'?'

He put his hands in his pockets and shrugged. 'Nobody wants a history graduate.'

Me phone vibrated in me pocket, so I got it out to see who it was, hoping it would be Rubi.

'Oh, so your phone does work?' Scott glared at me.

'It's Kai. She wants to talk.' I gestured with the phone. I didn't want him to ask me why I wasn't messaging him back. 'Who are all those kids on the wall?' I pointed to the stairway wall, which was head-to-toe with pictures of the Wrights with kids.

'That's all the kids they fostered.'

'Which one's you?'

'I'm at the end. Last one.' He pointed down the stairs.

'So they stopped when they adopted you?'

'We're not related, you know. It's dumb! There's no way.'

'Don't call me dumb.'

'Sorry, it's just... I saw a picture of my dad. And he looks nothing like yours.'

'Really? Can I see it?'

'I don't have it anymore, didn't want it.' He put his hands down onto me shoulders. 'But trust me! If we were related, don't you think it would feel weird? We'd sense it somehow?'

'I dunno.' I shook me head and put me phone away. 'Not sure.'

I didn't want him to be a Saint. For his sake, and mine. If me trip into the past with Granny had confirmed anything - it was that we Saints were a natural disaster. Maybe the only way to save yourself was to join a different tribe, a pride of lions like the Wrights. I wanted to believe him, but a sort of instinct kicked in, telling me something wasn't quite right and I didn't know why.

'I am sure.' Scott had U-turned from the distant and aloof mystery guy I fell for, to me struggling to get space between us. It was as if he was afraid I'd get away, afraid that I would escape, leave. His hands were hairier then I remembered. His fingers dug into me arms. He pounced towards me, but I shrunk back.

'Hey sprouts!' Clive shouted from the hallway, out of sight. Scott froze. 'Am home! Going out to the den.'

'OK!' Scott stared at me like he was stalking deer. It reminded me of when I used to work at the local Tesco and this guy would come to me checkout to ask me where I lived and what I got up to, and he'd just stare so hard I swear he was trying to hypnotise me or something. I never left work on me own, never walked back alone.

'Clive?' I shouted. 'Can I borrow the computer for a sec?' Scott backed away and me back eased up.

'Sure! Now?'

'Yeah. Won't take long.' I pulled away from Scott and ran down to see Clive in the kitchen at the open window. 'Just something I want to look up.'

'Sure... just a second.' In Clive's hand was a long gun that he'd rested on his shoulder, and aimed outside.

'What y' doin'?!'

'These blasted pigeons keep eating the cherries on me tree.'

'You can't shoot them!'

'Don't worry, it's just to scare them. I'm not that good an aim.' He took a shot and the pigeon flew off. 'Now come with me, follow me to the den, to me lair... Mwahaha. Hey, is that my slipper?'

'Yeah, just found it on the stairs.'

'You're a Saint!' Clive's pun made me wince. He winked. 'Don't know what we do without you.'

I glanced at Scott behind me, who hated me right now. I wanted to tell him I just needed to be sure. That I just needed to be 100%. You can't always rely on instinct, especially mine, because I'd got it all so wrong already with Mum, and the neighbour and Kirsten.

Clive's den at the back of the garden was where he worked some days. It was packed full of stuff, suffocating, as thick as a thicket. A jungle. The table was growing upwards with papers and books, ropes and garden hoses drooped down like vines over shelves, and dust hung in the air like pollen. Hazy sunlight dripped through and landed on the desk where there was a computer screen and a glass case with a scorpion inside.

'Liz never comes down here. So I'm free to be as filthy as I like!' He laughed.

'You have a scorpion? Why?'

'Have you ever seen one before? Oh, they're fascinating.'

'What does it eat?' I bent over, peering into the glass cage. It didn't move. It's bulging tail, its sting, its leathery pincers - it made me wonder how high up the food chain we could be, if even a lion could be taken down by something as small as a scorpion.

'Crickets. About twice a week.' He turned on the screen. 'It's the circle of life. Want to see me feed it?'

'No, no, not sure I'm ready for that.' I waved him away.

The computer came out of standby, and on the screen there was an open webpage - looking at wedding rings. 'Oh, whoops!' Clive tried to click it away. 'Busted!'

'What was that?'

He turned to look at me, eyes wide, a deer in headlights. 'Promise you won't tell?'

'Promise!' I held up me hand.

'Well... I'm not one for all that gushy, lovey-dovey stuff.

When I first proposed to Liz, it was without a ring and while she was cooking, so...'

'Cookin'?'

'Yeah, it just sort of... well, anyway. We got married at a registry office because I thought she didn't want a big thing, but... Well, long story short. I thought I would try again.'

'You're going to propose? Again?'

'Yes! Renew our vows. What do you think?'

I wanted to say no, that he shouldn't, that Liz wasn't exactly worth marrying again. But I remembered what Scott said about keeping out of it, about keeping the pack together. So I swallowed down the canary in me throat. 'Uhhhh, yeah... That's nice. If you think that...'

'The ring is on the way. Hope she likes it. But if not... Well, it's not the end of the world. I'm glad you saw that. I feel more excited now!'

'You've not told Scott?'

'No, he's a bit of a blabbermouth. Not sure he could keep a secret.' He crossed his arms.

'You might be surprised!'

'Here you go.' He turned the keyboard towards me and went to leave.

'Thanks. Just a sec... What was Scott's surname before you adopted him?'

'Scott? Oh, I dunno.' Clive looked in at the scorpion. 'We wanted to give him a fresh slate. Let him forget all that. He's a Hopkins-Wright now!'

'Yeah, sure, makes sense.' Me phone went again. More messages from Kai.

'It's a bit like he stalled at some point - from his past life,' said Clive. 'He's such a closed book. Hard to get a look in. Get close. But he'll get there.'

'I know what you mean.' I nodded. No matter what we talked

about or how physically close I got to Scott, it always felt like there was this barrier, that I was only skimming the surface.

'Scott's still got a lot of growing up to do. Liz spoils him. But with someone like you around...' He smiled and winked. 'He'd be a lucky man.'

'Ha.' I laughed nervously. The pressure flushed to me face.

'I'm going to go make a tea.' Clive patted me hand. 'Want one?'

'No thanks.'

'Back in a mo.' He walked off, humming the tune *I'll be getting married in the morning*. I opened up a private tab in the browser to see if I could order a DNA testing kit. But sibling tests cost over two hundred quid. No way I could spend that when there must be adoption papers or something around. So I closed down the window and began roaming the computer.

The shed was silent. Nothing moved, not even the scorpion. I was click-click-clicking like a cricket, exploring places I shouldn't be in, trespassing on private land. I found old photo files, work files. Then deep, deep down into the hard drive, in boring folders, I found locked folders, locked documents. All of them were called X1 or X2. I found fostering documents and pictures of children, but Scott's folder was empty. Nada.

So I dug around for hard copies in the den. I pulled at the drawers and cupboards, but nothing opened. Clive started walking up the garden, and I knocked something metal off the table. I reached down to pick it up; me head leaning on the desk, staring at the scorpion who I didn't trust to break out and attack me. The fake rock it sat on was tilted to one side. Underneath the hollowed rock was a ring-pull and the side of a key.

'So I've been thinking?' Clive put down his mug as I grabbed the ring of metal I'd dropped. 'About your fundraiser.'

'Are we still doing that?'

'Oh yeah, wheels are in motion. We'll have it in the backyard. Give us a chance to get to know the neighbours. But I think we should have a theme!'

'What sort of theme?'

'Up?' He raised his eyebrows. 'That film with the old man and the balloons who took his home to the falls. I know somebody who could lend us the... What you got that for?' He pointed.

'Huh?' There was a door knocker in me hand. It was a brass lion's head with a ring in its mouth for the knocker. 'I knocked it over.'

'This came from our last house.' He took it from me, tilted his head to one side and smiled. 'It's supposed to be a guardian. A display of strength and power. Me dad always said that this knocker would never ring out in the house if the visitor was unwanted or if they were bad news.'

I got up to leave. What about the woman that Granny and Mum had both turned away, the woman whose knock went unheard? The woman Mum thought she'd hit with her train. For so long, I had doubted me mum. But what if I was wrong?

'Feel free to knock on me door any time. I'm always here.' Clive lifted the knocker up and down.

'Thanks.' I was unsure of what he was getting at. 'Can I check one more thing?' I grabbed the computer mouse. 'Will only take a sec.'

'Might need to help get your own laptop with this fundraiser, too! Necessary piece of equipment.'

I smiled, opened up the browser on the computer, and typed in one last thing - the date of me mum's worse nightmare:

12/02/2010 train suicide in Gloucestershire

A newspaper feature appeared first, but it was short with no details. I kept scrolling until I found a newspaper who didn't care about privacy. Granny couldn't remember much. But she had remembered one thing - she had remembered the name of the woman who came to the door, asking for me dad, asking for his help.

Her name was Mari Tammii.

And it was the same name in this article. Me mum was right, she had hit the woman who she'd turned away. Maybe she was right after all.

10

---

7 DAYS UNTIL COURT

'I've seen things you've only seen in your nightmares.
Things you can't even imagine.
Things you can't even see.
There are things that hunt you in the night.
Then something screams...

Afraid?

You don't even know what afraid is.'

Jumanji.

I shouldn't snoop. There are things you shouldn't play with; boxes that should never be opened. But Clive's den called out to me like drums in the distance. I couldn't help but wonder why he'd hide a key in a scorpion's cage. Maybe he was hiding something about Scott's adoption. Or maybe the drums were all in me head, and there was only ring-brochures there.

But I wanted to throw the dice, to see what number would

come up. I could get lucky and roll a 5 or an 8. Because maybe the answer to everything was in that desk, maybe even the answer to a long-lost boy who got sucked into a game decades ago. The shed creaked. It pulled away from its hinges as the chilly night breathed into its limbs. At 2am, the moon was a spotlight. Everything was black and white and grey, and appeared bigger with their moon-shadows. Even the scorpion seemed twice as big, stalking around its glass cage, almost pacing. I stood, staring, waiting, wondering if I'd start sinking into the floorboards.

'Oh, come on you wuss!' The office chair spun around with Granny sat on it, and I knocked into a jar full of empty ink-pen cartridges, but caught it before it fell. 'Get on with it.' She sniffed. 'Be 'ere all night otherwise.'

'There are lots of things you could do.' I put the jar back. 'Like go back to haunting Dad.'

'He's passed out. And I really want to know what's in the desk.' She stood up and peered into the glass tank. 'Go on, it won't bite.'

'No, it'll sting!'

'It's not that hard. Can't you try to put a glass over it or something?'

'Actually, that's a good idea.' I scanned around for an empty jar. I picked up an old Nutella jar, the 1kg kind, and tipped out the paperclips in it. But it wasn't all clips. There were earrings on top of the pile. A bunch of hoops and studs, silver and gold.

'He wouldn't look good in those.' Granny snorted. 'He'd make an ugly woman.'

'They're probably Liz's, aren't they?'

She shrugged. 'Maybe he likes to dress up.'

I took the lid off the scorpion's tank. Its shadowy shape moved to the right, and me skin crawled with it, as if ten of them just ran up and down me body.

'Ger-on with it.' Granny elbowed me. 'Haven't got all night.'

'Yeah y' do! You've got eternity, Gran.'

'This *feels* like an eternity.... just....'

I lunged forward as Gran was about to rev up and stopped above the scorpion. 'The jar's too small.'

'Try this.' Granny pointed to an empty ice-cream tub I hadn't seen next to the tank. I picked it up and, without thinking, without letting the idea sit and crawl up me skin again, I reached in and put it over the top of the scorpion. I lifted the hollow rock and picked up the key, and used it in the top drawer that was locked. As it travelled around, it clicked.

'D' you even know what you're lookin' for?'

'Adoption papers?' I pulled open the drawer and rifled. 'To find out Scott's surname.'

'Why?'

' 'cause he might be Dad's kid.'

It made sense. Scott was cagey and distant. He didn't care that we might be related. Something had happened to him. It must have. Clive had said his past was rough. If his mum had jumped out in front of me mum's train, then it would explain why I felt so nervous around him, so worried. Me instinct about him being me brother would be right.

I pulled out wads of paper, and on them were pictures of ears, closeups of different earlobes and earrings in them.

'What are those?' Granny leaned over me shoulder.

'Ears? Earrings? Why would he lock these away?'

'Maybe he's a kleptomaniac? Loves to steal earrin's.' Granny took a photograph from me.

'Probably a surprise for Liz. To match the ring.' I picked up the earrings on the table next to me and held one to the picture. They looked the same. But the ears sort of looked different. But one of the pictures was zoomed out, and it was a picture of a girl sleeping on a deck chair in a bikini.

'I know this girl.' I pointed. 'That's Sophie.'

'Sophie who?'

'The one who attacked me. Who said I set fire to the care home. Tried to frame me.'

'Why he's got a picture of her?'

'Weird. And what is with all the ears?'

In the house, the bathroom light came on.

'Shit.' I locked the drawer back up, put the key back, freed the scorpion, and put the earrings and paperclips back into the jar. Granny followed me through the garden. All I could hear was the drum-drum-drum of panic getting louder, as if a stampede was running through me. The bathroom light turned off. I waited next to the back door, listening for movement. But there was nothing.

'Maybe it was Clive sleep-walking,' I whispered. 'He wanders about sometimes.'

When I got to me room, I lay down on me bed and Granny lay down next to me. I checked me phone for messages, but there was nothing. Not from Scott. Nor from Rubi. Not a word since that argument outside her parent's. I missed her. She'd know what it all meant: the photos, Sophie and Scott. Maybe I should meet up with Kai, see what she has to say, see if she can give me some look in with Rubi?

'I have more questions than answers now.' I turned on me side towards Granny.

'I found that when I died.' Granny gazed up at the ceiling. 'Only more questions... You'd think someone would know what was going on around 'ere. Bloody useless.'

'Shhh... D' you hear that?'

'What?'

'Someone's up again.' Me door opened, and I closed me eyes, pretending to be asleep. Footsteps crept closer to me. It must be Scott wanting to talk, but I wanted him to go away. So I kept me eyes shut. Me heart was boom-boom-boom, pounding in me ears.

'What you doin'?' Granny poked me arm. 'Why are you pretendin' to sleep?'

I couldn't reply. I wanted Scott to leave. I figured he'd go if I didn't wake up, but he got into me bed.

'Do something!' said Granny.

But he started kissing me neck, and then his hands moved down between me legs. Me eyes sprang open.

'Mmm Liz,' said Clive.

It wasn't Scott at all. But no part of me would move. It was as if I'd been cornered by a lion and me body was playing dead, thinking he'd get bored and leave me alone.

'Gordon Bennet!' Granny stood on the bed. 'What you doin'? Why aren't you screamin'?'

I managed to break free of me freeze and pushed his hands away from going up me leg further, but they kept coming back. 'Is he sleepwalkin'? Can you wake a sleepwalker?'

'You can castrate a sleepwalker if he's tryin' to molest you, the perve.' Granny bounced. 'Just do something!'

'What if he wakes up? It'll be embarrassing.' I tried to move across the bed.

'Then he'll stop and you can knock his block off.'

Clive pulled at me top, pushing it up. In times like this, you think you'd fight, you'd face the fear. But in the moment, when it sneaks in at night, when it's the person who's been looking after you, saving you, whose given you a roof over your head, a home you've always wanted, a family you always wanted, then something in you stops working right. All I could do was push his hands away, and it wasn't working.

'Right!' Granny pushed up her sleeves. 'You disgustin' perve. I don't care if you're asleep...'

There was a thump and a grunt. She'd shoved Clive onto the floor.

'What the hell? What's going on?' I could make out Clive's silhouette, lifting a banner of the realm off of him.

'You're lucky I can't draw blood.' Granny was sparring, holding up her fists like a boxer. 'I learnt a thing or two watchin' your father.' She leant forward and punched him in the face, knocking him backwards. 'Oh yes! Direct hit!' She threw her fists up into the air like a champion. The light turned on, and she vanished. Scott stood at the door, and then Liz. Clive was on the floor, pushing a cardboard castle off of him. His nose bled.

'Clive! Are you OK?' Liz went towards him.

'What happened?' Scott glared at me.

'I'm not sure. I woke up on the floor...' Clive pinched his nose. 'And then... I guess something hit me or I hit it.'

'Scarlett?' Scott raised his eyebrow.

They were all staring at me, waiting for me turn. Granny was gone. I had no-one in me corner. Dad was passed out somewhere. Kirsten had gone awol. Rubi had disowned me. Me mum was locked up. Granny, dead. Where would I go if they chucked me out? If I made things difficult, I'd be homeless on the street. And he was just sleep walking, he couldn't help it. Wasn't like anything happened. Thanks to Granny, it was all just a horrible, embarrassing moment that could go away if I said nothing. If I could forget about it, then it would be like it never happened.

'He was sleepwalking. And I was having a nightmare, and I thought... Sorry Clive.'

'Oh no!' Liz pulled a tissue out of her pyjamas' trouser pocket. 'He's on medication to keep him in a deeper sleep... I used to wake up with... Oh god. This isn't good...'

'No, it's fine! I'm OK.' I crossed me arms.

'I'm sorry, Scarlett.' Clive got up, wiping his nose, and turned to Liz. 'How embarrassing. Did we lock our door?'

'Yeah, but doesn't seem to make a difference. Let's get you downstairs. Get you some ice.' Liz put her hand on Clive's back and guided him out.

Scott just stared at me, cold. He looked me up and down as if he was looking at me morph into something else, as if I had grown a tail. It was like he knew I had lied. He was disappointed in me. As if I was the one who had done something wrong. As if he'd known I'd gone into places I shouldn't be in.

11

---

5 DAYS UNTIL COURT

'Winds in the east, mist coming in.
Like something is brewing and about to begin.
Can't put my finger on what lies in store,
but I fear what's to happen all happened before.'

Mary Poppins

At work, I couldn't get Sophie out of me head. The first time I had met her, all I could see were tattoos and piercings. Her nose was pierced, one ear was chained up in hoops, one arm had a tiger on it. Her inner wrist had a compass, and on her neck, behind her left ear, there were three butterflies surrounded by music notes. It took me a while to see the girl behind them. But what got to me was that in the picture in Clive's shed, she had none of them. Nothing. Not a single mark or hole in her. She was whole.

Sophie's story was just beginning, and it wasn't just Sophie's story, it was mine; it was Kirsten's. But the thing was, I didn't want to see it. I didn't want to face it square on. But like the wind that had swept in that night, that was sweeping across the Cotswolds and blowing over power-lines, it didn't matter if I didn't want to see it, because the force of it was going to cause damage, anyway.

'D' you hear the M5's shut?' Tamara walked into the dining hall, where I was preparing for breakfast. She wasn't no temp no more and she had to drive an hour every morning from Bristol to get there. 'Wind blew over a truck of Redbull and it went all over the motorway. I just missed it.'

'That was lucky.' I placed out knives and forks.

'Oh, me god! Would you look at this place? Did y' come in at the crack of dawn or what? It's spotless.'

The small dining room looked like a Premier Inn canteen, but it looked almost new, with a good deep clean. 'I had trouble sleeping.' I stopped to survey me work. What I didn't say was that I had trouble sleeping even though I had moved a dresser and some dumbbells in front of me bedroom door.

'Well, be careful, love.' She raised her eyebrows. 'The cleaner is already complaining, sayin' it's like you think she doesn't clean well enough.'

'Did you see the floors, Tamara? Footprints everywhere. I swear she just looks at it and thinks that's enough.'

'I think she's worried you're doing her out of the job. But to be honest, love... It would be best if you didn't. It's hard enough keeping on top of everything. I don't want to have deep-cleaning added to me rota too.'

'It's just a one-off.'

'I'll start gettin' the residents up, shall I?' She pulled on plastic gloves. Tamara was a morning person. You could tell by the way she swayed when she walked out, as if rocked by the breeze.

When all the residents were up and sat down with a cuppa and toast, I noticed how the entire home was howling. It creaked and whistled with the gales, as if we were spinning on a Mary-go-round. Something about the wind was good, like it was blowing away the dust, blowing away the dirt.

But then thoughts and images crept in: Destiny taken by the Eagle Owl, Mr Post's flowers falling on the bed, Kirsten cradling a tiny box, Mum put in cuffs, Rubi walking away, Dad pointing at me, Kai bowing her head, Granny disappearing on the bridge, Sophie's untouched skin, Clive's shed, his hands, Scott's piercing glare and his head shaking. I got out me phone and told Kai to meet me after work. She hadn't stopped messaging me.

' 'ere love, what's going on with your house?' Doreen brought me back into the room. 'With it being burnt and all.' Doreen had white, short, curly hair, and still insisted on wearing makeup, even though she struggled to get it to blend well. She couldn't recognise her own kids when they came in, so when she remembered me house had burnt down, I dropped everything. She often had these moments where she was super with-it, proper together-like, and they would never last long. But when they happened, it was as if we'd stepped into a from her past. As if we were on a jolly holiday away from her dementia. She was the Granny I wish I always had, a textbook soft and kind old lady.

'Me house?' I pulled over a chair to her dining table. Most residents had moved into the sitting room. 'Well, I'm living with another family until I get back on me feet.'

'Oh, that's nice.' She smiled.

'And they have this huge event planned to raise money so I can start replacing some things that got burnt up.'

'Oh, they sound like fine people.' She nodded.

'And they've got press coming, the mayor, the son of that famous artist around here, and a ton of famous people who I didn't even realise lived round here. Everyone who's coming has to bring their pets too for a contest and whoever wins gets to meet David Beckham.'

'Who's that dear?'

'The footballer who married a Spice Girl... Anyway, so many

people are coming. It's huge! Everyone in Stonecloud is talking about it.'

'Sounds like it couldn't be better.' She sipped her tea. 'You'll never want to leave!'

The thing was, I relied on Doreen not remembering what I told her. I had told her many things I would tell no one, so many things I wouldn't admit to a soul, and she was always so good with me, so kind. So I didn't see the harm in telling her one more thing and I needed to get it out, because it was beginning to eat me up and I had no-one else to talk to. 'Doreen, is... I mean... It was perfect at first, but it went a bit...' I glanced around to see if anyone was listening, to check that Tamara was out of earshot.

'Come on, dear... you can tell me.' She leaned in and played with her hearing aid.

'Scott's dad, Clive, he sleep walks. But, well, I'm not sure if it's just an excuse...'

'Excuse for what, petal?'

'He came into me room the other night and did stuff...'

'Shhhh.' Doreen put her forefinger to her lips. Shook her head. 'No good talkin' bout that sort of thing. Does no good.'

'But...'

She shook her head again. 'I'm sure it was nothing. Maybe you were being too flirty with him?'

'No, I don't think so...'

'He just a man and you're a young girl. You should cover up when you walk around the house. Make sure you don't give him any temptations. Not fair on him, otherwise.'

'But I was in bed, he didn't...'

'Saw it all the time when I was growin' up. All these girls just showin' whatever they got. Flirtin' and then wondering why...'

All the times I spoke to Clive, all the times I had been with him, had he misread me? Had I given him the wrong messages? Made him think I wanted something else? But he said it himself, that I was like a member of the family. He made me his daughter in the game. He wouldn't do that if he thought we were anything else. Doreen was still shaking her head at me and it was the first time in me life I was glad to have had Granny. To have had someone who'd punch a person in the face for me.

'Scarlett?' Tamara beckoned me over to the doorway and I went to her. 'Have you seen George?'

'Uhhhh...' I stalled. 'Sorry, I think I forgot to get him.'

She clamped down her lips together like she was stopping herself from getting carried away, stopping herself from calling me a liar. 'Hmmm.' She squinted. 'I'll go get him then.'

When she left, Mr Post blew in through the front doors and into the reception area and everything in me tensed. He was holding onto his hat and coat, stopping them from blowing away. He searched around the room and spotted me watching him. Then he pointed at me and rolled his finger towards him.

'Looking for a new home, Mr Post?' I smiled.

'I'm 'ere for you!' He shook his coat.

'What, why?'

'Just saw your mum. She wants me to pass on a message.'

'What d' mean? What message?'

'You're not to visit her again before the trial.' He was staring over me shoulder.

'What? Why?'

'Summat about you blabbin'. She doesn't want you giving something away.'

'No, I have to see her. I have to. Please, Mr Post, you've got to tell her to let me see her.'

I was no closer to finding out who really set the fire, to save me mum from making a stupid mistake. Scott was still making out we weren't related. Before last night, I was sure he'd cared about me enough to send that message to tell me it wasn't me mum, but now... It was like he was looking down on me, as if he thought he was better than me. And me last resort was being able to convince Mum to withdraw her confession, or to confess to the guards that she'd made it all up.

'She doesn't know what's best for her. She'll go to prison. And she don't need to.'

'It's her choice.' He shrugged. 'She don't want savin'.'

'She does! Everyone does. And what about me?'

He shrugged again and opened the front door, holding on to his hat before the wind hit him.

'Please say something to her!' I shouted after him, but I knew the gale force wind had blown me voice away.

'Scarlett?' Tamara walked towards me.

'Yeah?'

'George just told me that you went up to see him, but that you just stared at him and walked off.'

'I did? Ah, god I'm such an idiot!' I slapped me forehead with me palm.

'Yeah... You can't just leave him, y' know. Isn't that what got that last girl fired?'

'It was a mistake.' I reached out for her arm. 'I meant to go back. I just slept so badly I must have forgotten...'

Tamara bit down on her lip, tilting her head, wondering what a lie looked like on me face, wondering if this was it. And she'd be right. I had gone up to George's room and stared at his hands and wondered what he'd done, and to who, and thought about Clive's hands, and I saw Sophie's tattoos come to life in George's room. There was a tiger at the foot of the bed and butterflies in front of me, and I followed them out of the room and downstairs, wondering if Sophie had followed them too.

12

5 DAYS UNTIL COURT

'You, me, or nobody is gonna hit as hard as life.
But it ain't how hard you hit; it's about how hard you can get hit,
and keep moving forward. How much you can take, and keep
moving forward. That's how winning is done.'

Rocky

Kai told me to meet her at me dad's gym, where she had a boxing lesson. She had something to talk to me about. The gym was so empty there may as well have been tumbleweed. One guy was rowing, and another was on weights. I searched for me dad, but it was just Ceri behind the desk. She waved and ran over to me. 'Do you know where your dad might be?'

'Sorry.' I shook me head. 'He's not been in?'

'Ad hoc. He's all over the place. Gone AWOL.'

'Have you seen Kai?' I grabbed her arm to stop her from leaving. 'Black bob and...'

'Oh yeah, she's just getting out of the ring.' She pointed to the back of the warehouse, to a black and red platform. 'Stu has been taking over lessons. Thank *God* for Stu!'

'Sorry about me dad.' I couldn't look Ceri in the eye.

She crossed her arms. 'Just give me a ring if you see him or tell him to get his ass down here.'

Kai waved a big sweeping arch with her boxing gloves on. There was something about Kai that got me back up, that grated on me. Not just because of Rubi, but because she was a bit of a know-it-all. That was what she was. Thought she knew better than everybody else. Interfering in our business. She talked down to me, even though she wasn't that much older. Like those kids used to be at school, the hall monitors or prefects. Soon as they're given a badge or some responsibility, they believe they can tell everyone what to do. So seeing her laced up in gloves made me want to fight her, made me want to show her a thing or two about taking a punch. It made me want to teach *her* a lesson.

I strutted towards Kai, passing through sweaty gym equipment that nobody wiped down after them. It was humid, damp. Wind rattled in the metal roof.

'Hey.' Kai leaned on the ropes. 'Wanna spar? I know you want to punch me. I know I would.'

I didn't want to give her anything. Me teeth were clamped shut. I didn't even want her to know she was right. Why did she want to see me? Why can't we just get it over with? But I wouldn't see Rubi again if I didn't find a way to like Kai, to hang out with her. 'Sure, I can show you a few things.'

Dad used to say I was a firecracker. Unpredictable. He said I needed more control over myself to pack a proper punch. But right now, I didn't care. Kai rocked back and forth on her feet and punched her gloves together as she waited for me to get mine on.

'Everything alright?' I laced up.

'Just, you make me a bit nervous.' Kai dropped her hands.

'Me?'

She took a big breath. 'I never wanted to get between you and Rubi. Honest.'

'It's not about you.' I glanced away from her. 'Is this why you wanted to see me?'

'I know she misses you. Maybe if you came round and...'

'And what?'

'Say you're sorry?'

I rolled me eyes. 'Look, no offense, Kai, but I think I know Rubi better than you.' It wasn't easy staying away from Rubi, but she had told me so many times before that I can be over-the-top and smothering. So I had to hang back and wait for her to be ready. She didn't really want to see me, and I very much doubted she missed me when she had Kai to hang around with.

'I just want to help.' Kai walked towards me. 'I feel like it's all me fault.'

'You didn't lie to me.' I bounced back on the ropes. Anger was burning up in me. 'Or keep secrets.'

'She didn't mean to.' Kai shook her head, and her bob swished from side to side. 'Rubi was just so worried about how you'd be, how you'd react. With everything that was going on, and with your gran... She didn't want to put more on you. This big revelation. She was trying to look after you. She knows maybe it wasn't the best way to do it. But...'

I snorted. 'That makes no sense! Do you hear yourself?'

'What do you mean?'

'That's a nice way of basically saying that Rubi was worried I was homophobic! D' you know how much that hurts that she thought that?'

'She just thought it would be a big shock.' Kai tapped her mitts together. 'But I just think, if she saw how much you really do care, then...'

'Rubi has known me for most of me life, and I have known her most of me life, and we... you won't understand. It's not about you, OK?' I thumped me gloves together - hard. Me teeth gritted. So much fight was buried inside me. 'You ready?'

'OK.' Kai lifted her hands in surrender.

'So what were you learning?' I held me gloves up near me chin.

'Just focusing on stance and form, and a bit on rhythm.'

Kai staggered her feet: one, two. Me hands already felt hot in the gloves. I thought of Granny punching Clive and how I wished I had been the one to launch forward. Kai and I circled and then I launched forward, punching her arms that had blocked me.

'And blocking, apparently. You're good at that.'

She smiled. 'Apparently, I have a habit of sticking me elbows out when I punch, just like you.'

'What do you mean, like me?'

'Your dad always said I had to twist more. Keep it all in tight in the middle. Fire from the chin.'

'I just did that!' I stood upright.

Kai cocked her head. 'He said you never could get your arms straight.'

I gritted me teeth and fired at her again, pushing all me weight behind them. She dodged back, but took the blows. 'Better?' I said, sarcastically.

'Sure.' She shook out her arms. 'He never could stop talking about you, though. Said I reminded him of you. It was always Scarlett this, Scarlett that. You're lucky.'

I rolled me eyes again. 'You have a really low bar.'

Kai's face twitched. 'Yeah I guess so.'

'You're welcome to him. Not that he'll stick around.'

'You've not seen him?'

'No.' I danced from foot to foot. 'He ain't Father of the Year.'

'Is it all because of the fire that he's like this?'

'What d'you think?' I danced some more, but Kai wasn't

moving. 'Are you going to try punching me? Or is this a free pass or summat?'

'Sorry.' She jumped onto her toes and bobbed. 'Just a bit distracted. How *is* the investigating going?'

'Good. Turns out I have a long-lost brother somewhere.'

Kai was mid-lunge, her arm outstretched. She lost her balance and fell flat on her face. 'Ah fuck.'

I laughed. This was the first time I'd seen a different side of Kai - the fuck-up side and something in me broke, collapsed, eased. She was like the rest of us. 'Oh god, are you alright?'

She turned over, looking up at the ceiling. 'Yeah. Am OK. Bloody hurt, though. Aren't these floors sprung?'

I shrugged.

'Think I'm done for the day.' She panted and gazed up at me.

I felt bad. Had I beaten up Kai because I was mad at myself for not fighting Clive off? I put out me hand to lift her up, and we walked to the edge of the ring, ducking through ropes. I didn't want to punch her anymore. Me jaw had unclenched.

'Did you say you found out you have a brother?'

'Well, a half-brother.' I sat down on a bench.

'Where? How?'

'I dunno. No idea. All I got is this picture I found of a baby, the name of the mum, and nobody will tell me shit-all.'

'What's that got to do with the fire?' Kai used her teeth to untie her gloves.

'Think he might be the one to have set fire to our house. But...'

'Why?'

'Revenge?' I went to me bag and got out the photo to look at. 'On the whole family. That's usually why arsonist do it, right? Angry guys with a match.'

'Not all the time.' A drip of sweat ran down her temple to her neck.

The photo was getting creased. Wrinkles ran through it. It

occurred to me at that moment that this baby, this half-brother, was all I had left. Maybe we deserved it. Maybe some people don't deserve to be happy, to have a home, a mum, a dad, a family.

'Is this it?' Kai reached out for it. 'The picture.'

'Yeah.' I passed it over. 'Were a cute baby, whoever they are.'

I often wondered what life would be like if things had turned out different. I was so excited when I thought I'd got pregnant, but Rory wasn't. In the end, it didn't matter because it was a false positive. I still wonder if we'd be together if I'd really had been pregnant. Maybe that kid would have made all the difference in the world. I'd have me own family. Kai took hold of the corner, and her hand was wobbling a bit and I wondered if falling over had shaken her up a bit and I felt bad for taking out me rage on her, for making her feel bad for loving Rubi. I guess I was jealous of them, for having each other, and thinking that I'd never get a look in.

'That's no boy.' She tapped the picture. 'That's a girl.'

'What?' I took the photo from her. 'A girl? You sure?'

I'd been back and forth on this. Boy, girl? Boy, girl? Since talking to Scott, I'd landed on it being a boy because of the blue clothes, too. But the more I looked for her, the more I saw a girl too, and it made me think about Sophie again. Could she have done it after all? Could we be related? Maybe the alibi was a false one, like the one Rubi had given for me? Maybe Scott would do that for her.

13

4 DAYS UNTIL COURT

'Magic Mirror on the wall, who is the fairest one of all?'

Snow White

I hoped Granny would show up in the mirror and mock me outfit. But it was just me and Liz, finishing off our characters in the service station loos on the way to an out-of-town LARP. A big event in the calendar.

A heavy mist pressed up against the postbox windows and even though it was supposed to be warm, me fingers were numb. People came in and out of the loos, staring at us. I checked me phone for messages from Rubi, but there was nothing. Even Scott had stopped. I was desperate to talk to Rubi about everything, but her voice echoed in me head: *you're obsessed.* I couldn't ask her. So I was no closer to figuring out who set fire to the house, or where Dad's missing kid was, and whether it was Sophie or Scott and whether it mattered. The days until Mum's court date were disappearing. After what happened that night in me bedroom, I was wondering if I had been the one sleepwalking. Maybe I had ruled out Clive as a suspect too soon?

I eyed Liz up and down. The line between the real world and fantasy was being drawn with eyeliner. And with each line I drew on me, the further over it I went. The less I cared people were staring. I'd put on a long, blonde, wavy wig and pulled around the green cape Rubi had made me from a curtain, hugging it tight. I didn't see myself anymore. I was Skyla Goode, part wood nymph and part royalty. Scarlett was left behind. I could leave the homeless, friendless, boyfriendless, parentless girl behind. Skyla Goode was none of those things. She had a family; she had guts. Smart and brave. She stood up for herself.

Liz was drawing on her eyebrows, thick and black, between bites of an apple she put on the side of the sink. The idea of eating in a public loo made me want to throw up.

'You have quite the skill there!' She pointed to the drawings on me skin. 'What made you draw butterflies this time and not flowers?'

'I might do a tiger on me arm, but could be too hard.' I licked the end of me blue make-up pencil.

'A tiger? Why a tiger?'

'To feel strong.' I coloured in a butterfly's wing on me cheek. 'Or make people think I am.'

'That's what I love about being a police officer.' Liz stood up straight. 'People treat you differently when you have the uniform on. You get more respect, more command. You need something that will give you authority.' She picked up her apple. 'A don't-mess-with-me item.'

'Exactly! I want people to see me as someone not to mess with.'

'I don't think you have any problems with that.' Liz took a bite of her apple, crunching through a thought. 'Maybe you need something to make you feel it in the game. Oh, I have the perfect thing for you!' She put down her apple and rummaged in her make-up bag. 'You remind me of her, with that wig on.'

'Of who?'

'That elf from the Lord of the Rings...'

'Arwin?'

She shook her head. 'No, that other one...'

'Legolas?'

'Nooooo, silly!' She pulled out a silver headpiece. 'Cate Blanchet.'

'Oh Galadriel!'

'Yeah, that's the one. And with this...' She stood behind me and placed the silver, dangling crown on me, and a blue stone hung onto me forehead. 'If I pin it in... I mean, wow - you'd be the fairest of them all!'

She placed her hands on me shoulders and smiled. Liz loved to dress me up. She'd gaze at me and tell me how cute I was. She'd say if she had a daughter, she'd want them to be just like me. Over the past few months, on Friday film nights, we'd sit on the floor and paint our toenails together, ignoring complaints about the smell. I was reliving a childhood I'd never had. A picture-perfect one, the stuff of films. It was the way I had always wished it to be with me mum.

'I've got clip-on earrings to match.' She let go of me.

'You don't have your ears pierced?'

'No, I was a wimpish child.' She shook her head. 'Too scared to do it. Always got told I was a fraidy-cat, but I proved them wrong.'

'Most people I knew had their ears pierced as babies.'

Liz stopped putting on lipstick and faked a shocked look. 'Bordering on child abuse! Clive's always going on at me to do them, but needles gives me the willies.' She smiled in blood-red lipstick, which she'd blotted onto her fingers, staining them too. None of the pictures in the shed would have been of her. The earrings wouldn't be hers. So whose the hell were they?

I gazed at Galadriel in the mirror and stood up taller. Granny always used to say *fake it until you make it*. Life was one big game, and you had to play your part well. Take a bow at the end. And if I didn't play this out, I may never find out who set fire to me house. I had to turn the tables on Liz, and leave the daughter-act behind.

'That girl from the game, Sophie, d' you know her?'

Liz's face changed as if she'd put on the wrong one, the wrong character. Her pencilled eyebrows looked more like storms rolling in and lipstick smudged onto her front tooth. She didn't look at me; she gazed only into the mirror, into her own reflection. 'Sophie stayed with us for a while when we were foster parents.'

'What? Really? For long?'

'Her mum was *absent* for a bit.' Liz rummaged in her makeup bag for something she couldn't find. 'So she went through foster homes until she got back out. I mean, got back. Has Sophie said something to you? We try to keep at arms-length from her now.'

'Why's that?'

'We had some issues with her, and we still do a bit. What did she say to you?'

'Like what issues?'

Liz glanced down at an old woman washing her hands next to her. The old lady had a big hooked nose, stared at us and smiled, showing us some missing teeth. We watched her leave. The loos were empty, apart from us, apart from our reflections echoed in the mirrors around us.

'Don't take what she says at face value.' Liz glared at me. 'We often get messages from her. Or she tries to get close to Clive in the game. I keep telling him we should find another campaign, but he's pretty sure she'd follow us anyway.'

'She stalks you?'

'She had a bit of a crush on Clive. Which sort of made sense, since she had no dad in her life. And then Clive showered her with so much affection. It all went a bit... It's why we didn't end up adopting a girl.'

'That's a shame.'

'It was a tough decision. I'm not sure it's something we should talk about... But if she's saying stuff to you, we have a right to know.'

'No, she didn't.' I channelled Galadriel's calm. 'I just found a picture of her in the house.'

'A recent one?'

'It looked a long time ago.'

'Oh... she used to send pictures of herself to Clive. She claimed she didn't. But Clive told me everything as it happened, and well, then there were the text messages. But that's all I'm saying.' Liz picked up her lip liner and began painting on thicker and thicker lines over the top of the ones she had as if she'd forgotten she'd done them, or as if she couldn't cover up enough. 'I just wish it could have been different.' She sighed. 'I'm a really good judge of character. You don't get into the police force without knowing a thing or two about people. What their backgrounds do to them. It's a sad state of affairs with Sophie.' Liz leaned into the mirror and began to use her finger to tidy up her eye makeup. 'We've been as lenient as we can be with her. But there comes a point where people have to be punished or it doesn't register...'

'Like Kirsten?'

'The law was on our side, Scarlett. She dropped the charges because she knew she had nothing.'

'But...'

'Now, I know what you're thinking... But from the moment I met Clive, I knew who he was. Deep down, he's a big softy. He's just so charismatic and interested in people, and women just think he's flirting. He is a big flirt, but he doesn't realise he's doing it. But I know the real him. I know he's not as confident as he seems. That's why I married him. Why I'm with him. If only he could...'

A kid ran into the public bathroom, interrupting her. Why was she cheating on Clive if she was so in love with him? If she wasn't off with other men in the game, maybe Clive wouldn't be sleepwalking into me room? Maybe he wouldn't need to go looking elsewhere, like Doreen said. Maybe Kirsten never would have lost her job? Maybe he would have kept to himself if she was a good enough wife to him?

'Why you cheating on him then?' I hadn't planned to say it out loud. It was as if I was possessed by Skyla, or as if Galadriel had seen the ring dangled in front of her and imagined the terror she'd cause, the temptation to be all powerful, and she let it rip through me.

'Did Scott tell you?'

'No, I saw you.' I carried on colouring in me butterfly.

'Where?'

'Last weekend, in camp. I followed you. Thought it was part of the game.'

'It is, it is part of the game!'

'It is?' I raised an eyebrow.

'Yes, it's all just part of me character.'

'But... doesn't that upset Clive?'

'No. We have an agreement. It's a personal one, and it works for us and our marriage.'

'Does it?'

I could tell that Liz was lying. She wasn't looking directly at me. There was no way Clive had a clue what was going on. She was covering.

'What's that supposed to mean?' She put her hands on her hips.

'Maybe if you didn't sleep around, Clive wouldn't be sleep-walking into me room at night? Maybe there wouldn't be any

278

flirting going on. Maybe you wouldn't have all these problems with women.'

'You're blaming me?'

'Maybe you don't know Clive at all.' I turned to face her head-on. 'Where was he the night me house burned down?'

'Excuse me?'

'Because maybe he was out for revenge or wanting to hush Kirsten up?'

'You better remember who you're speaking to, Scarlett.' Liz had her policewoman's voice on. 'We're already running late. Pack up your stuff and let's go.'

'What?'

She closed the gap between us. 'I suggest you have a bit of a think about what you just said here, and what you just accused us of. After having taken you in, treated you like one of our own, loved you like one of our own. We're even trying to help you get your house back, to raise money. We helped you find Destiny! Do you really think we'd do that if he wanted revenge?'

She made a good point. None of that would make sense if he was consumed with rage and fury. 'No, I guess not.'

'Do you think we'd jeopardise our jobs, and our lives, and Scott's, to burn down your house?'

I gulped. 'No.'

'I didn't think so.' She grabbed her make-up bag and walked out.

'Sorry,' I called after her.

I didn't see a powerful elf in the mirror anymore. All I saw was me, dressed up and pretending to be somebody I ain't.

14

4 DAYS UNTIL COURT

'And some things that should not have been forgotten were lost.
History became legend. Legend became myth.'

Galadriel, The Lord of the Rings

Clive had gathered everyone from the LARP game. We were all waiting inside the mouth of the Rollright Stones, a mini-Stonehenge that looked like rotten teeth. There was something bigger than us there. A presence. The mist had lifted, leaving dewy tears clinging to the grass. There was a strange faraway feeling about it all. Voices were hushed. The air was still.

Sophie stood opposite me on the other side of the circle. Her face was rock hard. She looked like Legolass, wearing olive green, with a plait snaking down one shoulder. Arrows poked up from behind her, and her bow hooked over one shoulder. The last time we spoke, I accused her of burning down me house. Since then, I'd found out that she'd been involved with the Wrights in a way I never would have guessed. She wasn't someone to mess with.

Scott stood next to me, golden sunrays lit his face. I edged closer to him, but he moved away. He'd gone stone cold on me, as if freezing me out, as if Liz had told him about our chat at the service station. But it wasn't possible because I'd been with them the whole time. I should have believed him when he told me we weren't related. I'd told him about Kai thinking it was a girl and not a boy, but he didn't seem to care. The damage was done. I'd messed it up. He didn't even like me anymore.

'Why are you staring so hard at Sophie?' Scott tucked his thumbs into his belt.

'What? I'm not...' I straightened me headpiece that kept falling down.

'Do you think *she* could be your sister?'

'But Sophie has an alibi.'

'For what?'

'For burning down me house?'

He blew out his cheeks and rolled his eyes. 'Who said they had to be the same person?'

'Because then who...'

'Ladies and gentlemen of Mardon!' Clive yelled with his hands up in the air, commanding the troops. Everyone hushed and fell in line, apart from Sophie. She stared at the ground and chewed her lip as if she were taking her rage out on it. Not a hint of obsession. She sensed me staring at her, because our gaze met across the ring of people.

'Before we begin our campaign, I have some things to say...' Clive clapped his hands together. 'First, a warning. I've been told the Eagle Owl has been sighted again recently and attacking people. She isn't part of the game, OK?' People smiled and laughed. 'So if you spot her, they say to protect your head. Do not turn your back on her.'

'Sounds like me ex wife!' A man grinned.

Clive pointed at the crowd and placed an index finger on his nose. 'Good one, Pete. Can't all have treasures like mine.'

'Which brings me to me second point... There's a special reason I booked the Rollright Stones for today. Such a magical place on midsummer's eve. Legend has it that if a woman wishes to see the image of the man she will marry, then she has to run around here naked at midnight on Midsummer's eve.'

People wolf-whistled and made suggestive noises, but they felt muted, distant, as if they'd happened yesterday. The sun went behind a cloud shaped like an erupting volcano.

'But, for one person here, the image of the man she married is already standing in front of her. She's a wonderful, kind-hearted woman, full of imagination and spirit.' He walked towards Liz and grabbed her hand. 'I've been truly lucky that she said yes to marrying me all those years ago. She deserves so much more. A proper wedding for one and a proper proposal, which is why...' Me eyes almost blew wide-open when he knelt down on one knee, in front of everyone. 'I want to ask her if she would do me the honour of marrying me - again.'

'Yes!' Liz reached down to take the ring from him. 'Of course!'

People clapped and cheered. Scott breathed in and out with an enormous sigh. Sophie was as unmoving as the stones, and as ancient as them. A penny whistle played, and everyone danced like wild folk, swinging round each other's arms. It reminded me of me mum, and how she got swept up into the weird 'religions' and whatnot. Was this any different?

I only had four days to save me mum. Four days to get her out. Scott was on to something, and I needed to dig deeper, follow me instincts, any leads I could get hold of. So I walked around the circle towards Sophie and leaned into her ear, making her flinch. 'Meet me by the King's Stone.'

'What? Why?'

'Please.' I walked away.

Everyone else was still setting up while I waited for her. I held onto the railings around the King, waiting. The King looked different from every angle. Sometimes he was like a man. Sometimes it was a hand pointing to the sky. And sometimes he was a monster, hunched, erupting from the tuffs of grass. The stone's face was pocked, covered in yellow and white lesions of lichen. I didn't know what to think anymore. What should I believe? I was being taken over by something. A spell had been put on me.

'Do y' know what happened to the king? The legend of that rock?' I turned around to see Sophie coming towards me, light on her feet.

'No, what?'

She stood next to me, dropped her bow and arrows to the ground, got out her phone and typed into it. She read it out:

'As Long Comptan thou cannot see
king of England thou shalt not be
Rise up, stick, and stand still, stone,
For king of England thou shalt be none
Thou and thy men hoar stones shall be
And I myself an Eldern tree.'

'What does it mean?'

'A witch turned the King into stone. I should have chosen a witch as me character.' Sophie crossed her arms. 'I feel Eldern. Could get rid of him then.' She nodded towards the crowd.

I adjusted the Elven headpiece again to stop it slipping over me eyes. Words and questions jammed up inside me. How can I ask her? How do I start? It was as if I was holding onto something dark and powerful that would consume me. I didn't want anyone to know about it. I didn't want anyone to see it. I wanted to keep it to myself, to throw it into Mount Doom and never talk about it again. But it ate away at me. What if I'll never be the same? If I said something to Sophie, things would change. And if I asked questions, we couldn't pretend to be who we used to be. It would always be a weight around our necks.

I held me breath. 'I found a photo of yours.'

'Where?' She uncrossed her arms. Softened. I thought she was a lot older than me, but now I couldn't tell. She looked like a kid.

'In his office.'

'Do you have it?'

'What?'

'Did you take it?'

'No, sorry.' I shook me head.

'Shame.' She leaned on the railings, dropping her bow to the ground.

I took a deep breath. I should've taken it just in case it got into the wrong hands. Rubi had an ex-boyfriend in college who had naked pictures of her, and he sent them around his friends. They ended up online, all over the place. It ruined her for a while. After that, Rubi started changing her hair colour every week, until her hair began to fall out.

'Wish I didn't know he had that.' She glared up at the King's Stone.

'Is it true?'

'What?'

'That you had a crush on Clive?'

'What? Did he say that?' She glared at me, repulsed.

'Liz said *you* sent him pictures.'

She shook her head and turned away. 'What do you believe?'

'Whatever it is you want to tell me.' The headpiece slipped down over me ear.

'I'm not sure how much I want to tell you, to be honest.' Her jaw clenched. 'It's not something I've... It's not a place I like to revisit.'

'Then why did you stay doing this game with him here?'

'Stay?! He follows *me*.' She put her hand to her chest. 'And I'll be damned if I let him ruin everything for me.'

I nodded. 'He said he sleepwalks...'

Sophie squeezed her eyes shut. 'Scarlett, I really can't re-live it...' She shook her head. 'It's hard to... explain.'

'What do you mean? Did you start summat with him?'

'I thought... I thought he cared about me. He made me feel special, and then it was... off you go!'

'So, there was *something*? You wanted...'

'I was fourteen years old, I just... He made me believe... I did things because I wanted him to be happy. I wanted to be wanted.'

'To have a home.'

She nodded. 'I thought I was old enough to look after myself. Been doing it for ages, anyway. It's only looking back...' She kicked a stone away from her. She shook her head. 'History's only ever written by the winners, right?' She reached down to pick up a stone. 'Guess I can't blame people for wanting to believe him.' She threw the rock at the King's Stone. 'Denial is so much easier, right?'

I wasn't sure. Who would be considered the winner out of me parents? Did I believe their version more? There was this one time a few years back when me mum told me that dad couldn't swim. I didn't believe her. It made no sense. I remember him being in the water with me when I was a kid. I remember him teaching me, holding me up with armbands. Going swimming was me best memories with Dad, and I didn't want that to change.

'But if you'd have stopped it....' I scratched an itch under the headpiece. 'Do you think he'd of backed off?'

'What?'

'I mean, maybe he really fell for you.' The itch got worse.

'Scarlett, I was fourteen years old. Can't you get that into your thick skull?'

'Yeah, but... you said it yourself. You probably came across as older than that.' Me head was even itchier. I couldn't stop scratching.

'No, I didn't. Look, I will not stand here and have you try to tell me that what that man did was OK.' She picked up her bow and arrows. 'And I know it's hard for you to understand, because I've been there. I wanted to be part of that family, too. I know how much you want it, want Scott? I get it. But for fuck's sake, Scarlett, I can't say this loud enough... Get the fuck out of that house! OK?' She slung her bow and arrow over her shoulder and towards the circle.

'Wait!' I shouted and the Elven crown slipped down entirely, hanging around me neck.

'What?' She turned around.

'What's your surname?'

'Why?'

'I'm looking for someone with the surname of Tammii.'

'Tommy?'

'No Tammii. Two i's on the end.'

She walked backwards, away from me. 'Mine's Knight, with a K. Like them over there.' She pointed to a cluster of rocks called the Whispering Knights, who were said to be plotting treason behind the king before getting turned to stone, forever denied. They were collapsing in on each other, as if they'd seen horrors that had left them forever scarred.

15

2 DAYS UNTIL COURT

'You cannot conquer it. It has conquered you!'

Dr. Jekyll and Mr. Hyde

I didn't have to take Sophie's advice to leave the Wrights, because everything I had ever feared was about to happen anyway. I was about to lose everything and there was nothing I could do about it.

Ryder Cliftone, son of Oswin Cliftone, defender of the weak, aka - Scott, sat on the roof above his window. He'd been avoiding me since the LARP. When I went looking for him, I only saw his legs dangling at first. His nostrils flared at me when I stuck me head out of the window to look up at him, and I should have taken that as a sign to leave him alone.

But I didn't because despite Rubi's warnings, I can't help myself. I smother. I wanted him to be near him. I missed him. I wanted him to tell me everything would be OK. Rubi said if you clung on to people too tight; it suffocated them. Human instinct, when something got too close, was to run away. But I could never understand that. We were meant to be, Scott and I. We had a connection, something that was out of this world, supernatural. And it had nothing to do with us being related - I was sure of that now. That connection had to be soulmates. I wanted him to know that I was holding me breath and closing me eyes, making a wish whenever I looked up at starlight. I plucked clouds of dandelions and I sent them away so that we could be together. And I wanted him to know how I felt in case the reason he was cold to me was because he thought I didn't want to be with him. And I didn't want to lose him.

'How d' you get up there?' With me head out of the window, I searched for the best way up.

'Shimmed along the ledge and then up the tiles.' He gazed at the houses head.

'Can I come up?'

He nodded, but it was twinned with a shrug. I lifted myself up onto the window ledge and then shimmed across, holding onto the guttering. The lead along the side of the tiles and the window was rough and patchy, making it easier to climb up and onto the flat roof. Scott's room had been built into the loft space, and his windows came out of the roof like frog eyes.

'Think I saw that owl...' he said.

'Really?'

'Probably just a pigeon,' he said, facing away from me so I couldn't see his expression. Up on the roof, you could see across all the other roofs, their chimneys like bottlenecks poking up out of them. You could see all the upstairs windows open to let out the heat, sticking out like ears trying to listen.

'You alright?'

He shrugged. And it was the first time I realised a shrug could cut so deep. I wished for Granny to show up at that moment and make a joke of it, so I could pretend it wasn't so bad. So I could roll me eyes and let the hurt roll off me too.

'Have I done something?' I said. He shrugged again and

looked away. All the wishes I'd made sunk down to the ground, clouds had covered the stars, and dandelions were just weeds. It didn't feel like the supernatural was between us. It was a gulf. 'I was only avoidin' you because I was worried we're related. But maybe I was wrong. Maybe Kai's right? It's a girl.'

'You *are* wrong,' said Scott.

'Do you remember what your surname was before you came 'ere?'

'Of course I do,' he said. 'I'm not an idiot. I told you already that I'm not related, but you wouldn't believe me.'

'I'm sorry,' I said. 'I just wasn't sure you'd...'

'Be telling the truth?' He rolled his eyes. 'My surname was Hyde.'

'Like hide and seek?'

'No, as in Jeckle and Hyde.'

'Oh... is Hyde the doctor?

'I try not to live up to the name,' he said. 'But... maybe these things just follow you. Like legends. Family curses.'

'You think your family has a curse?'

'Maybe I have the curse,' he said. 'First Sophie, and now you...'

'What d'you mean?'

'He's off limits, you know. He's married.'

'Who?'

'My dad.'

'What?'

Scott rolled his eyes. And I wished for Granny again, for her to come in and punch him in the face, like she did to Clive.

'He came into *my* room. Y' have to believe me,' I said. 'It wasn't me...'

'I thought you'd be different. Actually, I thought you liked *me* but...'

'I do. You have to believe me, Scott. I'm mad about you. I just...'

'You barely know me, Scar,' he said.

'Don't call me that,' I said. 'You know I hate it when me dad calls me that. And I do know you. I do.'

'And I don't you,' he said.

'Of course you do,' I said. 'I'm right here.'

'I've seen the messages you've sent him.'

'Messages?'

'To my dad. They're already talking about turfing you out.'

'Wait, what? Where?'

'I'm not sure they have a choice to be honest.'

I sat there in silence, waiting for the words to sink in. But it was as if I had been poisoned. 'I never sent him any messages.'

'Can I see your phone?'

I handed Scott the phone they had given me, unlocked. He clicked and clicked and then shook his head and handed it to me. On the screen, there were messages. All I could see was Clive's name and then messages from me saying I-want-to-see-you-alone-and-I-want-to-kiss-you-and-I-can't-control-myself-around-you. And I dropped the phone in me hand so that it fell from the roof and down onto the path and smashed into pieces.

'I didn't send 'em,' I said. 'Y' have to believe me. That ain't me. Honest.'

At me feet, I saw Liz come out of the house, and then Clive, looking down at the phone and then up at us.

'Scott, please, he did this...' I said, pointing at Clive. 'Y' have to believe me. He's lying. I don't think he was asleep. Please, believe...'

'Scarlett,' shouted Liz. 'We will go inside and talk about this.'

'But I...'

'Don't you even dare,' she said. 'If you so much as say a word out here... We have rights too, you know, especially over false allegations.'

Liz and Clive went back inside. Scott was beginning to move off the roof, his back to me.

'How can you do this to me?' I said.

'Do this to you? You did this to you, Scarlett! We took you in and this is how you repay us?'

'You don't know what he did to me.'

'Did to you?'

'When he was sleepwalkin'...'

'Are you trying to set us up or something? For Kirsten?'

'What? No!'

'I knew things were messed up with you. I got it. I did. I knew it. I went through it too. But this is something else...'

'But it's true.'

'Then why didn't you say something when it happened?'

'I was scared. I thought maybe he was *actually* sleepwalking...'

'He *was* sleepwalking. I've seen him do it a million times. You knew it too. How convenient. I mean... You're the only witness in that case. He's a good man. You saw what was happening with them, how weak they were, what she got up to, and you thought you'd make a move. There's no way...'

'Please, Scott. That's not it at all. Please. This isn't fair. I didn't ask for this.'

I heard me voice, but I didn't know it. I always thought if this sort of thing happened to me, I'd be like a warrior princess, like Xena or Buffy. I wouldn't take this shit. I'd be up fighting, not begging. But to be accused of being someone you're not, to be talked to as if you're someone else, as if you're a kind of evil, the first thing you want to do is convince them that you're not. You want them to see you as kind, as caring, innocent. A victim. To fight, to get angry, to accuse - wouldn't that make it worse?

'I'm done talking to you,' he said. 'You better pack your stuff up.'

'And go where?'

'Not our problem. You're not a kid. You're the state's problem now.'

Scott went the way of the wishes I'd made, and shimmed down the roof, sinking to the ground. I had thought Scott was a lot of things, but he'd morphed into someone, or something I couldn't recognise. He was no defender of the weak. No hero. He was the last person I had and losing him, losing his faith in me, pushed me someplace dark, and I felt something expanding inside me, something explosive, something worse than Jeckle could ever Hyde.

16

2 DAYS UNTIL COURT

'What do you get when you cross a mentally ill loner with a society that abandons him and treats him like trash?

You get what you f**kin' deserve!'

The Joker

When you've got nothing, when nobody wants nothing to do with you, when even your haunting Granny doesn't show up, when you wonder if maybe you've lost it like your mum, that maybe you're proper-wrong too, and you're walking in circles, going around and around in your own head, and people walk on the other side of the street from you, and you sneer at them because you know that they're all the same and that they ain't going to do a thing to help you, even when you're dragging everything you own in a black plastic bin bag, because why would anybody want to help a Saint, why would anybody want to come near us when we're clearly cursed to hell, and I dunno what to do with myself or where I'm going to sleep, and the sun has gone in just like everyone else and when the sun has gone you can feel the darkness growing in you too, and when that happen's you got nothing to fight it, no light in you to fend it off, so when the dark came for me I knew it was time, and I knew I wanted it to have me because there was no point in trying anymore, no point in trying to be a good person for no-one, no point in trying to look after them, because I had failed me mum and was going to lose her forever too, and so no-one was going to come save me from them, from the ones who took everything, from those smug-rich-posh stuck-up toffs who've got it all and who swim in their own gold-lined shite, and who tell you they love you and that you're like the daughter they never had and dress up like morons to prove that they're something they ain't, trying to prove they've got something more than what they have, but underneath all that stupid getup and gear they're something else altogether, grim and pathetic, and when you see all that, when you see what they are, what they took away from you to make them look good, what they'd do to make sure that they stay on top and you're treated like you're something not worth having, like you're something that should get chucked out onto the street, when you see the world for what it is in the darkness, for what it is when you got no roof over your head, nobody to put an arm around your shoulder, when there's nothing that's going to keep you warm when the cold comes in, when the shivers shake you so bad you're convulsing, a step-away from foaming at the mouth, when you know you've only two choices and one is to die on the street, out in the cold, or to get up with a lighter in your hand, and take all the injustice, and all the stuff you've been burying deep - so deep that it has become its own grave, but you're going to raise the dead, you're going to raise hell - and you use it for fuel, because you're gunna make yourself a fire, make yourself a great big f-you fireball to warm your graveyard bones, and you'll start at the roses, beneath the woody stems, near where they dumped a bunch of wood from when they ripped out the shelves in the front room, and you know it'll go up without them knowing because you disabled their smoke alarms before you left, and so when you hold the match, hold it to the kindling you made yourself since learning how to make fires with them on LARPs, and you go to do the thing you've always wondered in the back of your mind if it was you who'd done it to your own house, when you're ready to change lives to look like yours, to burn with you, to keep you warm on cold nights,

there's only one thing left to do,

light a match,

and watch them get what they deserve,

watch them burn.

17

I DAY UNTIL COURT

'It's like my heart is a tooth,
and it's got a cavity that can only be filled with children.'

Despicable Me

At first, when I lit a match under the roses, in the early hours of the morning, under the Wright's house, it blew out, even though there was no wind. The second time, I gritted me teeth, and the match snapped because I pressed down too hard.

There was an out-of-control rage burning in me. The rage hulked-me up. I wanted to smash things, step on anyone who tried to hurt me. Was I the bad guy or the hero? I didn't know who I was, what to believe, what was real or true or good or bad anymore. I had nothing and no-one. But I was done being the walk-over. Done with rules, with being Miss Nice Girl because it had got me nowhere. Actually, worse than nowhere, it had destroyed all that was good in me. Nice girls finished last, and I was done being at the bottom of the heap, treated like I was worth nothing.

I would not be quiet for the Wrights. I would not be made to be no-one. They will remember me. Feel fear like I did. They'll wish they never messed with a Saint. Not this Saint. I would not turn out like Dad, punishing himself when I could punish them instead. I'd seen Clive Wright in battle. I knew his moves. They were empty. He was nothing without his men. This, was war.

An eye for an eye.

A tooth for a tooth.

A house for a house.

When I lit the third match under the roses beneath the Wright's house, it blew out. When I tried it again, that blew out too.

And again.

'*Most* stupid idea I've seen in me entire life.' Granny's head was close to mine.

I jumped. 'Stop blowing 'em out.'

'Your plan is to set their house on fire and go to prison to join your stupid mother?'

'At least I'd have somewhere to live.' I kept me voice low, a hiss in her ear.

'You really think that burnin' down his house is going to work?'

'I don't care what it does, I just want to see them pay! To see what it's like.'

'Get up off the floor.' Granny pulled me arm up. 'All you're gunna do is make him a victim and burn up all the evidence. He ain't gunna pay. He'll have insurance. It'll be you who pays. It'll always be us who pay. That's how this works.'

'No, leave me alone...' I shook off her grip. 'He deserves this! He deserves to go to hell!' A light came on in the upstairs hallway.

'Sec.' Granny pointed to the light. 'Told you so.'

'Shit...'

'Better get movin' you plonker.' Granny nodded.

'I got nowhere to go.' I backed up.

'Go home.'

'What, why?' I jogged away from the Wright's house.

'I got summat to show you.'

'What?'

'Just do it.' She disappeared.

The mansion house, the Wright's stately looking home, still stood proud, untouched, unmarked. Its climbing rose stretched out in full-bloom, mocking me. *I'll be back. I'll come for you. Ain't nothing going to stop me.*

They say that home is where the heart is, but me home was a rotten tooth, a black cavity along a street that was gleaming with Cotswold cream. And I was no different. For so long I had been a decaying tooth, needing to be pulled out. Everything was black: the house, the night, me soul. It had that black hole feeling to it; light doesn't escape, it just gets sucked in.

I walked around the back, calling out for Granny. The house was streaked with soot like black scars, and through the rips and the charred walls, it was proper-bleak. I walked through our outdated kitchen into the TV room. Each room was haunted with memories.

'Gran! You here?'

The house creaked, but I didn't hear a call back. The house whispered secrets to me. There was still so much I didn't know about me family and nobody wanted to talk about it, and when they did, it was like being in a funhouse of mirrors, all bent and warped. Even the dead can't seem to get it straight.

'I got summat to show you.'

'What?' I turned round. The yellow streetlight coming through the window barely lit Granny up.

'We're going to play a game.' She put her hands on her hips. 'A spot the difference.'

I laughed. 'There's a big F-ing difference everywhere, don't you think?'

'This ain't no scrabble.' She paced, hands behind her back. 'Mark me word. This one... It's going to change everythin'.'

I crossed me arms and rolled me eyes. 'Is that right?'

'It's going to tell you who burned down our house.'

'What?! How? Why didn't you say summat before...'

'Because you already know who did it. I'm just 'ere to bring it out of that thick skull of yours.'

Me head went a hundred miles an hour as I went through the last couple of months. 'Did... did I do it?'

'What?'

'It's me, ain't it? I knew I was all wrong... I mean, it sort of makes sense, right? Why else would I be speaking to me dead granny, and try to burn down the Wright's house, and...'

'For god's sake, it's not all about you.' She threw her arms out, wiping away the idea.

'I didn't say it was... So it's not me?'

She huffed. 'You're taking all the fun out of this.'

'Fun?!'

'You know the wonderful thing about bein' alive, Scarlett?'

'What's that?'

'You can change things. Being on this side of everything - I can do F all. All I can do is drag up the stuff that haunts me, the stuff I wish I did summat about. But you... if you could see it all from 'ere. It ain't just one fire. It ain't just one house. You could bring the whole thing down.'

'What you talkin' about?'

'There's summat missing.'

'Understatement.' There was a lot missing: Rubi, Dad, Kirsten. Me entire family was missing. I was missing, too.

'Right 'ere in this room, there's summat missing.'

I glanced around, but it was all the same, except blacker, darker, covered in soot. I walked over to the dresser, the glass one with all the special plates in that granny would pretend was her wedding China.

'Cold. Colder.' She shook her head as I walked past the 'sofas' and to the melted TV. I reversed and went towards the marble fireplace.

'Warmer.'

'Did there used to be a picture here?'

'Nope, keep going...' She bounced up and down on her toes, smiling, eyes wide like search lights.

'Can't you just tell me?'

'Nope. You need the first spark to get the rest of 'em lit.'

'Why?'

'You got to remember Scarlett, there's more than just who *you* know to be missin'.'

'You're literally making no sense.' I made fists and gritted me teeth. 'You're getting on me last nerve.'

'Yous got a family member that you've never had before.'

'You mean Dad's kid?'

'Not just your dad's kid, but your sister.'

'Sister? It *is* a girl?'

'You're so blind half the time.' She rolled her eyes.

'I have a sister?' And it was the weirdest thing, because that one word changed everything. A sister. Another Saint, like me, out there. For so long, I'd been thinking of them as my dad's kid, and not as *my* sister.

'Colder...'

I turned back to the fireplace and to the mantle. 'It's funny because I always thought it was boys who set fires, right? Except me, I guess...'

'HOT HOT HOT.'

I looked around, back to the mantle, to the clock that was Grampa's, to the vase that used to have Granny's dried flowers, but was now ash in the bottom. 'I DON'T SEE IT!'

' 'cause you're looking for the wrong thing. This ain't no film Scarlett. Stop lookin' for a cartoon villain. Look for a person.'

'What are you talking about?' I picked up the glass paper-weight and wiped it down with me sleeve so I could see the glass rose swirl in the middle.

'Maybe the one who set fire to the house wasn't doing it to hurt us,' said Granny. 'Maybe they just wanted a reason to get close. To be part of our lives. To 'ave a family too. Who's the only person who's reached out to you? Who's the only person who's come into your life since?'

'That's a weird way to get a family.'

'No weirder than dressin' up as a bleeding troll.' She gestured to me costume I was still wearing from the LARP.

'I'm an Elf, actually.' I turned so she couldn't see me squirm.

I had done some pretty weird things just so I could have someone. To have the perfect family. Now Granny believed someone, somewhere, was lookin' at the Saints in the same way, looking for a way in. 'So you think me half sister did it? That's why she didn't want me mum to go to prison for what she did? Because she cares about...'

I put the glass paperweight back. At me feet, a square was free of soot. Something missing from the hearth. I was so used to it being there that I didn't even notice it wasn't there anymore. And just like that, the pieces came together. Me sister. A sister who'd been abandoned by the Saint family. A sister whose mum had been killed by me own mum. A sister who was just as alone as I was, who had taken to lighting matches to keep her warm too, and who had taken something from the Saint house, not because she wanted us to pay or because she wanted revenge, but because it was her family heirloom too. It was as much hers as it was ours. She was me sister, just like me, who needed me, just as much as I needed her.

'You see who it is now?' Granny stared down and the pale square on the hearth too - the gap in the soot.

I stared up at her. 'I can't believe it. I can't believe she's me sister. We don't look anything alike.'

18

I DAY UNTIL COURT

'It's a dangerous path I bounce... but I bounce it alone. Because the Hundred Acre Wood needs a hero, Pooh Bear! And I'm the only one.'

Tigger, Winnie the Pooh

I heard a car door slam outside the house, and Granny vanished before answering any of me questions. I ran through every time I had met me sister, re-living it, seeing it all with fresh eyes. She was there, always in the background, trying to help, trying to explain, and I didn't see it. Why didn't I see it? It was so obvious.

I heard a noise by the front door. Who'd be here at two in the morning?

I crept forward. 'Whose there?'

Black and amber eyes glowed in the dark from the kitchen doorway. They stared into mine. I held me breath. It was the Eagle owl perched on a pile of rubble. Its head turned towards me and it opened its wings but didn't fly off. I backed into a corner of the living room with no way out.

I never truly saw myself as Skyla Goode when I dressed up as her. She was a wish, a dream. But when I stared at the owl, it felt like a mirror image. It was all alone too - an outsider. Just like me and me sister. I wanted to reach out to it. How lonely it must be, being the only one...

'Scar?' A voice had come from outside, making the owl turn its head and fly up. It flew past me, went through the doorway and into the hallway. I backed towards the fireplace, trying to edge towards the kitchen.

'Scarlett?!' Dad was at the front door. Torchlight flickered through the hall.

'Dad?' The owl was between us. But I couldn't see him. 'Watch out!'

It was too late. Dad had walked towards us. He was face to face with the owl - shining a light on her. She screeched at him. Was she protecting me? Was she defending me?

'It's OK. It's me dad.' I edged forward, softly. Hands out.

'Not this time. This is our 'ouse.' Dad brought up a fist near his face, as if in the ring. 'You in there, Scar?'

'In the TV room.' I grabbed me throat to soothe the hoarseness. It must have been irritated by all the ash in the air.

'It's time to get loud and angry, alright?' Dad was calm. His voice, low.

'What?' Me voice cracked. 'But it's just scared, too. It don't mean to.'

'It took Destiny, remember? It'll turn on you if you ain't careful. Lash out. Need to show it who's in charge. Now - shout like a beast, both of us. On three.'

'On three?'

'One. Two. Three.' Dad threw up his arms like a bear and growled, and I copied him, pushing through the burning in me throat.

The owl glanced back and forth, flying up into the air, screeching like the damned, and came towards us. Dad then hit his chest like a gorilla, and I threw up me hands like a raging warrior. We were a tribe defending our land. The owl backed off, hovering and screeching, flapping back and forth. Then it flew towards us both, but turned just before, and flew out through the kitchen.

'Argh!' Dad lifted his fists into the air and roared again like he'd just become WBO Boxing Champion.

I lifted me arms up too. 'ARGHHHH...'

Something broke in me.

Something snapped.

Me throat was done-in. I held me neck and swallowed and swallowed. I tried to speak, but nothing came out. It was lost.

Dad shone his torchlight on me and smirked. 'What the hell happened to you? You look like an angel that went to hell and back.' Me elf clothes from the LARP were smeared in black soot. 'Want to get out of 'ere?'

I wanted to ask how he found me, but nothing came out of me throat. I rubbed me neck and pointed to it.

'Come on, get on the bus.' He didn't understand me pointing. 'Careful over the boards.'

He waved at me and walked off towards the front door. I followed the light, gulped, and tried to speak again. I wanted to ask him so many questions, to tell him I was sorry, to tell him what had happened, but...

'Come on. What's taking you so long?' He waved me over. Then sighed. Hung his head. The torch light from his phone shone on the wall, but up-lit him. 'I know.... I know... You're me daughter. I don't care how old you are. I'm still your dad. I should never of... I let you down. I know that...'

He looked back up at me and nodded. I'd never seen his face so soft, resigned, at ease with itself. I didn't see the weight pulling at his skin anymore. He seemed lighter somehow. I pointed to me throat and opened me mouth to silence as I stared down at the gaps in the hallway. Ever since falling through upstairs, and finding out we had a basement, I've been nervous about the hallway.

He tilted his head to one side, shone the light back on me. 'You can't talk?'

I shook me head and decided I should make a run for it. I dodged the missing planks at the bottom of the stairs. But I lost me balance.

'Stop running.' Dad stretched his legs over the holes, coming towards me. 'Scarlett!' He caught me just as me leg slipped down a hole. He had me by the arm. 'What the hell you doing? You scared the bejebus out of me.'

I mouthed *sorry*.

'No 'arm done, yet.' He tutted. 'You melon.'

I tugged on his arm, and shook me head, and mouthed: *For everything.*

Because I was sorry. I was really sorry for not believing him, for not believing Kirsten, for not giving them the benefit of the doubt, for not trying to help him when he fell apart after granny died, for not coming to his aid, or Kirsten's or Granny's. I was stupid and sorry for bringing disaster into our lives, and for blaming them for everything that had happened, and believing that they were maybe the villains in all this, that we deserved to have our house burned down. Because there was just so much more to it than what I could see. So much more to it that I even knew now. It wasn't black and white, nothing ever was. They were trying their best with what they knew, with what they had.

Dad shook his head. 'Nah, Scar. This ain't on you. This is on me.' He lifted me up by me arms. 'I royally screwed up. You were right. I wanna to be a fighter. I do. I should've come after you. I shouldn't have let you stay with that man. I don't care how old you are. You're still my kid. I know men like him. I've seen them. They could convince the Pope that they're Saints. And you're still figuring that stuff out. I should've stepped in. I should've fought for you - then and now.' He put his arm around me shoulder and squeezed me. 'I dunno if it's too late...But I do know one thing. I want back in the ring. I'd rather get bloody and pummelled, trying, than to sit on the side-lines. I'm gunna fight for us. Try to get this family back together. You up for that?'

I nodded and smiled. I couldn't remember the last time he hugged me. The last time we were together, just the two of us. Our pack had fallen apart long before the fire. But something had shifted. Not just in me, but in dad too. Granny was right. On this side of it all, we could still change things. We could still do something about it. For me sister, things could be better. I wasn't alone at all. I was never alone. It wasn't about me. This was about me dad, this was about Kirsten, this was about me granny, and Sophie. This was about me half-sister.

I should've tried harder too. It ain't at all like the fairy tales. Happy endings don't all depend on one person. There won't be one person to save the day. In real life, we're all main characters, and we all need to save the day, every day. And Dad was showing up, and Granny had showed up. Mum had showed up. It was time for me to show up, too.

Dad had left the bus running. Its beams lit up the road. The street was still and quiet, with the smell of cut grass and damp moss. I still couldn't get a word out of my throat.

'We are going to get Kirsten.' The bus doors opened with a hiss. He walked up the steps.

I raised me eyebrows and put me palms up in the air.

'I've half an idea.' He got his phone from his pocket and opened up the map app. 'Of where she is.'

I grabbed his phone off him, opened up the texting app, and started typing.

I typed: *Do we have time?*

He read it and then looked up at me. 'I'll get you back in time for your ma's hearin'. I promise.'

I typed again: *Can we make a stop on the way?*

'Where to?'

I typed: *Rubi's.*

'But it's 4am.' He squinted and closed the bus doors. 'Maybe we should get some kip first.'

I gave him a thumbs up and turned to go upstairs.

'Y' know what Scar...'

I turned back around.

'I think I know who may have you-know-what?' He frowned and pointed to the house. 'Who burned down our 'ouse.'

I smiled, pointed to me chest and nodded, because I knew too and I wanted to be there for her when everyone found out.

19

---

28 HOURS UNTIL COURT

'Oh, it's good to be home!'

Wall-e

＾

The next morning, Dad talked about the bus and how he'd been working on it, and how he'd been trying to work his way back to getting dry. He was talking and talking as he drove towards Rubi's house, more than I had ever heard him talk before. We bounced our way over potholes in the road, trying to swerve to avoid them, but they didn't faze him one bit. It was so unlike him to talk this much. He kept looking at me, waiting for me to nod because me voice still hadn't returned. It was as if losing me voice had pried open a space, a gap that he just had to fill, and he was reaching for me, looking for me, trying to get me approval. He talked about how he had to work through some stuff, but never said what, and that he'd come out the other side.

'But I realised summat.' He squinted. 'It's all in past. Ain't nothin' I can do about it, but I can stop it from ruining your life, and Kirsten's. I can be better than I was. I know it. I can.' He rubbed his nose. 'I see your Gran everywhere... I know it can't be her. I know.' He shook his head.

I was standing up, trying to hold onto the rail next to the driver's booth. Dad seemed bigger to me somehow..

'But still, she gave me the push I needed...'

The bus launched down the hill and I put me legs out wide to get more balance.

'You can't start a fire without a spark.' Dad glanced over at me. 'Can't sit round cryin' over a broken heart. Y' know who said that?'

I shook me head. Me knuckles around the bar were going white.

'The Boss of course. Bruce.' He glanced at me again. 'Y' know, Bruce Springsteen. And it's so simple, Scar. Maybe the person who did it, who burned it down, didn't want to hurt us, right?'

I nodded.

'I found out all this stuff online about arsonists and why they do it, and it ain't always about revenge. Sometimes they get a kick out of puttin' the fire *out*. Don't forget that. Alright. Remember that.'

I nodded, and he turned a corner, pulling into the Dunn's driveway. The wheels crunched and popped the gravel. There was a flower growing up through it, a dandelion. Granny said *dandelion* means *Lion's tooth* and that if you give it to a loved one, then it will give them happiness and faithfulness.

'Y' know, I'm not sure this is smart. After what I said last time I was 'ere.' Dad's eyes were jumping from side to side like a boxer dodging jabs. He put the bus in park and it jumped back and forth too. He turned around in his chair to face me. 'So I was listenin' to that song. That one by Bruce. And it was like I got this massive sucker-punch to the face. Everything made sense, Scar, like I went flyin' across the room.' He unlatched the door and got out of the driver's booth. 'You was right. Someone did set the fire. Someone who was smart. But not someone who wanted to hurt us. Know what I mean? They don't want to hurt us. Ever since you started pokin' around, digging up stuff. It got me thinkin'. First, I thought maybe this other kid of mine was tryin' to get revenge. I mean, they had every right to be mad. They was just acting out and...'

BANG BANG BANG.

The glass in the bus windowpanes rattled. It was the Dunn's knocking on the bus. Dad smirked. 'Dunn Dunn Dunnnnnnn.'

'You better have a good reason to be here, Jason,' shouted Rubi's dad.

Dad pressed the button to release the door. 'Hear, sorry about this. It wasn't my idea.' They all looked at me and I tried to speak, but only air came out and lips moved. 'She's lost her voice.' Dad pointed. 'But I think she wants to see Rubi before we head off.'

'They're in The Haunting. The big house. But I'm not...'

I pushed past Rubi's dad, plucked the Dandelion from the gravel, and went running over to the big house. It wasn't proper-big. Dad spent a long time doing this one up to look regal. A single-storey, tiny house, made up to look the bees' knees. Proper columns stood on the outside in Cotswold stone. I knocked on the blood-red door with me fist, and when Rubi opened it, I held out the Dandelion, hoping it would say the words I couldn't.

'Scarlett.' Her eyes were wide. 'What you doing here?'

Dad caught up behind me. But didn't compute the situation. 'She's lost her voice. I think she's trying to tell you she's sorry.'

I nodded, but it wasn't just sorry I wanted to say. I needed Rubi more than ever. She took the Dandelion from me. And behind Rubi was the person who'd burned down our house. I pointed in and then struck a fake match, and hoped me charade skills were up to scratch.

'You think Rubi did it?' Dad frowned.

I shook me head and tried to say no, but still only air came out.

'Did what?!' Rubi frowned too.

'Burned down our house,' said Dad.

'I didn't burn down your house!' Rubi put her hands on her hips.

'I know that.' Dad didn't realise Rubi wasn't alone. 'She's been through a lot. Don't take it personal.'

I shook me head, leaned forward, and guided Rubi aside. On the sofa was Kai, her stare on warp-drive, and on her lap she was scratching the chin of Destiny, Granny's micro-pig.

'Kai, what you doing 'ere?' Dad took a step back.

'Me boat's getting serviced.' She cleared her throat and hung onto Destiny.

I smiled. When I had picked up the treasure chest that was exactly like ours, I didn't realise that it was ours. She had said it was a family heirloom, and she wasn't technically lying. She'd wanted to get caught. That was why she'd told me the photo was of a girl. She'd wanted us to work it out!

Kai got up from the sofa, but was crouching as if about to do a runner. Destiny jumped to the floor and ran towards me feet.

'So she's staying here for a bit.' Rubi took Kat's hand. 'Not that it's any of your business.'

I didn't realise that I was jumping, that I was leaping up and down and pointing at Kai like some demented circus animal. Not just because Kai was the person who set fire to our house, but because I had found me sister. A sister I never knew existed, a Saint we never knew was out there. And I didn't realise how much I had wanted a sister until then. It was like being at the birth of something amazing, watching a miracle. Because everything was different. Our family was growing.

Dad put both of his hands on me shoulders to hold me back from entering outer space. 'I know, I know.'

'Know what?' Rubi's dad came up from behind us.

'Kai is the one who burned down our house.' Dad said it as casually as that, as if he were ordering a Maccy D's.

'What?!' Rubi stared at Kai. 'That's mental. Have you lost your mind?!'

'She's a fire*fighter*.' Rubi's mum peered over Rubi's dad's shoulder. 'She wouldn't do that. And why? Why would she do that?'

' 'cause she's me daughter.' Dad pointed towards Kai. 'She's a Saint. And we ain't exactly normal.'

For a moment, I thought maybe Kai had lost her voice too. Her mouth gaped; she glanced back and forth from Rubi to Dad, and then at me.

'That can't be true.' Rubi's dad laughed. 'She looks nothing like you...'

'She has a right-hook like mine though.' Dad smiled.

'But... but... I don't get it. Why would you do that to them?' Rubi turned back to Kai.

'I... I didn't mean it to... I just thought if I could... It got out of control so fast. I didn't expect it to...'

'But you're supposed to stop fires,' Rubi yelled. 'Not start them.'

'It's quite common, y' know.' Dad crossed his arms. 'When there's been a spat of fires, they look at firefighters first. Which I guess makes sense, 'cause they like to be the heroes. Get a kick out of the whole thing. And they love fire, which is why they get into it...'

Rubi dropped Kai's hand and backed away from her. 'I don't feel like I know you at all.'

'Rubi, please.' Kai tried to hold Rubi's hand again, but Rubi's were dodging her. 'It wasn't like that. You have to believe me. I just wanted to meet them and I thought I had it under control...'

'Were you just using me to get closer to them?'

'Of course not!' Kai turned to us, angry tears welling up in her face.

'Kai, I think you need to leave,' said Rubi's dad.

'Leave? Where to?'

And I saw myself in Kai. I felt for her. Because she knew what it was like to lose a mum, she knew what it was like to be pushed away by Dad; she knew what it was like to be told to leave by another family and to feel you have no one. And now she knew what it was like to lose Rubi.

'Kai, get on the bus!' Dad looked at his watch. 'We need to get on the road. I hate driving at night. And we're out of gas.'

'What?' Kai scanned around, confused.

'Come on. On the bus. Bring that stupid pig too.' Dad turned to the side and held his arm out to the bus, signalling.

Kai stared at me. But the look was searching, getting in deep, trying to work out what might happen if she got on our bus. Where might we take her? I picked up Destiny and handed her to Kai. Then, she walked towards the bus with wide steps and long gazes, as if walking to the end of the line. Dad followed her.

Rubi's face had caved in. I didn't want her to be hurting. I wanted to tell her it was all way more complicated than that. It wasn't simple. Nothing was like the films. Life wasn't black and white or even technicolour - it was all chaos. But Rubi wouldn't look at me. She wouldn't look at anyone. Her arms were so tightly folded, she looked fit to lock herself in them for the rest of her life.

And it was so hard, because I got no words to say sorry, and she was so fenced off it was like barbed wire. So I took a deep breath, ready to cut myself up, and I launched into wrapping me arms around her so tight she couldn't wriggle out. She didn't want it. But this might be the last time I saw Rubi. I didn't have words, so the hug became more than just a sorry or a goodbye. The hug became a thank-you too because Rubi had been the best friend I ever had, and she deserved better from me.

I stared at the yellow dandelion and how it was still in her hand, and I wondered if it could be a new start, whether it was a sign that things weren't as toxic as I thought. That maybe... things might grow again.

'Scarlett.' Rubi's mum touched me arm. 'Your dad's leaving.'

I let go and went towards the bus that was holding hostage the person who actually burned down our house. And it occurred to me then that I could actually save me mum, but it would mean I'd lose a sister too.

27 HOURS UNTIL COURT

'Just because you can't see something, it doesn't mean it's not there.'

Pirates of the Caribbean:
Dead Men Tell No Tales.

W e were leaving the Cotswolds, heading towards the coast. Dad had drawn a bit of a map on a well-creased piece of paper. Rain was pelting down on the bus faster than the wipers could move. Our breath was sweating up the inside of the windows. It was more of a ship than a bus. More like being at sea than on the road. And on our voyage of the damned, we had a stowaway.

Dad wouldn't say where we were going. He'd ramble about getting the family back together again. But he insisted we'd be back in time for Mum's court hearing, even though I still had no idea what I was going to do. I finally had what I wanted, but it was far from I had imagined. Granny was right. I'd been looking for a villain, a pirate. For someone who'd want us dead.

Someone who wanted revenge, to rob us, to curse us. I had been looking for someone who wanted to settle the score, to take our treasure. So I didn't see Kai. A sister who wanted to be a Saint. How could I hand her in? But how could I not? With me mum walking the plank.

I couldn't stop staring at Kai on the bus. I kept wondering what it would have been like to have grown up with her, to have not been the only child, to have had someone who'd know what it was like. This deep ache settled in me. A loss.

Kai sat upfront on bus seats next to the luggage holder, biting her nails like me. Destiny was asleep on her lap. Most of the first floor of the bus was still waiting to be converted. A cardboard box kept swerving round the luggage holder. A box of treasure, knocking into the sides. I glared at Kai, and then pointed at the box, and lifted me hands to ask what it was.

'Uh Jason?' Kai leant to one side. 'I think Scarlett wants to know what's in the box here.'

'That's me!' Granny showed up next to me, making me jump.

'That's part of your Granny.' Dad yelled from the driver's seat. 'Picked her up t' other day.'

I pulled a disgusted face at Kai.

'Cat got your tongue.' Granny stuck out her tongue at me. 'That's the lightest I've ever been, mind. Death does wonders t' your figure.'

'What happened to your voice?' Kai nodded to me.

'I reckon it's from the soot in the house. Or stress.' Dad spoke on me behalf. 'But don't worry, if I know Scarlett, she'll find her voice in no time.'

Kai put her hands around Destiny, cupping her and staring at her. 'What you going to do with me?'

'Hang her up!' Granny laughed and slapped her leg.

'Well, we will not send you to Coventry, ain't that right, Scar?' Dad cleared his throat.

'Send me to what?' Kai didn't blink.

'No, I mean, we *won't*...' Dad swerved a bit to avoid a bin that had fallen into the street and the bus dipped and bumped. 'Girt bloody potholes!'

We all slid to the right. Dad's driving was questionable at the best of times. I got up to see if there was a police car where they sometimes sat for speed checks. Something reflected through the rain. I got out me phone and started typing, then showed the message to Dad, who had to read it, bit by bit, while looking back and forth from the road.

'But you've never driven a bus before, have you?'

'She wants to drive?!' Kai got up from her seat, still holding Destiny, who was wriggling.

'She wants to drive?' Granny rolled her eyes. 'Daft cow.'

'She wants to drive,' said Dad.

'Why?' Kai shook her head at me.

Dad swerved again. 'Police checks. Says if they pull me over and if I've been caught before and if I'm not sober...'

'Are you not sober?'

'I am! I think... How long d'you have to not be drinking to be safe?'

'I dunno.' Kai struggled to keep hold of Destiny. 'Does it stay in your blood stream longer if you drink regularly?'

'I do remember someone sayin' that because of the football, the police were going to be checking people more. But how long does... Ah, damn it. I don't want to risk it.' We all held on as Dad pulled over and unfastened his seat belt. 'Right Scarlett. Don't kill us, OK?'

'Too late for me!' Granny bent down and made a face at Destiny. The pig snorted.

Dad slid off his seat and opened the door to the driver's booth. I got in and closed the door, stretching out me arms. Everything was bigger, further away. The wheel reminded me of those spinning merry-go-rounds in a park.

Dad pointed to the mirrors. 'Now, can you see alright?'

I nodded.

'Go slow. Pull away slow.' Dad waved his hand.

Kai tapped on me arm. 'You got a licence? A bus one?'

I nodded, lying.

'She ain't driven the bus before. Not had to. Since the fire we just... y' know...'

Dad put his head down. Nobody moved. The weight of what Kai had done sank in. We may have gained a Saint, but we had lost everything because of her. We lost Granny, Kirsten and her little babber, even me mum. Our ship had sunk to the bottom of the ocean, forever lost at sea. There were no warnings, no chance to get up a white flag.

Sometime curses, family curses, they don't come about because somebody wishes you harm. They are legacies. They are the ripples of something bad that happened a long time ago. The sort of things that plunge you deep into the sea. Two boys drowned that day in me dad's garden, and Kai and I were forever cursed, forever diving in search of him. But now he was swimming back up. Should me mum pay for that? Should me mum go to prison because of something that happened to me dad? And then to Kai? She had her own curses to deal with, her own sea monster under the surface to wrestle with.

'Look, about before...' Kai shrunk inwards.

'Wait, Kai.' Dad held up the palm of his hand. 'Just gimme a second to talk to Scar about how the bus works.'

'You're nuts if you let her at the wheel!' Granny shook her head. 'Bonkers.'

I buckled in as Dad went through the motions, talking about being 'aware' of the size of it. I watched and nodded. Behind the words, he was having separate thoughts, a separate conversation with himself.

Dad held on to the rail as I edged out onto the road. 'You're insured, right?'

I nodded. Kirsten had put me on for emergencies. Dad

stayed up front while I drove, keeping an eye on me. Granny kept shouting that I'd be the death of them all.

'You alright for a bit?' Dad waited for me to nod. 'Just stay on here 'til I say otherwise.'

I wanted to ask him where the hell we were going. He swaggered down the bus, swinging like a gorilla from rail to rail. I watched them in the mirror. Kai perched there like a parrot. She looked smaller, shrunken like a little doll.

'So, don't know how to knock, eh?' Dad smirked, and sat down.

'Like a normal person...' Granny tutted.

I wished I could talk. Granny knew full well that Kai and her mum had tried that once and had the door shut in their faces. It's no wonder she burnt it down. It's no wonder she needed to get into a ring and fight with Dad. I'd been there. I got it. The Saints were thick headed and stubborn. She needed a sledgehammer to get through to us.

She sat upright. 'Not after what happened to my Mum. Nobody let us get a look in.'

'Fair point.' Dad nodded. 'Sorry about that. You were just a little babber too, eh?'

'I remember it pretty clearly though,' said Kai. 'Hard to forget something like that. My mum was desperate, she'd heard you were doing well, had got back on your feet. She was convinced you'd help but then...'

'I would have if I'd have known. They were trying to protect me.'

'From what?! Being a parent?'

'Your mum and I had a bad thing going. We made each other worse... The only thing I could do was leave.' He patted Destiny's head. 'She never said nothing about being pregnant. And I guess I cut off all contact 'cause I knew if I got near her then I'd be back to square one, because I still loved your mum.'

'I tried calling,' said Kai. 'But then I'd freeze and go into work-mode.'

'Oh, you were the one who kept calling about installing free smoke alarms!'

Kai nodded. 'But you already had some. And then everyone just seemed to get annoyed with me after the first call. I didn't know how to say it... I mean, like - Hi, remember me, the daughter you may or may not know about... How are things? Am I allowed to see you now?' Kai voice was high-pitched, strained. She gazed out of the window, grabbing onto Destiny's ears for comfort, but she jumped free. Kai crossed her arms.

'Y' know, only a Saint can set a small fire and accidentally have the whole thing go up in flames.' Dad smirked. His teeth were like a white flag.

Kai put her head in her hands. 'It wasn't supposed to get that bad. I should have emailed or phoned, or whatever... I know that!'

'How *is* your mum?'

I swerved down the road. Granny and I looked at each other. How did Dad not know? Kai stared out the window, and shook her head. 'She's, uh, not with us anymore. She died.'

'What? When?' Dad's face dropped.

'When I was ten.'

He went silent. I wanted to ask Kai if her mum knew it was me mum driving the train, if she'd wanted to get Dad's attention or revenge on Mum and Granny for turning her away. But when you looked at her, the utter devastation on her face, I knew it couldn't be that.

'I went into care after that.'

'Turn right 'ere Scarlett,' Dad yelled up to me. 'Then keep on the M5 when you get to it.' Dad's movements shrank each time Kai said something. And now he wasn't moving at all, like he'd dropped his anchor in a storm, letting waves crash and plummet into him. 'I'm surprised you'd want to find me after everything...'

'Wanted to know where me love of Bruce Springsteen came from.' Kai smiled.

'Ah.' Dad nodded. *'I got debts that no honest man can pay...'*

But I knew why Kai came for us. I got it. She had no-one, and that was always way worse. She was like Sophie and Scott, like me - just wanting to have someone in her corner, someone to be there for her.

'I'm so so so... sorry.' Kai pulled at her jumper sleeves. 'For ever showing up.' It came out like she was pushing it. Like she should've had some All Bran to get it loose. She was so like Dad, the Dad I used to know. So closed up.

'Don't...' Dad shook his head. 'This ain't on you.'

'But I was the one who...'

'A tiny spark. You had no idea it would lead to all that, did you?' Dad lifted up his arm, awkwardly at first, and then threw it around Kai's shoulders and squeezed her tight. And the more he squeezed, the more she loosened. 'Right?'

She nodded. I wanted to be next to them because maybe they'd forgotten about me up front, driving. Maybe they'd always forget about me. Maybe Kai would be the kid he always wanted. Maybe Kai was more like Dad than me? But it was her time. When I tried to see things as she saw things, I felt lucky and guilty. We were all going to have to make up for what happened to her, especially me dad.

'Y' know what Kai?' Dad sat upright. 'I couldn't be happier that you burned down our house.'

I turned back to look at him and swerved in the road.

'What? But what about Scarlett's mum? What's going to happen to her?'

'We'll work it out. I done you wrong in so many ways. Worse than any fire. You screwin' up, sort of helps me feel... well... Feel free to burn down whatever you need to burn down. You too, Scarlett.'

That was as close to a sorry as we were ever going to get.

Considering we had nothing left, it wasn't exactly an invitation. But maybe when Kai burnt down our house, she'd done us a favour. Maybe that was the only way to get rid of a family curse.

Granny and Destiny went upstairs. I listened to Kai and Dad talk while I drove the bus across the country. Kai talked about her mum a lot, about how hard life was for her. She had a diary of her Mum's that came with a book care-services had made about her past (from what they could find out about her life before the council took her on). Her Mum's diary talked about Dad and coming to the house - it even had an address, but it had taken Kai years to pluck up the courage to come. But her job as a Fire Inspector gave her courage somehow, a sense of being part of something - like a family. So it made sense that it was this part of her that came to us. She literally had to light a fire under us to get this whole ball rolling.

Cars backed up behind us on the motorway because it's hard to get up to speed on a bus. We went over the bridge Granny took me to, the bridge where Dad would go metal-detecting as a kid, and over to Wales. It was as if we were revisiting something, as if we were on a voyage. And I wondered what waited for us at the other end.

When we pulled up in front of a white-ish lighthouse, I saw a pirate flag out front, blowing in the wind like the one on Kai's boat. We were on the edge of a cliff and some podgy woman in a white dress came out of the front door to see us, arms crossed.

'I don't believe it.' Dad rushed off the bus. 'D' ya see that?! I don't believe it.'

He ran towards the blue front door. The wind stuck his Nike jumper to his front, overflowing behind him. The shoelace of his trainer was untied. I got out and watched at a distance, and even though this woman had got her arms crossed like Rubi had, and even though Dad hates to hug, he threw his arms around her like a lifebuoy.

At first, I thought it was Kirsten's mum. But I watched them talk. She shook her head at him, and then he took her hand, and they walked towards us. It was Kirsten. Except Kirsten wasn't walking. She was waddling as if she was carrying an enormous chest of treasure in front of her, smuggled under her dress, and I could finally see what I couldn't see before.

She hadn't lost the baby like we thought at all.

Some things had been saved from the fire.

21

'A woman doesn't know how powerful her voice is 'til she has been silenced.'

The Little Mermaid.

W hen Kirsten came towards me, waddling, with a plastic bag in her hand, I couldn't look at her. I stared up at the white lighthouse and the grey roofs of the houses clumped around the base. When she put her hand on me shoulder and said: 'It's a girl', I still couldn't look at her. I stared at her enormous belly and felt the wind almost cut me in half. When she waddled like a seal over to Kai and hugged her too, I couldn't look at either of them for all the shame I had in me. It explained why Kai was always looking at her shoes.

It was one thing to lose your voice when you want it most, when you need to sing. But quite another when it has been taken from you. Me voice had left me as if it was making a point, but Kirsten had hers taken from her by Clive. I should never of doubted her.

'Well, I never...' Granny got up from patting Destiny. 'She's a whale! Gi-normously fat.'

'These were knitted by my mum.' Kirsten handed me the bag she was carrying. It was a bundle of knitted baby clothes, the ones she'd saved from the fire. They were so small - the pastel yellows and blues and pinks looked like a coral reef wrapped up in plastic. Our lives were about to change forever. I was no longer going to be someone that Kirsten tried to be a mum for, and I felt me legs go, like they were turning to something else, disappearing from me.

'Woah, steady on.' Kirsten grabbed me arm. 'Shall we go inside? Get you some water?'

'Are you OK?' Kai took the bag of knitting from me. Granny peered inside.

I nodded, holding on to Kirsten's hand, thinking it should be the other way around. I should be holding her up.

'You sure you should be climbin' all those stairs?' Dad followed us. 'Lemme help.'

'No, no, get the stuff in. The climb's good for us. Been doing it for weeks.' She patted her belly. 'Come on Scarlett. It's not too far. You're just a bit faint.'

Did the lighthouse still work? Could it bring me back? Light me way through the dark? The others all stayed back at the bus, together, loading Kirsten's things inside. It felt like I was swaying up the spiralled stairs, up and up, around and around, like we were stuck in a whirlpool.

'My sister in Spain let me stay here.' Kirsten huffed her way up, grabbing hold of the railing ahead of me. 'It's usually a holiday home. But when she heard about what happened... Sisters are good like that, you know. Don't know what I'd do without mine.'

When we got to the top, the glass window opened out to a calm sea, rocks and boulders and dried out seaweed, below. A long, blue line stretched out on the horizon.

'The Atlantic ocean.' Kirsten breathed in and closed her eyes. 'I'll miss it. There's something about looking out to sea. They say that if you feel seasick, you should stare at the horizon.' She poured water into a glass etched with a lifebuoy and anchor, and passed it to me. 'Completely gone, then? Your voice?'

I nodded, trying to fix me gaze on the horizon.

'Do you know why I left?' She stared straight at the horizon too. 'It wasn't because of you. Or even because of him.' She poured herself a glass of water. 'I wanted to protect the baby. I was so close to losing her. I was bleeding and I thought the stress would finish it. I had to leave.' She sighed and sat down next to me. 'I couldn't lose another.'

There was a swell, an undercurrent in me belly because I wasn't actually full of shame like I thought. I was mad at her for leaving. And it had never even registered to me before that I'd be upset that she'd left me, that she'd left us, that like Dad, she didn't even try to keep Clive away from me. I mean I wasn't no kid, but sometimes it's hard to remember that, to feel grown up.

'Y' know, I got laryngitis once. Couldn't even whisper. Doctors said it was stress. Started getting really sick all the time back then. That's why I dropped the lawsuit. I couldn't cope with it. Even though I knew I should have kept going. I shouldn't have quit. But he'd literally taken my voice. He'd have ruined my life.' She sniffed. 'I wasn't sure it was worth it. The system's rigged. I wasn't even sure if, after sacrificing everything that I would even get anywhere. That would have undone me.' She breathed in as if she hadn't breathed in all day. 'The problem is Scarlett, I didn't have any good options. Once something like that happens to you, and you think you have this courage to do the right thing, to protect other people, you realise suddenly that no matter who is around you, you really are alone in it.'

I was underwater, drowning in a sea of so much stuff that I didn't know how to break the surface. I could see Scott's face when I tried to convince him, and sweet dementia-Doreen's words when I tried to tell her. And it was like a bad dream, when you can't get no-one to believe you. And I turned away from Kirsten because I felt so bad that I'd done the same to her.

'Anyway.' She shook her head. 'I just wanted you to know I was sorry. For all of it. For what I said about your mum, for leaving, for not taking Clive to court, for... Well, I've not been a good whatever-it-is-I-am-to-you.'

It was as if something dislodged in me throat. Whatever I was choking on was coming up. 'I'm the one who should be sorry.' Me voice was cracked and horse, but it was coming back, along with everything else. I push tears back up me face.

'What? What do you mean?'

For a minute, I lost it again. For a minute, I went right back under. Because it served me right, it served me damn right. I deserved it. I deserved to have had Clive do that to me, after what I did to Kirsten.

'Scarlett...' She put her arm around me. 'Did something happen? Did he do something to you?'

I nodded because that was all I could do.

'This isn't your fault.'

'I should have believed you.' I put me head in me hands.

'This isn't divine justice.'

'Poetic justice though.' I sniffed.

'Oh Scarlett... It's not justice at all. There hasn't been any. I should have fought. I'm so sorry I was a coward. I did this to you. This is my fault.'

'No.' I grabbed her hand. 'You did your best. On your own.'

Her back rose as if she'd been given legs. 'You're right. I may have been too weak to fight for me, Scarlett. But for you, I'll take on anyone. You hear me? I'll never stop. Promise.' She pulled me hand towards her as if dragging me out of the water. 'We're in this together now, OK? You and me.'

I nodded, wiping me face and squeezing her hand back

because it might have been the worst and most terrible bond to have with someone, but it was ironclad. 'We should get Dad to teach us some moves. Knock him out.'

'Good idea.' She smiled and laughed with tears in her eyes. 'Glad your voice is back. I've missed it.'

'You have?'

'Oh yeah, I've missed you guys. I even miss your Gran - god forbid.' She rolled her eyes.

I smiled. 'Me too. Bet she's loving that.' I stared at Kirsten's stomach, the bulging baby swimming around inside, and took a deep breath. There would be another soon. Kai was just the beginning. I met Kirsten's gaze for the first time as she held onto her stomach.

'I was thinking of naming her after your Gran. What do you think?'

'Oh god, don't do that.' I laughed and sniffed.

'Why not? Scarlett and Henrietta.' She gazed up at the ceiling. 'I can see it now. A great duo. No doubt she'll love you.'

'You think?' I held me hand over her. 'Can I?'

'Course.'

I placed me palm on Kirsten's stomach, the bulging promise of a new start, and leaned over. 'Hello tadpole! It's Scarlett, your sister... D' you think she can hear me?'

'Oh yeah, I talk to her all the time.'

I leant back in and whispered. 'I will teach you how to punch a man like Granny, 'til he's seeing stars.'

Kirsten laughed like a loon, snot came out of her nose. 'Oh god. What a handful. What a day, eh? Two sisters in 24 hours.'

I nodded and rubbed me throat.

'What you going to do about Kai? Your dad's worried you might hand her in.'

'What's the right thing to do?'

'I'm not sure there is one.' She shook her head. 'Some things just have to play out. Some things just seem like they are meant to happen, you know? They feel like they've already happened. Do you get that feeling? That what's about to happen has already happened?'

I shrugged because I had no words for her. I didn't want to voice the decision I was making in me head. Did I think that what was about to happen had already happened, that somehow I had already made the decision for all of us?

22 HOURS UNTIL COURT

'Just for once, let me look on you with my own eyes.'

Darth Vader, Star Wars

The whole Saint family, including Granny and Destiny, were on a bus going back to the West Country. Kirsten was driving, even though none of us felt comfortable with her being so pregnant at the wheel. She was doing it for me, speeding for me, to make sure I'd get time to do what I needed to do before Mum's trial. Dad was napping upstairs, and I sat downstairs on the bus. Even though I could talk again, I didn't. Because when I didn't talk, I could hear better. Kirsten didn't tell anyone. The clouds were heavy, thick, pushing us down like an unseeable force. Every time the bus hit a pothole, I grabbed for me seatbelt, but didn't find a thing.

When I was a kid, me mum used to say that Darth Vader got messed up because of a car accident, and so if I didn't want to end up like him, I'd better wear me seatbelt. I'd sit in the middle of the back seat and reach across for the belt on the right and the left, criss-crossing them over me so that I was double-belted. Safe as houses. She'd ask me if I wanted to go to space in a ŠKODA, then told me to hold on tight and to use The Force while she shouted *lift off*. She'd zig-zag down the empty street, slamming her foot on the brake again and again, throwing me forward, the seatbelt holding me back. That was me mum before the train accident, before I realised seatbelts were never enough to stop someone from getting proper-messed up. I stared at the back of Kai's head. Her black, cropped hair reminded me of Vader's helmet. I got up to go speak to Dad.

'Scarlett?' Kai grabbed me as I walked past. 'I never meant for your mum... it didn't occur to me that she'd...' I lifted me hand as a signal for her to stop and not worry. 'I'm sorry. What should we do? I can hand myself in?'

I pointed to me chest and then tapped me temple. I climbed up the stairs, slamming into the side as the bus turned. I walked to Dad's bed. He was lying down with his back to me.

'Dad?' I whispered. 'Dad?'

He didn't move. 'You're thinking about handin' her in, aren't you?'

I stared at his back, willing him to turn around. 'I just think we have to find a way to save Mum.'

'But your mum doesn't want t' be saved.'

'Mum doesn't know what's best. She's never been able to look after herself. You know that.'

'But you got to stop doin' it for her.'

'She's doing it for me, Dad. How can I live with myself?'

'You'll manage. This might be your Mum's only chance to get help.'

'She could go to prison.'

He turned to face me and it was as if something was wrong with his face. 'Her lawyer said different. Anyway, with your Mum's history... She's been lucky *not* to be in prison already.

She's done things most people go to prison for. This could be the best thing for her.'

'Best thing for you, you mean.'

He sat up. 'Don't you dare. I said I would fight for you from now on. Well, that also includes Kai. You're both me daughters and I just don't see the point of ruinin' Kai's life at the same time. We'd lose her again. She'd lose everything. And she's been through plenty enough already.'

'And Mum? Hasn't she? Why should she pay for our shit?'

'Your mum already lost everything, that's why she did it. You were the last thing she had.'

'She hasn't lost me.' I swallowed. 'I'd never leave her. She knows that.'

'You already did. Don't you remember?'

'Remember what?'

'When you left her. When you begged me to take you away.'

'From Mum?'

'Haven't you wondered why you came to stay with me in the end?'

'I thought the courts made you.' I crossed me arms and turned me back on him.

He leaned in. 'You ran away from your mother. You were just a little thing, and you got on a bus, came all across town, and you sat on me doorstep waiting 'til I got home. You was crying with that little Mary Poppins' brolly. Not in a fit state. Heavin' mess, actually. Kept sayin' summat about one of your Mum's boyfriends scaring you. I didn't let you leave after that. I may not have been a good dad, but I knew I could keep you safe.' He signed. 'I couldn't risk sendin' you back. That's why your mum was the way she was.'

The bus was zipping past trees on the motorway, zipping past buildings and MacDonalds, edging closer and closer to home. Back when I was small and Mum had bad news, she'd take me to MacDonalds. She'd sit me down with a Happy Meal, which I referred to as the 'Sad Meal' because at some point after eating me way through the floppy cheeseburger and chips and playing with the toy, she'd tell me she'd lost her job, or that we'd have to sell the car, or that I couldn't go swimming no more.

I still always wanted to go to Macky D's though, because it was the year you could get a hundred different Disney characters to celebrate a hundred years of magic. So she'd go up to the people at the counter and come back with extra toys wrapped up in plastic. I got thirty characters by the end of the year. When Mum's boyfriend came along, that all stopped. She didn't need to break bad news to me over Happy Meals because we had money again, but it came at a cost.

I clung to me Mary Poppins figurine from MacDonald's - she had her bag in one hand, her umbrella in the other, and wore her hat with the flowers. As soon as I got her, I knew what it was I had to do whenever Mum had her bad days. I'd bring her medication and sing 'with a spoon full of sugar,' and when Mum stayed in bed, I'd go out and do the food shop. And that was when Mary took over who I was, when there were more days as Mary than there were days as Scarlett. And Mum's boyfriend would ignore her or yell at her, and me, and then one time I heard him hit her and I wasn't Mary anymore.

Even now, I still thought about what Mary would do. There really was only one thing that would make everything right. One thing in me power, for justice to be done. So when we got into West Stonecloud, I pressed the red buzzer that said 'Stop'.

'I want to get off.'

'What now? Here?' Kirsten's voice squeaked.

'Please Kirsten.' I went to the front of the bus.

'But...'

'Please.'

She nodded, then slowed and pulled over the bus in front of the Police Station. Kai and Kirsten stared at me with long looks. But they didn't move.

'Why we stoppin'?' Dad shouted from upstairs.

Kirsten opened the door to let me out. 'Sure you don't want me with you?'

'Need to do it now before I lose me courage.' I stepped off the bus.

'OK, I'll drive on.' She pointed ahead.

'Cheers drive.' I saluted her as the doors closed and turned towards the Police Station.

Granny had got off the bus too. She was waiting for me at the entrance. A silk scarf wrapped around her head. 'I haven't got long... This is it. The last hurrah.'

'This is it?'

'This is why I am still 'ere.' She adjusted her pointy sunglasses.

'What why?'

She pulled down her sunglasses to look me in the eye. ' 'cause there are some things in life that no-one should have to do on their own. This is one of 'em.'

'What about you? When you died. You were alone.'

'No, I wasn't.' She stood upright. 'Me sister showed up, and your Grampa, me mother and me father. And I got to meet me little boy. Ah, t' was the best day of me life.' She guided me towards the doors. 'Nobody dies alone, Scarlett. Now come on. Get a wiggle on.'

I took a deep breath. I was about to lose someone forever. But I had finally figured out what was worth fighting for, what wasn't worth losing myself to. That maybe villains didn't look like Darth Vader and breathe like a dodgy phone sex-pest. Maybe villains dressed up as heroes.

23

17 HOURS UNTIL SENTENCING

'All at once, everything looks different,
now that I see you.'

Tangled

Once upon a time, there was a girl called Scarlett, who wasn't particularly important before her house burned down. In the evening light, she climbed the highest tower, on the highest hill, on the edge of the Cotswolds to be safe, where nobody could catch her. Could she see better from up there? Would she be able to see the entire story clearer, even see into the past?

Would she be able to see her house burning?

The ghosts roaming at Rubi's?

Mr Post spying?

The owl swooping overhead?

Or even see her mum behind bars?

I wanted proper walls, to be far away, looking over the town. I wanted to be safe as houses, except they weren't so safe these days. I had climbed Tyndall's monument, where Rubi and I used to come. Where we'd scratched our names, *'Scarlett and Rubi, friends 4eva'* into the brick after too much cider and hash. I traced the engraving with me fingertips, remembering it like it was yesterday. I stared out at a golden streak of light zigzagging across the setting sky. The river mirrored it like flowing locks entangled in towns and green fields. Ponytails of trees sprang up around the neck of the hill, knots of clouds hanging in the sky. But it was like I'd been undone since going to the police station.

'Thought you'd be here.' The voice came from behind me.

I turned away from the iron bars of the window. Rubi stood at the top of the stairs in her Green Day hoodie. The horror I remembered on her face had gone away. Instead, her gaze was limp. I didn't run up to her with me arms out. She told me so many times not to be so needy, not to be so desperate. So I resisted. I didn't want to ruin it.

'I remember when we used to come here as kids.' She glanced around. 'Feels like so long ago. Why were you always Rapunzel?'

'I had the long hair.'

She pointed at me. 'So your voice is back?'

I nodded.

'You always made me the prince, remember? It's no wonder I turned out gay, right?' She smiled, a glint in her eye.

It was so hard not to run up to her, to wait for her. The energy was busting out the top of me head. It would leak out of me somehow in beams of light that would blind us all.

'What does it take to get a hug?' She tossed her arms up. 'You know, it's not easy to track you down and climb all these stairs at 9 O'clock at night...'

'Rubes...' I leapt forward and tied me arms around her. This time she hugged me back, and we were like our own messy knot.

'Can't breathe!' She faked choking.

'I'm so glad to see you. And I'm sorry.' I pulled back, but all the stuff I had been holding was spilling out. 'I'm not sure how to say this so that it doesn't sound weird or rude or... crap. Not even sure it's possible. I just know it's a big deal for you. But for me... I mean. I'm glad your gay. Wait, not glad - it's not like... Can you be glad someone is gay? I guess I'm glad you can be yourself. I was just hurt that you didn't think you could be *you* before. With me. Y' know? But you're right, totally right that I made it all about me and...'

'Scarlett, Scarlett.' Rubi put her hand over me mouth. 'Shhhhhh.'

I pulled her hand away. 'Sorry, I got so much I want to say...'

'It's OK.' She sat down on the stone floor, back against the wall. 'You know, I was still me before. Honest. I was just a little late to the party. It took me longer than most to work it out. Which is more than embarrassing.'

'Better late than never.' I sat down next to her.

'I guess. Man, it's cold up here.' She rubbed her arms. 'You won't treat me different, will you? I'd really hate that.'

'As long as you don't treat me different!' Everything will change now I'd gone to the police station. 'I don't want to lose you again.'

'Lose me? To Kai? You're such a drama queen.' She nudged me.

'Oi! Am I that bad?'

'If the crown fits!' Rubi smirked.

'It's genetic.' I poised like Granny would, head held high and proud.

'You're my best mate, Scarlett. There's nothing that can change that. I've seen you have a tantrum over a haircut, seen you wet your pants going down a slide, and I've seen you accidentally punch yourself in the face.'

'Eh, it goes two ways.' I pointed back and forth between us.

'What I mean is.... We both have dirt on each other. We're stuck together now whether you want it or not!' She laughed.

'Even if I did something you didn't agree with?'

'I didn't agree with that haircut, the one with the undercut, and we're still...' A chilly wind cut her off. 'Good god, that's freezing.'

'You should sit on me other side. I'll block the breeze then with me beef.'

She moved to the other side. 'Good plan. Your beef is a good blocker.'

I laughed. And she knocked into me again. 'Is it me, or does it still smell like White Lighting in here? Oh look!' She pointed out of the barred window. 'Someone's sending up those lanterns.'

We stood up to look out. Three floating paper lanterns rose up from the valley, as if sending out some sort of signal, as if trying to tell me something, but I didn't know what. I felt lighter, more hopeful. But I shouldn't feel like that. I shouldn't feel good when I saw them. 'Bad for owl's I heard.'

'Well, maybe it's time some owls got taken down.' Rubi cleared her throat. 'Especially the Destiny stealing kind.'

'Maybe.' I stared out into the distance. 'I went to the police station earlier to make a statement.'

Rubi paused for a second. 'Did it go OK?'

'Not sure it'll be enough. Just me. They said they'd need more people to come forward...'

'If I'd have known about Kai, I'd never have... I still can't believe she did it.'

'You weren't to know. But...'

'The whole thing made me realise how you must've felt. About me not telling you I was gay.' Rubi pulled away from the window and paced, staring at her feet.

'Well... I guess, but it's not quite the same. Your secret doesn't get you in prison.' I leaned back against the cool wall.

'Not anymore!' She grabbed me arm, and hooped hers

underneath. 'Was she only with me to get close to you? To your family?'

'Hmmm. Only one way to find out, I guess.'

'What d'you mean?'

'You should speak to her.'

'Nah way... after what she did. That's not right.'

'You should cut her some slack. Her life has been...'

'What? Why? She set fire to your house! That's messed up.'

'Who isn't?' I shrugged. 'Her Mum... Everyone turned her away. Do y' know what that's like? To have nobody? To be all alone?'

Rubi shook her head and squeezed me hand. 'I guess you do.' She took a huge breath and when she breathed out the wind picked up too, and it was as if the world had breathed out with her. 'She did have a shit time. Kai, I mean. Reallllly shit. Especially when she went into care. I guess that's why I was so shocked. She told me all about this really personal stuff, especially about this one foster parent who used to pretend he was sleepwalking as an excuse to walk in on her... I mean, it's...'

'Wait, what? He pretended to sleepwalk?'

No no no no, it couldn't be. Could it? Not another person. Not someone else close to me? What were the chances? There was no way...

'But she never said anything, about your family and her, and the fire and...'

'Rubi! What was his name?'

'Huh? Who?'

'The foster carer that pretended to sleepwalk.'

'Oh I dunno, she never said. She reported him and got moved to a new home, but she said they never did anything about him. Anyway, there's no more Kai to worry about now. So no point worrying about it. She'll be in cuffs soon enough.'

'In cuffs?'

'You said you went to the police station.'

'I did. But not to hand Kai in. She's me sister. You can't rat out family.' I ran to the stairway.

'Where are you going?'

'We've got to go to Scott's house.'

'Why?'

'Because the more of us there are, the better chances we have of taking Clive down.'

Rubi's footfall spilled down the stairs behind me. I ran wild. She threw out questions as we raced to the house I never wanted to see again, to see a wall I never thought I'd want to see again, to make sense of a story I wish I was never a part of, to put away a man who should of been put away a long time ago.

24

16 HOURS UNTIL SENTENCING

'The very things that hold you down are going to lift you up.'

Timothy Mouse, Dumbo.

S cott's house was a circus. The lanterns we saw were like breadcrumbs leading us there. People spilled out of the house and onto the front lawn, holding onto cats and dogs, ponies, sheep and goats. Music and fairy lights were dancing out into the street. A TV van was outside. The front door was open. A hot-air balloon like the one from the film Up, bobbed from behind the house.

'What's going on?' Rubi tapped me shoulder.

'Nah, they wouldn't still be...'

'Still be what?'

'They were doing a fundraiser to raise money for our house, but...'

I felt dizzy and out of place. I shouldn't have gone there. I should have just asked Kai outright. Me body fought against me being there. But I had this weird draw to be there too. Not only to find out who else he'd hurt, but because I wanted to see it: the freak show. I wanted to see them. For better or for worse, I wanted them to regret what they'd done to me.

'Why don't we ask Kai? Just call her up?'

I frowned at her. 'Have you tried that before? Just ask someone something like that?'

She shook her head, and I pulled her into the house. We ducked and dived through the nest of people, through the garden and through the hallway. There was no sign of the Wrights. Just memories of West Stonecloud residents clotting together. I drew on a smile for the Vicar, the shop assistant, and people I recognised from the LARP. I waved and kept me head down. I still felt like the elephant in the room, wondering if anyone knew the Wrights had thrown me out.

When we got to the 'wall of fame' on the stairs, the wall of kids who'd been through the Wright house, I finally recognised Sophie sat on a swing in one of the pictures, wearing all black and eyeliner. I scanned the wall for a girl who might look remotely like Kai. A girl with soft black hair, a girl with a blue fleck in her eye. Rubi pointed to a picture below her and looked at me. 'That's her.'

I got close to the photo. The girl had a pixie cut. Her eyes were a bit closed as she was mid-blow in front of a chocolate birthday cake.

'How can you tell it's her?'

'That feather she's holding.' Rubi pointed to a white feather in the girl's fist. 'She takes it everywhere. Said when her mum died, she kept finding them. Said she felt like she was watching over her.'

I felt myself plummet. First Kirsten, then Sophie, and now me sister?

Rubi put her hand on me shoulder. 'Look at them all. Do you think he tried it on with all of them?'

I stepped back to see all the girls on the wall. There was

Sophie and Kai - two that I knew of - but there were more of them. And there'd be more to come. 'God, there's loads.'

She nodded. 'But *they'll* be the ones who put him away.'

'You think we could get Kai and Sophie to report him, too?'

Someone bumped into the back of me. 'Oh, aren't they just incredible?' A woman stood next to us, dressed as a zebra, holding a martini glass. 'To have looked after all these kids. Practically saints, aren't they?'

'They wish!' I laughed.

Rubi glared and crossed her arms. 'If heaven is filled with sex pests, I'd rather go to hell.'

The woman raised her eyebrows and carried on upstairs. I grabbed Rubi's phone from her, swiped across and took a photo of the wall of kids.

'Have you seen Scott?' Rubi scanned around the crowd.

I shook me head. 'He's probably in his room. He's not much of a party person.'

'I'll hang out down there.'

I had a funny sort of power walking around, knowing that Clive's days were numbered. To see this party, raising money for me house, and know that it would end, to know he'd soon be going through a living hell, that all these people would soon know, soon find out, soon start seeing him differently. But poor Scott was about to lose everything and I'd probably lose him forever too. He was about to lose his dream of a happy-ever-after. I didn't want him to hate me. He had to know I wouldn't do that to him; I wouldn't make up something like this. Maybe if I warned him... Maybe if I told him again, he'd hear me. Maybe he would want to help us report Clive.

I ran up the rest of the stairs and knocked on his bedroom door.

'Come in!'

There was a lion sat on the bed, hunched; Scott was in a

fluffy onesie with paws and a mane. Not the king of any jungle, mind. Just sat, imprisoned in a circus act.

'You shouldn't be here.' Scott scowled.

'I know... Why aren't you downstairs?' I shut the door and sat down next to him.

He gave me a side-eye look. 'You know exactly why. Whole thing is... Why do you care, anyway? What you doing here?'

'I do. I just wanted to warn you...'

'Look, there's no evidence he did anything.' Scott stood up. 'He sleepwalks, and that's it. I've seen him do it.'

I took a deep breath. The sound of music and people vibrated up through me feet. 'There is evidence, actually. I've told them where to find it.'

'What? Told who?'

'The police. There are pictures, mementoes, girl's earrings.'

'What sort of pictures?' He shook his mane like he was shaking off blame. 'That doesn't prove anything. He was probably sent those. They were always falling for him. That's why they adopted me instead.'

'And what about Kirsten, Kai, Sophie?'

'I don't know those people. But I know him and he wouldn't do that.' Scott pointed at me as if his finger were a sword.

'What about me?'

Scott looked away. He was the second person to have turned his back on me. Before all this happened, I'd have changed me mind and bent the truth to please him. I'd have caved. I'd have done whatever it was he wanted so as not to lose him, to not end up on me own. Just like I did before. But now I saw it wasn't me losing him, he was losing me. I got up from the bed, knowing that he'd be better matched if he'd dressed as an ostrich, considering where his head was at.

'I'm sorry, Scott.'

'For what?'

'I'm sorry you didn't get picked by better people. And I'm

sorry your life is about to turn upside down. But I ain't sorry for something *he* did.' I turned away and opened the door.

'No, you're not.' He spat. 'You're not sorry. This is you all over. First you send your mum to prison, and now me dad?'

'Not the same.' I shook me head.

'When this gets out, I'm going to make your life hell.' He closed the gap between us. 'I'm going to make sure that you can't even walk down the street because everybody loves me dad and hates the Saints. We're a respectable family. But you... nobody wants the likes of you ruining their town.'

'I don't care.' I shrugged. 'Because I ain't doing it for me.'

And it was true. His threats would have worked before. They would have freaked me out. But I didn't care anymore what the street thought of us. I knew the best of me family and the worst. All the rest seemed so tiny, so pathetic in the light of day. It was nothing compared to what the Wrights had done.

'I'll tell the police that you planted all that stuff as revenge, that you told me about it, that you had a sick crush on him and I'll clear his name.'

'What? You wouldn't.'

'It wouldn't be just your word against his; it'll be your word against mine and Liz's too. There's no way you can win. He's got the whole of Stonecloud behind him. He's an MP. Liz is a police-woman. Who's going to believe a homeless care home worker like you?'

Scott had moved in close to me, too close. I was penned in with a beast. 'You don't scare me.'

'I'll wear you down, just like I did to Kirsten.'

'What?'

'I'll stalk you everywhere. I'll make sure you wished you were never born.'

'You were the one harassing Kirsten. Sending her messages?'

'Defending my family from liars like you.'

'Y' know what Scott, I've done everything I could for you. I tried so hard to get you to like me, to get you to love me. I don't even recognise myself. I don't even talk like myself no more. I tried to be someone for you, but I don't even know why. I don't even know why I was trying so hard to impress you, to impress all of you, when you ain't people worth trying to win over. You can have your deranged family. You can have the whole fucking village. I got people who will listen, who will fight for me too.'

'That's what you think... They all bottle it, eventually.'

'Maybe on their own. But this time it's different. Because I ain't the only one. I ain't alone. There's a whole wall downstairs of girls who I've no doubt have got something to say about Lord Bannon, who'd like to see what's right come to the Wright's.'

I closed the door on Scott, proper, in more ways than one. I wished Rubi had been there to hear me because she'd never believe that I stood up for myself like that. The music stopped and someone rushed past me on the stairs.

'It's starting, it starting,' shouted a man dressed as a panda.

'What's starting?'

'The ceremony!'

'Ceremony?'

The whole circus of people moved outside. And Rubi came running up the stairs and grabbed me hand. 'Where's best to see the back garden?' She pulled me along.

'In there.' We opened the spare bedroom door where I used to sleep and leaned on the windowsill, opening the window to hear.

The back garden was swarming in the twilight. Fairy lights twinkled. A huge red circus tent propped up in the corner. TV crews were set up next to the hot air-balloon that was tethered down, and Clive and Liz were inside the basket. Clive was in red coattails, a black top hat and a whip. Liz wore a glamorous sequinned leotard, with a feather coming out of her head.

'Ladies and gentlemen! Clive stood up on the side of the

basket, holding on to the string. 'Thank you all for coming to this wonderful occasion to celebrate the marriage....'

'Scarlett?' Rubi grabbed me hand and placed something in it. 'It's time to take the hot air out of him.' She had a moustache-twirling villain's grin. In me hands was a rifle, the one Clive used on the pigeons who'd eaten all his cherries.

'Where did you get this?'

'Found it snooping.'

'I can't shoot him!' I passed it back to her. 'They'll put *me* away.'

'Not him.' Rubi pushed the gun back into me hand and pointed. 'That!'

I followed her finger and smiled, aiming the gun at the hot-air balloon. Squeezing the trigger, I didn't just take one shot. I took a shot for every girl on that wall for as long as the gun would let me, hearing each bullet sing, feeling the force of each one punch through more than just the air and the balloon and the atmosphere. And the balloon floated down like an elephant with big ears as people screamed and ran for cover, turning their backs again and again on Clive and Liz and their performance.

25

THE DAY OF SENTENCING

'The real thing Ivy taught me, is you gotta live like there may not be a later.'

Paulie

This was the day of judgement. The day I had been waiting for. The day we'd find out if Mum would go to prison or whether Kai would storm the place and stop the whole thing and sacrifice herself and we'd forever name stuff after her. This would be the day that would mean we'd get our insurance pay-out because we'd finally hear what I knew all along - that someone burned down our house.

No birds sang that morning, no wind blew. There was just a waiting in the air, a held-breath, a heavy, loaded question hanging out to dry. Dad, Kirsten, and I were on the bus again. Dad had worked it out with Rubi's family. We were all back to queuing for their shower. Dad stared at me, but said nothing. What was he wishing for? Did he go to the tunnel and make a wish to save Kai? Would his wish undo mine? I still hoped the jury would take pity on Mum and let her go with a slap on the wrist. Or that maybe Dad bribed someone or blackmailed Liz into getting Mum out. Because what Mum wanted wasn't what I wanted. I wanted her on the outside with me.

Despite having all the Saints back under one bus, I stared at granny's empty bed. Not even Destiny could bring herself to go there. And there was a voice missing, no nagging at me to do this or that. I hadn't seen her since she left me at the police station - cool as a cucumber in sunglasses and a scarf. Her bed was like looking at an empty wall where a picture had been. That was what Granny's shadow was like. What did she look like? Am I forgetting? Every morning, Granny used to say 'time for me medicine' and I'd bring her a toffee before she put her teeth back in. Even though she wasn't around, I got off the bus and went to take her a toffee, anyway. I hoped she might show up.

Her grave was a wooden cross waiting for its headstone. Dad scattered some of her ashes there and kept the rest on the bus, wanting to take her some place nice, some place high up. I untwisted the blue wrapper and placed the round toffee on the damp ground.

'Time for your medicine, Gran.' I pulled down on the suit-skirt Rubi lent me that kept trying to shimmy up. 'Get that in your chops.' I glanced around, waiting for her to show, wanting to say thanks for being there. 'You don't show up when people want you, do you?' I sighed. 'You ain't no fairy godmother but... I dunno... It's weird you not being here to tell me how dumb me skirt looks.'

'Too short if you ask me.' Mr Post shuffled up the path behind me.

'What d' you want?'

'Free country. 'ere to see me son.' He leaned forward to dust a petal off the engraved stone. I had never seen this grave before. Gran had been put right next to him, and gramps was on her other side. 'Your Mum's day in court today.'

'Yeah.' I nodded.

'You lot got what you deserved, if you ask me. Your Mum's a hero. You all actin' like you all own the place. Your like weren't meant for our town. She should of finished the job if you ask me and burned that bus down too. Right common as muck.'

'OK Edward.' I smiled.

'I should get me son removed from 'ere. So close to his own murderer.' Mr Post's eyebrows twitched up and down.

'It wasn't me Gramps.'

'Oh, like you'd know...' He dismissed me with his hand. 'Was before you was born.'

'I do. Granny told me. She said it was an accident. Said he drowned. Nobody's fault at all, just a horrible, horrible accident.'

He stuttered and shook his head. 'No. Not true.'

'It *is* true!'

'No no no....'

'Our family aren't evil, just had some bad stuff happen to us. But that don't mean that we....'

He was shaking his head as if he was trying to avoid the words flying through the air. He didn't want them to find their way into his thick head. He was like I was. There are some things that people can't hear, or see, they don't wish to. No amount of telling or explaining is going to make them change their mind. They have to get there on their own terms and in their own time. He needed someone to blame so he didn't have to look too close to home.

'If it weren't for those holes, it never would never have happened. And who made those holes? *Him!*' He pointed to me gramps' grave. 'That man and your father helped him.'

'For god's sake, Mr Post.' I wanted him to see us as I saw us, to forgive us, to live next to us happily ever after. But Mr Post wasn't ever going to change. Mr Post wasn't ever going to see us as anything else but the demons next door. And so I gave up because it didn't matter anymore what he thought of us. If that was what he wanted to think, if it helped him in some way to have someone to blame for his son's death, then why bother to take that away from him.

'Bloody murderers.'

'I'm real sorry, Mr Post.'

'What?'

'Sorry that you lost your son. That you lost me gran. Sorry that me family has been hard on you.'

'I don't want your sorrys.'

'I know you don't. But you got them anyways.'

'Put a sock in it.' He turned, stared at his son's grave and then at Granny's.

I sighed and for a moment we were both silent. A breeze blew and a bird sang on the telephone wire. I closed me eyes and lifted me head to smell the air.

He whispered. 'That's a blackbird up there. Good omen for your mum.' I opened me eyes. Mr Post had his hands supporting his back, looking up at the tree. 'Be careful of the magpies, though.' He started walking away.

'What d'you mean?'

He pointed up to the red smoke bush tree where a single magpie sat. 'One for sorrow, two for joy, three for a girl, four for a boy, five for silver, six for gold, seven for a secret never to be told, eight for a wish, nine for a kiss, ten for a bird you must not miss.' He saluted the bird, and another two magpies flew up and perched next to the first.

'Wait - can you tell me just one thing...?' I called out as he walked away further. 'Why you letting me mum confess to something she never did if it gets us our house back? When you hate us.'

'I ain't as selfish as you. Your Mum's been locked up for a proper long time as is. This could help her. Gives her a fightin' chance at survivin'. A hard world this... to live in.'

Mr Post walked out of the graveyard, whistling, seeming to

know something about me mum that I didn't. Seeming to have some sort of bond that I'd never get. But he was right. It wasn't that I didn't want me mum to get help. What I wanted was for me mum to be better, to be well. I wanted to look after her. I wanted that to be enough. But I'd been trying to do that me whole life, and it had got both of us nowhere. I turned back to look at the magpies and wondered, was it one bird or three, one for sorrow or three for a girl?

26

THE DAY OF SENTENCING

'You'll hunt me. You'll condemn me. Set the dogs on me.
Because that's what needs to happen. Because sometimes truth
isn't good enough. Sometimes people deserve more.
Sometimes people deserve to have their faith rewarded.'

Batman

They said that we'd have our day in court, but they
didn't say that our day would also be a Fathers4Justice
former-Army-Sergeant's day in court. Outside the
courthouse, dozens of people were dressed up as Batman. They
held signs that said: 'Free Tim Grouse!' The court itself was a
section of hard honeycomb. Each side with a window. The one
in the middle, facing out, was glass. But the two on either side
had been blocked in. It looked like a face with its eyes closed.

Dad, Kirsten, Kai and I, walked towards the crowd, heading
towards the last judgement. But I didn't want to stop it anymore.
I didn't want to save the day. I didn't want to lose me new sister,
Kai. I didn't want to lose our house. Maybe they were all right.

Maybe Mum's fake confession was the very best thing we could wish for. Or maybe it would be the worst thing. Maybe she'd actually end up in prison and not in hospital at all.

'Hear? What's all this for?' Dad tapped a guy's Batman-padded chest with the back of his hand.

'He just wanted to see his kids.' The guy balled his fists. 'What sort of crime is that?'

'What he do?'

'Camped out on top of the judge's house for *thirty-six hours* as Batman. Did it in the wind and rain. Dedication! That's a good dad, right there.'

Dad nodded. 'Sounds like a good man.' Dad stared at his shoes. 'What judge?'

'Uh Tristan Bale, I think.' Batman joined back into the chanting.

Dad watched his shoes the whole way into the court, up into the gallery, and until we sat down on the curved benches, which looked down to the main stage. Was he having second thoughts? Would he tell the judge Mum didn't do it?

'Is it bad?' I leaned over to Kirsten, who was readjusting her underwear. 'To have the same judge as that guy?'

She looked up at the white ceiling above us, rubbing the back of her neck. 'It means the media will probably report on it. So it's either a really good thing. Or a really bad thing.'

I leaned forward and held onto the rail, waiting for the signal for when it would start. Kai and Dad barely said two words. Kirsten babbled about the benches, how hard they were, and how there was no back to them. She sat with her legs wide apart to make room for her belly. She made bad jokes - one about how we should pay for better seats next time, and another about me having passed 'the bar' exam, and pointed to the rail I was holding on to.

I turned around to Dad. 'It's OK - right?' He stared at me as if he was seeing more than one version of me: a baby, a kid, a teenager, and a nineteen-year-old. He considered all of them and nodded.

Down in the docks, tables with green leather padding were dotted around. There was the jury box that would stay empty. The judge's box was in the centre. All the chairs were lined in red leather, and there were so many wooden panels dividing sections and lining walls, even the ones behind us, that it felt like the inside of a coffin.

Doors on the side opened. People walked through. It was starting. I held on to me breath until I saw me mum. She was dressed smart, but her entire body was moving like a robot. She didn't look up at us. We all stood when the judge came in. Then some guy with a wig said things I couldn't follow until I heard 'victim's statement'.

'I'll be opening the case with a statement from one of the victims.' The lawyer gestured to a bloke who looked like me dad. I turned to look at our bench, and Dad wasn't there.

It *was* him. I glared at Kirsten, and she nodded.

'Your honour.' Dad bowed his head slightly. 'Me name is Jason Saint. The defendant and I have a long history. And we are no stranger to the courts, as you'll know. The title of this sheet o'paper is misleading, because I don't feel like a victim.' He shuffled to-and-fro on his feet as if squaring up to fight. 'Actually, I feel like I should be on trial today because I'm ashamed to say that I failed me family.' Dad glanced up at us, and then down to Mum.

'And I failed her... When she - the defendant - needed help, your honour, I ignored her. When she asked me to take our daughter, I refused. I dragged her through the courts and through hell. When the defendant asked for support, I took it away. But I'm not the only one to have failed the defendant your honour...'

Me heart collapsed. Was he going to say me? Was he going to tell the courts how I failed Mum? How I pushed her away.

'The state failed her, too. When she needed a lifeline, they made her suffer more. When she witnessed a suicide, somethin' went in her that was never mended. And nobody wanted nothin' to do with her.'

I glanced at Kai. I hadn't told anybody about her mum and about mine being connected. It was too much. How much did it matter now it was done? Kai might want nothing to do with us if she found out. Maybe she didn't remember what had happened? Did she even know?

'Her mental health... Nobody wanted to help. She wasn't well, and they cast her out. When I wake up in the mornin', I have to remind myself that the home we'd been buildin' for so many years has gone. But that's nothing compared to what the defendant has suffered, and it's nothing compared to what me daughter will suffer if you put her mum in prison.'

'The only person who was there for her was our daughter. When we failed her mum, we failed her, too. When I go to sleep at night, I can't sleep. Not because I'm afraid, but because I'm full of regret. She needs help, not punishment. She needs to be cared for, not cast out. It's not every day that you lose your house. But your honour, houses can be rebuilt. A *home,* though, is made of its family, no matter how broken. We cannot afford to lose another mother. We've already lost so much in our house. But we can't afford to lose our home too.'

He folded up his piece of paper, his hands shaking, and sat down. It explained why he was so quiet. He had been getting ready to fight, for me, for me mum, for our family. Kirsten grabbed me hand and smiled as if she'd known, as if she wrote it with him.

Chanting started up outside. I only heard parts, the words muffled by the walls.

'__ DOWN THE __

__ Tim Grouse.'

I stared at the back of me mum's head, trying to work out the

357

words in the chant outside because even though they were chanting for this Tim guy, I couldn't help but feel it was for us.

The man on Mum's side listed her mitigating circumstances:

No previous.

Handed herself in.

History of mental health problems.

Steps taken to address problems.

And the chanting got louder and I could hear the words now.

'BURN DOWN THE HOUSE.'

'FREE Tim Grouse.'

'BURN DOWN THE HOUSE.'

'FREE Tim Grouse.'

I turned to Kai, sat beside me, and she stared back with eyes like the bat signal. I wanted to chant with them. Because, like Dad said, I didn't care about the house; I wanted me home, me family, together. I wanted to stand up and shout.

'BURN DOWN THE HOUSE.'

The judge stood up.

'FREE Tim Grouse.'

'Tamzin Spencer, please stand,' said the judge.

'BURN DOWN THE HOUSE.'

'You have pleaded guilty to arson, but not with the intent to endanger life.'

I grabbed onto Kai's hand and squeezed.

'FREE Tim Grouse.'

'You will be given a hospital order and a restriction order under sections 37 and 41 of the mental health act 1983. A restriction order...'

Kirsten let out a huge exhale, squeezed me hand, and gave me an unfiltered smile. I didn't hear a single word after 'hospital order.' Kai pushed back her hair and then put her head between her knees, as if all the tension in her had been holding her spine upright. Me mum turned up to look at me and gave me a thumbs up. Me body that was locked up before, tied up in knots for so long, spread out all at once and out of me chest burst the most insane laugh. And I wanted to float up to the ceiling, laughing like they do in Mary Poppins, ignoring her eye rolls, and spin around and sing and laugh until I couldn't come down. Because for the first time in forever, me mum was happy, and that mattered to me more than I realised.

'BURN DOWN THE HOUSE,' they shouted outside.

'FREE Tim Grouse.'

Disgraced Local MP Clive Hopkins arrested on sex abuse allegations

By Martin Johnson   09:55 7 Aug

The independent MP, Clive Hopkins, has been arrested on suspicion of sex abuse allegations, sources in Gloucestershire have said. Police arrested the MP last week after officers raided his constituency office and home, removing documents and computers for investigation on Friday after he held a fundraiser that was targeted by protesters.

The arrest came shortly after he publicly celebrated his twentieth wedding anniversary to Elizabeth Wright, a local police officer, now also being questioned alongside the allegations. The couple had been well-respected in the area for being devoted foster care parents for over twelve years, finally adopting a child in 2009.

Clive Hopkins, an independent MP, is alleged to have assaulted one woman in 2014, but the civil action filed against the MP was dropped amid public pressure and online harassment. He was never prosecuted. Now, three more people have now come forward to claim they've been victims of abuse while in the couple's care between 2002 - 2008, and more are expected.

Mr Hopkins, 45, is due to appear at Westminster Magistrates' Court on 6 September. A Crown Prosecution Service spokesman said it had made the decision to charge Mr Hopkins 'after reviewing a file of evidence from the Metropolitan Police.'

Mr Hopkins has submitted paperwork for his resignation as an MP for Gloucestershire, dated for when parliament returns in September. Constituents have complained that casework has not been dealt with in the MP's absence. Allegations that have been denied.

When asked for a comment, the Gloucestershire police said they could neither confirm nor deny the identity of someone who has been arrested.

A spokesman for local Liberal Democrats said: 'We have been calling for the resignation of Clive Hopkins for a long time. With crucial votes coming up in Westminster, the people of Gloucestershire need an MP they can count on to stand up for local communities and justice.'

27

'Sometimes what's left behind can grow
better than the generation before.'

The Lion King

The people of Stonecloud would cross the street to see the new Saint baby. They were like moths to a flame. They came from all around to see a new life arrive, cooing at her through the bars of a crib. They wanted to squidge her tiny feet, smell her head and ask how heavy she was when she was born, and how she was sleeping. Baby Henrietta, the newest member of the Saint family, was born with red hair that had a stripe of white on the side of her head. So Kirsten got no end of lip from people in the village who thought she'd died her baby's hair.

Hetty was the cutest thing ever to have blown snot bubbles in West Stonecloud. One of the nurses called her tiger when she was born and it stuck. The whole family came together on her first birthday, celebrating in our house that had been rebuilt from the fire. Kirsten was a big fan of wallpapered accent walls and lamp-lighting, and of course, hundreds of fire alarms. They decorated the entire house beyond recognition. Me old room was an office. Granny's room was now Hetty's, which always felt weird to me but fitting. Henrietta never left.

'Happy birthday, Tiger.' I leaned over her crib and tickled her tummy. 'This is for the wind and the rain. Watch out for those easterlies.' I hung me Mary Poppins' umbrella on the side of her crib.

We'd all given Baby Henrietta the things we had saved from the fire. She was wearing the clothes knitted by Kirsten's mum. She snuggled up to Dad's boxing monkey in her crib. And Destiny liked to sleep nearby, next to Kirsten's new doll house in the corner of the bedroom.

'Any luck on convincing Sophie to testify?' Kirsten picked up Hetty from the crib.

'Reckon she's close. But it's so much harder for her...'

'I've started getting messages from Scott again.' She bounced Hetty on her hip.

'Oh god.'

'Doesn't seem as threatening when you know it's him, though.' She walked towards the door. 'Plus, he doesn't know me, so... It felt more personal when I thought it was your mum.'

'Saw her last week.' I followed behind them both, and Destiny followed me, so I picked her up, too.

'Oh yeah, how's she doing?'

'She's all zen-like. Keeps talking about having entered this higher plane of existence. But I think she just enjoys having not to worry about the basics, y' know?' I put Destiny down when we reached the bottom of the stairs. I pointed to the new fire guard in the front room, near where I discovered the box Kai had taken. They told her to keep it. 'Hear, I didn't think you used the fire.'

'We don't!' Kirsten lifted Hetty up like she was flying. 'But I keep finding Hetty in the fireplace. Can't keep her out of it. Yes you, you mischief. We'll have to block it off soon.' Hetty grinned back at her, mouth open, dribble coming down her chin. 'Come on, Tiger, time to eat some cake.'

Kai was in the kitchen with Rubi, putting candles on the cake. They were giggling. When they fixed the house up, I never moved back in. I moved in with Kai, living on her boat with Rubi coming by most nights. We were making up for lost time while I saved up to buy me own boat. Kai taught me how to knit, and we'd joined this knitting society where you make knitted hats for post boxes and whatnot. We had lots of yarnbombing planned. I'd call in on Kirsten and Dad on weekends to help with Hetty.

'Kai, could you get the other candles out of that drawer?' Kirsten pointed to a dresser behind her. 'And Scarlett, could you get your dad?'

'Where is he?'

Kirsten rolled her eyes and nodded to the backdoor. 'Guess.'

Hetty laughed at the ceiling, and we all looked up. I'd often catch baby Hetty laughing at nothing, or she'd be watching a blank space for a really long time. One time, I swear she tried talking to nothing, too. But maybe it wasn't nothing? Because one time, I caught her rattling a box of matches in her hand, with no idea how she got them. I always looked for Granny, but never found her. Even though the house was so different, as if the past had burnt down, there was still some smoke damage left behind, a lingering smell every now and again.

I found Dad outside with a spade, patting earth with the flat side. 'What you doing Dad?'

'Moles.' He nodded. 'Keep finding holes everywhere.'

'We're gunna do the cake now.'

'I'll be a minute. Can't have this.' He pointed to the ground. 'So dangerous.'

'You sure it's badgers?'

'What d'you mean?'

'Well...' I had never told Dad I knew about what had happened to him. I didn't want to drag him through the pain of it again. But the fact the garden was opening up, holes springing up again, seemed too... 'Maybe there's something down there?'

'Like what?'

'A sink hole? I saw this thing online...'

'Get inside. Now.' He dropped his spade and pushed me into the house too. 'Could be an old mine, couldn't it? We should get a survey done.'

'Maybe.' I shrugged. 'Or something else.'

Dad ended up leaving his spade out in the garden for three months, until one week after putting the 'Sold' sign up on the house, the spade was swallowed up as half the garden collapsed into a giant, gaping hole.

'Can I hold Hetty?' I put out me arms. 'For the birthday cake!'

'Sure.' Kirsten passed me the tiger cub, and I sat down at the kitchen table with her. Hetty looked tearful, and tired, and about to cry. 'We may have to make this quick.'

'I'm on it.' Dad picked his phone off the counter. 'Camera's ready.'

'I'll do that!' Rubi took his phone from him. 'So the whole family is in it.'

Kirsten and Dad stood on either side of me. Kai took out the matches and strummed it over the sandpaper.

'Eh, who let the arsonist have the matches?' Kirsten smiled.

A flame zipped up the match and Kai cupped it, grinning as she edged it towards the candle. 'Stand back, citizens! I've got this.'

We all laughed, and Hetty's mood lit up too. She grinned and clapped and giggled as we sang her Happy Birthday. I bounced her on me knee. Me sister. Me tiger. And in her eye I saw the flame of the candle and a spark in her eye, just like Kai's.

'One, two, three...' we said. 'Blow!'

But the flame didn't go out.

'Did you get the magic ones?' Kirsten turned to Kai.

'No. They're normal. I think. See - there's no glittering.'

'Try it again,' said Rubi. 'On three.'

'One, two, three, blow!'

But the light wouldn't go out. It just wavered in the wind, and burned brighter than ever, and Hetty laughed and laughed and clapped, not at the candle, but towards a blank spot in the corner.

ACKNOWLEDGMENTS

This book wouldn't be here today if it wasn't for the generous support of the Arts Council whose funding helped me to take the time out (in a pandemic I might add) to finish this wonderful mash-up of a book.

I want to thank all the editors, beta readers, friends and my partner, who have helped me to whip this novel into shape. Thank you for enduring early drafts of the novel in complete Bristolian dialect. That was no easy task! Although part of me would still have loved to have published it all in dialect, I'm also a pragmatist, awright me lover?

Thank you to the every Bristolian and West Country person I have ever met and grown up with. This book is entirely for you and for me. May we forever be proud of our heritage and our love of cider. And shout gert lush from the roof tops!

ABOUT THE AUTHOR

Zoe J. Stark grew up in the West Country and found herself unable to leave, despite many valiant attempts. *Burning Down the House* is a YA Mystery Thriller and her debut novel funded by the Arts Council.

Zoe is now always on the hunt for people who say 'cheers drive' and 'babber', and hates anyone who asks for her consonants (sorry Carol). But she promises she would never burn down anybody's house for doing so... You can find in middle earth, talking to trees, wondering where her hobbit family went and whether they'll ever leave the shire.